THE RIDDLE

PUBLICATIONS:

Conflicts in an Estuary (1973)
Tall Ships (1976)
Salt Water Palaces (1979)
Yachtsman's Naturalist (with Paul Rodhouse, 1980)
The New Forest (with Philip Allison, 1980)
The Riddle (1985, first edition)
West Highland Shores (1990)
(Ed) *Lord Bute* (1996)
The Book of the Solent (with Robin MacInnes, 2001)
After You Mr Lear (2007)
Roving Commissions (editor)

THE RIDDLE

Illuminating the story behind *The Riddle of the Sands*

Preface by Robert Childers
Illustrated by Martyn Mackrill

Maldwin Drummond

UNIFORM

First published by Uniform,
an imprint of the Unicorn Publishing Group LLP, 2016
101 Wardour Street
London
W1F 0UG
www.unicornpublishing.org

First published in Great Britain 1985 by NAUTICAL BOOKS
an imprint of CONWAY MARITIME PRESS LIMITED
24 Bride Lane, Fleet Street, London EC4Y 8DR

British Library Cataloguing in Publication Data Drummond, Maldwin
The Riddle.
1. Childers, Erskine. Riddle of the Sands.
I. Title
823'.912 PR6005.H52Z

ISBN 978-1-910500-39-2

Cover and interior design by Vivian@Bookscribe
Printed and bound in Great Britain

To Aldred

CONTENTS

ACKNOWLEDGEMENTS

I am particularly grateful to Robert and Christobel Childers for unfailing kindness and support throughout my efforts to discover more about Erskine and also for writing the Foreword. This book would not have been possible without their help.

I have also benefited from the encouragement and the papers of Hugh Popham and his late wife, Robin. If any stimulation or ideas were required, they were readily given by David Cobb, the celebrated marine artist, a line by-line student of *The Riddle of the Sands*. He shares this devotion with Frank Carr, one-time Director of the National Maritime Museum and now Chairman of the World Ship Trust. I am indebted to them both.

Walter Childers gave me a private view of the life of his father, Henry Childers, Erskine's brother. Lord Runciman helped me with his family history and Dr Paul Kennedy, with his specialised knowledge of naval history and Anglo-German relations, clarified a number of points. My thanks to them all.

The Childers Papers are held in the libraries of Trinity College, University of Dublin, and Trinity College, Cambridge. Dr Bernard Meehan and Mr Trevor Kaye were unstinting in their help, as was the Imperial War Museum which looks after Erskine Childers' war records. John Hawkesworth also lent me his papers and the correspondence he had with Molly Childers while writing the screenplay for a film of *The Riddle*. I am most grateful to him too.

I followed *Vixen's* course in a variety of small boats, including *Vivette* whose owner, Roderick James, took a particular interest in the research.

Thank you to Charles Hanrott who allowed me to reproduce the 'Childers Charts'.

Cyril Ray, Ted Watson, Group Captains Frank Tredrey and Frank Griffiths, and many others in the list below sent snippets of information and photographs which were enormously useful in my detective work.

The following people and organisations have provided invaluable help in bringing to light much that is new: the late John Atkins; Doug Baverstock; James Bayes; Vice-Admiral Sir Patrick Bayly, Director, Maritime Trust; Commander Richard Beach RN; Bill Beavis of *Yachting Monthly*; A. S. Bell, Assistant Keeper, National Library of Scotland; Jules Van Beylen, Director, National Sheepvaart Museum, Antwerp; Howard Biggs; R. M. Bowker; Lieutenant-Colonel Dr Donald F. Bittner, Military Historian, US Marine Corps; Mrs Christina Boyle, The British Newspaper Library; Alistair Brown; David Brown, Naval Historical Branch, Ministry of Defence; Commander and Mrs Vernon Bullin; Miss K. Byrne, Charity Commission; Peter Cameron, Regional Controller, HM Coastguard, Brixham; Commander R.J. Cardale RN, Coastguard Training School, Brixham; Mrs Ian Carr; Mrs Gill Coleridge; Adlard Coles; R. M. Coppock, Naval History Branch, Ministry of Defence; Jack Coote; Dr Edwin Course, University of Southampton; Colonel V. F. Craig; Mrs Carainn Davies RNE; Dawe Central Library, Folkestone; Captain Henry Denham RN; Deutsche Bundesbahn; Deutsches Hydrographisches Institut; Donal Dunne; D. T. Elliot, Chief Librarian, London Borough of Tower Hamlets; Mr and Mrs Seymour England; the late Grahame Farr; Major James Forsythe, Hon. Secretary, World Ship Trust; John Francis; Colonel R. C. Gardiner-Hill; Dr Michael Gilkes, Hon. Librarian, Royal Cruising Club; Mrs Elizabeth M. Gordon; Mrs Seton Gordon; Sir Peter Green, Chairman of Lloyds; Maurice Griffiths; Fred Harnack; Mrs Kathleen Harrison, Isle of Wight County Council; Graham Harvey-Evers; C. G. Harris, Bodleian Library, Oxford; Mr and Mrs Eric Hiscock; Maurice Hochschild; W. H. Honey, Maritime and Local History Museum, Deal; Humber Yawl Club; J. A. Hunter-Rioch, Marketing Director, Valor Heating (owners of Rippingille); Mr and Mrs Colin Mudie; Ralph Hammond Innes; L. Jenkins; Bruce Jones; Lord Kennet; the Curator, Kodak Museum, Harrow; Professor I. Lambi, University of Saskatchewan; David Lyon, Department of Ships, National Maritime Museum; Mrs Mandy McBeath; W. R. McKay, Committee Office, House of Commons; Mrs Margaret Mann; Bryan Matthews, Records Office, Uppingham School; Phoebe Mason, Stanford Maritime Ltd; David Messum; Meteorological Office; Lord Montagu of Beaulieu;

Professor H. R. Moon, Sangamon State University; Mrs Francesca Morgan; Mrs Virginia Murray of John Murray (Publishers); Colonel G. A. Murray-Smith; Mrs Joan and the late George Naish, National Register of Archives; Susanna Nockolds; Stadtdirektor, Stadt Norderney; Lord O'Neill of the Maine; William O'Sullivan, Trinity College Library, University of Dublin; T. R. Padfield, Public Record Office; J. C. Parker, Royal Commission Historical Monuments; Captain R. H. Parsons RN, Director, Royal Naval Museum, Portsmouth; Miss M. J. Perry, Curator, Hydrographic Department, Taunton; the Editor, *Portsmouth Evening News;* Sir David Price MP; David V. Proctor, Head of Printed Books and Manuscripts Department, National Maritime Museum; A. A. Raines; Adrian Rance, Director, Department of Leisure Services, City of Southampton; Registrar of British Ships, HM Customs and Excise, Southampton; M. Reid; Colonel John Richards; Stephen M. Riley, Research Assistant, Department of Ships, National Maritime Museum; Royal Cruising Club; the Director, Royal Marines Museum; Royal National Lifeboat Institution; D. F. Saunders, Curator, Hydrographic Department, Ministry of Defence, Taunton; David Scurrell; Sidney Searle; Lieutenant-Commander Derry Seaton RN; Bill Smith; Major Ewen Southby-Tailyour RM; the Editor, *Southern Evening Echo;* D. S. Stonham, Historic Photographs Section, National Maritime Museum; Dick Stower; R. W. A. Suddaby, Imperial War Museum; Hardo Sziedat, Commercial Director, Esens-Bensersiel; Dr Christopher Thacker; Mrs Imogen Thomas, Assistant Librarian, Haileybury College; Dick Tizard; R. G. Todd, Historic Photographs Section, National Maritime Museum; Richard Tubb, Ministry of Defence Library; Commander F.C. Van Oosten, Historical Department, Naval Staff, Ministerie van Defensie, Amsterdam; Mr and Mrs L. E. Wainwright; Neal T. Walker, Secretary, Slocum Society; Korvettenkapitän Dr Walle, Militärgeschichtliches Forschungsamt, Freiburg im Breisgau; Rear-Admiral John Warsop, Port Admiral, Rosyth; Ted Watson; Jack Whitehead; Stadt Wilhelmshaven; Burke Wilkinson; W. T. Wilson, Imray Laurie Norie and Wilson Ltd; John Wyllie; WZ Bilddienst; the Editor, *Yachting Monthly;* the Editor, *Yachting World;* Elizabeth Yeo, Assistant Keeper, National Library of Scotland; Jim Young; J. Zwaan, Rijksinstituut voor Oorlogsdocumentatie, Amsterdam.

Finally I would like to thank both my wife, Gilly, for her lively encouragement and Rosalie Hendey who typed the manuscript and, with her usual skill, saw that all went well.

I am most grateful to Martyn Mackrill, the artist, who has done the admirable sketches for the new edition and to Lord Stratchcarron, Chairman of Unicorn Publishing Group who produced this edition.

FOREWORD

When Maldwin Drummond first started to work on this book, it didn't seem possible that he could unearth any more appreciable or significant information about Erskine Childers than had already appeared in previous biographies. As I got to know him and his wife Gilly better, however, I realised that they are both perfectionists in their own fields and that any task to which Maldwin set his hand would be exhaustively studied and researched.

The Riddle is really two books, each with a different focal point, but closely entwined. One is a comprehensive study of *The Riddle of the Sands*, from the original cruise in *Vixen*, through the years that covered the writing of the novel, and going on to describe in a fully documented manner its effect on public policy in Great Britain during the years leading up to the First World War. The other is a delightful biography of Erskine Childers through his early years, bringing to the reader a wealth of quite fresh knowledge about his work, his interests, his sailing and, perhaps most importantly, about the close friends who clearly played such a significant role in his life.

That this abundance of new information about a way of life that has long since vanished could be collected some eighty to ninety years later is a truly remarkable achievement which I would not have believed possible.

A son must necessarily be the last person fitted to comment on a book about his own father, but that doesn't prevent me from expressing my very warm thanks to Maldwin for the endearing picture he has produced for us.

Robert Childers
Glendalough House
Annamoe
Co. Wicklow
September 1984

THE LIFE AND TIMES OF ROBERT ERSKINE CHILDERS (R.E.C.)

1870 *25 June* R.E.C., 2nd son, born to Professor Robert Caesar Childers (1838–76) and his wife Anna Maria Henrietta (*née* Barton), who had married in 1866.

1883 After the death of their mother, R.E.C., his brother Henry and their three sisters go to live at Glendalough, Co. Wicklow, with their Barton cousins.

1883–9 R.E.C. at Haileybury School.

Trinity College, Cambridge, where R.E.C. gained his BA. A permanent limp from sciatica began, contracted on an Irish walking tour. Owner with Henry of the cutter *Shulah*.

1895 (Liberals defeated at the general election. Salisbury again Prime Minister. Jameson Raid: the unsuccessful invasion of the Transvaal by Dr Jameson of the British South Africa Company.)

R.E.C. joins the staff of clerks in the House of Commons. R.E.C. awarded the De Horsey Cup for their exploits in *Marguerite (Mad Agnes)* by the Cruising Club.

1896 *3 January* (The Kaiser, Wilhelm 11, congratulates President Kruger by telegram. The British government mobilises a flying squadron. A Select Committee of the House of Commons is set up to enquire into the Jameson Raid. Admiral Otto von Diederichs, chief of staff at the High Command, produces his operational plan against Britain.)

1897 (Sir Alfred Milner appointed Governor of the Cape. Queen Victoria's Diamond Jubilee celebrated. Admiral Eduard von Knorr presents his plans to the Kaiser for the possible invasion of England. Germany seizes Kiaochow; Tirpitz appointed Secretary of State of the Imperial Naval Office. Tirpitz Memorandum.)

11 August–14 December R.E.C. sets sail in his new cutter *Vixen* for the Baltic, returning to Terschelling, so providing the background to *The Riddle of the Sands*, published later.

1898 (Fashoda Incident – a territorial dispute in Africa between Great Britain and France. The German Navy League founded. Tirpitz first Navy Law. William Gladstone dies.)

R.E.C. sails for the West Indies aboard SS *West Indian*.

1899 (The Kruger Ultimatum. War breaks out. The Boers lay siege to Mafeking and Ladysmith. 'Black Week' in early December.)

R.E.C. and William Le Fanu go cycling in the Dordogne. R.E.C. joins the City Imperial Volunteer battery of the Honourable Artillery Company.

1900 (Lord Roberts appointed commander-in-chief with Lord Kitchener as chief of staff. Ladysmith and Mafeking relieved. Salisbury wins the 'Khaki' election. Tirpitz 'Risk Fleet' theory and second Navy Bill. Von der Goltz invasion plan put forward.)

3 February SS *Montfort* with R.E.C. and the CIV aboard leaves the Thames for the Cape.

7 October Returns to Southampton aboard the SS *Aurania* with his battery.

1901 (Queen Victoria dies and Edward VII accedes.) R.E.C. part exchanges *Vixen* for *Sunbeam*, owned in partnership. *In the Ranks of the CIV* published by Smith, Elder & Co.

13 December R.E.C. begins to write *The Riddle of the Sands*.

1902 (Salisbury resigns and Arthur Balfour succeeds as Prime Minister. Peace Treaty signed at Pretoria.)

R.E.C. immersed in *The Riddle* and duties in the House of Commons.

1903 *27 May The Riddle of the Sands* published by Smith, Elder & Co. and later *The HAC in South Africa*, in which R.E.C. collaborated with Basil Williams. Good reviews. R.E.C. cruises to the Baltic on *Sunbeam*. Made clerk of petitions. Towards the end of the year R.E.C. goes to America with the HAC and meets Mary Alden (Molly) Osgood in Boston.

1904 (The Entente Cordiale between Britain and France strengthened. Kaiser tries to persuade the Czar to join France and Germany against Britain.)

5 January R.E.C. and Molly Osgood married in Boston and father-in-law presents them with a new yacht, *Asgard*, to be designed by Colin Archer and built in Norway.

1905 (Balfour resigns. Liberals under Campbell-Bannerman come to power. Sinn Fein Party organised in Ireland. Russian fleet destroyed by Japanese at Tsushima.)

Erskine Hamilton Childers, R.E.C.'s eldest son, born. He was to be President of Ireland, 1973–4. *Asgard* sailed home from her Oslo fjord builders by Ivor Lloyd-Jones.

1906 (Liberals win a landslide victory in the general election.)

Asgard cruises to the Baltic.

1907 (Hague Conference, Germany refuses armament limitations. Triple entente of France, Russia and Great Britain.)

Times History of the War in South Africa, vol. 5 by R.E.C. published.

1908 (Campbell-Bannerman dies; succeeded by Herbert Asquith.)

R.E.C. converted to Irish Home Rule on a motor tour of Ireland with cousin Robert Barton and Sir Horace Plunkett. He begins to take an intense interest in Irish affairs – his 'watershed'.

1910 (Edward VII dies; George V accedes. Liberal majority reduced at the general election.)

Publication of *War and the Arme Blanche* by R.E.C. with Preface by Lord Roberts. R.E.C. resigns his post of senior clerk in the House of Commons to take an unimpeded interest in political matters. Robert Alden Childers born.

Captain Trench and Lt Brandon found guilty of espionage by German court and imprisoned.

1911 (German gunboat *Panther* sent to Agadir – Agadir Crisis.)

Edward Arnold publishes two books by R.E.C., *The Framework of Home Rule* and *German Influence on Cavalry*. In the former he argued for full dominion status for Ireland. Gordon Shephard arrested in Emden.

1912 (Franco-British Naval Agreement. French fleet to guard Mediterranean, Britain north and west coast of France.)

R.E.C. candidate for one of the Devonport seats but resigns before the election. Brandon and Trench released and they meet R.E.C.

1913 (End of the first and beginning of the second Balkan Wars.)

Asgard cruises to the Baltic. Gordon Shephard brings her home via Shetlands and the West Coast and wins the Royal Cruising Club Challenge Cup.

1914 (Irish Home Rule Act. Ulster Volunteers oppose integration with the South and import arms into Larne. The Curragh Incident. First World War begins.)

R.E.C. and Molly run guns for the National Volunteers into Howth. Lt Erskine Childers, RNVR, joins seaplane carrier HMS *Engadine*. Writes memorandum 'The Seizure of Borkum and Juist'. Flies as observer on the seaplane raid on Cuxhaven, the first time aircraft, surface ships and submarines are used in concert.

1915 (Battle of Ypres, Dogger Bank. SS *Lusitania* sunk by a German submarine.)

R.E.C. joins seaplane carrier HMS *Ben-My-Chree* as intelligence and reconnaissance officer and steams to the eastern Mediterranean.

1916 (Battles of Somme and Verdun. Allies leave Gallipoli. Von der Goltz defeats British at Kut and dies. Sir Roger Casement executed. Easter Rebellion in Dublin. Lloyd George succeeds Asquith as Prime Minister. Tirpitz resigns as Secretary of State in the Imperial Navy Department.)

HMS *Ben-My-Chree* at Port Said. R.E.C. becomes an aerial photographer. Posted back to England for naval intelligence and staff duties, then to Coastal Motor Boats at Queenborough, near Felixstowe.

1917 (Battles of Passchendaele and Cambrai; Russian Revolution.)

R.E.C. a lieutenant-commander with Coastal Motor Boats at Dunkirk. Awarded DSC for past services in the Mediterranean in addition to several mentions in despatches. Seconded as assistant secretary to the Irish Convention which failed to agree on Home Rule.

1918 (Armistice 'Coupon Election', Civil War in Ireland.)

R.E.C. bitterly disappointed by the continued delay in giving any form of self-government to Ireland. Brig. Gordon Shephard killed.

1919 (Treaty of Versailles. Rebel MPs form unofficial Dail Eireann.)

R.E.C. demobilised; determines to accept nothing less than Home Rule for Ireland. Attended the Versailles Conference with the Irish Republican envoys to argue the case.

1920 (Fourth Irish Home Rule Bill. 'Black and Tans' introduced by British government.)

R.E.C. and family leave London and move to Dublin. He argues the case against the 'Black and Tans' in a pamphlet 'Military Rule in Ireland'.

1921 (Irish Treaty gives Southern Ireland dominion status.)

R.E.C. elected member for Wicklow in the Dail Eireann. Minister of Propaganda. Goes to London as a member of the De Valera delegation and was secretary to those who negotiated the Irish Treaty. He soon repudiated this, joining the Republican Army, publishing their news-sheet.

1922 (Resignation of Lloyd George, end of coalition government. Bonar Law Prime Minister. Irish election endorsed dominion status though rejected by Sinn Fein. Michael Collins, Irish Leader, assassinated.)

1922 10 November R.E.C. arrested at Glendalough House by Free State soldiers. Found to have a miniature pistol given to him by Michael Collins.

17 November R.E.C. court-martialled in Dublin for possessing arms.

24 November R.E.C. shot by firing squad at Beggars Bush Barracks on the orders of the Irish provisional government.

PART ONE

Pages From The Past

Dollman aboard *Mędusa* shouted to *Dulcibella*, 'Follow me...'

Chapter 1

A VOYAGE TO FRANCE

'There were reasons,' I read, 'there are reasons still – which well make it *a tangled business*.' The words came from a book with a yellow cover. An iron cross half obscured by an Imperial German eagle with a gaff cutter sailing through the bird's reflected image gave some idea of the contents. I stood by the bookcase in my study and thumbed idly through the pages in an attempt to recapture the story, the rolling descriptions of a small boat at sea, the pages of detection and chase, the amalgam that had so encouraged my first cautious efforts at cruising under sail.

The book was the early Edwardian adventure tale, *The Riddle of the Sands*. The plot came flooding back, much like the tide repossessing the sands of Frisia where the tale is set. I remembered how I had been gripped before, how a cocoon had surrounded and supported, relaxed and transplanted me into the Childers' world of a small, black yacht worked by two opposites, Davies and Carruthers, who had stumbled across a scheme of invasion aimed by the Kaiser's Germany against England's then unprotected flank. 'A tangled business.' I had certainly been entangled in the story as soon as I opened the book in the saloon of *Runa VII*. It must have been the summer of 1953, for I had become the owner of the five-ton sloop just after my twenty-first birthday. My brother Bend'or and I were 'going foreign' for the first time.

Making east from the Solent, we spent the first night in Newhaven. I remembered the fog that had disfigured the port the morning we left for Boulogne. I hate fog now – all sensible sailors do. The departure had been difficult, for when dawn came

Runa

we found the yacht stuck hard on the mud in Sleeper's Hole. There were just a few mooring buoys there in those days, coloured pimples upon the water. The boats were dotted about; there was no marina. The Kim auxiliary was persuaded to wake up. It was usually reluctant when there were droplets of moisture in the air. A windless day was just breaking, disguised by a thick blanket that threw a veil around us, leaving the masts of twenty or so yachts to fade into the background with no order, like a spinney with few branches. The water churned uselessly under the counter. We both went forward and jumped up and down to encourage the yacht in her efforts. The boats around us suddenly revolted; reacting to such antics so early in the day. One hit us a glancing blow. We tumbled back into the cockpit, realising that they were not to blame; they had been dozing, and we were at fault. We had suddenly left the mud and had struck our neighbour. No damage was done and they were soon at peace again.

The engine had to do most of the work for the next twelve hours, as the wind did not seem anxious to help. Our world was a small circle of sea, caught under a tea-cosy of fog. The opaque wool of white could have been little more than fifty yards across. Bend'or steered, dutiful as always when things were not easy, while I fiddled with my new toy – a BEME Loop radio direction finder. Hitherto we had only used it for weather forecasts and news. An old compass in a box had been screwed on to the cockpit floor. It had once acted as a reserve aboard *Britannia* and had come to my father through the sale of her effects in 1936, just before that famous cutter was scuttled, on royal instructions, off the Needles. The near seven-inch card and the polished brass pedigree on the lid gave me confidence. We were 'going foreign' on our own for the first time.

Runa slid by Beachy Head and I picked up the Boulogne beacon on the loop soon after. The engine made communication difficult and I had to shout directions up through the companion hatch. I wondered how we would ever find our way between the piers when even my brother's outline was distorted by fog. The forecast was that conditions would improve, but there was little sign of that happening. Morse from Boulogne beckoned us on and after an age of worry as we crossed the Channel, we went straight through the harbour entrance. My astonishment at seeing the gap in

Runa off Beachy Head

the stone wall is difficult to describe. I thought it was an anchored ship until I picked up the hole in the middle. *Runa* entered with some pride and some odd noises from the overworked engine but she was soon secured to the railway jetty – surely the proper place for vessels from far-flung shores?

Bend'or, wearing his yachting cap, was accosted by an angry traveller. 'Where's my Vespa?'

'Your Vespa?' he replied in surprise.

'Yes. I'm on holiday; it was put aboard but has disappeared.'

'I am terribly sorry to say, sir,' said my brother, to my surprise, for he was not usually so fastidiously polite, 'that while we were craning your vehicle ashore, the rope broke and it's in there.'

His gesture toward the brown and frothy harbour water could not have been misunderstood. I could almost see the 'vehicle' as it disappeared in a khaki eruption while being hoisted from the railway steamer down the quay. Bend'or went on in his best railway voice to explain that the company could, of course, take no responsibility. I took off, making for the iron ladder and *Runa,* whose welcoming sand-coloured deck appeared as a tiny oasis far below.

'He's gone to see the captain,' said Bend'or, with a smile, half-heartedly helping with the warps as I started the engine, anxious to be off before the holiday-maker returned.

The fog had cleared enough now to take in our surroundings. The devastation showed how important Boulogne had been to both sides in the war. Wrecked buildings were all around. It was like standing on the tongue of an aged giant, looking outward at a skyline of ill-used and decaying teeth. The little white yacht seemed out of place.

Against the mole wall to the south lay a gigantic, floating crane, a whisp of steam and a slight smudge of smoke mingling above her funnel. Her master welcomed us. Our triumphant entry and rapid escape from the railway jetty had taken my mind from the signs of trouble coming from the engine, but it was now clear that the dog clutch was not working properly and even with the ahead/astern lever secured forward with hambro line, it was still slipping. We needed expert help.

Bend'or's French then was of the varnished kind, gained from grammars and old wooden desks. There was far less shine to my efforts and so I sheltered behind his ability. He warmed to the captain, who told him that the crane's engineer would look after our mechanical problem in the morning. He could fix anything. He smiled in a way reserved for those who may not know of French mechanical skills. I felt cautiously optimistic in the face of such obvious understanding of our problem, though he had hardly glanced through the cockpit floor.

Bend'or, feeling a bit of an ambassador, prattled away, accepting a starved and wrinkled cigarette from the crane master. It looked as if it had spent some time naked with strange companions in our host's blue-denim pocket. Occasionally, glanced up at the companion to see figures looming above me, Bend'or wearing an old Coles military flannel shirt and his deceptive cap. Our benefactor had a day or two's growth of beard which softened a care-worn face. The puffy, lidded eyes looked as if they had been opened with a knife and they blinked in protest at the smoke that rose from the nicotine-stained stump in his mouth.

'He's been lifting bits of wreck in the harbour,' Bend'or explained later, after a meal of scrambled eggs. We were sitting in the cockpit and the fog had returned.

'Apparently a lot of ships were sunk here during the war.'

'Why, has he stopped working?' I asked.

'Yes, he's worried about that too; he can't get a crew and can't understand why. Apparently a week ago they had some sort of disaster, a wire broke,' he said sombrely. 'Ten men, I think that's the number who were killed or badly injured. Anyway the accident seems to have dissuaded others signing on.'

We both looked up at the steel jib that stretched into the mist above *Runa's* thirty-foot wooden mast. The whole contraption looked like the captain – old, over-worked and under-maintained. Still, he would need a good engineer to keep that lot going, I thought to myself.

Aboard *Runa VII* – Maldwin Drummond's yacht

There is nothing quite like the first night in harbour after a successful crossing, especially if it is the first time over. I didn't feel tired. I lit the oil lamp over my bunk, pulled the sheet up round me, disregarding the damp embrace and the coarseness of the army blankets the linen was meant to disguise. I dragged a book from the shelf and looked across at Bend'or. He, too, was deep in something. I glanced at the worn cloth spine through my fingers. The gold letters were difficult to make out, but what was left shone out, reflecting the warm light from the bulkhead – *The Riddle of the Sands*. I skipped past the title-page, just noting the name of the author – Erskine Childers – and past the introduction by someone or other and a Note dated April 1931, by M. A. Childers – his wife, I learnt much later. I thumbed quickly through the Preface, anxious for the first real taste.

> *I have read of men who when forced by their calling to live for long periods in utter solitude – save for a few black faces – have made it a rule to dress regularly for dinner in order to maintain their self-respect and prevent a relapse into barbarism.*

I looked up at the white deckhead crossed by yellowing oak beams, then at Bend'or, who had not moved much, though his glass was empty. I shifted, to make a more comfortable hole in the mattress, then rearranged the covers, turned up the wick and leafed back to the Preface, in case it was important. This was my sort of book. I was sure the author would not let me down now he had caught me with his first sentence.

I do not remember Bend'or turning down his lamp or his 'Good night.' I read on – one more chapter and then I would go to sleep, I promised myself, but page followed page. I only let go when I noticed that I was reading too deeply into tomorrow's pleasure.

The hammering inside the crane barge slowly persuaded me that the engineer had returned and was active. Bend'or went over and returned with a youngish man, also in blue denim and powered by Gauloises. He was armed with three or four depressingly unsuitable tools, all of great size. They appeared part of him and I had the feeling that if I had asked him to repair the yacht's clock, he would have arrived similarly equipped.

The engineer belaboured the dog clutch with his weapons, looking fierce rather than expert, until just before lunch a particularly savage clunk was followed by a clank. Bend'or said in English, 'Well, that's done it.' I peered down. Somehow or other our friend had managed to break a casting.

'He says it will be all right,' said Bend'or, optimistically, after the man had explained what he had done as a triumph rather than the disaster it looked. His solution now was to secure the gear lever in the 'astern' position to go ahead. There would, of course, be no neutral or astern. The captain beamed at us and said to Bend'or, 'I said that my engineer would fix it.' He patted his expert on the back and as we wanted one more night alongside we did not argue. It just might work and at least I would be able to return to my book.

Those Boulogne days come back so easily. We wandered around the broken city in the afternoon and had an early dinner in a little restaurant among the ruins not too far from the harbour. Yachtsmen had even more reason to go to France in those days. Restaurant fare in an English port the size of Boulogne, perhaps Southampton, would have been the standard 'meat and two veg' – probably a wafer-thin piece of meat rimmed with fat, afloat for most of its length in watery gravy. At that French table you could easily forget the damage outside. It was with unusual contentment that we returned, complete with enough bottles to fill the cellar in the bilge. I was back with *The Riddle* before many minutes and Bend'or sauntered off to have another look at the town.

There is a special feeling reserved for those who have finished a good book. 'What a marvellous story,' I find myself saying and may seize hold of those nearby and demand that they share the experience, as some sort of miracle cure that must be taken three times a day. My brother had to go through this on his return.

We left Boulogne on another windless, high-pressure morning. The fog had cleared and the coast stretched away southward in a clear, unbroken line, the sun catching the green of the cliff top, picking out buildings and sending us occasional flashes of reflected light. Shafts from the sun passed deep through the calm surface as *Runa* headed south-south-westward for Dieppe. We were half an hour out when the engine quickened but our pace slowed. The dog clutch was slipping again. *Runa's* tool box held no cure for an engine that had endured such crude doctoring. The engine could no longer help and died with a flick of the switch.

The tide was on our side though and soon a cat's-paw reached out from the coast as though Mother France were apologising for the actions of her ham fisted son. The southeasterly soon filled the sails and we enjoyed lunch on a broad reach, the yacht responding well to the wind off the shore. It was not to last, for the breeze died towards evening. For thirty-six hours we were becalmed, carried only by the tide. The lights on land marked our backward and forward progress by night and familiar shapes helped by day. We made Dieppe eventually, ate cod cooked by those who understand that fish, and drank wine full of French summer sunshine before returning to the Solent.

Are all first cruises like that one? I wondered. Then looking down at *The Riddle of the Sands*, I remembered again the contribution that those pages had made to the adventure.

The twists and turns of the story and the contrasting characters take a powerful hold on the reader, but it is more than a 'rattling good yarn.' The book had sounded an alarm, a 'watchword', showing the 'nearness of the enemy', to quote the definition of Old Rider.[1] It would be difficult for anyone to say now that Erskine Childers was misinformed, that no threat had existed.

The publishing history, though, in the front pages of the yellow paperback showed that the first edition had been published in 1903, when surely the British were more worried about the intentions of the French. At that time they would only have raised a quiet eyebrow at the activities of Edward VII's nephew, Wilhelm II, I thought.

Erskine Childers leads the reader to believe that his characters had stumbled on something and that they had brought their discovery to his attention as the editor. The plot is so well worked out, so plausible, and the descriptions of the Frisian coast so accurate, that I believed Childers must have had inside knowledge, intelligence that may have been denied his peers.

I was blessed with a little knowledge myself, gained a year before I read the book on *Runa*. I had stayed in a farmhouse at Neuharlingersiel, rising early after geese, while on leave from my regiment, part of the British Army of the Rhine. It was not possible to read the book and have an inkling of those places without feeling that the author had been there. It took only one further step to believe that he knew more of German plans through these wanderings than he or any of his biographers had admitted.

Questions with incomplete answers and answers without proper questions rolled forward in my mind. What had the Germans been up to? Were they really planning to use the siels, tugs and barges to invade us? Had Childers been to the Baltic and bumped across those endless sands, rejoicing at the comparative freedom of the channels? Did he know the dark streets of Essen or the approaches to Norddeich? Had von Brüning or the spy Dollmann existed under different names? And what about the helpful Bartels, was he real? If Childers had been there, what was his purpose? Was he gathering information and, if so, for whom? What happened to *Dulcibella?* Was she just a fiction too?

The book was so well constructed, so professionally put together, Childers must have put pen to paper before. His ability to describe the ways of small boats, I thought, took him briefly alongside Conrad, Stevenson and Jack London.

I was suddenly fired with determination, filled with a need to find the answers to these questions. I would start by taking another close look at the book and I picked up *The Riddle of the Sands* again.

PART TWO

The Dulcibella File

Chapter 2

THE RIDDLE

The plot of *The Riddle* is rather like the sea. At first, the waves look simple; propelled by the wind they move up and down according to a pattern, their rank and file bent on a common course of advance. Closer inspection, though, reveals more, for on top of this purpose is another. There are secondary wavelets crossing their hosts at different angles, so the main aim may be obvious enough but there is more to their onward march.

In this chapter, the story of *The Riddle of the Sands* is retold. The theme and the principal characters are given touches of brilliant white so they stand out in this necessarily brief synopsis. The overtones, or the waves on top, are highlighted and some of the best passages quoted. The reader, so encouraged, should reach for the book itself, for no one should be deprived of that experience.

Erskine Childers felt much the same way, for from the very beginning he was anxious to assure the reader that the story was no flight of fancy or fiction, but an account of what had actually happened on a yachting cruise that took place shortly before October 1902. The tale unfolds with such force that the reader is left in little doubt that the cruise, or something very near to it, actually occurred.

The Preface is, in part, responsible for this, for the author is very much a part of the story and introduces his two principal characters by bringing one of them to his chambers with the strange story of a voyage in a small boat. Erskine Childers' visitor was 'Carruthers'. He was given an alias to protect his real name, and his companion, the owner of the yacht, was similarly disguised as 'Arthur H. Davies'. Carruthers was persuaded to seek out the author because of the attitude of those in power. He states that 'the important facts discovered in the course of the cruise had, without a moment's delay, been communicated to the proper authorities, who, after some dignified incredulity, due in part, perhaps, to the pitiful inadequacy of their own Secret Service, had, he believed, made use of them, to avert a great national danger.' Carruthers wanted Childers' advice for 'the information wrung with such peril and labour from the German government and transmitted so promptly to our own had had none but the most transitory effect, if any, on our policy.' Davies and Carruthers suspected 'some poisonous influence' persistently at work. The cure for the 'national disease' of do-nothing would be to make the whole story public. Childers was so impressed by what they had to say that he urged them to do so.

The Preface concludes with an agreement to bring out the facts in book form, written as from the mouth of Carruthers, the story told 'with its humours and errors, its light and its dark side, just as it happened'. To this end, Carruthers was to hand over his 'diary' of the cruise and to give further details of the 'quest', while Davies was to meet Childers with his charts and maps to do the same. They would endeavour to protect innocent persons who wandered haplessly in and out of the story.

Carruthers began the tale in London, painting a picture of a young man left in the capital in the middle of September by the receding tide of society bent on pleasures elsewhere. Carruthers, who had done well at Oxford, had lived in France and Germany, was a good linguist and a member of the right clubs, knowing the right people, felt he 'may be excused for a sense of complacent martyrdom, when, with his keen appreciation of the social calendar, he is doomed to the utter solitude of London in September'. His job as a junior functionary in the Foreign Office required such martyrdom as declining the invitation of Lady Ashleigh to go to Morven Lodge after grouse. So to 'quench a passing thirst', as he put it, and thousands have done the same since, he spent a few evenings in some shady haunts in Soho and further eastward, being finally cured by the reeking atmosphere of a low music hall in the Ratcliffe Highway, where he 'sat next to a portly female who suffered from the heat, and at frequent intervals refreshed herself and an infant from a bottle of tepid stout'.

Drinking warm beer was but one of the peculiarities of The Highway, as it is now known. The street stretched from The Tower and East Smithfield (A1203) to the Limehouse Basin and was described at one time as 'the Regent Street of London Sailors'.

Freed at last to enjoy a month's leave, Carruthers found he had nowhere to go. 'My own people were at Aix for my father's gout; to join them was a *pis aller* whose banality was repellent. Besides,' he adds, 'they would be leaving soon for our home in Yorkshire, and I was not a prophet in my own country.' While in this depressed and depressing mood, Carruthers received a letter from his friend from Oxford days, Arthur H. Davies. Davies, he remembered, had failed for the Indian Civil Service and had gone into a solicitor's office.

'He seemed to know none of my friends, he dressed indifferently, and I thought him dull.' Such opinion was hardly an encouragement to an invitation for a little yachting and duck-shooting. The address on the letter showed that it had been written from the yacht *Dulcibella*, then at Flensburg, Schleswig-Holstein. Davies said that he had a feeling that he was in luck, so he larded the letter with requests for Carruthers to collect his gun from Lancaster's together with a good lot of No. 4 cartridges, a prismatic compass and a pound of Raven mixture. The envelope, too, had a scribbled postscript for rigging screws.

Carruthers had sailed before, at Cowes, with a pleasant party aboard, and quite liked the idea of a steam yacht in French waters, or off the west coast of Scotland, but yachting in the Baltic at the end of September made him shudder.

In the end he was persuaded, for 'after all it was a good-natured piece of unselfishness to join Davies and he really seemed to want' him. The matter was clinched when one of his colleagues returned to work 'offensively sunburnt', with the greeting 'Hullo, Carruthers, you here? Thought you were away long ago.' That was the final straw and Carruthers telegraphed Davies with his time of arrival at Flensburg and received, almost instantly, the classic reply, 'Delighted; please bring a No.3 Rippingille stove.'

The two met at Flensburg railway station. Carruthers, who had taken the precaution of packing his portmanteau with cool white ducks, neat blue serge and a

No. 3 Rippingille stove

snowy-crowned yachting cap, felt oddly guilty when he first caught sight of the drab appearance of his new yachting companion.

Davies was apprehensive about the size and solidity of Carruthers' luggage, saying that it would have to be stowed somewhere in the confines of *Dulcibella*. Carruthers, on the other hand, was put out when told there was no crew. Paid hands and yachts were indivisible in his mind. His worst fears were confirmed as they transferred the mountain of luggage and stores from the dinghy to *Dulcibella*. 'The bitterest touch of all was a growing sense of inferiority and ignorance, which I had never before been allowed to feel in my experience of yachts.' The taming of Carruthers had begun.

Dulcibella was no Cowes swan, nor was she a sleek ocean greyhound, but a 'scrubby little craft of doubtful build and distressing plainness.' She began her career as a lifeboat and was exceptionally strong, being of double diagonal teak construction. The transformation into a yacht was contrived by adding a counter to the lifeboat's double-ender stern and dressing her with a yawl rig. Of seven tons, she was something over thirty feet in length and nine in the beam, a size suitable, Carruthers thought, for the Solent rather than a cruise from Dover to the Baltic.

Dulcibella presented a strange appearance to those more used to the creations of famous yacht designers such as Fife and Watson. 'The hull seemed too low, and the mainmast too high; the cabin roof looked clumsy, and the skylights saddened the eye with dull iron and plebian *[sic]* graining. What brass there was, on the tiller head and elsewhere, was tarnished with sickly green. The decks had none of that creamy purity which Cowes expects, but were grey, and showed tarry exhalations round the seams and rusty stains near the bows. The ropes and rigging were in mourning when contrasted with the delicate buff manila so satisfying to the artistic eye as seen against the blue June sky of Southsea.' Carruthers, though, warmed a little towards her. 'That the ensemble was business-like and solid even my untrained eye could see.'

This down-at-heel appearance was carried below decks. The companion ladder led down between the saloon and the sleeping cabin aft. Forward was the fo'c'sle, a rabbit-hutch of a place in which lived the paraffin-fuelled No. 3 Rippingille stove and so acted as a galley.

The saloon was dominated by the centre-board case, a long, low triangle that also acted as the support for the table and had an odious habit when lowered of spouting jets of water through its chain lead onto the cabin floor. The deck overhead was very low at each side, but rose shoulder-high for a space in the middle where the coach-house roof with a skylight gave additional cabin space. Across the forward bulkhead was a bookshelf crammed to overflowing with volumes of all sizes, many upside down and some coverless. They included an ancient ledger that did duty as the yacht's log, a nautical almanac, *Sailing Directions* by Cowper, several books on cruises in small yachts, including E. F. Knight's *Falcon on the Baltic*, Brassey's *Naval Annual* and two works of Captain A. T. Mahan, United States Navy, the much-thumbed *The Influence of Sea-Power Upon History* and his *Life of Nelson* (see Figure 2).

Below the bookshelf 'were a pipe rack, an aneroid, and a clock with a hearty tick'. All the woodwork was painted white, and, Carruthers' description continued, 'to a less jaundiced eye than mine the interior might have had an enticing look of snugness.' He concludes his description of the saloon by noting that there was a Kodak print of a young girl over the doorway, whom Davies identified as his sister.

The sleeping cabin was through the companion lobby and complete with two 'short and narrow berths, with blankets but no sheets'. Beneath these were drawers, a set for each of them; 'a princely allowance of space' to Davies but little enough to swallow the contents of Carruthers' yachting wardrobe. The food and drink were stowed, not too exclusively, in the saloon, as Carruthers soon discovered. The food was in one of the sofa-lockers, while the drink was under the floor in the cool of the bilge.

Dulcibella sailed from Flensburg on 27 September and put her nose into Ekken Sound, briefly revealing a view of 'tantalising loveliness' before anchoring in thickening weather in the open Als Sound roadstead, near the approaches to Sonderburg.

The character of the narrator, the characteristics of the boat and the first beginnings of the adventure are introduced in this way to the reader. Arthur H. Davies takes a little more getting to know.

Carruthers recollected that he 'liked him for his physical energy, combined with a certain simplicity and modesty.' His dress reflected his absence of show. *Dulcibella's* appearance was a mirror image, the only concessions were to the shining binnacle and the 'gaudy new burgee'. She never wore an ensign any more than he wore a yachting suit. Carruthers was to learn later that Davies was a 'master of his métier'. He also discovered how resourceful, skilful and alert his friend could be, even though 'he was liable to lapse into a certain amateurish vagueness, half irritating and half amusing'. Carruthers suspected 'that both these peculiarities came from the same source – a hatred of any sort of affectation'.

Through the Ekken Sound

Davies was reticent, anxious to please his friend, delighted when he showed signs of enjoying the sea life, careful to nurture the feeble beginnings of pleasure in the other, not wishing to lose him by explaining too early the part he hoped he would play in the scheme of things to come, for fear that he might take fright and flight. It was only with difficulty that Carruthers dragged out of him the course of the voyage before they met on Flensburg's lamp-lit quay, but at last it came out.

Dulcibella, with Davies and his friend Morrison, had sailed from Dover on 6 August and had made for Ostend. After two days spent repairing, they had a splendid sail to the East Schelde and then, foolishly as he put it, decided to go through Holland by river and canal. He enjoyed navigating the estuaries, but the canals were a wretched business, 'nothing but paying lock dues, bumping against shuyts, towing down stinking canals'. Peace was unobtainable; moored to quays and canal banks, because of the endless numbers of people and 'a perfect murrain, of stone-throwing boys'.

Davies had nosed his way through Dordrecht, and on to the great port of Rotterdam, through swarms of tugs, and then to the capital, Amsterdam, via the Vecht River. From there *Dulcibella* made again for the North Sea and had just entered the Zuyder Zee when the weather broke. However, this did not put Davies off exploring the northern part of that inland sea, before making for the Dutch and German Frisian Islands. Davies was particularly concerned about the poor state of Admiralty charts for this splendid sailing ground. 'You can explore for days without seeing a soul. There are channels, you see; they're very badly charted. This chart was almost useless, but it made it all the more fun.'

He went on to say how he had followed that chain of islands, 'really gigantic sandbanks', from, Terschelling, the third island from the east, making for the Baltic. Sometimes they sailed outside the islands, sometimes inside. *Dulcibella* went by Ameland, Schiermonnikoog, Rottum and on to Borkum, the first of the German islands, where they arrived on about 9 September. Morrison had to leave *Dulcibella* at Terschelling and Davies had been single-handed after that. From Borkum, *Dulcibella* took in Norderney before sailing, as E. F. Knight had done in *Falcon*, straight for the Eider River and the canal for Kiel. Davies was hesitant and avoided giving detail. He allowed problems of the minute to distract him from telling anything but the barest outline of his voyage to the Baltic and was silent about what happened after 9 September, when *Dulcibella* reached Borkum and German waters. Soon after, though, he displayed a wisp of a wish to return to the Frisians, an idea that Carruthers was quick to say he would loathe, infinitely preferring the sun and scenery more likely to be found, even at that time of year, in the Baltic, than the sand-girt southern fringes of the North Sea. Davies had already said that any bad weather in the Baltic could be properly employed after ducks – the worse the weather the better the chances on that score.

With this in mind, they made north through the narrow gut of Als Sound, past the fascinating town of Sonderburg. They visited the entrenchments of Duppel or Dybbøl, as Carruthers called them, and the thought brought out Davies' mixture of admiration and concern about the Germans, who had occupied that part of Denmark since the battle and siege of 1864.

It was late in the evening, while anchored under the monument commemorating this feat of arms, that Carruthers discovered a page had been torn out of *Dulcibella's* log and that a record of three days had been lost. The entry for 9 September was there, but the frayed and pruned edge of the page showed that the journal for the 10th to the 12th had been removed. Carruthers forbore to call attention to this signal maritime crime and determined instead to keep a notebook of his own, as Davies had earlier urged.

The continuing search for ducks took them south, into the narrow confines of Schlei Fjord, where they were at last successful, or rather the pilot who had taken the two sportsmen under his wing was successful, for he, knowing the best place to stand, bagged the fine mallard and three ducks that fell that evening.

The next day, 1 October, dawned in a wreath of fog. It was a day that was to signal a change of course in both their lives; the skipper of the ketch *Johannes,* Captain Bartels, was the herald.

Davies had good reason to be grateful to the little bearded man in oilskins and sou'wester whom he had met on the outward voyage. Now the *Johannes* was anchored in Schlei Fjord; Bartels spotted *Dulcibella* through the fog and so paid a call on his friend. Bartels told Carruthers a little of what had happened the day that Davies and he were last together and it was this that persuaded the owner of *Dulcibella* to confess to his friend from the Foreign Office and to seek his help.

Davies recalled how he had called in at Borkum and asked about the wildfowling. He had been advised by fishermen there to seek out the owner of the barge-yacht *Medusa,* for he was a keen shot and could no doubt give some tips. Shortly after this, in the evening; Davies came across *Medusa* lying off Norderney. He described her as a 'barge-yacht of fifty or sixty tons, built for shallow water on the lines of a Dutch galliot, with lee-boards and those queer round bows and square stern … She looked like a clipper of her sort and very smart; varnished all over and shining like gold.'

After dinner he plucked up courage and sculled over, and the steward led him down the companion into the saloon. His host, Dollmann, a tall, thin chap of about fifty with greyish hair and a short beard, was dressed in a dinner jacket. It did not make things easier for Davies when he found that Dollmann could not speak English. The interview was sticky, at least in the beginning. Dollmann was positively negative about ducks – there were none in these parts. It was only as Davies was about to go that Dollmann thawed and in quite a friendly way took an interest in the cruise so far and his plans for the future. However, this change of tack did not really improve matters, as Davies never felt at ease. Dollmann seemed to be sizing him up all the time.

Rather surprisingly Dollmann turned up for breakfast aboard *Dulcibella* the next morning, then Davies lunched or dined once or twice on *Medusa*. There he met Dollmann's daughter Clara, who seemed a very nice girl. Dollmann suggested that Davies abandon his search for sport and follow *Medusa* as far as the Elbe, leaving him free to continue to the Baltic through the ship canal at Brunsbüttel. They decided to sail in company to Cuxhaven. It was only a day's sail of about sixty miles and they left early on 13 September, the glass falling.

By the time the two yachts were off the island of Wangeroog, the most easterly of the German chain, it began to blow really hard. Davies had earlier taken in two reefs and he now thought it advisable to take in a third. He had half a mind to chuck it and cut into the Jade River but soon dismissed the idea. With the reduced canvas, *Dulcibella* dropped astern of *Medusa* and when she was about six miles southwest of the Elbe Outer Lightship, the German barge-yacht hove to, right ahead. Dollmann, lashing the wheel, leaned over her quarter and shouted, 'very slowly and distinctly so that I could under stand: "Follow me – sea too bad for you outside – short-cut through sands save six miles." '

Davies spoke with bitter gravity. He realised the sense of the plan and that the short-cut could avoid going outside the Scharhörn Reef, 'a great jagged chunk of sand that runs out from Cuxhaven'. It would also enable them to keep out of the rough and tumble off the point, where the two tides meet. It meant, though, following Dollmann into the Telte Channel and relying entirely on him. He admitted wryly that that was the only time he had taken a pilot. The story, now loosened, cascaded out of him, as though this admission had broken some sort of word-jam.

Davies kept *Dulcibella* in the wake of the *Medusa* but found that she was gaining. He seemed to be going for all he was worth and in a rain squall he lost sight of her altogether for a short time. Davies recalled, 'I had enough to do with my own tiller not to want to be peering through the scud after a runaway pilot. It was all right so far, but we were fast approaching the worst part of the whole passage, where the Hohenhorn Bank blocks the road and the channel divides.' He pointed out the difficulty to Carruthers. 'I knew perfectly well that what I should soon see would be a wall of surf stretching right across and on both sides. To feel one's way in that sort of weather is impossible. You must know your way, or else have a pilot. I had one, but he was playing his own game.'

He then recounted how he saw the surf wall clean across the horizon, shutting him in and booming like thunder. At that point he lost *Medusa*. 'She seemed to be charging it like a horse at fence, and I took a rough bearing of her position by a hurried glance at the compass.' Davies had no more time to worry about *Medusa*, because he was soon aground, 'grinding and banging'.

Carruthers gathered that this was where Bartels came in. His galliot was at anchor a mile away in a branch of the channel and he helped kedge *Dulcibella* off. *Johannes*, loaded with a cargo of apples, was bound for Kappeln in the Schlei Fjord, having come from Bremen; she was making for the Baltic via the Eider River when they met. Davies told how he changed his plans after this rather traumatic day and had challenged *Johannes* to the Eider, winning handsomely.

The breathless, racing account of near shipwreck was spell-binding enough, but it was Davies' reading of Dollmann's real face lurking behind the salt-stained drama which captured Carruthers: 'You see, I had come to the conclusion that that chap was a spy.'

Davies was all but convinced, too, that Dollmann meant *Dulcibella* to founder and her owner to drown. His so-called short-cut led straight onto the Hohenhorn West Sand. It was clear that Dollmann intended to pilot Davies into the next world, for *Medusa* had driven on out of sight on purpose.

Davies allowed that Dollmann's first intention had been to persuade him to leave the German Frisians in favour of the Baltic. However, when the weather worsened, he seized his chance and did his best to rid himself of the Englishman. The other argument, in favour of Dollmann being a spy, was not so clear cut. The theory came from doubt about Dollmann's nationality: 'He's not a German,' Davies said, 'he's an

Englishman.' He based his surprising claim on the way that Dollmann, who had professed little English in earlier conversations, had shouted, in what Davies was sure was his native tongue, 'short-cut through the sands; follow me!' Davies felt he was on safe ground in this – 'I'm convinced,' he said, 'that he's an Englishman in German service.' He had a house on Norderney Island and was friendly with a German naval officer, Commander von Brüning, who was in command of a fishery protection gunboat, *Blitz*. Davies met the latter on board *Medusa* and took to him. Showing his admiration for Germans and Germany, he continued, 'He looked a real good sort, and a splendid officer too – just the sort of chap I should have liked to be.'

Davies was much less forthcoming about Dollmann's daughter Clara. Carruthers sensed that he felt awkward, for some reason, about the girl. He was only too keen, though, to develop his theory about Germany, the Germans and their emperor's ambitions. Encouraged by his friend, he outlined his theory with some force.

The Germans have, unlike Britain, no colonies. They, like us, 'must have them'. He went on, 'They can't get them and keep them and they can't protect their huge commerce without naval strength.' He cited the writings of Captain Mahan, represented in *Dulcibella's* library, pointing out in an almost expert way the make-up of the existing small but highly efficient German Navy and how it was expanding under the leadership of the Kaiser.

Davies then turned to the geography of Germany and in particular to her coastline, split in two as it was by Denmark. To evade this block, the Kaiser built the Kiel Canal. Davies was certain that this would be smashed in war time and that the North Sea half was far more important than the Baltic one. 'It's where Germany gets her head out into the open, so to speak. It's there that she fronts us and France, the two great sea powers of Western Europe, and it's there that her greatest ports are and her richest commerce.' He emphasised that it was a ridiculously short stretch, compared with the coast of France and England, being only 200 miles from Borkum in the west to Schleswig in the east.

For the purposes of his argument, Davies divided the 200 miles into three parts: the first stretched from Borkum to Wangeroog, where there was a string of sandy islands backed by more sand, with the Ems River and Emden at the west end. The second stretch continued eastward from Wangeroog and consisted only of twenty miles, yet it contained the three great rivers – the Jade, the Weser and the Elbe, which led to the great naval base at Wilhelmshaven and to the commercially vital ports of Bremen and Hamburg respectively. The third stretch, he felt, was less important. This was the Schleswig coast, which was hopelessly fenced in with sand. The importance of the second stretch was undeniable, with Wilhelmshaven and the two giants of Bremen and Hamburg in need of defence. The approaches to both were well known and the fortifications could be viewed from the decks of steamers that endlessly plied those waters.

Davies was much more concerned and interested in the first part – that sand-strewn stretch from Borkum to Wangeroog. 'In event of war,' he stated, 'it seems to me that every inch of it would be important, sand and all.' The big estuaries, on either side, would be blockaded or attacked by an enemy. There was no lack of knowledge as their approaches were well known and charted and in peacetime they were buoyed and lighted. This contrasted starkly with 'the threads of channels', tidal for the most part, that run behind and between the islands, and were probably only known to smacks and shallow coasters like the *Johannes*. Davies warmed to his subject and emphasised what lay behind his interest in this first stretch.

> *It strikes me that in war a lot may depend on these [channels], both in defence and attack, for there is plenty of water in them at the right tide for patrol-boats and small torpedo craft, though I can see they take a lot of knowing. Now say we were at war with Germany: both sides could use them as links between the three estuaries; and to take your own case, a small torpedo boat (not a destroyer, mind you) could, on a dark night, cut clean through from the Jade to the Elbe and play the deuce with the shipping there, but the trouble is that I doubt if there is a soul in our fleet who knows those channels.*

Davies had earlier expressed his low opinion of Admiralty charts of the area, emphasising their 'pre-historic rottenness'. His researches had also persuaded him that this strip of Frisian coast and adjoining estuaries 'would also form a splendid base for raiding midgets, which could travel unseen right through from the Ems to the Jade and so to the Elbe, as by a covered way between a line of forts'.

There is no doubt that Carruthers was drawn to Davies, to his account and to his 'channel theory'. He was, however, not convinced that Davies had given good reason why an Englishman should be watching these waters and ejecting intruders like Davies, nor did he provide sufficient motive for Dollmann to send his friend to a watery grave. However, Carruthers was willing to take a good deal for granted 'until we find out more'.

These last few words were the very ones that Davies wanted to hear but had not dared to hope for. His delight was obvious. He saw in Carruthers his only way of obtaining an answer to 'The Riddle', for he felt hopelessly out of his depth, not speaking German and being 'a dull chap all round'. Davies was embarrassed by his lack of frankness with his friend, feeling he had brought him to the discomfort of his scrubby little vessel on the false pretence of providing innocent pleasure, rather than letting on the true purpose and enlisting his friend's help in unravelling this 'tangled business'.

The two decided, there and then, to return to the North Sea, this time via Kiel and the ship canal, with two objects, the first of which was to work back to Norderney, exploring on the way all the channels to the estuaries behind the islands. The other objective was to find Dollmann and discover what he was up to, and, if necessary, settle with him.

Dulcibella left Bartels and *Johannes* in Schlei Fjord and headed for Kiel. Carruthers realised that he had committed himself; he had 'signed the articles' and he began to savour the call of adventure.

The yacht passed through anchored warships and anchored off the town of Kiel at 1 am. The next day they bought sea boots, rough woollen breeches, jerseys, helmets and gloves, all chosen to harmonise with paraffin stains and anchor mud. They purchased all manner of other stores, so as to be independent of the shore in their seven-tonner. Importantly, they also managed to secure 'German charts of excellent quality'.

On the evening of 2 October, they left for the Kaiser Wilhelm Canal, entering at Holtenau, taking two days to reach Brunsbüttel at the North Sea end. Then Bartels arrived, so they secured alongside the *Johannes* for the journey, relying on Karl, the shock-headed, stout-limbed deckhand to steer both vessels.

The enforced idleness of the canal trip allowed the two to get to know each other better, for Carruthers to learn more about his friend and his past failures. Davies' ambition had been to enter the Royal Navy, but they would not have him. Davies thought it a waste that people of his bent and ability could not serve his country and he expressed strong feelings about this:

> *There must be hundreds of chaps like me – I know a good many myself – who know our coasts like a book – shoals, creeks, tides, rocks; there's nothing in it, it's only practice. They ought to make some use of us as a naval reserve.*

Davies blamed Britain's 'blockheads of statesmen' for not waking up to Germany's growing commercial might. She was Britain's great trade rival and would be our great naval rival in the future. Davies was certain that we were not ready for her. 'We don't look her way. We have no naval base in the North Sea, and no North Sea fleet. Our battleships are too deep in draft for North Sea work. And, to crown it all, we were asses enough to give her Heligoland, which commands her North Sea coast. And supposing she collars Holland'; he had heard some talk of that. Carruthers saw that Davies was determined to contribute to the cause of the maritime supremacy of Britain and to use, with his friend's help, his seven-ton pleasure boat and 'a taste for amateur hydrography' to forward this end.

As *Dulcibella* nosed out of the great sea-lock at Brunsbüttel, Davies discovered that *Medusa* had called only the day before and that Clara had enquired about the English yacht and had been difficult to satisfy. *Medusa*, it appeared, was bound outward and for Norderney.

The tide took them swiftly down the Elbe, 'drab, dreary miles like the dullest reaches of the lower Thames', until they passed Cuxhaven and, a little later, 'the long, low fort, with some great guns peeping over'. A couple of sea miles further out of the great estuary of the Elbe, they picked up on the port and the entrance to the Stickers Gat and soon entered the waters of the 'Sleeping Whale', the name that Davies gave to areas where the receding tide left 'sleek, mauve humps, surrounded by streaks and circles of white breaking sea, marking where the sand appeared to have risen from the deep'. They had returned to that intricate stage of the short-cut selected by *Medusa* on that memorable day.

Carruthers, who had earlier asked the meaning of 'kedging off', soon began to learn by experience, for *Dulcibella* was barely three miles into the channel that pierces the Steil Sand when she went aground.

With the help of a large-scale chart, the two planned the next few days. Davies pointed out the estuaries of the Jade, Weser and Elbe, that split the sands into two main groups. Davies named them by their appearance on the chart. To the west, those caught between the Jade and the Weser he called 'The Pike'. The sands they were about to cross to the east he nicknamed 'The Fork'. They were the three deadly prong of the Scharhörn Reef, the Knecht Sand and the Tegeler Flats, pointing northwest, separated from each other by deep water-filled cavities through the sand. It was their duty, Davies explained, to explore The Fork and The Pike and the channels that ran through them.

Dulcibella spent the night anchored in the shelter of the Hohenhorn Sands, in the intimate embrace of the east and west banks, protected as securely as if she had been within a stone breakwater. Even so, at high water and with the wind against tide, much to Carruthers' discomfort, *Dulcibella* began to roll. Davies, though, was unmoved. Eventually, maddened by all the noises caused by the wind and the rolling, Carruthers suggested half in jest that they make the best of the night and explore the shore. The two wandered over the East Sand, Davies reliving his narrow escape when following the false wake of *Medusa*.

During the next ten days they explored The Fork and The Pike. The meaning of their work became more clear with experience and, as their knowledge of the sands and channels grew, they both began to realise 'that the whole region would be an ideal hunting ground for small freelance marauders'.

Davies saw that a small boat in sheltered waters could play a mighty role in a naval war, especially in the final stages of the conflict. He held that 'the heavy battle fleets are all very well, but if the sides are well matched there might be nothing left of them after a few months of war. They might destroy one another mutually, leaving as nominal conqueror an admiral with scarcely a battleship to bless himself with. It is then that the true struggle will set in and it is then that anything that will float will be pressed into the service, and anybody who can steer a boat, knows his waters, and doesn't care the toss of a coin for his life, will have magnificent opportunities.' The same was true on the British side of the North Sea. Davies cited the Mersey estuary, the Dee, the Severn, the Wash and best of all the Thames, with all Kent, Essex and Sussex banks around it. He despaired: 'We've nothing ready – nothing whatsoever! We don't even build or use small torpedo boats.'

For all these theories, they found nothing to substantiate their suspicions, nor anything that suggested a really adequate motive for Dollmann's treachery. To cap it all, Carruthers was due back in London – unless he obtained an extension – and their supply of paraffin and oil was running low. Wangeroog, the easternmost of the Frisians, was selected for re-victualling and as the island had no harbour *Dulcibella* was run on to the sand on a rising tide.

The yacht was high and dry by the time they finished supper and Davies set out into the fine, starry night to replenish the water-breakers and oil-cans, leaving Carruthers to lay out the anchor and ensure that the riding-lights burned brightly to guide his return.

Carruthers was almost asleep when he heard 'the pad of a boot on the sand', and realising that the furtive step was not that of Davies he kept quiet. He heard the intruder climb aboard, made a grab at him and was left holding a big sea boot as the owner vaulted overboard. Carruthers followed in hot pursuit but ran headlong into the wire bobstay and was sent sprawling. The visitor had doused the riding-light on boarding and the short chase that followed, after Carruthers had picked himself up from the sand, was nearly fatal, for he had the greatest difficulty in finding the boat again.

Davies' verdict on the escapade was that it could not have been a thief; 'They're not like that in Germany,' he said. 'In Holland, if you like, they'll do anything.' At any rate, he was convinced that the intruder was after the ship's log and the charts with all the corrections and notes. They kept two sets of charts – German and

English. The former they used and annotated; the latter, 'being relatively useless', they decided should be left for all to see. In the circumstances, the two decided that their alibi, the purpose of the voyage as far as the outside world was concerned, was still to be duck-shooting, even though it was very early for that in the islands.

Carruthers noticed on the chart that the mainland dyke was punctuated at intervals by infinitesimal villages, all ending in 'siel', indicating that they were drainage outlets for the lowlands behind and possessed a sluice or a lock. Davies, with his usual aversion to any place with a population, was not too keen on spending time on the mainland shore, though he spotted some sort of quay arrangement at Neuharlingersiel and Dornumersiel. He was still sold on his channel theory, arguing again, with a strength that impressed his companion, that the space behind the islands was like 'an immense tidal harbour, thirty miles by five' and 'absolutely made for shallow war-boats under skilled pilotage'.

Bright and early the next morning, 16 October, Carruthers took the turn ashore and walked to Wangeroog with the water-breakers. He visited the village, half lost in the sand drifts. A friendly grocer told him sceptically that he had heard of plans to expand the 'mud-holes', as he called the siels. It was part of a scheme to develop the islands as health resorts.

The yacht required yet more fresh water and Davies made the next trip while his companion stalked some small birds with a gun and managed to bag a jack-snipe.

On leaving the anchorage at one o'clock, they saw a galliot with *Kormoran* painted large on her stern. The name remained in their minds. They noted, too, 'the great church tower', standing in the water on the north side of Wangeroog, a witness to the encroachment of the sea.

Dulcibella soon entered the Muschel Balge, the channel inside of Spiekeroog, the next island to the east, and they anchored there for the night.

The days were getting shorter, with sunset soon after five. High water was awkward at this time, too, arriving at twilight, morning and evening. About this time, on the 16th, they spotted a small grey, single-funnelled German gunboat going east, which Davies identified immediately as *Blitz*. He was contemptuous about her low freeboard and they both agreed that she was an 'ugly, cranky little vessel'. From the edition of Brassey on *Dulcibella's* bookshelf, they discovered her further details. She was 140 feet long by 25 feet in the beam. She sported one 4.9-inch gun, one 3.4 and four maxims. There was no doubt that she was an old type. In addition to *Blitz*, Davies thought he saw the galliot *Kormoran* again in the offing.

The next day, the two explored the gap between Spiekeroog and the next island, Langeoog. In the evening, they made a bad mistake, running aground on the top of the tide in worsening conditions. The two worked furiously to lighten ship and had to undertake 'the horrid business' of 'handling pigs of lead, heavy, greasy and black'. The saloon was 'an inferno, the deck like a collier's, and ourselves like sweeps'. This was Carruthers' description of the scene as they transferred ballast to the dinghy. The operation was a success and they came off on the tide.

They spotted *Blitz* at anchor in the Schill Balge, inside Spiekeroog, about a half mile from them. Her draft of nine feet ten inches convinced Davies that she must have entered between Spiekeroog and Langeoog, seeking respite from the gale.

The weather went from bad to worse, for 'at 3.30 a black ragged cloud, that appeared to trail into the very sea, brought up a terrific squall'. They decided to seek shelter and in so doing Carruthers lost the anchor, for the chain slipped and whizzed out of the hawse pipe on the first heave on the winch lever. There was nothing for it but to run for Bensersiel and with the gale-force winds increasing in strength from the northeast, they certainly arrived in style. 'Once in the small square harbour, there was no time to lower sails. Davies just threw the kedge over, and it just got a grip in time to check our momentum and save our bowsprit from the quay-side.' The natives were so surprised, they seemed to think the two had 'dropped from the sky' and were disappointed that there was no salvage work to be done. The yachtsmen, for their part, were equally astonished to discover a customs officer, who duly searched *Dulcibella* for spirits, salt and coffee. In the end, Herr Schenkel was full of kindness, thinking the two 'were mad, wealthy aristocrats' and therefore 'worthy protégés for a high official'. He insisted 'they take the yacht's cushions to dry in his cottage near the quay, just over the bridge that crossed the sluice.

Davies and Carruthers talked 'ducks and weather' in the Gasthaus and took a closer look at the harbour, which boasted five to seven feet of water for two hours out

Vixen's saloon

of the twelve, and catered for the Langeoog post-boat and a few lighters that came down stream with bricks and other produce, from the interior, bound for the islands under tow.

Carruthers was introduced for the first time to Commander von Brüning of the gunboat *Blitz* early the following morning and they arranged to meet in the inn for a talk at twelve o'clock. The idea of such a close encounter with authority put a question mark over their plan to conceal the log and the marked charts. Von Brüning knew of Davies' weakness for exploration, having met him on the outward voyage, and there now seemed little point in this subterfuge.

The galliot *Kormoran* had come in on the same tide as *Blitz*'s steam-cutter and they discovered her business by talking to the twins who manned the post-boat. *Kormoran* was a salvage vessel employed in the attempt to recover the bullion from a French warship that had foundered ages ago on the western end of Juist, the island that lay to the west of Norderney. The twins pointed out *Kormoran*'s master, whom Carruthers christened Grimm.

When the three met in the inn, von Brüning was alarmed by Davies' account of the crossing of the Hohenhorn Sands. Davies told the story in an everyday way, leaving out any hint of treachery on the part of Dollmann. The commander seemed puzzled at the story and not a little astonished at the route taken. He thought *Dulcibella* was lucky to survive those conditions in such a dangerous place. He accepted the explanation that Davies and Dollmann had failed to meet up later because the former had decided to cross to the Baltic by way of the Eider. Carruthers thought his friend had told the tale well.

Medusa was apparently back with Clara aboard, but without Dollmann.

The conversation was wide-ranging and took in the night-visitor from Wangeroog. Carruthers tried to discover more about the treasure ship off Juist. The German explained that the casualty was a frigate, 'the *Corinne*, bound from Hamburg to Havre in 1811'. He gave a history of the subsequent salvage efforts, pointing out that the wreck had at one time been owned by Lloyds. It was now the turn of a local firm. Von Brüning went on to say that 'an engineer from Bremen was the principal mover, and a few men from Norderney and Emden subscribed the capital.' Dollmann was 'largely interested in it too'.

The meeting at the inn concluded with the commander urging them to take a local man as a guide in their search for wildfowl, but they declined the idea on the ground that their plans were uncertain until Carruthers should receive news of how long he would be allowed to stay by his masters in the Foreign Office. The three agreed to meet again in Norderney where the telegram deciding Carruthers' fate was expected, and with this von Brüning declared he had to leave them to drive to Esens where he had business. Drawing Carruthers aside before departing, he urged him to keep Davies clear of Dollmann.

Davies' mind was on other things. He was worried about being stuck for days in the little port. Strong onshore winds made departure very difficult. Von Brüning spotted Davies' concern and offered a tow with his launch that evening when he returned from Esens, where he had a fishery-protection case. Apparently a Dutchman had been caught trawling inside German waters. Von Brüning added, in a way that Carruthers thought might have deeper meaning, 'That's my work, you know – police duty.'

Davies and Carruthers returned to *Dulcibella*. There was something intriguing about Memmert, the western extension of the Nordland Sands that stretched from the shallow water under the belly of the Island of Juist to surface in the form of a scimitar of sand. The island was nearly two miles long but only 150 yards wide, except for a bulge where this measurement expands to a quarter of a mile. The German chart marked a house where this occurs, while on the English edition the nakedness was absolute, save a beacon on the southern end. The island was remarkably isolated, yet conveniently near the wreck of the *Corinne*, two miles out on the Juister Reef.

Carruthers noticed a barrier growing between Davies and himself which their natural interest in the strange island of Memmert could not conceal. He apologised to Davies for having chaffed him about Clara Dollmann. Davies admitted, 'I find it very difficult to tell people things like this,' and added, 'I did like her – very much.' Carruthers thought that Davies should realise that Clara Dollmann was as deeply involved as her father, a would-be murderer and a traitor and that it was not possible to pursue him without harming her. Throughout, Davies held to his theory about the importance of the channels. It was a clear tenet of his faith. He seemed to see threat in Carruthers' growing belief that Memmert played a significant part in the story.

Carruthers was certain that two principal clues had shown themselves in the conversation at the inn. The first, already mentioned, was the significance of Memmert; The second clue was that as it was only a matter of time before those on *Dulcibella* realised that von Brüning, Dollmann and Grimm were concerned together in the Memmert operation, it was important for the naval officer to emphasise that 'buried treasure was at the root of any mystery the pair may have scented.' Secrecy, after all, was essential because of the great sum involved and any midnight visitors could be put down to worries about the activities of Lloyd's agents.' Any Englishman on this coast is open to such a label,' the commander had cleverly implied. Carruthers was now convinced that Grimm had been the midnight visitor.

Davies listened patiently as Carruthers developed his theory about the importance and the meaning of Memmert. The island commanded the entrance to the eastern Ems. They had neglected the importance of this river in favour of the vital and much publicised roles of the three greater estuaries that commanded the quays of Hamburg and Bremerhaven and the great naval dockyard of Wilhelmshaven. The Ems, after all, only served the small and drying port of Delfzijl on the Dutch side and Emden, which required locks and a mile of canal, on the German side.

This short dismissal, though, neglected the fact that Emden was a flourishing port and of growing importance with a network of canals suitable for craft of shallow draft that would soon be able to reach the Rhine at Dortmund. Davies added that 'even the heaviest battleships could approach within striking distance of the land, while cruisers and military transports could penetrate to the level of Emden itself'. Emden, he repeated, was 'connected by canal with Wilhelmshaven on the Jade', and was 'a strategic canal designed to carry gunboats as well as merchandise'.

At the entrance of the two arms of the river, the western and eastern Ems, lay the protecting islands of Borkum and Memmert. Memmert was part of the 'outer rampart'; it therefore commanded the eastern branch and was essential to its defence.

> *No more admirable base could be imagined; self-contained and isolated, yet sheltered, accessible – better than Juist or Borkum and with a ready-made excuse for shrouding the nature of any work with absolute secrecy by having a valuable wreck conveniently in the offing right by the main fairway. Further, Memmert, with a depot for salvage operations, required dredging and diving equipment that was precisely the same as would be needed for serving port defences such as mines and dirigible torpedoes. All the details of [von Brüning's] story were suggestive: the 'small local company'; the engineer from Bremen; the few shares held by von Brüning, enough to explain his visits; and gear coming from Wilhelmshaven, a naval dockyard.*

Davies and Carruthers felt drained, and decided on some fresh air to clear their minds. They donned their oilskins and set forth. They looked at the little port of Bensersiel for clues and then decided, on impulse, to look at the dyke. They wandered east along it and looked inland at the 'square of pasture ringed with ditches'. They returned by a short circuit inland, crossing the Esens road and coming to the banks of the Benser Tief, the stream that gave into the harbour. Their brief survey had produced no answers.

Back in the harbour itself, the Imperial steam launch was already afloat and *Kormoran* was preparing for sea. By the time the customs had cleared *Dulcibella* and Carruthers and Davies had said their goodbyes to those in the inn, the yacht was afloat. Commander von Brüning offered to tow them to the anchorage under the island of Spiekeroog, near where *Blitz* was lying and not too far from where they had buoyed the anchor. In a friendly way he joined the two Englishmen for the tow out. Before the steam-launch set them free, the commander reminded Carruthers of the warning he had given earlier.

The next day dawned cold and vaporous. There was a light and fitful northeasterly to help them on and an oily swell to support them. They went westward outside Langeoog, after they had recovered the anchor, and eventually anchored in the lee of Baltrum for the night, engulfed in fog. The next day, 21 October, was clearer and they managed to thread their way west behind Baltrum and along the inner flank of Norderney. Davies spotted a scrap of white in the distance and recognised it with some emotion as *Medusa's* dinghy. They anchored quickly, Davies setting out in pursuit in *Dulcibella's* tender, Carruthers watching as Davies and Clara met on the sand on the north side of the creek. He soon realised that it fell to him to make *Dulcibella's* saloon worthy to receive a lady. He had just about finished when the dinghy prepared to come alongside, 'Davies sculling in the bows, facing him in the stern a young girl'.

Once aboard, the girl cast a seaman's inquisitive eye over everything. She said her father would be back tomorrow to join *Medusa*. She and her stepmother were staying ashore at their villa in the Schwannallee. The conversation carried on in a happy vein but the banquet that had been anticipated was never celebrated. Catastrophe came and passed so suddenly that Carruthers scarcely had an inkling of what caused it. Something on the bookshelf caught her eye and seemed to disturb her; she jumped up, exclaiming that she must go. Carruthers accompanied her as she rowed back to her stranded dinghy. There she urged him to forget about visiting her father – he did not like foreigners much and, she was sure, did not want to see Herr Davies again.

On his return, Carruthers found Davies surrounded by a litter of books. He was handed a volume shrouded in a cheap cloth, the binding of rather antiquated style. The tide showed it to be a guide for yachtsmen to a certain British estuary. He was astonished when, in an excited voice, Davies explained that Dollmann was the author.

Sure enough there on the title page was a rather poor illustration of a man 'in his shirt-sleeves; a well-knit, powerful man, young, of middle height, close shaven'. Davies went on to say that although he was now fifty and bearded, you could tell that the man was Dollmann by the shape of his head, how it widened on the top and then flattened to a sort of wedge shape, with a high, steep forehead. The man's height and figure, coupled with the dates of publication, evaporated doubt. They spent a few minutes discussing what they now knew about Dollmann. Sixteen years before he had been an officer in Her Majesty's Navy. Now he was apparently a German. The girl was about nineteen or twenty, so she would have been four at the time the book was published. The family must have been hiding in Germany ever since.

Dollmann must have seen the book when he came aboard for breakfast on the morning after his first meeting with Davies. The sight of it had determined the plan to drown the young Englishman. It was clear that there were two accounts of the doings of that day. Dollmann had evidently indicated to his daughter, who had seen and heard little because she was below, that *Medusa* had come by the inside route, but that *Dulcibella* had taken the longer haul, stayed in the main channel and left the Scharhörn Reef to starboard. Clara, thinking this was the reason that Davies had been left behind, had apologised for not waiting for him in Cuxhaven, explaining that her father had discovered pressing business in Hamburg.

The other account, the true one, was now known to Commander von Brüning and he was likely to tax Dollmann with it when they met, while Dollmann would probably maintain his own account. This would sow the seeds of distrust. It was clear that the Englishmen's best interest lay in preserving the status quo for as long as they could in order to discover more. It was clear to Davies that nothing would be gained by cutting and running now, by returning to England and seeking the assistance of either the Admiralty or Scotland Yard. They had to stay and unravel the mystery themselves: Dollmann was likely to be on the 8.30 boat from Norddeich, the ferry port that served Norderney. *Dulcibella* must be in the island harbour when Dollmann returned and they should convince Dollmann that they had no suspicion of foul play in his account and that they, in their turn, were just innocent travellers. They had to assume that von Brüning had been taken in by their story when they met at Bensersiel.

Dulcibella was soon under way, though the wind was not long with them.

To maintain progress they had to tow the yacht with the dinghy largely through fog, and in due course anchored in the five-fathom roadstead, close to Norderney's eastern pier at about 9 pm. The two decided that their objective should be 'to get Dollmann, secrets and all, daughter and all, away from Germany altogether'.

They watched the steamer arrive just after nine o'clock on the morning of 22 October. They spotted Dollmann through *Dulcibella's* oval ports, so managing to remain out of sight. Carruthers was particularly taken by Dollmann's companion, whom he caught thoughtfully contemplating *Dulcibella* as the little paddler entered the harbour. Wearing pince-nez, this short figure had little to commend him. They could not identify him. Neither he nor Dollmann left the ferry, which (they learnt from the harbour master) on Saturdays continued her journey to the neighbouring island of Juist. She was due to return to Norderney at half-past seven that evening. Just before she steamed away, Davies and Carruthers spotted Grimm aboard.

They walked to the Four Seasons Hotel. There, with the help of a cigar, Carruthers was able to examine his long-awaited mail. There were two letters from Whitehall; the first, of 6 October, suggested that Carruthers take another week's holiday. The second, forwarded from home, demanded a return to London without delay, though handwritten on the corner of the envelope was a note from his colleague M., 'Don't worry, it's only the chief's fuss.' Carruthers handed the letter to Davies, saying 'I'm afraid I never got this!'

Before they reached the harbour, the fog had swallowed them once again. With difficulty they found their way back to the yacht. As a joke, Carruthers suggested that they go to Memmert. To his surprise, Davies took him seriously and he was soon dazzled by the idea himself. It was clear that something was going on at Memmert that day. They decided to take the route that passed inside Juist, making use of the tide across the watershed, following the booms (saplings planted in the sand as guides through the channel) of the Memmert Balge that wriggled its way between Nordland and Koper Sands. *Dulcibella*'s dinghy was equipped with 'grub and whisky, the boat-compass, lead, riding-light, matches, small boathook, grapnel and line'. Carruthers suggested a fog-horn and a gun, so preserving the idea that they were after ducks, and Davies added a whistle and set to to muffle the rowlocks with cotton waste.

It was 11.25 am when they left *Dulcibella*'s side. Carruthers was at the oars, while Davies sat in the stem acting as pilot. The course was sou'west, half-west. By keeping the stern on northeast half-east, Carruthers looking at the compass as he came forward on each stroke, they saved taking way off the boat with the helm and gradually their progress became smoother and they could keep silent. 'Plump went the lead at regular intervals' in the Buse Tief, and Carruthers had to redouble his efforts as the tide was stronger in the deeper water and the dinghy required more control.

Shortly after three o'clock, after an exhausting journey, they reached the sandy shore of Memmert. Davies agreed that the land expedition should be left to Carruthers. Armed with a pocket compass, a scrap of chart, a watch, matches and a knife, Carruthers set out to inch his way to the depot. The two had arranged to meet at the foot of the big triangular beacon on the southwest tip of the island, if Carruthers took more than an hour and a half.

As Carruthers walked over the firm sand, he was surprised by the three double strokes of a bell, followed by a bugle call: *Blitz* must be there too. He soon stumbled on the base of a giant tripod. This 'ghostly polyp' was the beacon. Carruthers struck out northwest in rapid stages of ten yards, pausing then to listen.

He soon found himself at the end of a corrugated rectangular building, much like an 'Aldershot hut' (see Figure 7). He strode past the window and took a deliberate look inside. Grimm was sitting at a counting-house desk, facing 'a burly fellow in seaman's dress holding a diver's helmet'. Looking towards Grimm with their backs to the window were von Brüning, Dollmann and his companion last seen on the

Norderney steamer, whom Carruthers later discovered was Herr Bohme. Nothing could have looked more innocent: 'Relics of the wrecked frigate abounded.' What seemed to give the final touch of authenticity to the scene was 'a balk of curved timber, garnished with massive bolts' that lay on the table and seemed to be the object of earnest interest. Carruthers wondered where his mines, torpedoes, submarine boats and the Imperial conspirators had disappeared to and felt 'the ladder of proof' he had mounted tottering and shaking beneath him. It was only the presence of the four men that kept him at his post.

The view was soon barred by the drawing of a curtain. He could hardly hear a word, though he caught three of Bohme's sentences in their entirety: 'What was that?' 'They went no further?' and 'Too long: out of the question.' Then came Dollmann's voice sounding distinctly uncomfortable: 'Very well, sir, you shall see them at supper tonight; I will ask them both.' Carruthers looked quickly at his watch in surprise, realising that they were referring to Davies and himself and that there was little enough time if they were to be back on board the yacht to receive the invitation.

Carruthers caught little of the report that Dollmann made, though he was startled and put right back on the scent by a word, easy to catch, rapped out as though a heading – Chatham. Dollmann must have been there last month. He heard little more, try as he might to capture the sound that was circulating within the room. By employing a marlinspike, he managed to pry half an inch between the sash and the sill. Dollmann's report was now over. They seemed to be talking in cipher or relaying a string of statistics. The seven letters ran backwards from 'G', with remarks added to each thus: 'G ... completed.' 'F ... bad ... 1.3 (metres?) ... 2.5 (kilometres?).' 'E ... thirty-two ... 1.2.' 'D... three weeks ... thirty.' 'C ...' and so on. Straining to catch any sound, Carruthers picked up five pearls – 'four sibilant nouns' and a name he had heard before. The nouns were *Schleppboote* (tugs); *Wassertiefe* (depth of water); *Eisenbahn* (railway); *Lotsen* (pilots). The name, also sibilant, was Esens.

Although time was running out, Carruthers felt he must stay a little longer. Grimm and another left the room. When they had gone, Bohme announced, 'He insists on coming,' to which von Brüning expressed both surprise and protest. A meeting was to take place on the 25th: 'The tide serves well. The night train, of course', and Grimm was to be ready. There was a query from von Brüning which caused Bohme to say 'No, any weather,' and then, 'Only one, with half a load' and '… meet?', to which the reply came, 'At the station.' Carruthers returned to the dinghy. They could go direct now, as the water covered the banks. Carruthers had explained why they had to return with all speed, but had left the clues until later. As he sculled eastward, he puzzled over the significance of the letters A to G, and asked Davies what there were seven of 'round here'. 'Islands,' was the reply. The few clues that Carruthers gave him convinced Davies that his channel theory was right. Carruthers could not see how this outworn creed could square with Esens, tugs, depths of water, railways and pilots. They both soon realised 'that the substance of the plot was still a riddle.'

The fog began to lift just before they reached the harbour, Carruthers spotted lights and Davies identified them as those of *Blitz*'s steam-launch. They would not be able to reach *Dulcibella* before von Brüning, so they settled for the pretence of returning from a search for ducks. The naval officer and Dollmann were below by the time they were within hailing distance. Their explanation for being aboard *Dulcibella* was plausible enough. Dollmann had seen the yacht in the harbour in the morning and he had called on his return from Memmert to ask them to supper. They had been down below to leave a note and for Herr Böhme, the distinguished engineer from Bremen, to have a look around, for Dollmann knew that Davies would not mind.

Prompted by Carruthers, Davies asked Dollmann to stay while they dressed, but the other two would not have it and when they had left Carruthers remarked that 'they don't trust Dollmann'. He had noticed this on Memmert, when Grimm was sent to keep an eye on him and that he was not in the room when they fixed the rendezvous for the 25th. It looked as if Dollmann had been at the bookshelf and pushed 'his book' behind the others to ensure that von Brüning and Böhme did not see it, which suggested that they knew Dollmann's real name, but not his motive for trying to get rid of Davies.

Carruthers stopped in the middle of changing for dinner and reached for the Bradshaw, the railway timetable. He was puzzling over who Böhme, von Brüning and Grimm were to meet at a railway station on the 25th and what was its location. It must be somewhere by the sea because Böhme had said, 'The tide serves' but it could have been anywhere from Emden to Hamburg.

As they walked through the town, Davies emphasised the importance of watching for a chance to tackle Dollmann privately. They were determined to detach him from Germany. His attempt on Davies' life proved that he would probably go to any lengths rather than abandon his position in his adopted country. They also had to follow up the two valuable clues they had picked up that day, the rendezvous on 25 October and the name Esens. If they were to succeed in unravelling the mystery of what was going on, they would have to prove that they themselves were harmless. The best way to do this was to separate; Carruthers to go back to London under the cover of the letter that had urged his return – and he had brought these with him to show if necessary – while Davies could stay in Norderney laying up the yacht, taking some time about it. Davies agreed on the plan, with reluctance, just as they arrived at the villa, where they found Dollmann and his wife, von Brüning, Böhme and Clara, the last looking a little apprehensive.

During dinner the commander was interested to learn that Carruthers had been recalled to London and that he would be on the 8.15 steamer the next morning with Böhme, who was heading for Bremen. Von Brüning went on to try to discover what the pair had been doing all day and was a little sceptical when Carruthers replied that they had felt it best to remain on board because of the fog. Carruthers then teased them provocatively about the secrecy of their salvage operations on Memmert.

The evening had been some sort of success. They had managed in a skilful, but it must be said uncoordinated and unrehearsed way, to let Dollmann and his companions know that Carruthers had to leave for London and that Davies would be staying on to do a little duck-shooting, perhaps search for a crew and, failing that, would lay up at Norderney. Carruthers was convinced that their adversaries now thought that Memmert was the centre of any suspicions that the two Englishmen might have, rather than that they had caught any wind of Imperial designs. It was clear that the German side would not wish to take strong action against the young men, for this would bring publicity, which would be fatal to their enterprise.

As for Davies, he was trying to occupy a space between Clara, the girl he loved, and Dollmann, the man he despised and hated. In these circumstances, it was going to be difficult to accomplish the end they had decided on the night before: that of disarming Dollmann, without noise or scandal, and aiding him to escape from his allies.

Davies ensured that Carruthers was up, reasonably presentable and in time to catch the Norddeich ferry. He had burnt some of *Dulcibella*'s lamp-oil that night looking through the Continental Bradshaw to find the train times, both for a journey to England and for possible clues to the activities and destination of Böhme and his friends. Davies put it all in a note which he gave to his friend.

Carruthers found Böhme on the ferry and they shared a carriage on the train as far as Emden. There the engineer met a friend who talked of a feeder canal to the Ems. Böhme rapped a goodbye on Carruthers' carriage-window at Leer where the engineer changed trains. Carruthers eventually threw off his mantle of lethargy at Rheine, the last change before Amsterdam. He began to see the hopelessness of investigating Dollmann's past at the Admiralty in London. It was now the 23rd and so he only had three days to reach England, see the Admiralty to discover more about the supposed traitor Dollmann and return to *Dulcibella*. 'What a scramble! No margin for delays, no physical respite.' Carruthers recalled 'Davies' wistful face on the quay, heard his grim ejaculation: "He's our game or no one's."' He realised at the time that it would be difficult to keep the story secret and yet extract the information about Dollmann. The only way was to stay in Friesland. He and Davies had to finish the work in their own way with their own weapons – after Carruthers had enjoyed a good night's sleep in Amsterdam.

He breakfasted in an hotel by the waterfront after his train journey, and sleeping the day away, bought a pea jacket, peaked cap and comforter, all props for his new role as a young seaman. Much refreshed and now without his moustache, Carruthers caught the 8.28 back to Germany. His sea boots, a few other garments and necessaries were in an umber bundle, parcelled with tarry rope, resting in the rack above his head together with a stout stick. His Baedeker of northern Germany was in the new jacket pocket. His story for the curious was that he was an English seaman going to Emden to join a ship, though his actual plan was to be in Norden, a town seven miles south of Norddeich the following night, 25 October. That would tie in well with the 'night train', for the only one arriving at Norden late at night coincided with high water in the creek. That left a little time in hand, which he decided could be usefully spent taking a close look at Esens.

Comfortably wedged in his seat on the train, he studied Davies' note again. His friend had not lost the opportunity of putting his channel theory on paper. Carruthers did not doubt Davies' idea that Germany had a plan for the defence of the North Sea coast. The seven islands and the seven channels and the ring of railway around the peninsula, with Esens at its apex, fitted in with the theory and pointed to secret plans for mobilisation for defence, but they would not 'require for their elaboration so recondite a meeting-place as Memmert. Dollmann was another weak point.'

At Rheine, Carruthers took on the guise of a German seaman. He felt that 'there was little risk in a defective accent – sailors are so polyglot; while an English sailor straying about Esens might excite curiosity.'

At Emden, the railway crossed a large canal, which interested him in the light of his discovery the day before that Böhme was not just a submarine engineer but an expert on canals. 'It was dusk, but light enough to see an unfamiliar craft, a torpedo boat in fact, moored to stakes at one side.' He 'remembered that page in the North Sea Pilot, where the Ems-Jade canal is referred to as deep enough to carry gun-boats, and is used for that strategic purpose between Wilhelmshaven and Emden, along the Frisian peninsula.'

The creek at Norden was dry and there were barges lying aground. The train rattled on and with the help of a map Carruthers 'assembled all his threads, and tried to weave them into a cable whose core should be Esens.' Esens lay four miles inland from Bensersiel and 'standing up to get a better light and less jolting', Carruthers searched the ordnance map again. There was a road and something else. A stream running to Bensersiel. It showed as a 'rough little corkscrew, like a sucking pig's tail'. He remembered it as the muddy stream or drain they had seen in the harbour during their earlier visit, issuing through the sluice or the siel from which Bensersiel took its name. 'It inclined away from the road to Esens and passed the town about a mile to the west, diving underneath the railway. Soon after it took angular tracks to the eastward, and joined another blue line trending southeast, and lettered "Esens-Wittmunder Canal".'

The jigsaw was beginning to fit together. 'Those shallow depths and short distances, fractions of metres and kilometres' which he had heard from Böhme's lips at Memmert could be depths and distances in the canal. He remembered the barges in Bensersiel and talk of expansion of business in the islands themselves as bathing resorts and Dollmann's part in this. He had heard, too, of the growing trade in bricks and grain passing from the interior by canal to the islands and in an obscure connection with these things he saw the torpedo boat in the Ems-Jade canal.

At last he arrived at Esens station, and reached a humble Gasthaus at 9.10. He told the landlord that he was on his way to Bensersiel, 'to sleep there, and take the morning *Postschiff* to Langeoog Island' and went on to ask 'how are they getting on with the Benser Tief and the connection to Wittmund?' When his landlord replied that he thought that the Benser Tief was finished but the connection was still under construction, Carruthers pressed his advantage and continued with a speculation that the development of Langeoog would be going ahead too. The Frisian, whom Carruthers summed up as a bigoted old conservative, conceded that a few more barge loads than before of bricks, timber, coals, etc., might result, but it would come to nothing, he knew.

Carruthers left the hotel and following the owner's instructions for the Dornum road, headed for the Tief. After a short reconnoitre he found that his stick gave a depth of barely three feet. The torpedo boat melted from his speculations. It seemed moreover only wide enough for two barges to pass with comfort.

To the south of the road and railway 'the towpath, after half a mile, plunged into woods, then entered a clearing and another fenced enclosure; a timber yard by the look of it.' This was confirmed by stripping from the waist downwards and wading over. There was a long tin shed that strangely reminded him of Memmert. Below it, nearer the canal, loomed a dark skeleton framework, which proved to be a half-built vessel on the stocks. Nearby was another almost completed, and in a backwater seven or eight finished barges lay in tiers.

After pressing on for a further three miles, it was clear that the canal was in the process of improvement, though it was as yet little used for traffic. He had nearly reached the end of the blue line on the map and 'his boots were heavy with clay'. He retraced his steps. Rather than knock up the inn-keeper, he decided that one of the empty barges in the backwater of the yard he had passed earlier would provide free and accessible lodging. He returned and surveyed his quarters for the night. It was clear that she was designed not merely for canal work, but for rough water. He knew from experience what vicious surf the waters inside the islands could be whipped into by a sudden gale.

With the aid of a series of matches he studied the ordnance map. In concentrating on Esens and Bensersiel, he had forgotten that there were other villages ending in 'siel', connected by corkscrew streams. 'Five miles eastward of Bensersiel was Neuharlingersiel, and further on Carolinensiel. Four miles westward was Dornumersiel; and further on still Nessmersiel and Hilgenriedersiel. There were six on the north coast of the peninsula alone.' Böhme's statistics of depth and distance had been marshalled in seven categories – A to G. Carruthers added the solitary Greetsiel, a good way south of Norden on the Ems, so making up the numbers. 'From all seven points of issue dotted lines were marked seaward, intersecting the great tidal sands and leading towards the islands. And on the mainland behind the whole sevenfold system, ran the loop of railway.'

The morning broke mild and showery and Carruthers made his way back to the road. Hoping to make his way to Dornumersiel and Nessmersiel, he found himself instead trying to evade the company of a rascally beerhouse proprietor who suspected him of being English. Carruthers resolved to do no more exploring by daylight. The experience that day with the towns and their siels made him wonder about the 'rendezvous' supposedly in Norden. It could in fact be in any of the seven towns that boasted *Tiefs* leading to the sea. However, the more he thought about it, the more he was convinced that the last train in the evening from Norden junction to the east could be described as a 'night train'. He had used the same service the night before and determined that he would wait for the conspirators at that station, catch their train, or, if they did not turn up, decide that Norden itself was the rendezvous and, therefore, wait for the very last train at 10.46.

It still being light, he cut across the 'oozy fens and knee-deep drains' to the Harke Tief, the stream that issued at Nessmersiel. South of the town of Nesse work on a deviation was in progress and he spotted a lighter-building yard.

Fatigue left him when he reached Norden by train from Hage. He turned up the collar of his pea jacket and donned a heavy muffler, which was just as well, for he nearly walked into von Brüning in the booking office. He followed hard on the commander's heels and caught a muffled double syllable from the official who checked the naval officer's ticket. It must be Esens, he thought, and so made for a fourth-class carriage, noticing two cloaked latecomers, whom he could not identify, boarding the train. They had been waiting till the last moment at the end of the platform. The train would reach Esens at 8.50 and 'the tide serves' at Bensersiel at about eleven.

Carruthers was the first off the train, through the barrier and into the shadows, awaiting the commander and his two cloaked friends. He followed them down the road to the highway, where, to his surprise, they turned right, out of Esens and away from the sea. The level-crossing gate brought them all together at the barrier but they were soon off again into the darkness.

Carruthers went past them and then noticed that they must have turned off. He found the track to the west of the road that led to the Benser Tief and, guessing where they were bound, made for Bensersiel himself by the more direct route.

It was nine by the time he made the diminutive port. There were the makings of a fresh, wild night 'with a halo round the beclouded moon'. The post-boat was making ready for sea. The only other vessels in the harbour, apart from the odd rowing boat, were a deserted tug and two lighters, which he peered into. There was no trace of Grimm, whom he had expected.

The lights of a steamer suddenly appeared entering the harbour and it was not long before a small tug berthed ahead of the lighters and the elusive Grimm jumped ashore. Carruthers hurriedly pulled his oilskin jacket and trousers over his clothes and, when the two crew left for the inn, he seized his chance and concealed himself in the tug's lifeboat on davits swung out on the starboard side.

Grimm returned, followed soon after by von Brüning's party. The tug got under way with a lighter in tow. Carruthers' earlier inspection of the barge told him that it contained common household coal and was by no means full, giving substance to the phrase overheard at the depot, 'Only one – half a load'.

Grimm was steering, occasionally relieved by a seaman. Böhme, von Brüning and he who 'insists on coming' (the phrase heard at Memmert) were gathered aft, leaning over the taffrail. The fourth man was not to be seen, and it was not clear where Böhme had sprung from.

'Any weather' – was another Memmert phrase, and 'it was a dirty squally night, not very cold for the wind hung in the S.S.W. – an offshore wind on this coast causing no appreciable sea on the shoal spaces.' From his eyrie, Carruthers could gather the direction the tug was making as he identified the lighthouse on Wangeroog and that in the centre of Norderney. They seemed to be in the gap between the islands of Langeoog and Baltrum, heading for the open sea, when the engine-room telegraph rang and the tug slowed. The next order – 'To lower away' – froze Carruthers to the marrow, but it was countermanded almost at once by an unknown but strong, imperious voice which indicated that they should jump, and the three left the comparative comfort of the tug for the lighter.

They headed out for the North Sea and 'swung to windward over the troubled bar'. Grimm shouted orders and the tug and her charge executed a number of evolutions 'steering on each point of the wind in succession, after that worked straight out to sea till the water was a good deal rougher, and back again at a tangent, till in earshot of the surf on the island beach'. The manoeuvres completed, the observers were recovered from the lighter and the tug pulled westward, heading, it appeared, for Memmert, though 'it was the course for England too'; Carruthers understood at last and the significance of what he was watching burst upon him. He was 'assisting at an experimental rehearsal of a great scene, to be enacted, perhaps, in the near future – a scene when multitudes of sea-going lighters, carrying full loads of soldiers, not half loads of coal, should issue simultaneously, in seven ordered fleets, from shallow outlets, and, under escort of the Imperial Navy, traverse the North Sea and throw themselves bodily upon English shores'. He remembered 'that, recent as are the events' that he was witnessing, 'it is only since they happened that the possibility of an invasion of England by Germany has become a topic of public discussion'. Davies and he had been trying to unravel secret plans of defence rather than of offence. Orthodox invasions start from big ports and involve a fleet of ocean transports, while none of their clues pointed that way. To neglect the obvious methods, to draw on the obscure resources of an obscure strip of coast, to improve and exploit a quantity of insignificant streams and tidal outlets and thence, screened by the islands, to despatch an armada of light draft barges, capable of flinging themselves on a correspondingly obscure and theretofore unexpected portion of the enemy's coast; that was a conception so daring, and so quixotic in some of its aspects, that even now he was half incredulous. Yet it must be the true one. 'Bit by bit the fragments of the puzzle fell into order' until he felt that he understood what was going on.

'Broad on the port beam were the garish lights of Norderney town and promenade.' There was a change of course and it became clear that they were heading for the landing-stage at Norddeich. Carruthers wondered what Davies would have done in such circumstances. Surely there was a way out. 'For an answer there came that familiar *frou-frou* of gentle surf on drying sands. The swell was dying away, the channel narrowing; dusky and weird on the starboard hand stretched leagues of new risen sand. Two men only were on deck; the moon was quenched under the vanguard clouds of a fresh squall.' A madcap scheme danced before him and after checking the time, he put on Grimm's oilskin, which had been left over the cabin skylight, and made his way to the bridge. He jogged the helmsman's arm and pointed forward, just as he had seen the owner of the coat do earlier. The man went like a lamb and took up his position again as look-out in the bows. Carruthers edged the tug slowly to starboard and then, spinning the wheel hard over, he drove for the sands. Panic followed, the look-out dashed aft, there was a cry from the lighter and Grimm and his companion came tumbling up on deck. Carruthers threw off Grimm's coat, stepped behind the smoke-stack and made for the boat. On the way he cannoned into one of the passengers, pressed him into service, incidentally seeing his face and verifying an old conjecture. 'It was one who, in Germany, has a better right to insist than anyone else.'

The tow-rope to the lighter parted with a report like a pistol shot, the tug listed heavily to starboard. The boat was soon in the water and Carruthers aboard. The wind and tide took charge and by the time he had shipped rowlocks and sculls he was being swept merrily back towards the lights of Norderney.

Davies was astonished to see his friend and all Carruthers could blurt out was 'It's the invasion of England' and then went on hurriedly to ask him if Dollmann was still in his villa.

They warped *Dulcibella* astern of the ferry so that she should not be caught, as *Medusa* had been, by the receding tide. They made their way back through the sleeping town, 'rain driving at their backs'.

As they walked, it was evident that Davies was still reluctant to see his channel theory dashed. 'I was right – only upside down – these channels are the key to the whole concern.' He muttered that Chatham was Britain's only eastern base – there was no North Sea base or squadron – and that the Germans would land at one of those God-forsaken flats off the Crouch or the Blackwater or, on second thoughts, at the Wash, for it was much the nearest and as sandy as the Frisian side.

They reached the villa in the Schwannallee. Dollmann, in his dressing gown, opened the door. He was greeted by Carruthers as 'Lieutenant X' which nearly caused the door to be slammed shut in their faces. However, Dollmann let them in with a plea for silence and was told that *Dulcibella* was to leave for Holland or England in half an hour and that he and Clara should accompany them. Carruthers promised immunity.

Dollmann at first protested, called them meddlers, marplots and all sorts of fools, for he was in *British* service. The fierceness of his come-back left them momentarily speechless, until Carruthers asked him why he had tried to wreck Davies. He rapidly went on to recall the night on Memmert, explaining how he had taken notes of Dollmann's English tour and his visit to Chatham. Then there was the English scheme of attack and the German plan of defence. He repeated the snatches of conversation as though he had heard the lot. Dollmann's protest continued, though without any urgency, and he gave in when Carruthers told him that he had just witnessed the demonstration of the invasion of England. The fight left Dollmann and he asked what it was Carruthers had said about immunity and about Clara. Davies assured him of their friendship and that if he did not hurry it would be too late, as his erstwhile companions were now after them all.

Dollmann left it to Carruthers and Davies to tell Clara, who already had her light on and was standing apprehensively by her bedroom door. She was soon sobbing in Davies' arms. Below, Dollmann busied himself in stuffing papers into a smouldering stove.

Somehow, they reached the yacht and *Dulcibella* made her way out of the harbour unnoticed and unmolested. Soon Dollmann came on deck. 'He held on by the runner, and stared to windward at Rottum, as though he knew the place quite well.' He must have forgotten the earlier incident on the Hohenhorn Sand, for he offered help, asking for the helm, saying 'sea's too bad outside – there's a short-cut there.' His help refused; he settled on the counter, 'his feet against the lee rail.'

Dulcibella was beating in towards the coast to get behind Rottum when Davies turned round and noticed that Dollmann was no longer there. He must have gone in the 'bobble of sea' between Rottum and Bosch Flat. They searched, but never found him. He must have gone down quickly, clad as he was in his ulster and heavy sea boots.

They reached Oostmahorn and left the yacht in the charge 'of some astonished fishermen', making their way back to England by road, rail and steamer from Harlingen.

✦ ✦ ✦ ✦

Childers, who had introduced the story in the Preface, now takes over again in the Epilogue. It is this technique that gives the book such power. As a yachting story, it is a rattling good yarn by itself, but the lasting power of the book comes from the way that 'the important facts discovered in the course of the cruise' are introduced to the reader in the Preface, together with the remark that, in spite of their moment, they were poorly received by 'the proper authorities'. Bumbling by civil servants is always easy to believe and so the reader has been put in the right frame of mind to absorb Carruthers' tale.

It is left to the Epilogue, though, to bring the reader back to reality, drag him from the Frisian sands, from adventure and brightly painted scenes, back to the world of 1903. The Epilogue lifts Carruthers' yam to a clear message that readers of *The Riddle of the Sands*, from publication day to the present, can easily see as a warning of things to come.

It begins with the statement that Carruthers had rescued from Dollmann's stove a confidential memorandum to the German government setting out the plan for a German invasion of England, clearly drafted by Dollmann. The memorandum emphasises the German genius for organisation and Germany's great Army, and declares that Germany:

> *... studies and practises co-operation between her army and navy. Her hands are free for offence on home waters, since she has no distant network of coveted colonies and dependencies on which to dissipate her defensive energies. Finally, she is, compared with ourselves, economically independent, having commercial access through her land frontiers to the whole of Europe.*

The memorandum then contrasts Britain's situation, summarised by *The Riddle's* 'editor':

> *We have a small army, dispersed over the whole globe; and administered on a gravely defective system. We have no settled theory of national defence, and no competent authority whose business it is to give us one. The matter is still at the stage of civilian controversy. Co-operation between the Army and Navy is not studied and practised; much less do there exist any plans, worthy of the name, for the repulse of an invasion, or any readiness worth considering for the prompt equipment and direction of our home forces to meet a sudden emergency. We have a great and, in many respects, a magnificent Navy, but not great enough for the interests it insures, and with equally defective institutions; not built or manned methodically, having an utterly inadequate reserve of men, all classes of which would be absorbed at the very outset, without a vestige of preparation for the enrolment of volunteers; distracted by the multiplicity of its functions in guarding our colossal empire and commerce, and conspicuously lacking a brain, not merely for the smooth control of its own unwieldy mechanism, but for the study of rival aims and systems. We have no North Sea naval base, no North Sea fleet, and no North Sea policy. Lastly, we stand in a highly dangerous economical position.*

Next the memorandum discusses the method of invasion. The suggested plan is that worked out by Carruthers except that Norden rather than Hilgenriedersiel was one of the seven launching spots on the Frisian littoral. Dollmann reduces the possible landing places in England to two: 'the flats on the Essex coast between Foulness and Brightlingsea, and the Wash – with a decided preference for the latter'. East Holland, more precisely, would be the ideal target area.

Dollmann also remarks on the Royal Navy's ignorance of the tides and shoals around the siels amid claims that the British charts are of no value.

The 'editor' concludes the Epilogue by denying the value of 'an axiom, much in fashion now, that there is no fear of invasion of the British Isles because, if we lose command of the sea, we can be starved, a cheaper and surer way of reducing us to submission'. He argues that nothing short of a successful invasion could finally compel us to make peace.

The final Postscript of March 1903, tacked on just before the book reached the shops in May of that year, showed movement by the government, as it reacted to the dangers that were so apparent to Davies, Carruthers and Childers.

Chapter 3

ERSKINE CHILDERS – CORINTHIAN SAILOR

Erskine Childers, Corinthian Sailor

Robert Erskine Childers became an author by chance. Just as circumstance introduced me to *The Riddle,* Erskine became an author through fortune. His life was like that. There are many major turning-points in most lives, usually recognised with hindsight. Erskine Childers seems to have seen the marks on his course only as he rounded them, pressing ahead in between, with a determination and confidence born of attention to detail. This dogged progress is well illustrated by one of the two principal characters in *The Riddle,* Arthur H. Davies.

It is time to look closely at the man who wrote a book that was to be his lasting memorial.

Erskine Childers has been the subject of three biographies and two special studies; two of the former borrowed *The Riddle* for their titles. The first of these, Michael McInerney's *The Riddle of Erskine Childers*, was published in 1971. This was followed in 1977 by a major work, employing the same title, by Andrew Boyle, who is believed to have started his hunt for Professor Blunt, the spy, just before its completion.

Boyle had been selected and entrusted with the task of writing the life of Erskine Childers by his son, also called Erskine, who was by then the President of Ireland.

Molly Childers, Erskine's wife and the President's mother, would have welcomed a biography by Lord Longford in her lifetime. Longford was a natural choice for as chairman of Sidgwick & Jackson he had published many editions of *The Riddle*. In a foreword to their paperback edition[1] he wrote: 'In my reading of Irish history no one emerges during the twentieth century with more unassailable claims to intellectual and moral elevation.' However, Longford was unable to accept the task, for he knew that Molly Childers would have insisted on her own interpretation of Erskine's every action. (Her will allowed the Childers' Papers to be released from the bank ten years after her death.)

A year before Hutchinson published Boyle's book, Burke Wilkinson brought out *The Zeal of the Convert*, perhaps the most readable of the three and the one that Childers' youngest son, Bobby, regards as capturing the sense of his father.[2] Childers' life can be distinguished in these biographies as dividing into two – the adventurer and the zealot. This division though may be too simple, for in the adventurer there is much zeal and in the zealot there is both the courage and single-mindedness that is the stamp of the real adventurer. This side of Erskine is well illustrated in a collection of his wanderings, *A Thirst for the Sea* edited by Hugh and Robin Popham, published in 1979.[3] In this the editors have gathered together his logs and writings about the sea and his stories of cruising in small boats. Another study, *Damned Englishman*, by Tom Cox, was published in 1975.[4]

Perhaps the most sensitive overall look at the man was written and privately printed in 1925 by one of Childers' greatest friends and admirers, Basil Williams.[5] Burke Wilkinson found this sketch a great help and quoted from it liberally in his biography. Williams also contributed the last word, Childers' entry in the *Dictionary of National Biography, 1922–1930.*

Williams knew both the adventurer and zealot. He could mark the dividing line in Erskine's character and describe how, for his first forty years, he had tasted life, grasping at the joy of open space where land and firmament, sea and sky meet. He knew how he enjoyed his friends, drawing on them and returning in full. Williams wrote of him, 'By his friends Childers will always be remembered as a man of indomitable courage, of winning modesty, of extraordinary generosity and, in his earlier and happier days, of a most engaging sense of humour.'[6] Basil Williams was puzzled by the zealot. Molly Childers confirmed this when she wrote to Basil and his wife Dorothy in September of the year (1922) in which he was shot at Beggars Bush Barracks, on the orders of the provisional Irish government, for being in possession of an automatic pistol:

> *May I say this to you both – you are right still to love him even though you disagree, for his work has been so fine in every way and our unending effort to promote the only solution that will still this strife and benefit both countries alike.*[7]

Williams saw the changed personality. So did others less able to judge. A leader in the *Irish Times* headed 'Erskine Childers' was emphatic:

His strong will and great talents, not only failed to bring happiness to himself and others; they were lavished on a cause that has devastated Ireland and has darkened a thousand homes with sorrow. What is the mysterious difference which sometimes in ardent minds, perverts the ideal of freedom from a blessing into a curse? Erskine Childers was an idealist, a thinker of high thoughts and a brave man: that last tribute not even those who condemn most fiercely the work of his closing years need hesitate to lay upon his grave. He fought against the tyranny of the Boers many years ago, in a brilliant book he foretold the German attack on the liberties of Europe and when his vision was fulfilled he defended those liberties on sea and in the air. He sought freedom, too, in Ireland and during the better part of his life he sought it in the right way.[8]

The bones of his early life were set out by Childers himself in the *Daily Express* of 27 November 1922.

> *These are the facts of my life very briefly. According to rules laid down by your own government, and some such rules have to be laid down by any government, I am by birth, domicile and deliberate choice a citizen, an Irishman.*

Childers was naturally defensive over his part-English background. He had been referred to as a 'damned Englishman' and as having spent a lifetime in the British Secret Service in an attack by Arthur Griffiths in the Dail in January 1922. Childers went on to explain: 'My father was English, born in England. My mother Irish, born in Ireland, Anna the daughter of Thomas J. Barton of Glendalough House, Annamoe, Co. Wicklow.' Robert Caesar Childers, his father, was a noted orientalist who occupied the chair of Pali and Buddhist Studies at University College, London. He died of tuberculosis in 1876, aged thirty-eight, six years after the birth of his younger son, Erskine. His wife, Anna, followed him, suffering from the same disease, in 1883.

Robert Caesar Childers' finest work was the Pali Dictionary, an invaluable insight into the canonical books of the Buddhists. Robert Caesar was responsible for that dogged determination referred to before that wracked his youngest son and pushed him onward, either in adventure or in pursuit of political ideals.

Henry, Erskine's elder brother, and his sisters, Dulcibella, Constance and Sybil, moved to Ireland in 1883 and, as Childers says, 'from the age of thirteen I was brought up at Glendalough House by my uncle and aunt, Charles and Agnes Barton.'

The Barton family had lived at Glendalough since the end of the eighteenth century. They prospered early by smuggling wool to France, returning to Ireland, equally illegally and profitably, laden with wines and spirits. They owned, and, the family still own, Chateaux Leoville Barton and Langoa Barton. The chateau attached to the latter was built in 1758 on the west bank of the Gironde and is one of Medoc's most elegant houses. The wine is reputed to be a typical St. Julien.

Anna Barton came, therefore, from adventurous stock. If there is anything in blood lines, Robert Erskine Childers was a predictable outcome, looked at from the stands of horse-racing. The family tree tells its own story, for the Bartons claim descent from Thomas Erskine, the first Baron Erskine and Lord Chancellor of England.

Thomas Erskine had more than a silver tongue, for before he gained his unrivalled reputation as an advocate at the English Bar, he had been a midshipman in the Navy. While serving on board *Tartar*, cruising in the West Indies, he was struck by lightning, an experience he recorded in the *St. James Chronicle* of 5 December 1765. On return to England, he joined the Army and met Johnson and Boswell. The latter recorded of him: 'On Monday, 6th of April, 1772, I dined with him Johnson] at Sir Alexander Macdonald's where was a young officer in the regimental of the Scots Royal, who talked with a vivacity, fluency and precision so uncommon that he attracted particular attention.' On another fated occasion, Lord Mansfield, drawn initially by his uniform, asked Erskine to sit alongside him in court and this kindness changed a life. The sailor turned soldier was turning again, this time to the law.

In his new career, Erskine first gained fame by his defence of Captain Baillie, Lieutenant-Governor of Greenwich Hospital, who was accused of libel, having imputed corruption against Lord Sandwich, then First Lord of the Admiralty. At the trial, Erskine rounded on Lord Sandwich, subjecting him to a fierce onslaught. Jekyll, the wit, politician and one-time advocate, coming into court in the thick of this found 'the court, the judges and all in a trance of amazement'. Erskine said afterwards that he had found courage by 'feeling that his children were plucking at his gown, crying to him that it was now time to get them bread'. He certainly achieved this from then on.

The young lawyer successfully defended Admiral Lord Keppel, accused of incompetence, and Lord George Gordon, following the Gordon riots. He obtained an acquittal in the 1790s for William Stone, who was accused, with strong evidence in support of inviting a French invasion. Erskine defended James Hadfield in 1800 for attempting to assassinate George III in Drury Lane. Perhaps it was not surprising that when he was raised to the peerage as Baron Erskine of Restormel, he took the motto 'Trial by Jury'. The name Erskine was clearly well worth preserving in the Barton/Childers mix.

The Childers family came from Yorkshire, Hugh Childers having been a mayor of Doncaster in 1604. The name derived from the Middle English 'Childre', meaning a youth of gentle birth. The Royal Navy named two sloops *Childers*, one in 1778 and one in 1812, after the legendary racehorse *Flying Childers*, bred in 1715 by Leonard Childers of Carr House, Doncaster, and later referred to by the family as 'our most illustrious ancestor.'

The Childers' Yorkshire blood was twice reinforced by the strain of Sampson Gideon, the oracle and leader of Jonathan's Coffee House in Exchange Alley, afterwards the Stock Exchange, in Threadneedle Street. Sampson's son became the first Lord Eardley, in the Irish peerage, a title taken from the name of his wife, the daughter of Sir John Eardley Wilmot (1709–62), the Chief Justice of Common Pleas. Lord Eardley's third daughter, Selina, married Colonel John Walbanke Childers of Cantley, near Doncaster, in 1797, and the Reverend Eardley Childers, who was vicar of Nice and father of the First Lord of the Admiralty, wed his granddaughter, Maria Charlotte Eardley.

This financial sparkle showed itself in Hugh Culling Eardley Childers, who spent the first seven years of his working life in Australia, where he became auditor-general. He returned to Britain as agent-general for Victoria and soon decided to stay in England and became the Member of Parliament for Pontefract. Preferment did not take long and, perhaps because of his knowledge of the colony, Hugh Childers was soon given the job of chairman of the Select Committee on Transportation. It was largely through his efforts that this invigorating form of punishment was abolished.

Childers' interest in the Navy came from his efforts to reform the dockyards. As First Lord of the Admiralty he was the first to aim at making the British fleet equal to the combined strength of any two other maritime powers. It was, perhaps, because of this that he backed Captain Cowper Phipps Coles, the inventor of the British turntable turret system for mounting guns in ships. HMS *Captain* was to his design and Hugh Childers reinforced his approval of Coles' ideas by ensuring that his son moved from the traditionally armed and stable HMS *Monarch* to HMS *Captain*, then under the command of Captain Hugh Burgoyne, VC. HMS *Captain* capsized on 6 September 1870, just at the time that Captain Burgoyne's father, Sir John, was rescuing Napoleon III's Empress Eugenie from Deauville on his yacht *Gazelle*. They were all caught in the same depression.

Hugh Childers became Secretary of State for War in 1880 and pushed through the territorial system in the Army, which linked regiments to places rather than their number in the line. He abolished flogging in the Army and made better use of the militia and territorial forces. He became Chancellor of the Exchequer in 1882, succeeding his great friend Gladstone. Hugh Childers ended his political career as Home Secretary. Throughout his career he had strongly supported Gladstone's policy of 'a large measure of Home Rule for Ireland', an idea he had done much to forward himself.

The combination of the Barton line, descending from the great advocate Lord Erskine, and that of the Childers, stemming from Yorkshire and the financier Gideon, was to come through in Hugh Childers and in his young cousin Erskine in more than name. Hugh shared a further common bond with Erskine's grandfather, Canon Childers – that was the friendship of William Gladstone, for the latter had been a close compatriot of the canons at Oxford. The cleric Charles and the politician Hugh were to have a good measure of influence on the young Erskine. Grandfather recommended Haileybury as a suitable public school and Hugh suggested his old college, Trinity, Cambridge, as the proper place to continue his studies afterwards. Erskine followed this advice and in 1889, no doubt to the great pleasure of his cousin, won an exhibition to Trinity. Erskine's elder brother, Henry, had not inherited either his father's or his cousin Hugh's application or brightness but progressed steadily through Harrow to Sandhurst.

Erskine sums up this period of his life in a sentence: 'I was educated in England, travelling to and from school and college.' He misses out that it was while at Haileybury he made a friend for life in Ivor Lloyd-Jones; nor does he mention in his necessarily short account that he, 'Perk', as his sisters affectionately called him, valued the communion and spiritual advice he received so readily from the Very Reverend Edward Hardress Waller, the rector of Annamoe, the village whose few buildings embraced the Lodge and the start of the main drive to Glendalough House. Wailer was to become not only a person to turn to but, like Ivor Lloyd-Jones, a close sailing

Meeting Clara, Dollman's daughter

companion. 'Perk' was a late starter and had an undistinguished scholastic record until 1888, when he reached the upper sixth form. He was consistently better at languages than mathematics. Perhaps he responded, as he matured, to the achievements of his companions, for in his last few terms he was with four boys who already held Oxbridge awards. Whatever the stimulus, in his last year he won the school prizes for Greek iambics, Shakespeare studies and the study of art, and his form prize. He was second in the Latin prize and, not surprisingly, won the English essay prize. In the words of a legion of schoolmasters before and since, it was a creditable effort. Three exercise books of this period survive and Erskine received seventeen out of twenty for an essay, 'Revolution, Evolution'. His tutor scribbled underneath, 'You have taken too liberal a view of revolution.'[9]

Erskine's pursuit of the outdoor life started during his holidays from Haileybury. The call of the Wicklow mountains persuaded him to walk for miles, enjoying the solitude and the onward call of that magnificent part of Ireland. Not far from the back drive entrance of Glendalough House, past the diamond-paned lodge, lies the challenge of Lough Dan. His brother Henry learned to sail there and Erskine followed in his wake. The lough is trapped among the hills and the road wanders in search of it, not quite sure whether to touch water, as though the lake itself possesses a strange liquid secret. Perhaps this dark stretch of water, pebbled in parts with rocks, gave Erskine the added dimension that water offers to those who would wander alone, touching only natural things. His experiences on Lough Dan may have persuaded him, while at Haileybury, to seek solace in a strange craft on the River Lea.

Erskine's love of water, though, never lessened his passion for walking. In 1889, while in his first year at Cambridge, he went to the far west of Ireland, beyond Galway City, to that wild part of Connemara, dominated by the Twelve Pins. His young, wiry frame was ideal for this country where, in the downward descent of the hill, the tacking, checking and stumbling awkwardly between boulders across sprung heather and purple moor grass, navigating past tussocks of mat grass and outcrops of bilberry, and skirting the edge of sphagnum bog, racks calf muscle and ankle joint. The going down is more tiring than the measured tread upward, where the promise of the unseen draws the walker onward.

It is a land of fulfilment, where violent winds and driving rain can lift to reveal a new heaven and new earth. Connemara is also a place where the hill walker is well advised to wrap up against such cold, watery onslaughts. Erskine failed to take this precaution. As a result, he was lamed for life with sciatica in his left foot. His love of walking was not lessened by this complaint, for in later life and in less wild places, from 1908 onwards, he was prominent among the 'Sunday Tramps', who rattled out of London on the Sabbath, catching a suburban train from Charing Cross to Knockholt, Liverpool Street to Billericay or Paddington to Windsor, just to wander fifteen or twenty miles, and return, puffing, from some other station into London, refreshed not only by the walk but by the company. Robert Bridges, the Poet Laureate, Lord Haldane, the Lord Chancellor, and Ralph Vaughan Williams, the composer, shared his addiction.

Erskine added the dimension of speed provided by the bicycle to the pleasures of the trek. The 'safety pattern' had not long been introduced and, though a bone shaker, it was a relatively dependable way of touring. Erskine's tale of his 'Ride Across Ireland – An Account of a Bicycle Tour',[10] from Glendalough to Leenane on Killary Harbour, that finger of cold Atlantic cutting into the northern fringe of Galway, was not only rigorous – it was Erskine's first attempt at logging a journey and is, therefore, worth reading.

Although Erskine continued to tour on a bicycle, especially in France, his slight disability may have made such adventures less appealing and turned his eyes seaward. The young undergraduate was certainly helped towards a new view by another, Walter Runciman, later the first Viscount Runciman of Doxford.

Walter Runciman was five months younger than Erskine, but he already owned the cutter *Edith* and was later to sail many hundreds of miles in the twenty-one-ton schooner *Waterwitch*, built by R. Aldous of Brightlingsea nine years before either of the two were born. Runciman was a dedicated sailor; he had salt-water for blood. His grandfather had been master of a schooner and had served in the Coast Guard. Young Walter's father, 'Old Waiter', ran away to sea at the age of twelve and was bound apprentice in the brig *Harperley*, sailing with coal from the Tyne to Mozambique. He gained his master's ticket by the age of twenty-four and a couple of years later was given command of the barque *F.E. Althausse*. The sea captain's only son, Erskine's friend's father, was fourteen years old before he left the sea to become a South Shields shipowner. The boy must have had his head filled with tales of the sea and the ships that his father had sailed in, such as the brig *Maid of Athens*.

Young Walter inherited his love of sailing from his grandfather and passed on the art of navigation and the ways of small yachts to his friend Erskine. The present Lord Runciman is in no doubt that his father taught Erskine Childers to sail.

Erskine and Walter were to have another love in common, the love of their two yachts *Sunbeam*. In 1922, the year that Erskine died, 'Old Walter' bought Lord Brassey's three-masted topsail schooner of that name which had been made famous by Lady Brassey's record of world voyaging. Seven years later 'Old Walter' built a second *Sunbeam* of even greater dimensions. His instructions to the designer were to produce the sort of vessel that Brassey would have built if he had wished to replace his old yacht. Erskine Childers was part-owner of a *Sunbeam* too, a fifteen-ton yawl, built as *Zephyr*, destined to play a significant part in this story.

'Old' and 'Young' Walter Runciman enjoyed equally successful careers in shipping and politics, the two of them being raised to the peerage within four years of each other. 'Old Walter' died, aged one hundred, in 1937.

His son may well have introduced Erskine to the writings of E. F. Knight, and in particular to *The Falcon on the Baltic – A Coasting Voyage From Hammersmith to Copenhagen in a Three-Ton Yacht*. The book was first published in 1889 by W. H. Allen, the year Erskine and young Runciman met. The little blue volume, showing in red a converted ship's lifeboat running before a breeze on a lumpy sea, was to become Erskine's 'bible'.

Books played an important part in Erskine's life. He was clever with words himself and enjoyed writing to those who shared his passion for the printed word. While at Trinity he wrote to his sister Dulcie, recalling lines of Tennyson's *Ulysses*: ' ... Come my friends, 'Tis not too late to seek a newer world.'

'These lines,' Erskine continues in the letter, 'send a strange thrill through me and are half responsible for any longing I ever have to desert civilisation and ...wander far away. On from island unto island, to the gateways of the day ... and so on ... So if I ever disappear suddenly for a year or two, you will know what sent me!!'

These lines were recalled in 1925 by Basil Williams in his sketch of Erskine, referred to earlier, and capture that restless spirit better than anything else.

They are perhaps Childers' best epitaph. Although the first line, 'Come my friends, 'Tis not too late to seek a newer world,' is pure Tennyson, the remainder is word for word Childers. As Williams remembered, Erskine had 'the poet's gift of hitting off the places or people he sees in a few happy words'. Erskine's progress through life had an urgency about it, as if responding to a call. The striving of both the adventurer and the zealot had a direct result on the man, as though his eyes were fixed and his arms outstretched toward 'the gateways of the day'.

He continues the summary of his early life: 'In 1895 [I] entered the British Civil Service as a Committee Clerk in the House of Commons, remaining there until 1910.' Erskine had already shone as a debater in Trinity's own society, the 'Magpie and Stump', and led a motion, within a few days of joining, in favour of the Channel tunnel.[11] He was successful too at his studies and came down from Cambridge with his law tripos and BA degree in 1893.

Within two years, urged on by cousin Hugh, he passed out well in the Civil Service exam and became a committee clerk. He joined a hierarchy of four principal, six senior, twelve assistant and the same number of junior clerks, thirty-four in all.

Erskine's quiet manner was exactly in tune with those he found at the clerk's table in the Commons or Lords. Their backgrounds were similar too, stemming from old county families attracted to the place through a family connection, being sons of or closely related to members of either house. Rupert Palmer Colomb arrived there in 1893. John Horsbrugh-Porter, who was to become senior clerk before he retired in 1934, was another; but the one who was to make the most impact and become both a firm friend and confidant was Arthur Frederic, known as Basil, Williams.

Basil Williams came from almost the same mould. His father, a barrister, lived in London but was proud of his Somerset background and his seventeenth-century Lockyer ancestors around Ilchester. He arrived at the House a couple of years before Childers. However, their acquaintance soon ripened and they discovered they shared the same indoor and outdoor enthusiasms, declaimed similar political views and were both skilful with the pen.

Rupert Colomb, John Horsbrugh-Porter, Herbert Warington-Smyth, Stephen Simeon (his cousin by marriage), Basil Williams and Erskine Childers had another common bond – they were all keen on the sea and the ways of small boats. To this band were added a few friends from outside the Houses of Parliament – William Le Fanu, Erskine's brother Henry, and Ivor Lloyd Jones. William Le Fanu had been at Haileybury, though they would not have known each other there as he was some nine years senior to Erskine Childers. Ivor Lloyd-Jones was a contemporary of Erskine's, both at Haileybury and Trinity, and his father had been chaplain at Newgate Prison. These friends all played a part in the story of *The Riddle* and helped Erskine 'seek a newer world'.

The coming together of this shoal of seafarers, though, was a slow business. Judging from Basil Williams' account, they were hardly 'press-ganged'. In his *Sketch* he remembered that it was with some astonishment that 'we heard that our quiet friend was wont, in the long recesses from parliamentary business allowed us in those comparatively placid times, to go away, often alone, sometimes with only one friend, in a little cockle shell of a yacht, the seven-ton *Vixen* (see page 130), navigating through the storms of the Channel or the North Sea or threading his way through the complicated shoals of the German, Danish or Baltic coasts.'[12] Childers had progressed a great deal from his first hesitant sorties on the dark and usually placid face of Lough Dan. He had learnt a great deal from Runciman and from exploits with Henry. One of his brother's girlfriends, Edith Picton-Turbervill, later to become a Socialist MP, remembered the several summer visits that she paid to Glendalough House in Co. Wicklow. She was keen on archery and tennis: 'Much as I enjoyed those visits to Glendalough, sailing on Lough Dan with Erskine and Henry Childers, nothing, in spite of their kind entreaties, would induce me to stay a day longer when by doing so I missed the tennis or archery tournament at home. We were all keen archers and aimed straight.' She recalled the long passage at Glendalough that stretched the length of the house on the ground floor in terms of the arrow: 'It stretches to the length of a full archery range, no less than 60 yards.'

Erskine turned from the Lough to the sea. Perhaps as a consequence, the two brothers bought *Shulah*, a thirsty, nine-ton, thirty-five-foot cutter, drawing no less than eight feet of water. She was designed and built by Arthur Payne in his Southampton yard in 1890. Payne was then at the high point of his career. In six years' time he was to build the first *Cariad* for another famous Irish yachtsman, the Earl of Dunraven, who challenged unsuccessfully for the America's Cup on two occasions.

Erskine's sea learning was the usual mixture for a new owner – days packed with 'makey learn', served up by paid hands, hired before learning how to choose the right man. The little ports were full of hawk-eyed, would-be mariners, eager for a berth. They were topped up with blarney and their faces were as worn and wrinkled as their oilskins, giving some hallmark of respect to their boasted knowledge. Many fishermen would take a summer berth and some were pure gold to the amateur salt. However, not many of these longshoremen, although they had the right leathery face and narrowed eyes from long hours of staring to windward, were deep-sea men. They were not used to spending more than a night away from land after fish. They were not navigators but local pilots who knew every fathom and furrow of their own waters but were lost a day's sail away from their beach.

It was difficult for the young yachtsman in these circumstances to discover the skills that he had to depend upon. Childers records his view in an article he wrote for *The Times* on 11 May 1909, sixteen years after the experience:

> *We were ready to sail alone? Alas! not yet; but from what source to obtain help. In our depression fortune sent our way a young Scotch fisherman, rather slovenly, ignorant of yachts, but infinitely good-natured, and only too delighted to let us go where we pleased and commit all the gaucheries we liked, so long as he had nominal control of a spruce little cutter. He asked for no mate and best point of all, knew nothing of charts, so that we at once became responsible navigators, only relying on him for practical seamanship. We became fast friends and had a time of pure delight in the only perfect cruising ground which the British Isles afford; one too, in which our deep draught presented the minimum of inconvenience.*

These days of 'pure delight' were shared with Henry in a voyage from Kingstown, port-hopping to the Clyde, where the yacht found a winter berth at Gourock. Walter Runciman joined them the next year and added to the growing sum of sea sense the brothers were fast accumulating.

Shulah took the two to sea in their own boat. The bond between man and salt water forged in this sort of initiation is lasting and was to take Erskine on from boat to boat. Unlike so many yachtsmen, whose yachts grow in size with their years, he suited the size of his craft to the waters he wished to explore.

Childers was a true enthusiast for wind on the cheek and when he took up his appointment at the House of Commons in 1895 he secured a boat that was useful on the Thames, an eighteen-foot, half-deck centre-boarder by the name of *Marguerite.* Henry and Erskine sold *Shulah* to Captain C. P. Dean, a member of the Royal Thames Yacht Club. They changed ample accommodation for the owner, a guest and two crew, for a half-decked dinghy with a tent over the boom. No wonder she was nicknamed *Mad Agnes.*

Childers was not a great one for flags but he realised they had their uses beyond identification. Until modern times, a burgee or racing flag at the masthead was an essential method of discovering where the boat lay to the wind. The helmsman, glancing aloft, with that typical sweep of the head and eye, could, with the aid of fluttering bunting, know whether to pinch or free his boat, to luff or to bear away, in the continual war between holding course and improving speed through the water.

Childers gained a burgee of some distinction in 1895 when he joined the Cruising Club, a band of men who were to contribute greatly to his life, just as they received full measure from his membership. The Club was founded in 1880 by another trained in the law, Arthur, later Sir Arthur, Underhill. The objects of the Club were threefold and simple:

(a) To associate owners of small yachts, boats and canoes, used for cruising on sea, river or lake, and other persons interested in aquatic amusements.
(b) To give an opportunity to members who may wish to visit a coast, river or lake which is new to them to obtain information as to harbourage, boatmen and other local matters, by means of correspondence with members acquainted therewith.
(c) To circulate among members, by means of a Club Journal or MS (or otherwise), accounts of interesting cruises carried out by members of the Club.

Members flew a flag from their masthead which was described heraldically in the rules as 'white and red vertical; the white or inner portion charged with a black Maltese cross edged with yellow and bearing in its centre, a yellow naval crown.' The cross was later altered in shape and colour, perhaps because of the strong likeness of the black cross to that worn aggressively with a white edge in the Kaiser's Navy. These flags, the Club advertised, could be secured from Messrs Hunt & Co., of 119 Church Street, Edgware Road, NW.

The minute-book records, in careful ink script, that on 1 May 1895, R. E. Childers was proposed by the Hon. Treasurer, seconded by H. Stuart Moore, and elected. The Treasurer, J. G. Pease of 4 Paper Buildings, Temple, was also of a legal persuasion.

His cruise by Saone and Rhone to the Mediterranean, undertaken in the season of 1896 and recorded in the *Journal*, was to be the catalyst that started Erskine across the Channel to Boulogne the next year.[13] Erskine's seconder was a year older and had been called to the Bar in 1893. He became not only a yachtsman of note but one of the great experts on the law of the foreshore. Hubert Stuart Moore was wedded to the Strand and the sea in both work and play, for he married the founder and commodore's daughter and died in 1951 on board his yacht *Wildwave*.

Erskine, therefore, was well 'launched' and it was not long before his ability in small boats was recognised by his fellow members. Brother Henry became a member in due course too.

The Club's method of applauding their colleagues was by the award of a Club prize, an electro-plated cup. The second prize of a flask was, perhaps, more appropriate in light of the rigours of small-boat cruising as practised by Childers in *Mad Agnes*. This encouragement was before either Erskine joined or Vice-Admiral Algernon Frederick Rous De Horsey became an honorary member.

Admiral De Horsey gained fame by becoming the first British naval officer to engage an ironclad in action. This claim to immortality occurred in 1877 when, as a Rear-Admiral, he was Commander-in-Chief in the Pacific with his flag hoisted on the *Shah*, an unarmoured frigate of 6,250 tons. Some six years after the incident, Arthur Underhill met the admiral, a keen yachtsman, in Dartmouth when they were both aboard their respective yachts. As a result of this meeting; De Horsey was invited to become an honorary member of the Cruising Club and to join such legendary amateur sailors as Lord Brassey, who had been similarly recognised.

Writing to accept from his flagship HMS *Northumberland*, off Madeira, in February 1885, De Horsey summed up the Club and its objects in a way that emphasised a particular approach to sailing that distanced the Cruising Club from the majority of other Victorian yachting organisations. The others, in tune with the age, were bent on racing their boats. De Horsey's paragraph was scathing about this, no doubt sweet music to Underhill, as the gallant sailor knew well from his conversations in the saloon of his cutter *Wych*, or crouching uncomfortably below in Underhill's tiny two-and-a-half-ton *Wulfruna*. De Horsey wrote:

I have perused the Rules of the Club, and beg to be permitted to express my opinion that the objects for which the Club is formed, as detailed in Rule 2, are deserving of every encouragement as conducive to the study and practice of navigation on our coasts, and of handling small vessels in all weather – a far worthier object than that of most clubs which unfortunately encourage the winning of prizes by racing machines sailing under a fictitious tonnage measurement.[14]

The electro-plated cup, the flask and indeed other subsidiary rewards, such as a yachting knife, binoculars, compass, or brass riding-light, had failed to attract entries for some seven years. Indeed, there had never been an entry for the riding-light. Admiral De Horsey, recognising this, gave the necessary stimulus in 1895 with a 'handsome silver cup'. The first to meet the challenge in a sufficiently vigorous manner and so win the approval of the committee, was Erskine Childers, then of 16 Cheyne Gardens, SW. He managed this in the year of his election.

Childers described his diminutive *Marguerite*, or *Mad Agnes* (as he affectionately nicknamed her after his Aunt Agnes Barton) in his log published in the Cruising Club's *journal* for the year 1895. This short account of some fifteen pages was his first published writing and his powers of description were already evident.

The 'Marguerite' is a small half-decked sailing boat, 18 feet in length overall and 6 feet beam. Her draught, without plate, is 2 feet 6 inches aft and 2 feet 1 inch forward. The centreplate is 5 feet 6 inches long and, when down, increases the draught to 4 feet 6 inches. The boat is clinker-built, and varnished, and her canvas consists of a balance lug and jib. As to deck, she has a foredeck from stem to mast, and 18-inch waterways, with 3-inch combing, all round. She has one 20-lb anchor, with 20 fathoms of chain, a pair of sweeps, one of Norie and Wilson's spirit compasses (50s.) in one of their most convenient guinea binnacles.

As for sleeping accommodation, I have a specially designed bell-tent of oiled canvas, laced (when in use) round the combing, and bent to a halyard or runner by an eyebolt at the apex, and hauled taut. The bedroom under apex is 4 feet 6 inches. Our couches consist of two reindeer-hair mattresses, which make most efficient life-preserving gear.

I must premise that I have nothing new or valuable to relate. The only interest that I can hope may attach to my log is reduced to that of its being the record of a cruise in a, perhaps, unusually small boat, single-handed for the most part, and never with more than one additional hand, also an amateur. As to the boat, though I only acquired her this year, I had obtained confidence in her in a previous single-handed cruise to Folkestone and Boulogne in April, and in a week's sailing on the Essex coast in June. The drawbacks and difficulties of cruising in such a boat do not need enumeration, and I should not have tried it had my choice been free. But, on the other hand, I found many compensations in various unexpected ways, but especially in her shallow draught, which naturally told in navigation, the entering of tidal harbours, taking the ground, etc. As to the paramount consideration, her behaviour as a sea-boat, she was as good, I believe, as any boat of her size can be. In a high sea her openness, of course, made perfect buoyancy an essential quality, and this quality she possessed. Under such conditions she would go admirably to windward, and stay without fail, with or without the centreplate, for the latter was a luxury, and not a necessity. To go over everything was a 'sine qua non', as I need not say.

This was certainly a change from *Shulah* or sailing with his friend Runciman in either the comfort of the forty-five-foot, twenty-one-ton schooner *Waterwitch* or his earlier thirty-two-foot cutter *Edith*. Ivor Lloyd-Jones and William Le Fanu were among his companions in discomfort in *Marguerite's* early cruises.

Erskine wrote good-humouredly to 'Runcy'; contrasting his little vessel's limitations to the comparative space aboard *Waterwitch*, in a letter written in March 1896, a year after he joined the Cruising Club. Erskine was declining an invitation because of his involvement with *Marguerite*: 'I should have liked much a trip with you and Hurst in this braw new line of battleship! I'm sure you'll have a fine time. I will go and smell round your boat at Lymington at Easter perhaps and it will be interesting. A bathroom, ye gods what debauched luxury! A ladies' cabin, shades of our Viking forefathers!!'[15]

But to return to 1895, to *Marguerite* and her epic voyage. Erskine called the first part of this adventure his 'Dissolution Cruise', rejoicing in the loosening of his bonds with the land rather than harking back to Hakluyt's stern use of the word – 'Through meere dissolute negligence 'she' [a ship] perished on a sand.' However, as it happened, these words were within an ace of being apt. The cruise started from Greenhithe, a Thames village, two and a half miles from Deptford, on a hot, fine day. Childers' companion was Stephen Simeon, a fellow clerk in the House who was some thirteen years his senior and married to Louisa, the eldest daughter of his political cousin, the Right Honourable Hugh. After a 'rather tedious' beat to Sheerness, they left the boat with the Coastguard at Colemouth Creek – 'nice civil chap'. The two took rooms at the Port Victoria Hotel. Erskine recorded in his log: 'the only house in this high sounding port. Most lonely spot in the world, projecting point of limitless marsh. Accommodation better than the amazement of our appearance led us to expect. Going bedwards at eleven saw the moon had transfigured this dreary waste.' The next day they sailed to Rochester and returned to Port Victoria in time to catch the Southern Railway to London in the evening.

Erskine returned alone to *Marguerite* the following day, loaded with stores. He anchored in Herne Bay, setting tent, dining, and turning in at ten o'clock. *Marguerite* made her way slowly to Margate, Ramsgate and Dover, arriving in the last port on 10 July. Erskine explained his philosophy about harbours in his log:

> *I lay behind the Admiralty Pier (Dover) for the rest of the day and the night. I may say that I always made a point of keeping in open anchorage at night in preference to the inside of a tidal harbour, whenever and wherever this was possible. I have the strongest antipathy to the dirt, odours, publicity, and general discomfort of a quayside berth in a crowded basin.*

He described weighing anchor and setting sail aboard *Marguerite* as an easy job, even under the worst conditions, though he admitted he would have sought shelter if necessary.

Sheltering gave Childers time to read and write, an occupation woven through his pastime of sailing. Such a silver thread, an aid to patience, was a necessity in a small boat in those days, relying on wind and tide for progress, where prudence dictated a ready antidote to over-haste. Erskine was as keen on such paper prophylactics as he was on progress at sea.

Yachtsmen and commercial sailormen were used to anchoring in an open roadstead, tying themselves to the bottom to prevent losing hard-won miles, when the tide turned against them on a windless sea. Long waits in harbour for favourable winds were commonplace, particularly before steam tugs encouraged masters to chance departure.

Marguerite suffered such a delay after making Folkestone on the 11th, where Erskine's stay was made less trying by enjoying the kindness and hospitality of the Reverend F. E. Lloyd-Jones, father of his friend Ivor, who lived at 35 Millfield. However, neither the friend nor books prevented him setting sail in unfavourable conditions on 15 July. He lost *Marguerite's* tiller overboard off Dungeness and made good use of a mop handle in its stead. He sheltered in the East Road by the Coastguard station to wait for the tide before night-sailing on to Rye, anchoring in the Bay at 1 am when the wind left a glorious night.

He reached Hastings and while shopping there bought the papers and gathered that he was to have new masters in the House, for Lord Rosebery and his Liberals had been defeated and the Marquess of Salisbury was to be returned. The news would have added a dimension to the improving weather for the young clerk had written to Runcy during the Whitsun recess about this 'impotent and moribund government'.

His pleasure at the news was soon tempered by a disagreeable contretemps with the men who had rowed him to and from *Marguerite*. This short episode shows the dogged side of the Childers' character.

> *One came aboard and asked an exorbitant sum, blustered, and refused to leave my boat till paid. I offered more than a fair sum and said he might stay as long as he liked, but that I was going to sail with the weather tide. Then made tea and sat down to read. After an interval of silence, heard a much altered voice*

consenting to a somewhat less sum. Took no notice till the demand descended to my original level, when I promptly paid him and he decamped in low spirits.

In spite of the delay, Erskine made Eastbourne, turned in and went on to Newhaven the next day.

He avoided the Looe Channel, fearing the tide, in spite of a good whole-sail breeze. *Marguerite* took the outer course for the Solent, rounded the Owers Lightship and anchored close to Bembridge Fort in three fathoms. A wild night ensued, the wind blowing first from the relative shelter of the west and then backing south, armed with a deluge of rain. The tent arrangement was severely tested but stood up well, ensuring for Erskine a comfortable night. However, the wind was against him the following day, as it had been for most of the cruise, so he left *Marguerite* in the care of a Bembridge fisherman, after taking a pilot over the bar into the quietness of the harbour. On 19 July, the lone sailor took a train to Ryde, steamer to Portsmouth and railway to Newcastle to join his friend, Walter Runciman, for a cruise on *Edith*.

He was pleased to find *Marguerite* well cared for when he returned to Bembridge on 31 July, though there was no wind to tempt him westward that evening. In thick weather and light breeze the following day he made Poole. Erskine used Frank Cowper's *Sailing Tours* as his guide to the muddy intricacies of that harbour. Part II of this book was published in 1893 and was up to date.

The *Sailing Tours* were a great aid to the Corinthian yachtsman. The description 'Corinthian' was an American import that had become part of the language in the United States in the second half of the nineteenth century, where it was used to describe the ways of well-to-do amateur sportsmen. These men relied on their own expertise and prowess rather than enjoying the sport second-hand by watching a hired champion perform. In America the title was conferred widely from steeplechasing through to yachting. A *Harper's* correspondent of 1883 described being 'on a yacht of a friend who was fond of sailing Corinthian races'. In Britain the idea was embraced principally by yachtsmen. However, this was certainly not the rule, for almost every amateur sailor during this period employed a paid hand or two. Erskine and Henry had this experience with *Shulah*. When the Reverend Robert Edgar Hughes cruised to the Baltic during the Crimean War in 1854–5 in his eight-ton cutter *Pet*, he shipped two seamen at Southampton and garnered them in the small fo'c'sle.

The size of the yacht was not important, for a gentleman was used to having someone to fetch and carry at home and saw nothing strange in ensuring that the same advantage was available afloat. Washington McCoy shipped a boy in his three-and-half-ton *Lua*. Arthur Underhill, when cruising in the five-and-half-ton yawl *Cornavia*, in 1889, carried the idea to an extreme, for he shared the fo'c'sle with the paid hand, the ladies took over the saloon, there were two gentlemen under canvas in the cockpit well and the ship's boy slept in the sail locker, gaining entrance through a round hatch in the counter.

The Marquess of Ailsa, the father of modern yacht-racing, encouraged the Corinthian spirit in this country, and soon there was a rash of Corinthian yacht clubs. The Royal Corinthian was established at Bumham-on-Crouch in 1872, the Clyde Corinthian in 1876 and the Royal Portsmouth Corinthian in 1880.

Erskine, with his *Marguerite*, was certainly of Corinthian persuasion. He enjoyed giving pleasure to those less fortunate and so after visiting Poole town to shop, he anchored *Mad Agnes* off Ower Farm where the Church Lads' Brigade from Camberwell (London) were camping. Erskine's description in his log of sailing with them the next day gives a vivid picture of what it is like taking small boys to sea at any time.

> *3 Aug: Took 5 boys for a sail. They behaved well though wildly excited and formed a valuable shifting ballast. Unhappily we grounded on the ebb and remained stuck for 3 hours, 'alone in the woide, woide sea' as Tommy Atkins said. Boys demolished every ounce of food on board and then like a litter of puppies simultaneously dropped down and slept. In an hour all woke up simultaneously and were very rowdy. Another boatful passing finally towed us off. Camp at 5 pm.*

Erskine enjoyed his time with the boys and was 'delighted with Poole' and 'the beautiful land-locked harbour with the pine-covered, Norman Castle crowned, island in the centre'. He was, of course, referring to Brownsea Island. The boys were taken sailing again before he picked up Ivor Lloyd Jones and, with the wind free and under spinnaker, made for the Needles, Hurst and the Solent.

Cowes Week was in full swing and Childers noted that he 'ran straight on past Cowes' under the lee of the Kaiser's yacht *Hohenzollern* and the German fleet. He decided to play around in the shelter of the Wight for a few days. 'Cowes,' he records, was 'a bewildering brilliant spectacle. Every sort of anchorage occupied with every size and sort of steam and sailing yacht. The whole edged with English and German battleships, the *Hohenzollern* conspicuous, the latter a marvellous compound of destructive force and graceful luxury.' The Prince of Wales' *Britannia* and the new *Ailsa*, belonging to A. B. Walker, were lying near.

Hohenzollern's escort of four large cruisers emphasised her look of matchless determination and outclassed the American escort, the cruiser USS *Chicago*, commanded by the remarkable Captain Alfred Thayet Mahan. The captain first published his *The Influence of Sea Power Upon History (1660–1783)* in 1889. Wilhelm had read the book from cover to cover in the spring of the previous year and telegraphed his American friend, Poulteney Bigelow, son of the American minister in Berlin: 'I am just now not reading but devouring Captain Mahan's book and am trying to learn it by heart.'[16]

The Kaiser opened the Kiel Canal on 20 June that year, a considerable step towards achieving German naval parity and perhaps eventually superiority. Mahan's contention was that the prosperity and material progress of nations depended on the command of the seas.

Childers included in Davies' library aboard *Dulcibella* both *The Influence of Sea Power Upon History* and the captain's *Life of Nelson*. Talking of war, Erskine's hero from *The Riddle* was to say, 'It's a tremendously interesting subject …pulling down (in two pieces) a volume of Mahan's *Influence of Sea Power*.

The Kaiser was so pleased with the news of the Marquess of Salisbury's huge majority of 152 seats that he telegraphed the new Conservative and Unionist Prime Minister on 30 July with words that would have been more suitable for a pilot joining his ship at the Nab: 'Hope you are none the worse for your stupendous climbing of the ladder, considering the height of the tempest and the number of rungs.'[17] Childers was on his way to rejoin *Marguerite* in Bembridge when the telegram was received.

Lord Salisbury, whose administration Erskine now served, had been at Cowes earlier in 'The Week' and had had an interview with the Kaiser that was to prove highly significant in relations between the two men and to the world. The strange story unfolded at Osborne House on 5 August when the Prime Minister dined with the Queen, the Prince of Wales and the Kaiser, who had just arrived in his yacht. After dinner Salisbury and the Kaiser were able to talk. Their principal concern that August was Turkey, for the renaissance of Armenian culture in both Turkey and Russia had focused European and Russian attention on the plight of that minority, with particular concern for the Armenian Christians and the way they were being murderously harassed by the Kurds. The sultan, Abdulhamid II, was pressed by Britain, France and Russia to carry out reforms. He promised to do so, but instead massacres took place on a large scale.

Salisbury thought that these outrages might herald the break-up of the Ottoman Empire and in July 1895 he suggested to the French, Russian and German ambassadors in London that the sultan's rule should be ended. The German ambassador, Count Paul van Hatzfeldt, thought Salisbury's general idea sound and would bring the Triple Alliance of Germany, Austria/Hungary and Italy and the British Empire together. However, in reporting to Berlin and the Wilhelmstraße, he gave the impression that Salisbury already had a refined plan for dividing up Turkey.

Baron Friedrich von Holstein, senior counsellor of the German Foreign Ministry and the *eminence grise*, feared that such a plan and any discussion surrounding it would upset Russo-German relations, particularly as the German Foreign Ministry had lost faith in Britain since the Gladstone/Rosebery administration. Holstein saw it as a plot to cause strife between the Triple Alliance and the Dual Alliance of France and Russia, so that neither could oppose British plans and ambitions. His thinking even envisaged that Salisbury's scheme might start a war of diversion from which Britain might profit. The Kaiser was warned not to give the Prime Minister any encouragement and as Wilhelm was not the Anglophile he had once been, because both the British press and public were less enthusiastic about him, he readily agreed.

The German ambassador explained to Salisbury, in diplomatic terms, Germany's fear that the partition of Turkey would lead to war. He was reassured by the Prime Minister that no action would be taken without further discussion, and in addition it was indicated that Russia might receive Constantinople and Italy's part of North Africa, both ideas that were favoured by Germany.

The ambassador advised Holstein of all this and successfully suggested that negotiations should not be broken off, as Britain would then not help Russia or Italy. Holstein accepted this, having a complete change of heart, but too late to warn the Kaiser. Consequently, Wilhelm remained resolute, would have nothing to do with Salisbury's ideas and said so in no uncertain terms at Osborne House on the evening of 5 August. Baron Hermann von Eckardstein later said in his memoirs[18] that Lord Salisbury was deeply upset by the Kaiser's behaviour when they met at what is now famous as the 'Cowes Interview'.[19] He also reported that Salisbury spoke bitterly of the language used by Wilhelm – 'Your Kaiser seems to forget that I am not a Minister of the King of Prussia, but Prime Minister of England.' When Wilhelm received the belated telegram from Holstein reversing the position, he tried to make amends by seeking a second interview, but Salisbury failed to turn up aboard *Hohenzollern*, saying that he had been detained in conference with the Queen and that he had to go on to Portsmouth to be in London for further unbreakable appointments.

The Kaiser's behaviour and Salisbury's reaction at that meeting on 5 August poisoned relations between the two and Salisbury refused to meet Wilhelm subsequently when he was in England, even at the start of the Boer War when a change of heart by Germany would have been very much in the interests of Britain.

Childers was unaware of all this as he sailed through the milling fleets on that beautiful, breezy August morning two days later. *Marguerite's* course was for Portsmouth, Erskine being bent on returning to London, an idea soon discarded in favour of staying with the glitter of the Solent.

Erskine was to recall his time at Cowes in *The Riddle*, for Davies' friend Carruthers was to comment on the rough and ready charm of *Dulcibella* and to remember his time at Cowes: 'Hazily there floated through my mind my last embarkation on a yacht: my faultless attire, the trim gig and obsequious sailors, the accommodation ladder flashing with varnish and brass in the August sun; the orderly, snowy decks and basket chairs under the awning aft. What a contrast with this sordid, midnight scramble over damp meat and littered packing cases!'

The following day Erskine sailed to Southampton to arrange the laying up of *Mad Agnes* at Picketts Yard. He returned to Cowes and in the evening he and Ivor Lloyd-Jones went ashore for a stroll and pushed their way through streets packed with a 'heterogeneous crowd'. It was firework night and they spotted the emperor as he landed at the Royal Yacht Squadron steps. 'Bookstall' Smith, a frequent yachting companion of George V, knew the Kaiser well and described accurately the man Erskine saw:

> *Small and short, handsome, with clear blue eyes, a well-set-up little person, rather short in the neck and a little lop-sided owing to his left arm being shorter than the other and thin and, of course, nearly useless. He was exceedingly dramatic and obviously very vain. He appeared to expect flattery in public by his courtiers and those about him. He spoke English very well, with no marked or unpleasant German accent, and took a pride in picking up and making use of English slang expressions and the colloquial phrases that have become a habit to many English people. He would omit the 'g' in words like hunting and yachting, which was in him affected and grotesque, and in his anxiety to copy the colloquialisms of ourselves he would often get them wrong.*

The intense vanity and love of dramatic effect that the man possessed was tinged with a slight strain of commonness and vulgarity, which was sufficiently marked to be unmistakable.[20]

The Kaiser was particularly jealous of his Uncle 'Bertie', Edward, Prince of Wales. Uncle Bertie in his turn was finding the emperor tiresome. Edward was not one to allow political problems to cloud personal relationships but if he was offended personally, his dislike for the man could colour his whole attitude. In his *Appreciation* of Edward VII, E. F. Benson wrote: 'These constant irritations produced by his nephew's ill-breeding not only increased his personal dislike for him but the whole concept of an Anglo-German understanding.'[21]

The emperor's tactlessness was often demonstrated at Cowes. He was elected a member of the Royal Yacht Squadron on the proposal of Edward in 1889. While on the lawn of the Squadron Castle, he asked for his uncle and was told that he had gone racing with Tommy Lipton on *Shamrock*. With glee and a twist, he repeated this saying: 'They tell me he has gone boating with his grocer.'

Edward may have regarded the emperor as tiresome from an early age, for his nephew had distinguished himself at Edward's wedding to Princess Alexandra. Wilhelm, then aged four, resplendent in Highland dress, detached the Cairngorm from the top of the skean-dhu in his sock and tried to throw it across the choir. This incident followed an attempt to push his aunt's muff out of the window and his calling Queen Victoria 'duck', an early and inappropriate use of English slang and colloquial phrases.[22]

Running into Bensersiel

The relationship between the two men deteriorated further in their yachting rivalries. Count Philipp zu Eulenburg, a diplomat and friend of the emperor, managed to be neither when he came to write his book.[23] He quoted Edward as saying of Wilhelm aboard the Imperial racing yacht *Meteor:*

> *I can't precisely make out my nephew's colonial game. I can understand a man wanting to buy diamonds when he hasn't got any, but if he can't afford the big ones, it is more practical to chuck a hopeless game. The emperor's interest in ships is all very well, but when one sees him taking a hand in everything, with that paralysed arm of his, as he is doing now on deck, one can't help being afraid he'll do himself some damage.*

They were prophetic words. The emperor's enthusiasm for the sea was to encourage yachting in Germany. Shortly after he became the owner of *Meteor* in 1891, he became the commodore of the Imperial Yacht Club at Kiel, which then had 458 members. Within nine years of his stewardship, the membership had risen to 1,599 and the rise in the number of yachts followed suit. Steam-yachts rose from four to twenty-four and those under sail from thirty-seven to 165. Expenditure on yachting was similarly inflationary and rose from 375,353 marks to 4,111,709.

The emperor treated Cowes as though it were Kiel, so the Prince of Wales nicknamed him 'the boss of Cowes,' adding that 'the Regatta used to be my favourite relaxation; but since the emperor has been in command here, it's nothing but a nuisance. Most likely I shan't come at all next year.'[24]

The emperor denounced the handicap arrangement in that fateful week of 1895, his last year with the old *Meteor,* and withdrew, with others, from the Queen's Cup, allowing the prince's *Britannia* a walk-over. The new *Meteor* arrived the following year and had a very successful season, but the unpleasantness continued and by 1897 the prince had had enough and he made good his threat, for that was his final year of racing *Britannia.*

Erskine had seen the Emperor of Germany for the first time. He watched the fireworks and was in his bunk at midnight. On 9 August, *Marguerite* made for

Southampton to collect post and then, in torrents of rain, beat for Hamble, past the then great modern attraction of the military hospital at Nedey inspired by the late Prince Consort – with beds for 1,000 patients, 'as well as accommodation for military lunatics'.[25] He was anchored off the little village of Hamble at seven o'clock.

Childers probably anchored *Marguerite* off the salterns, opposite the hamlet, he and Ivor Lloyd-Jones rowing ashore. They 'got beds at Mrs Vivian's and dinner at the Bugle with seven other yachting men who had been racing that day; one of them turned out to be Linton Hope, the designer.' He and Erskine would have had a great deal in common. Hope had just established his name and worked at Greenhithe, the starting place of the 'dissolution cruise'. Shallow drafts were almost Hope's trademark and he and Erskine may well have discussed the finer points of *Mad Agnes*. Hope was more interested in racing yachts, but they would have been at one in later years, regarding the advantages of proper accommodation. The discomforts of the open boat were to become apparent to both, with Erskine graduating to the cabins of *Vixen*, *Sunbeam* and *Asgard* and Linton Hope writing, 'Increasing years have made me more inclined to sail larger craft with some sort of lid on to keep a change of clothes dry and some food of sorts.'[26]

The news that Hope had just finished working on a twenty-foot lugsail centre-boarder to be called *Vixen* would not have meant anything to Erskine at that time, for the significance of that name, again associated with shallow draft, was to come later. *Vixen* was a popular name then, with no less than ten gracing the pages of Lloyd's.

Marguerite was left at Southampton on 11 August. The 'dissolution' part of the cruise had ended and in five weeks the autumn part of the adventure was to begin. Childers makes no such distinction between the two voyages in his account in the *Royal Cruising Club journal*. There is just a note in *Mad Agnes'* log. Erskine treated the autumn as though it were summer, as far as sailing was concerned. He responded to two calls in those days – the sea and the corridors of Westminster. As one faded, the other gained time. The train made such a double life possible. On this occasion he returned to London in what he referred to in *The Riddle* as 'the dead season'.

Like most young men of his background, he divided his time in London between three principal places and was to associate this pattern with Carruthers in *The Riddle*, describing it as 'the dismal but dignified routine of office, club and chambers'. In Erskine's case, this meant the Commons, later his club – the Savile – and his rooms in Mitre Court Buildings. Savile Row used to be the Harley Street of the day but the medical profession were slowly squeezed out and No. 15 became the Savile Club.

To this day, London clubs, in August and early September, enjoy musical chairs, as the holidays drain away the staff, providing time for cleaning and redecoration. Providentially for Erskine, then as now, a few remain open as a refuge for those not taking some of August for their annual escape from the capital.

In *The Riddle* Carruthers gives further insight into this strange London happening. 'The Club which you are "permitted to make use of" on these occasions always irritates with its strangeness and discomfort. The few occupants seem odd and oddly dressed, and you wonder how they got there. The particular weekly that you want is not taken in; the dinner is execrable, and the ventilation a farce.' Such depression drove Carruthers to Davies and the adventures aboard *Dulcibella*.

Mitre Court Buildings was a quiet harbour out of Fleet Street. Charles Lamb lived at No. 16 from 1800 to 1809 and used to hold literary evenings on Wednesdays with Hazlitt and Coleridge. Carruthers, on the other hand, had chambers in Pall Mall, a street that gained its name from Charles II's game of 'Pellmell' or 'Pall-mall' – his improvement on bowls which later became famous under the rather tame name of croquet. Lamb once refused an invitation from Wordsworth, saying that he preferred the 'sweet, shady side of Pall Mall' to the Westmorland lakes. Carruthers was similarly affected by 'our home in Yorkshire', explaining in *The Riddle* that he was not a prophet in his own country.

In 1895, parliamentary sittings were orgasmic rather than organic. The House sat from 5 February to 10 April and from 22 April to 31 May. Sittings continued from 10 June to 6 July and from 12 August to 5 September. The House did not come together again until 11 February 1896. Clerks were usually at their desks while Parliament was in session, though it was not too difficult to obtain leave of absence. Erskine uses the lack of pace in the Commons to illustrate Carruthers' attitude to his employment: 'I might have to apply for longer leave, as I have important business to transact in Germany.' 'Don't worry, it's only the chief's fuss' is a line which appears later. Childers may have been glancing sideways at his own boss, Sir Reginald Francis Douce Palgrave, or his successor as Clerk of the House of Commons, Sir Courteney Ilbert. W. R. McKay gave the descriptive title 'Mild Drudgery' to his article describing the life of a clerk in the House in 1900.[27]

The two Childers brothers returned to Southampton and *Marguerite* on a glorious September day to begin their autumn cruise and by the 20th of the month the leaves were beginning to turn. They had no definite plan, 'but made up our minds to sail west for a little, as it was now late in the season for cruising'. It was certainly late for an open boat and Erskine recognised this.

Marguerite shot through the narrows at Hurst, tide and wind in concert. Childers aimed, in common with many yachtsmen going west, to spend the night in the shelter of Swanage, but fate intervened, for in the race off Peveril Point, they gybed to turn into the bay and clear the rocky point when the tiller broke off short at the rudder head. Judging from the log, it would seem that *Marguerite's* steering arrangements could have been improved, for this was the third time during that cruise that the tiller failed and the fourth occurred minutes later, remedied, again, by using the mop handle.

Marguerite nosed into Portland, a secure duck-pond constructed for the fleet by convicts held on Portland Island. This vast harbour was a bleak place for two men in an eighteen-foot, half-deck boat, so they went on to Weymouth. Erskine enjoyed his stay there, for it was a good place to leave the boat if the crew was also after partridges. Henry and Erskine had a day's shooting with the Stilwell family, most likely the Stilwells of Steepleton Manor, in that Dorset-sounding, double-barrelled village of Winterbourne Steepleton. Charles Stilwell was a friend of Henry's at Harrow.

The marriage of the sports of shooting and yachting was not only 'the cover' in *The Riddle*, it was recognised as proper employment for a yacht: 'I merely write on the offchance to ask if you would care to come out here and join me in a little yachting and, I hope, duck-shooting. I know you're keen on shooting and I sort of remember on yachting too.' Erskine gave pen to Davies to entice his friend Carruthers aboard *Dulcibella*.

'Shooting and yachting' were much in vogue. A. G. Bagot, known as 'Bagatelle' to his readers, recommended the advantages of welding the two sports in his book of that name.[28] However, Bagot was a bit more exotic than Childers – 'I was bound with a party,' he recalls in Chapter 1, 'to try our luck at woodcock and pig in Albania.'

A great balloon of high pressure had settled over the Channel and south coast and, on rejoining *Marguerite* at Weymouth on the 23rd, the Childers set sail with the occasional cat's-paw to propel them around the Bill. They never made it and had to spend a night in Church Cove where an ancient land-slip provided a convenient gorge, on one side of which is Pennsylvania and on the other, Bow-and-Arrow Castle. Between the two, a path winds down, through romantic scenery, to the pretty cove below.

Pennsylvania Castle was built to the designs of Wyatt for John Penn, the Governor of Portland and the grandson of the founder of the State of Pennsylvania, USA. Frank Cowper, in his *Sailing Tours*[29] did not have a very high opinion of Wyatt, 'whose Gothic is not successful, to say the least of it'. Bow-and-Arrow Castle appealed to him and was said to have been built by William Rufus. It stands on a pinnacle 300 feet above the sea.

Marguerite, bereft of wind and her crew suffering from the heat, 'landed at Castletown for a cargo of ginger beer'. A light westerly wind persuaded them against any further progress in that direction and after an hour's rowing, in dense fog, they made Lulworth Cove.

Frank Cowper and his *Sailing Tours* for the South Coast may well have acted as their guide, for Erskine included the book in *Dulcibella's* bookshelf. Cowper urged that 'everyone ought to go into Lulworth Cove. It is the most dainty, fascinating, little swimming-bath imaginable.' He recalls, too, that there used to be a convivial cricket club called the 'Lulworth Lobsters'.

Erskine's and Henry's decision the next day to cross the Channel was made after first planning to return eastward. Perhaps it was the beat against the light wind from that direction that first inspired them to greater adventure. Like many a decision taken for small reasons, the effect was momentous. The Royal Cruising Club's De Horsey prize, in all probability, would not have come Erskine's way had they not 'gone foreign', remarkable though the 'dissolution' and 'autumn' cruise had been up to that date. *Mad Agnes* certainly lived up to her name and the experience on board her made them determined to do more and to go further. This change of course led to *Vixen*, the Baltic and the sands of *The Riddle*. The decision to cross the Channel on this occasion confirmed Erskine as a worthy member of the Royal Cruising Club. Walter Runciman's early tuition and words of wisdom had taken proper root.

The Channel crossing was achieved in nineteen hours, an average of 3.3 knots. The wind decreased throughout the first day and night from a two reef fresh to a light breeze.

Marguerite moored in the shelter of Cherbourg's Avant Port, south of the gigantic breakwater that protects the Petite Rade and which was begun by Napoleon I in 1776 and completed by Napoleon III in 1853.

The two brothers celebrated with dinner at the Hotel du Louvre. There is still an hotel of that name at 2 Rue H-Dunant, though it does not now have a restaurant, according to the 1982 Michelin Guide.

Erskine recalled his experiences in Cherbourg in the *journal:*

> *Moored in the Avant-port at 2 pm alongside a revenue lugger and just below the Customs office, where we thought she would be safe, while we spent the evening together on shore. We did so, in spite of the interested representations of an individual who might have passed, as he stood, into service at Drury Lane as a pantomime pirate. Delicious hot baths, and a walk round, were the next things. My brother put up at an hotel while I was to sleep on board. Generally speaking we were disappointed with French soil. Cherbourg itself is very commercial and 'banal', and Cherbourg cuisine was, let us hope, not representative of French culinary genius. We spent a pleasant evening though with coffee and billiards and a concert. I returned on board at 10 pm and found all snug.*

Erskine did not beat about the bush in the log – 'Town mean, dirty and uninteresting. Dinner very disappointing.' This comparison shows the difference between the log, a record near the time, and the *journal*, polished, the cutting edge somewhat blunted by recollection, but flowing nicely from pen to reader's eye, and written some time after the experience. Erskine was a master of this chameleon change in words, a gift much prized by readers of sailors' tales.

The *Marguerite* weather continued for the high and was almost stationary. Heat, lack of wind, and their companion – haze over the land – together with a strong east-going tide, made hesitation on direction unnecessary. The helping hand of Neptune was lost off Cape Barfleur, but the point was passed and the wind became a settled easterly, the course southeast, pointing to a landfall just short of Havre.

At about 3 am, while Henry was asleep, Erskine noticed the yacht 'going very dead'. The wire on the centre-plate had parted and the plate was left hanging down vertically. *Marguerite* refused to sail to windward in this condition, so Erskine let her head drop away southward to make land.

At 1 pm on 28 September, they anchored off Ver sur Mer, a village dominated by a large lighthouse. Erskine determined to dry out but after a conversation with two fishermen, he decided against beaching as this might bend the centre-plate, an experience that was to dog *Vixen* in Dutch waters, two years later. *Dulcibella*, too, in her brush with the Hohenhorn Sands, at the entrance of the Elbe, had to dry out to repair the lower rudder pintle with the help of Bartels of the sea-going, apple-carrying ketch *Johannes*.

Marguerite was piloted into the oyster port and growing watering place of Courseulles, two miles to the east of Ver, and locked into the west dock. 'A sleepy, do-nothing place' Erskine wrote in the log. The unballasted *Marguerite* was placed alongside a collier-brig and, with the aid of a tackle and sling from her main yard, the bow was hoisted clear of the water and a piece of the yacht's chain shackled on to the centre-plate, as there was no wire to be had.

The Cafe au Parc des Huitres (now replaced by an ugly block of flats) claimed most of their spare attention in the day and a half that Erskine and Henry remained in port. They entertained the helpers, and the crew of the brig 'could talk amusingly on almost any subject whether within or beyond their intelligence. The one subject that irritated them was Germany.' This last snippet indicates the germ of worry that developed later in the cruise to the Baltic and found focus in Childers' experiences in South Africa, finally surfacing with force in *The Riddle*.

Havre lay twenty-five miles due east and so, at 10.30 in the evening of the 29th, after a hard day, *Marguerite* set sail in a light southeasterly, with a misty rain just setting in, and headed for the then Liverpool of France.

At last the weather had broken but it did not blot out 'the noble electric flash' of Cap de la Hève, just to the north of the port of Havre. The weather looked dirty. The *journal* recalls the watery violence of that night:

> *About 2 sighted the town lights of Havre, but had to run off our course to windward to avoid a heavy beam sea. Took third reef, and reefed the jib. Hove to for about an hour, not liking to approach the banks round the bar in the dark at low water, as it was now, and in so heavy a sea. About 4, bore up and ran for Havre but found the harbour lights very difficult to pick up. Violent rain squalls came on obscuring everything, even the electric light, except at intervals, and making the helm very hard work. Scandalised lug by topping boom and lowering halyards. In the first daylight approaching Havre, through piers still obscured by mist, when wind suddenly whipped round the compass to the northwest, causing us to gybe all standing (topping-lift adrift, but no damage), and making a most confused and trying sea in which, well as the boat behaved, she took a good deal of water. Blowing a gale. Sighted piers, but now to windward. Doubtful as to their position. We had been following a smack, also running for shelter, just in front of us. Brought the sheets flat in, but found when close up that we couldn't make the entrance, a strong tide being also against us. The smack couldn't stay (we suppose), and was smashed on the rocks at the foot of the 'Floride' fort, and we saw her keel upwards, just as we stayed ourselves without difficulty. We were very glad to read in the papers the next day that her crew of seven men were all saved with the rocket promptly. It was a terrible sight, especially as early attempts to help on our part would have only placed us also in their plight.*
>
> *Took a tack out and back, but made no ground against wind and tide; tried*

again, same result. Gave up Havre, bore up and ran to leeward along the coast eastward, past miles of sheer wall forming the docks and yards of the port.

Beyond, the charts gave nothing but mud flats, but it was now more than half tide and we calculated to find water enough and shelter somewhere, or at least anchorage. About five miles down identified the Pointe du Hoc by its tower, and ran in behind it in smooth water, and anchored in very shallow water, very wet and tired, and glad to be so well out of it. Then went on to a tiny creek in complete shelter, with just four feet in it at high tide, and moored across it, with the anchor and a pegged warp on the grass on either side. Set tent, changed and breakfasted. The comforts in prospect in Havre proved too strong to resist, and we recklessly left the Marguerite in this dreary expanse of marsh and mud, with only a fisherman or two in the distance and walked into the city and put up at an hotel.

This experience, along with the ability to record the ups and downs of excitement, the colour of the weather and, above all, through his own experience, to be true to a sailor's feeling and reaction, was to stand Erskine in good stead when he came to relate the story of *Dulcibella*, fighting for her life as she bumped across the Hohenhorn Bank.

Time was as hard to kill as the weather. The two 'tried nearly all the cafes from Tartonis, the principal one (fair), to a little place on the quay where you were expected to bring your own knife! As a great concession the host lent me his clasp knife!' They returned to *Marguerite* in 'that dreary waste of marsh and mud' by fiacre on the 5th, only to see their yacht being towed away by two piratical fishermen. They gave chase in a hurriedly chartered boat and eventually, the game up, the boat-thieves anchored *Marguerite* and offered a cock-and-bull story about the chain having broken, for which Erskine and the receding tide had little patience. Whisky, wine and chain had disappeared in the process of this claimed kindness. *Marguerite* limped back to Havre, and on Monday, 7 October, she was hoisted easily on board the mail steamer and early the following day deposited in the stained waters of Southampton docks at a cost, all inclusive, of £2.11.9.

The cruise had covered 462 nautical miles, included thirty days' sailing, with seven nights at sea, all achieved in an eighteen-foot open boat.

The blessing of the Cruising Club on the cruise of *Mad Agnes* was the turning of Erskine. The adventurer had chosen his environment. The walker, the cyclist, the embryo sailor in the cockleshell dinghy on Lough Dan had progressed. The experience with 'the strange craft on the Lea', Walter Runciman's example aboard his *Waterwitch* and *Edith*, the days spent on *Shulah* and now *Marguerite*, had had their effect. *Marguerite*, flying the burgee of the Cruising Club, set a seal on this combination of self-discovery and sea-learning, and lengthened Erskine's horizon. The 'dissolution' and 'autumn' cruise distilled the adventurer into differen parts.

Now a competent seaman and fine small-boat sailor, Erskine could add this record to a natural and growing ability with the pen. His first attempts at description, such as the Irish bicycle-ride, progressed to pages in the *journal*. 'The Cruise of *The Marguerite*' led to an article for *The Field*, 'A Week in French Waters', published on 6 December 1896. Remember the day wishing for wind off Weymouth before groping in Lulworth? In *The Field* he recalled just a little more than before, the picture is brighter, with more detail:

> *Who will forget those last days of September, 1895? Presently came the faintest of airs from the west; sheets are hastily trimmed, and we run before it whither? Will it carry us to Lulworth? We will try. Just where the cliffs begin to melt into the haze, a cleft in the hills can be dimly discerned. We steal sleepily over the blue expanse towards it. Abeam, to shoreward of us, a gun boat is practising at a target. Now and again a woolly cloudlet hovers over her black, ungainly hull and simultaneously, a mile away from her, a snowy fountain spouts from the blue; then a deep silence, broken by a dead, sulky report and the drawn sigh of the flying shell, then silence again, deeper in contrast. We are approaching the cliffs at last; but as the sun sinks, the vapours mass themselves, and then come tumbling down in dark eddys of fog. Soon the brow of the cliffs is enveloped, then the lower slopes, and, before we know it, there is nothing in sight, and the last breath has died.*

Compare this quiet unfolding with the anxious urgency of the attempt to enter Le Havre. The author was on his way.

The last days of 1895 were to be as significant as those of the summer and autumn in Erskine Childers' tortuous cruise towards the writing of *The Riddle*.

In the dog days of August, while he was aboard *Marguerite*, the match that was to set South Africa alight was struck; the flames were to leave few untouched. The spark owed its origin to the discovery of gold in the Transvaal and the struggle for riches between the Dutch and the British. The Dutch East India Company had founded a colony at the Cape of Good Hope in 1652. They, keen to distance their new land from Europe, called themselves Afrikaners – simply 'the people of Africa'. The nickname 'Boers' came from their word for the nomadic farmers, or 'trekboers', who wandered the veldt, spreading northward from the Cape in search of new pasture.

In January 1806, the British, under the command of Commodore Home Riggs Popham, were worried – not for the last time – about the strategic importance of the sea routes round the Cape, and so took possession of Fort Knocke and then Cape Town. The two nationalities lived uneasily together for a time, Britain recognising, in 1854, the Boer republics of the Transvaal and Orange Free State. The reversal of this policy, the re-annexation of the Transvaal, led to a successful rebellion by Paul Kruger – the first Boer War.

Early riches had been made from diamonds, but the gold rush, which began at Witwatersrand in 1886, fuelled the fires of discontent between the Boers and the Uitlanders, or 'outlanders', as the mainly British settlers were called.

The Boers made sure that the Uitlanders had few political rights, and this added to the seething discontent that persuaded Cecil Rhodes and the diamond millionaire Alfred Beit to try to retrieve the Transvaal for Britain and, of course, for the Uitlanders. A significant step in this and the beginnings of the second Boer War was a secret letter sent by Cecil Rhodes to Alfred Beit. The message it contained told the story: 'Johannesburg is ready ... [this is] the big idea which makes England dominant in Africa, in fact, gives England the African continent.'[30] These few lines were part of the fan that brought the spark into flame and led to the Jameson Raid, which was meant to cause an uprising in Johannesburg.

Cecil Rhodes had known Dr Jameson from their days together in Kimberley. Rhodes was a mining engineer and Dr Jim, as he became known, a doctor. When the British South Africa Company received its charter, Rhodes, seeing more in his friend than his outstanding medical ability, asked Jameson to take on the difficult, demanding job of administering the company's territories. The doctor's resourceful mind and dogged determination made him a signal success as an administrator and when he put down a local rebellion he also gained the reputation of a good soldier.

Rhodes learnt that the chances of Jameson's operation succeeding were seriously jeopardised by internal disputes among the plotters; some wanted to end up under the British flag while others wished to be independent. Few, though, were willing to contemplate a prolonged struggle with President Kruger. Rhodes, therefore, wished to postpone the raid but Jameson was determined to press ahead and launched the charter company's troops on Johannesburg, still believing that there was a strong body that would rise to support him.

The story went that Dr Jim, while pondering on Rhodes' call for delay, was reading *The Life of Clive* on the stoep of Government House, Bulawayo. Inspired, he said to himself, 'Clive would have done it.' This thought urged him into action and led to the dash towards Johannesburg with 500 British South Africa Company troopers on 31 December 1895.

The scheme was feather-brained from the start. Kruger knew what was afoot and so Dr Jim and his men were doomed. Kruger's commandos killed and wounded sixty-five and forced the doctor to surrender. Jameson, had, in the words of his fellow arch-conspirator, Cecil Rhodes, 'upset the apple cart'.

As Edward Cook wrote in 1901, 'Those who were essentially in the right were placed, by the action of Mr Rhodes and Dr Jameson, in the wrong. Those who were essentially in the wrong were placed in the right. Every bad influence was enormously strengthened. Racial animosities were intensified throughout South Africa. The retrograde ideas of policy prevailing with Mr Kruger and his set were now invested with a semblance of justification.'[31]

Reaction in Britain might well have been very different if it had not been for precipitous action by the Kaiser, for on 3 January 1896 he sent his sympathy in no uncertain terms to President Kruger by telegram: 'Sincere congratulations that, supported by your own people, without appealing for the help of the friendly Powers, you have succeeded by your own energetic action against armed bands which invaded your country as disturbers of the peace, and have thus been enabled to restore peace and safeguard the independence of the country against attacks from outside.'

Erskine's own views on the Kaiser's intervention were typical. Writing to his friend Walter Runciman from the Grand Hotel, Nice, he said excitedly, 'What a damned insolent puppy that Emperor is ...'[32] The British press had their own field day, expressing similar thoughts in many more words and going on to such an extent that even the German government was taken by surprise. The furore persuaded their High Command to think about Britain as an enemy and to plan accordingly.[33]

The British government responded to the raid and to the telegram, too, by mobilising a flying squadron to deal with any conspiracy between Germany and President Kruger and by trying Jameson and his men, who had been released by Kruger to the Imperial authorities. The raiders received short terms of imprisonment, with Dr Jim, through the Kaiser's ill-timed intervention, becoming a national hero. The government, meanwhile, set up the promised strict enquiry, giving the job to a Select Committee of the House of Commons.

Basil Williams, Erskine's firm friend at the clerks' table in the Commons, was given the duty of attending and serving the Committee of Enquiry. Later he was greatly influenced by Rhodes, who appeared as a witness. Rhodes' manner may well have persuaded Basil Williams to write his biography, published in 1921, a quarter of a century after the experience. At the end of this he remarks, perhaps recalling those hours, that Rhodes had 'the gift of dominating personality, which most interests the world regardless of whether its owner succeeds or fails.' Certainly Rhodes failed at both the enquiry in London and the one held in the Cape, and responsibility for the raid was firmly put at his door. Joseph Chamberlain, the Foreign Secretary, who had come under suspicion of knowing more about the raid than he let on, was vindicated by the enquiry, as was the Colonial Office.

Let us look ahead a little – the six-month interrogation in 1897 drew Erskine and Basil even closer together, the former fascinated by what the latter could tell of the seemingly endless proceedings. Perhaps it was because of the workings and demands of the committee that Basil Williams did not sail with Erskine in 1897. Nevertheless their friendship ripened and was truly confirmed during the year the two spent in South Africa with the volunteer London regiment, the City of London Imperial Volunteers, of which more later.

Basil Williams, like Childers, was very much taken with southern Africa and returned as a member of Sir Alfred, later Lord, Milner's 'kindergarten'. He was assigned to the Johannesburg town clerk's office, later moving to the Education Department as Secretary of the Transvaal Education Department. After three years of appearing to be a rising star, Erskine wrote to him on 26 March 1903 that Tupper, one of his erstwhile colleagues at the table, had asked him to say that 'he expects to see you Sir Basil W. K.C.B. soon!'[34]

But it was not to be. Basil Williams was axed and returned to London to write, specialising in the eighteenth century. He went to South Africa again in 1908 as a special correspondent. During this time his politics turned from Tory to Liberal, mainly because of his days in South Africa. He stood for Parliament twice, unsuccessfully, as a Liberal candidate for Mid-Sussex, and for Rugby, in 1910. The years of the Great War were spent as an education officer with the Royal Artillery and from then on he lectured full time, first at Oxford and then McGill, before settling down as Professor of History at Edinburgh, where he remained until retiring in 1937. Basil Williams died in Chelsea on 5 January 1950, aged seventy-three. His deep affection for Erskine is confirmed in many letters, as they wrote to each other off and on until the end of Erskine's life.

It is worth continuing this quick forward glance at the lives of those who spent time together aboard *Mad Agnes* in 1896, for they were the principal characters in Erskine's progress towards the writing of *The Riddle of the Sands*.

The mate of *Mad Agnes*, or at least the one who made the most voyages that year, was William Richard Le Fanu, who was elected a member of the Cruising Club after it became 'Royal' in 1902. William Le Fanu was a good sailor and a strong oar, important in the days before auxiliary motors. His career, which ended with his becoming secretary and treasurer to Queen Anne's Bounty, was not so demanding that he could not join Erskine, almost at whim, and so he shared a number of the early adventures. Many of the surviving photographs were 'Kodaked' by William Le fanu. The art of photography had progressed by then to the 'snap' and this was Le Fanu's way.

The quality of some of his pictures of yachts now allow them to be blown up to reveal hidden detail. It is likely that he used either a Kodak 'Bullet' or a Kodak 'Bullseye' camera, both of which were available in England in 1896. He was generous with his copies, for photographs appear in albums of others who shared the same experiences. Photography then was an improving but still magical art and the most amateur practitioner could expect a welcome for his capture of events on paper, however ordinary the results. Le Fanu remained a bachelor and lived at the Albany, off Piccadilly. He died on 22 March 1925. Ivor Lloyd-Jones, who was second only to Le Fanu in time aboard *Marguerite* in 1896, was a little more than a year older than his friend Erskine and a particularly close companion. He was a marksman, shooting both for his school and later for Cambridge University. Of more use on a small yacht was another of his accomplishments at Haileybury, for he was the 'meteorologist' in the school's natural science society. Of above-average intelligence, Ivor Lloyd-Jones won an exhibition to Trinity College, Cambridge, gained his MA, and like both William and Erskine left to study law. For some reason this did not suit him and he embarked on a life of teaching that was to take him through to his retirement, as a master at Uppingham School, in 1929 at the age of sixty. Ivor had another gift, for he was a talented musician, his chosen instrument being unusual – the bassoon. Of athletic figure, a strong face softened by a fashionable moustache, he was typical of his time. Men of his stamp were seen pictured in magazines of the day as 'well-dressed men' or as 'Army officers serving the Empire'. His face was military rather than naval. Ivor Lloyd-Jones died on 6 February 1947.

Erskine's other sailing companions in *Marguerite* in 1896 were Walter Runciman, of whom much has already been recorded, and the somewhat more shadowy figures of Graham Hughes, George Garland and I.S. Richards.

This muster leaves only the all-important figure of Henry Caesar Childers, Erskine's elder brother, senior by two years, the first-born of the family. (Their sisters,

Sybil Rose, Dulcibella Mary and Constance Isobella, were one, three and five years Erskine's junior, respectively.)

Henry was of the same slight build as Erskine, but an inch or two shorter at five foot six-and-a-half inches. He, like Erskine, was devoted to his uncle, Charles Barton, who had looked after them at Glendalough following their father's death. Although he did not have the same facility with words as his brother, he enjoyed Latin, Greek and mathematics at Harrow School. He was anxious to pursue a military career and was accepted for infantry training at Sandhurst in 1888. However, after a year it was discovered that he had a degenerative muscular disease of the back and doctors predicted that he had only six months to live.[35] This happened a year before Erskine's own debilitating sciatica. Henry's disability was more serious, but he showed the same brand of determination and immediately began exercises to strengthen the failing muscles. He may have had some form of operation, for his Army record notes that in addition to an appendectomy scar he had another scar on his back.

Henry's single-minded keenness to conquer this affliction took him to the Austrian Tyrol to hunt chamois and to climb. He shot at least three of these mountain deer and climbed many peaks entirely unaided, for where others employed guides and ropes, perhaps wisely, he went alone. This courageous treatment was successful and the doctors were proved too gloomy, for soon he was well enough to sail with his brother, sharing discomfort, damp and the normal strains and hazards of the small-boat sailor of that time. His modest inheritance from his father helped him to rebuild his strength and to enjoy life by fly-fishing for salmon in Scotland and acting as a 'whipper-in' for the County Carlow and Island Hunt under John Watson. Henry was a daring rider and was often referred to as 'Flying Childers'.

Returning from the epic voyage of 1897 to the Baltic where he crewed for his brother, and which is covered in detail later, Henry made a decision of his own. He determined that his means were not sufficient to marry the girl to whom he had been engaged, and instead crossed the Atlantic, landing at New York in search of fortune. These right-angled decisions were in the family, as may be seen in following Erskine's life. Henry set course for British Columbia, arriving in time to take part in the Gold Rush of 1898. His son, Professor Walter Childers, takes up the story:

Henry 'mushed' into Atlin, where he worked for a mining company. He bought a canoe, fixed it up and canoed up the Yukon River. He cooked sour dough and lived under the stars. During December word came through that the South African War had broken out and that Lord Strathcona was outfitting a scouting or cavalry unit. He decided to enlist. He mushed out of the Gold Rush country with the mail, taking turns in breaking trail with snow shoes in front of the husky dogs.

He enlisted in Victoria but had trouble being accepted as he was only 5ft 6in but he demonstrated his skill as a horseman and was finally accepted. He sailed away to South Africa with the Lord Strathcona's Horse. He was slightly wounded in the foot and was carried out by his friend, Langley Lefroy. While in a convalescent hospital, he got Erskine's mail and they met for exchanges of views, neither knew [before Henry received Erskine's letter] of the other's presence in South Africa.

He was discharged in South Africa and got permission to travel back to England where he received his medal from the King. Both my father and Erskine were devoted to sailing and shared a love of literature. Erskine would read aloud from 'Paradise Lost' while his brother washed the dishes in the confined spaces allowed aboard the yacht. Dad helped take numerous soundings to apply to the charts that Erskine kept and Erskine kept up the log of their journeys. While sailing in the Irish Sea, my father was on a tack when a British naval vessel collided with the bow of his yacht. My father didn't change his course to avoid the vessel. The Navy paid for the repairing of the damage. This trait of following principles regardless, is possibly similar to Erskine's devotion to a course 'whither it leads'.

At the conclusion of these voyages, my father returned to British Columbia and joined three brothers named Johnson on a farm. Conditions were rough, money was scarce and they had lard on their bread. Dad said one time – that a brother had said, 'easy on the lard boys'!

As a veteran of the Boer War, my father applied for a land holding. The land was situated across the Okanagan Lake opposite Kelowna at a location called Bear Creek. He cleared the land and planted tomatoes and fruits for the prairies market. He met and married my mother, who was the daughter of Major Allen who had served in India and Egypt. Dad raised carriage horses but with the advent of the Model T Ford, horses became expendable.

He volunteered for the 1914–18 War, although he was over age and had a young family. He thought young men weren't volunteering so he was setting an example. He lost money by this impractical act but his loyalty to country was ingrained. He rented his farm to a young farmer and sold his horses for a pittance. On his return from the Army, all prices were inflated.

We sold the farm in Kelowna and migrated to the Annapolis Valley in Nova Scotia. My dad memorised long passages of Virgil in order to improve his memory but really he was extremely forgetful. He named the Jersey cows by Latin names, Aurora, Elissa, etc., which brought howls of laughter from the farmers in the area. My father was a kind, self-effacing, stubborn man and found difficulty in communicating even with those he loved.[36]

Henry Caesar Childers died in 1963, aged ninety-six. He did not achieve the notice the world paid his brother. The two had similar strengths and overcame physical difficulties but they chose entirely different paths.

Parliament sat from 11 February to 31 March for the first session of 1896.

The Rt Hon. Hugh Culling Eardley Childers had died on 29 January. Erskine managed to leave two days early to prepare *Marguerite* for the Easter cruise that began on 2 April and lasted until the 8th, just in time for the new sitting of Parliament that was due to begin on the 9th. The crew consisted of Walter Runciman, William Le Fanu and George Garland. Erskine spent the night in the Crown Hotel, Southampton, in easy reach of Picketts Yard, which looked after *Marguerite* for him. The others came down by train in time to be under way by 11.30.

The vital ingredients in making a success of Erskine's sailing were a yard that could be relied on to see that the tiny yacht was at least afloat, a mooring near to a station that was served by a quick and reliable service, a reasonably sheltered cruising ground so that the best could be made of the weather and a good hotel in case all else failed. There were two obvious geographical alternatives – the Thames Estuary and the Solent. *Marguerite* had already spent some time in the London river and roaming that great sand-choked estuary that flowed to the North Sea. Erskine was an authority on these waters, as acknowledged by the Cruising Club, and so it was clearly the Solent's turn. He and *Mad Agnes* made the best of it that year, for from Easter onwards Erskine and his friends, or just he alone, made seventeen pilgrimages to these waters, sometimes escaping from the shelter of the Wight to reach westward to Poole, a place that he had very much enjoyed the year before. At other times he made Chichester in the east. He went round the Island, besting St Catherine's Point. He visited Cowes and put up at the Globe; they went to Newtown and stayed aboard; they sailed to Yarmouth, Keyhaven, Lymington and Beaulieu, sometimes including three or four ports or more in a weekend, stopping for lunch or tea aboard and dining ashore. The joy of the experience, the refreshment of it all, comes through so clearly in the log and stood him in such good stead when he put his mind to writing about the ways of small boats in *The Riddle* nearly five years later.

The summer of 1896 was spent weekend after weekend in this way. Erskine never seemed to tire of the Solent and in succeeding years he kept returning. He came to enjoy Bursledon. At that time it was a quiet place. Frank Cowper said in 1893, 'Bursledon is one of the sleepiest, cosiest, most snug places we know. There are delightful walks all about the hills and fields towards Netley and Bitterne.'[37]

Erskine sailed *Marguerite* up the Hamble on a number of occasions. He knew the river from the mouth to Hamble village but appears not to have ventured further until 14 June 1896 when he decided 'to risk Bursledon'. The element of uncertainty in such a voyage may appear odd today, but the river has a strong tide and is sheltered, so progress under sail alone could be chancy, especially when trying to fit so much into so few hours. Bursledon is important in unravelling one aspect of *The Riddle*, as will be seen. One of the principal yacht yards in the area then, as now, was A. H. Moody of Swanwick Shore, Bursledon. Alexander Moody set up his boat-building business there in 1878 and prospered. There is no evidence that Erskine met the boat-builder in the summer of 1896; though on 14 June he reached the bridge for the first time, he immediately went about and beat back to the mouth. He was there again on 14 July in search of a Mr Blakiston and 'returned to a nice berth near the bridge'.

On 12 September *Marguerite* was again at Bursledon, but no mention of Mr Moody, though his yard was well known and a point of interest on the walk Erskine took with Ivor Lloyd-Jones in the evening of that day, which Erskine recorded.

They had just returned from a visit to Gosport where they had been invited aboard HMS *Majestic*, the flagship of the Channel fleet. The flag captain, Captain Arthur Barrow, following Erskine's note, had invited him and Ivor aboard. Erskine records little of the meeting in *Mad Agnes's* log: 'Crossed river and boarded *Majestic*, inspected ship with curiosity and amazement and subsided with whisky and sodas with the Captain. Aboard again at 4.30 and sailed to Bembridge.' It was not a long meeting but the fact that the two knew each other and met in 1896 is significant.

Arthur Barrow was assistant director of the Intelligence Department for two tours of duty lasting five years in all, the first from 2 May 1892 until 25 April 1895, and the second from 19 November 1897 until 28 June 1899, when he went to command HMS *Prince George*.

The summer sitting of Parliament that year stretched for a full ten weeks, from 1 June to 14 August. The time-table showed no respect for Cowes Week – not that that would have really worried Erskine, for he had enjoyed those sights the year before. He was anxious, though, to sail *Marguerite* back to the Thames while still using the last days of autumn to enjoy the Solent and he certainly made the most of it, not leaving the confines of Spithead until 12 October. He took eleven days to reach Greenhithe, arriving there on 1 November. Single-handed, he had not made bad time for the back end of the year, especially as he had left *Marguerite* at Charles Grigson's yard at Shoreham for a week and had again spent a day at Folkestone with Ivor's father at 35 Millfield.

While Erskine was completing his year exploring the creeks and harbours of the Solent, another character in this story, Lieutenant Stuart Victor Seymour Craigie Messum arrived home from surveying the Queensland coast of Australia. He appears to have been helping chart the waters 'down under' for nearly ten years.

Stuart Messum was appointed on 12 September 1896 to HMS *President* for service as assistant lecturer, in the nautical surveying and meteorology department, at the Royal Naval College, Greenwich. Promotion was slow in the surveying service of the Royal Navy; Messum joined as a naval cadet in 1872 and took eleven years to rise to lieutenant. He was thirty-seven, and eight years from retirement. However, the spell at Greenwich was to enable him to achieve two things: the production of his *Pilot* to the Thames Estuary, published in March 1903, and his appointment as hydrographer to the Royal Cruising Club, in 1905. The two were closely linked. In the Foreword to *East Coast Rivers*,[38] the author paid tribute to H. Stuart Moore of the Royal Cruising Club, who it may be remembered had seconded Erskine for membership the previous year. Messum also mentions his grateful acknowledgement to the Club 'for their courteous loan of their private charts to which reference has been made'.

The Cruising Club had started to produce their own charts in 1893 as the vast majority of charts were produced by the Hydrographic Office of the Admiralty and designed for the use of navies or the merchant services. The output of the Hydrographic Office was supplemented by publications of a few independent companies. Yachtsmen's needs, however, were different in that they wished to use anchorages that would have been too cramped for larger vessels and therefore were largely ignored by the hydrographer. Equally, the private publishers failed to produce large-scale charts of creeks and inlets that were of particular use to yachtsmen. There were then at least three independent chart-publishing companies – James Imray & Company, H. Laurie, and Norie & Wilson. The three firms amalgamated at the turn of the century to form the well-known publishing house Imray, Laurie, Norie & Wilson.

Norie & Wilson's chart catalogue of 1892 illustrates the problem faced by the yachtsmen and the reason why the Cruising Club were prepared to vote £60 to fund the initial venture. Take the Norie & Wilson chart No. 54 as an example. The sheet covered the vast sea area, Spurn Point in the north to Beachy Head in the south, stretching eastward beyond the Zuider Zee, including the north coasts of France, Belgium and Holland. The chart had a large-scale inset plan of the entrances to the Texel, but nothing else, though you could buy, for an extra ten shillings, a *Book of*

Sailing Directions to go with the chart. This was not a particularly attractive package for the amateur sailor.

Also, yachtsmen and other coastal navigators had considerable reservations about the accuracy of the information given by the Admiralty on their charts of European estuaries and coastal waters, such as the Wadden Zee and the waters inside the Frisian islands. The Navy argued that they based their charts on the latest information provided by the state whose coast was described. Yachtsmen felt that if this was the case they were both slow and less than energetic in committing this to paper and that the Admiralty charts compared unfavourably with the local productions. Erskine was one of the foremost critics of Admiralty charts, both in *The Riddle* and later in a memorandum to their lordships.

There was yet another reason for the Royal Cruising Club series, and that was size. The chart table, in those days, was almost exclusively a piece of furniture for the naval ship, merchant vessel or salt-water palace. The great paper sheets were too large and inconvenient for a small yacht. The dog-house had yet to be fitted to vessels of under ten tons Thames measurement and there was little or no shelter in the cockpit.

The Club produced eight charts in the first series which were exclusively dedicated to the east coast of England and only available to members. The batch included a chart of the Thames Estuary, one of Orford Haven and another of Harwich. The Club's consultants were Commodore Hull, RN, who became the first hon. hydrographer to the Club, and R. C. Carrington, chief hydrographic draftsman to the Admiralty.

Lieutenant Messum was able to take advantage of this early work in his *East Coast Rivers* and through this association was known to members of the Cruising Club. This may have given birth to the legend that Messum was the 'Lieutenant X' in *The Riddle* and that the 'drab little book' was, indeed, his *East Coast Rivers*. There is a snag though, for this useful Pilot was published in March 1903, only a couple of months before *The Riddle* came out. However, there is little doubt that Childers, as a member of the committee and an expert on that area, knew of the book's imminent arrival and may have decided to weave the book into the story, perhaps as a strange reward for Messum's help in deciding where the Germans might land, little thinking that anyone would trouble to connect Dollmann, alias

'Lieutenant X', with Messum. The description in *The Riddle* and the appearance of the book itself are almost as one. 'It was old and unpretentious, bound in cheap cloth of a rather antiquated style with a title which showed it to be a guide for yachtsmen to a certain British estuary.' Carruthers then turned to the title page and noted that it was 'by Lieut. X-, R.N.' The two then identify Dollmann from the photograph that is included as a frontispiece in Dulcibella's copy but not in the published edition. This difference and Davies' reminder that their Pilot was published sixteen years earlier, is the variation between the story and reality.

Plate six of *East Coast Rivers* is a small folding chart of 'the River Blackwater and approaches' and this shows that Messum completed the survey in 1902. The area was well known to Erskine, for he had sailed these waters at Whitsuntide in 1895 with William Le Fanu. *Marguerite* had taken them 'into wild, weird country – rugged islands and Mehalah – recalling flats'. They went on to the Colne, bound for Harwich, sailing northeast through the Wallet, that deep channel that lies north of the Buxey and Gunfleet Sands, which provides a sheltered anchorage, particularly at low water, for sizeable vessels in view of Clacton.

The Easter cruise of 1897 returned to the rivers Crouch and Blackwater, again with the help of William Le Fanu. *Marguerite* safely navigated Ray Sand, Dengie and St Peter's flats, taking the shortest cut the tide would allow to reach West Mersea, a place they had looked at two years before and recalled as a 'beautiful little red village round an old church tower on a thickly wooded hill'. These voyages of discovery were to come in useful later, for the flats of the Essex coast between Foulness and Brightlingsea were one of the two invasion sites selected by 'Lieutenant X'. The alternative was on the Lincolnshire coast, on the north side of the Wash, known as East Holland. These two areas have much in common. From the water, the sky overpowers the land, squeezing it into a flat, dark grey ribbon floating above the shimmer of the sea. They share something else too, for both are protected by sands that dry at low water. The low-lying coast of East Holland on the Wash has the Long and Roger Sands which do much the same work as the Gunfleet and Buxey. The Wash, unlike the Thames, is unobstructed. It is open to the North Sea and only 240 sea miles, west by south, from Borkum Island, and so could be a preferred point of invasion from the German coast.

Erskine's log, the record of the wanderings of *Marguerite*, was to bring back memories and give life to his warning of invasion. The days spent groping through the creeks, beginning to know the bumps and grooves by 'pandemoniacal anchoring, looking for a deep spot and lowering and weighing, setting and lowering sails, sticking, floating, rowing, poling and sounding and all talking at once', were recorded in the old exercise books that were pressed into service as the log.

If 1895 turned Erskine into an experienced small-boat sailor and correctly shaped his quill, the next eighteen months gave the navigator the skills of a pilot. *Mad Agnes'* log ends on 25 April 1897 at Greenhithe with the completion of the Easter cruise. This was not the end of her career under Erskine's burgee though, for William Le Fanu's photograph album shows *Marguerite* under sail at Burnham-on-Crouch on Midsummer's Day. The pictures are also evidence that William and his brother, Hugh Barrington Le Fanu, were on 26 June aboard the latter's ship, the sixteen-year-old armoured cruiser *Warspite*. The Diamond Jubilee, the major event of that year, was in full swing. One hundred and sixty-four Royal Navy ships and those of ten visiting nations were in the lines at Spithead that day. The most impressive naval peacetime get-together ever organised, before or since, was witnessed by William and Hugh and by the 35,000 officers and men who manned the British men-of-war. However impressive the spectacle, there were those who saw weakness in such a show of might. W. Laird Clowes, describing the scene for the *Illustrated London News*, observed that: 'It is unfortunately true that nothing is more difficult than to convince the official Englishman of the practical usefulness of any new and revolutionary invention. One of the consequences of this national peculiarity of ours is that at Spithead on Saturday there were foreign ships which, although they are already beginning to grow old, embody improvements which with us are still in the experimental stage.' Others were going to be as perceptive in-due course.

The album also shows that Erskine spent some time at the Le Fanu house, Ringsall. Judging from a photograph taken on Rose Sunday, 11 July, it was there that he gained the nickname 'The Duke of Bilgewater'.

The combination of Erskine, *Marguerite* and the favoured crew, William Le Fanu and Ivor Lloyd-Jones, was to end, for *Marguerite* was to pass into other hands. *Mad*

Agnes had served them well. Erskine was now twenty-seven, William thirty-six and Ivor twenty-eight. The little yacht, in the way of ladies, managed to keep her age a secret.

Fond as Erskine was of his half-decker, he had another purpose in mind. He wanted to go further afield. He may have remembered his talk with the Greenhithe yacht-designer, Linton Hope, at the Bugle Inn on the Hamble River two years before. Linton Hope may have recommended 'a larger craft with some sort of lid on'. He looked first in *Marguerite's* home port.

Greenhithe, at the end of the nineteenth century, was a quiet retreat for short summer holidays. The pier was served by the Gravesend packets and the Pier Hotel looked after a growing number of yachtsmen. It was a good place to keep a small boat in those days, only twenty miles from London and well supplied with trains by the South-Eastern Railway's North Kent Line. There was no substitute for *Marguerite* to be found at that time in the port, but Erskine would not forget Greenhithe and it was not long before he was once again moored in the hollow of that great bend in the Thames.

Chapter 4

THE EPIC VOYAGE OF 1897

'On from island unto island to the gateways of the day'

The House sat from 17 June to 6 August in the summer of 1897. Erskine was only able to weekend occasionally on the water. A photograph in William Le Fanu's album shows *Mad Agnes* full of Childers girls, beating to windward at Burnham-on-Crouch on 21 June. The old-style Royal Cruising Club burgee, black and gold edged with a very German cross, flies at the masthead. This is the last-known photograph of the open boat that confirmed Erskine as one of the leading Corinthian sailors of his day. *Mad Agnes* remained in his ownership until 1898, when he sold her to Lawes & Hurst.[1]

It is not clear how he first heard of *Vixen*. Perhaps he received a tip from Frederick Lloyd-Jones or from his son Ivor, as the former lived not far from Dover and it was in that port that Erskine first set eyes on the yacht that was to have such an important part in the telling of *The Riddle*.

In the *Yachting Monthly* magazine of 1898, he wrote: 'To start with, no one could call *Vixen* beautiful. We grew to love her in the end but never to admire her. At first I did not even love her for she was a *pis aller*, bought in a hurry in default of a better, and a week spent in fitting her for cruising – a new era for her – had somehow not cemented our affections.' The phrase *pis aller* was used at the beginning of *The Riddle*: 'My own people were at Aix for my father's gout; to join them there was a*pis aller*, whose banality was repellent.' The alternatives to *Vixen* are not recorded. Her history is like an old family jigsaw: parts are missing and some of those yellowing in

Vixen's sail plan

the box are beginning to delaminate through attempts to mate with the unmateable. *Vixen* had a peculiar history and like *Marguerite* did not grace the pages of Lloyd's Register of Yachts. Hunt's Universal Yacht List, on the other hand, first mentions her in 1898 but loses interest by 1903. Her dimensions are given each year as twenty-eight feet between perpendiculars, bow and stern, with a beam of seven foot six inches and registered tonnage of seven. Erskine says in his article in the *Yachting Monthly* magazine that she was thirty foot overall with a draft of four foot or six foot six inches with the centre-board down. But there is no doubt that she is the same boat because Hunt lists her for the five years as owned by R. E. Childers of 20 Carlyle Mansions, Cheyne Walk, London SW, a member of the Cruising Club. The reason for the difference in the overall length will be seen later.

The yacht's certificate of registry states that she was built by J. Price of Albion Road, Ramsgate, in 1893, and the same date is to be found in Hunt's. A Joseph Price lived at 11 Albion Road (on Ramsgate's East Cliffe) in 1893 but had left by 1898. He would not have carried out his boat-building trade at Albion Road, though he used this as his trade address. In the 1880s and 1890s, Ramsgate's boatyards were clustered around the harbour, which was a step away from the East Cliffe. There is no record of a boat-building firm *of* the name of Joseph or J. Price in Ramsgate and he may have worked in another yard or, more likely and according to legend, built boats and undertook conversions on the beach by the harbour side. Legend has it, too, that he specialised in turning lifeboats into yachts and that they were all named *Vixen*.The only other boat attributed to him and recorded in Lloyd's Register is the five-ton cutter *Pet*, which he designed and built in Ramsgate in 1877.

There was a plentiful supply of lifeboats in the days when steamships carried the wooden type, for the Board of Trade required that these should be replaced every few years, so the discards were available at low prices. The well-known yacht designer, Maurice Griffiths, writing in a recent issue of *Yachting Monthly* about sailing in East Coast waters in the 1930s, remembers that clinker lifeboats of twenty-two to thirty feet, in good condition, could be picked up for £25 to £45 or so and damaged boats from £5.[2] It was the poor fisherman's and yachtsman's way of getting a serviceable boat.

The famous ship- and lifeboat-builders, Samuel White of Cowes, used to produce some fine boats, of double-skinned, teak construction, the outer horizontally and the inner diagonally laid. E. F. Knight had one of these, originally built for the P&O. He is reputed to have started the craze for lifeboat conversions with the publication of his book *Falcon on the Baltic*, the story of a cruise undertaken in just such a boat from the Doves Inn, Hammersmith, to Copenhagen in 1887. The P&O lifeboats had a hard life, spending most of it on deck through many crossings of the Indian Ocean, and had to be well built, of best materials and of double-skinned, horizontal and diagonal construction to be serviceable in such an environment. Group Captain Frank Griffiths recalls that these were also designed for 'working through the surf in the Bight of Benin'.[3]

The Lamb & White lifeboat was designed and patented in 1846, built on whaler principles, carvel, with air boxes at either end and along each side, specifically for the P&O Company. In 1850 the company perfected its own method of diagonal and longitudinal planking. One of the features of the White lifeboats, after 1851, was a very straight stern post and the rudder fitted close to it, so that wreckage could not be trapped and affect the steering.[4] From photographs, it may be seen that *Vixen* had the more normal cut-away Lifeboat Institution stern that employed a lifting rudder to overcome this disadvantage, while giving better control in launching and beaching. Indeed, the only craft that excelled and outclassed an ex-P&O lifeboat were ex-RNLI or Coast Guard lifeboats. These were superannuated rather less regularly and on average were replaced every ten to twenty years.

Writing in the *Cruising Club Journal* for 1897, published in 1898, Erskine says of his new boat *Vixen*: 'Our own boat was an ex-lifeboat,' and so there has always been an argument about the type of lifeboat that formed the basis of the conversion. Some held that the cutter had started life as a ship's lifeboat in the tradition of Edward Knight, whom Erskine admired, while others held that she had been in the service of the Royal National Lifeboat Institution.

The ship's lifeboat idea has quite a following. The designer and former editor of the *Yachting Monthly*, Maurice Griffiths, writes, 'I have always understood that Childers' *Vixen* was a diagonal carvel-built ex-lifeboat.'[5] The late George Naish, one-time deputy director of the National Maritime Museum and honorary secretary of the Society for Nautical Research, writing to the artist David Cobb agrees in a characteristic manner with a sketch of a banana-shaped, self-righting lifeboat. 'I send you a picture of *Dulcibella*. An RNLI lifeboat, she certainly wasn't.'

Eric Hiscock, who has done more to expand Childers' introduction to cruising in small boats than anyone else, felt that George Naish ought to know. In a letter from *Wanderer IV* in New Zealand he said, 'I knew George Naish for many years, indeed I used to cruise with him in his little half-decker *Dodo*, and I formed a very high opinion of his knowledge and his keen observation where boats were concerned. As you may know, George, with his parents, his brother John and his sister Una, at one time lived at "Flagstaff", the house near the top of the hard beside Moody's Swanwick Shore Yard, and ... just across the road on the mud beside the hard *Vixen* lay for a long time. George must have looked at her often, and probably went aboard, so if he says she was a ship's boat I feel sure she must have been.'[6] Joan Naish, George's widow, found a picture postcard in the family album which showed *Vixen* converted to a houseboat in this berth.

Ted Watson had *Vixen*, renamed *Dulcibella* by Erskine in his last year of ownership, in his yard at Fishbourne in her twilight years. He bought her with the 'good will' of that dilapidated place from an old chap called Hapgood and remembered her well. 'I think I only went aboard once or at the most twice fearing no doubt that the deck would give way under my weight! She had a certain amount of decking and a rather low cabin top. She was very bare inside – no cabin – or cockpit sole. She seemed to have had a centre-plate, but the slot had been filled in. There was very little in the way of a keel, and, generally, she struck me rather as an old ship's lifeboat than one built for the RNLI.'[7]

The opposite camp, those who feel sure that *Vixen* was an RNLI lifeboat, are just as impressive with their arguments.

Frank Carr, a past director of the National Maritime Museum and now chairman of the World Ship Trust, feels certain that *Vixen* was an RNLI lifeboat because of the difference in construction between station and ship's lifeboats.[8]

Dick Stower, partner in Laurent Giles, is equally emphatic on the construction. 'To my mind, there was never any doubt that *Vixen/Dulcibella*, which was at

Fishboume, was an RNLI pulling lifeboat. Having served an apprenticeship during which we built quite a number of lifeboats at John Samuel Whites, I feel that quite apart from the shape, which is quite different from a ship's lifeboat, the method of construction, as far as I can remember, gives good reason to believe that she was not a ship's lifeboat as at that early date, "pre-First World War", I think I am right in saying, a ship's lifeboat of this size would most likely have been clinker-built and not diagonal carvel.'[9] He was in a good position to know for he was a kinsman of Claude 'Happy' Hapgood, mentioned earlier, who had *Vixen/Dulcibella* in his yard at Fishboume. Laurent Giles and Partners did a great deal of research on the yacht before they bought and converted the old Brooke lifeboat (1907–35), *Susan Ashley*, for the Drummond Challis film of *The Riddle of the Sands*.

Despite the impressive support for the ship's-boat theory, there is no doubt from evidence of construction, dimensions and dates that *Vixen* owed her beginnings to the RNLI and in particular to the second *Thomas Chapman*, the Kingsgate lifeboat from 1880 to 1889. As Erskine so aptly put it in his *Yachting Monthly* magazine article, she enjoyed a 'new era'.

The Kingsgate station, two and a half miles from Margate, was established by the Royal National Lifeboat Institution in 1862. Kingsgate was a pretty little village made up of a small hotel, a few gentlemen's houses and very few cottages, according to the *Lifeboat journal* of 1875.

> *Abreast of Kingsgate, there projects from the general trend of the shore a rocky point, which, being covered at high tide, gives the appearance to coasters (who with northerly winds hug the shore thereabouts) of having the same depth of water over it as is found off the adjacent line of coast. The result is that wrecks occasionally occur on the point, and as the tide operates against the lifeboats at other stations making a rapid passage to Kingsgate while the shallow and rocky nature of the bottom is not suited for the operation of a large boat, life might be lost before assistance could be obtained from other lifeboat stations. Hence the necessity for a small lifeboat of light draught of water which could launch out under the lee of the wreck, and land the crew.*

The RNLI were prompted by the loss of the *Northern Belle* in 1857 and five years later a lifeboat house was built at the head of a tunnel bored through the chalk cliffs that was used by fishermen and farmers for gaining access to the shore.

The first boat to be conveyed on its carriage to the sea in this strange way was the ex-Dungeness lifeboat *Brave Robert Shedden*. The station proved successful and there were two boats called after Robert Shedden, built with the help of a legacy given by Mrs W. Shedden Watson. In 1870, the last of these was replaced by the first *Thomas Chapman*, named after the deputy chairman of the RNLI 'as a compliment to him for his long and valuable co-operation'.

The first *Thomas Chapman* was very narrow gutted, being six foot in the beam and the smallest conventional lifeboat ever built for the Institution. She was, of course, designed to go through the tunnel and perhaps because of this was rather unstable, for she overturned on exercise in 1873, but mercifully no lives were lost. An RNLI inspector witnessed the capsize and in due course Forrests of Limehouse were sent to the station and they increased her beam by four inches on the spot.[10] It may be that this was achieved by 'slicing' the lifeboat exactly in half, fore and aft, inserting a filler piece and then rejoining the two sides.

The increase in beam and the reduction in weight, by dropping one oarsman, did not really improve matters. Although the lifeboat records are a little mute on the subject, it is clear that the old boat was withdrawn to London and a new *Thomas Chapman* was on station in 1880. She was a double-banked or eight-oared boat of twenty-eight feet with a beam of seven foot three inches.

The second *Thomas Chapman* was built by Thomas William Woolfe & Sons of 46–47 Lower Shadwell, only a couple of streets away from the Ratcliffe Highway where Carruthers had had 'an hour's immersion in the reeking atmosphere of a low music hall'. The extra beam that the firm provided in the new *Thomas Chapman*, however, proved to be a problem, for the boat did not pass conveniently through the tunnelled gapway.[11] The normal drill for launching was for the boat to be pulled out of the boathouse on the trolley, swung round at the head of the gap and then rolled gently down, checked by winch and cable as the slope was very steep.[12] The tunnel had been widened for *Brave Robert Shedden*, but it only took a small deviation on the way down for the boat or its carriage to hit the sides and so lose valuable time.

The RNLI records only one service for the second *Thomas Chapman* and that was on 11 October 1885, when she went to the assistance of an unnamed barque, but in the event her help was not needed. This rather quiet time was presided over by two generations of honorary secretaries, Major Webb of Broadstairs and Colonel Isacke of North Foreland Lodge, Broadstairs, both serving in a joint capacity with William Jenkins, the chief officer of Her Majesty's Coast Guard at Kingsgate.

The *Lifeboat Journal* of 1 November 1889 reports her relief, under a heading which includes Kingsgate, that the Committee of the RNLI 'have also had satisfaction to send new lifeboats to these places, the boats bearing the same names as those which they superseded, *viz.* [amongst others] *Thomas Chapman*', the third to bear that name.

So ended the lifeboat career of the second *Thomas Chapman*. The records show that she was sold locally, though the name of the purchaser is not given. It is now almost certain that she was bought by Joseph Price of Ramsgate, just a step down the coast, and that he set to work on her to turn her into a yacht. The conversion of a lifeboat into a yacht is quite a task. The only part of the boat that is usually of any use is the hull. Traditionally this is taken as one third of the value of a boat, the other thirds being the mast, sails and rigging, and lastly the expenditure on the accommodation and interior fittings.

Francis Cooke, in reviewing the idea of such a conversion in 1913, in his *The Corinthian Yachtsman's Handbook*, is not encouraging. He could not see that the owner would have much change out of £120, after buying the hull for £8–10. 'What has he in exchange for his money? A boat that won't sail, that is uncomfortable to live aboard, and unsightly to look upon.' Cooke adds that when the unhappy owner comes to sell, 'he has an article which is drug on the market,' and that 'he will in the end be glad to cut his loss and accept a price at would hardly cover the cost of cabin gear that he bought for her.'

However, this thought does not seem to have entered Joseph Price's mind when he decided to turn the second *Thomas Chapman* into the yacht *Vixen*. To make her sail and to give her more directional stability he added, as was customary at that time, a false keel to supplement the centre-board. This was of wood and wedge-shaped and, with three tons of internal ballast, gave her a draft of four feet aft, while at the bow she drew the same as she had done as a lifeboat.

He set to with a will to improve the headroom. He must have recognised this as one of the major difficulties if any comfort were to be provided, for just placing a deck on a lifeboat will give crawling room only, so at least a coach roof must be added. Cooke had had experience of that. He recalls that 'despite a coach-roof of generous proportions, one could not sit upright unless seated on the floor, and the bunks were so close to the deck that it was as much as one could do to turn over in bed at night.'

To overcome this on *Vixen*, Price added six planks running fore and aft above the double diagonal lifeboat hull. Perhaps conscious of the widely held view that lifeboat conversions were unsightly to look upon, he included a counter which gave greater deck space aft and avoided renewing the sternpost. A sort of false counter was common on transom-sterned beach boats down the coast and gave a little lift and some protection as the boat hit the shore. Today this would be very costly, but in those days boat-builders were handy and, as we have seen, regularly sawed boats in half to give extra length and split them to give extra beam.

The counter gave *Vixen* added length and turned a twenty-eight-foot lifeboat into a thirty-foot yacht. Her extra beam from a lifeboat of seven feet three inches to a gentleman's cutter of seven feet six inches was due to the additional fore and aft planking. The increase in draft from the lifeboat's two feet nine inches aft to the yacht's four feet has already been explained. The discrepancy between the four feet mentioned by Childers in the account of his cruise and that recorded by the Registrar of British Shipping of 1899 is simple. Childers discovered that the wedge did not add significantly to the boat's performance and had it removed when the yacht was refitted at Moody's in the winter of 1898, just before she was first registered. The recorded three tons of ballast must have been an over-estimate.

Childers stated that *Vixen* had another advantage and that was that with bilge keels she would remain almost upright on the sand while drying out. As the wedge disappeared quickly as it ran forward, the bilge keels would still be able to help.

The low bulwarks that took something off the high appearance of the coach-roof and the new narrow-planked laid deck gave the lifeboat a more yacht-like air, gaining further emphasis from her tall cutter rig, which Childers described as giving a 'certain over-sparred appearance aloft'.

There was no cockpit, the helmsman had either to drop his legs through the little round hatch to the lazarette or to sit on deck, feet on the lee bulwark. This lack of shelter, common on larger yachts of the period, was not unique on cutters the size of *Vixen*. *Dorothea*, designed by Dixon Kemp in the 1880s, had a similar arrangement. The plans of this six-ton sea-going cutter may be seen in *Practical Boatbuilding and Sailing* by Nelson, Kemp and Davies.[13]

Although the helmsman was condemned to almost total exposure, the crew could stand in *Vixen's* sliding companionway hatch, which was unusually and usefully large, as it opened virtually the whole of the after end of the coach roof, exposing a conveniently placed sail store and bo'sun's locker to starboard and bunk to port, tucked under the side deck. In a *Yachting Monthly* magazine article, Erskine confirms that *Vixen* 'has three comfortable berths and plenty of accommodation for stores and sails'.

This hermaphrodite cabin gave directly into a saloon with two berths. The owner goes on to describe the comforts: 'In the saloon he would find but just enough headroom to allow himself to sit upright; and before he could well help himself the observation would escape him that the centreplate case was an inconveniently large piece of furniture.' In *The Riddle of the Sands* many features of *Vixen* are seen in the fictional *Dulcibella*, but on close examination the one is not a mirror image of the other. Take the beam measurement again. In the *Yachting Monthly* magazine, Erskine gives *Vixen* as seven feet while in Hunt's it is seven feet six inches, the same as that recorded by the British Registrar of Shipping. In *The Riddle*, *Dulcibella's* figure is given as 'something over … nine'. *Vixen's* tonnage would be right at seven. Using the Thames Tonnage calculation invented by the Royal Thames Yacht Club in 1854 and a hull of thirty feet, the figure comes out at 6.732 tons TM, a figure that would usually be rounded to seven.[14]

Carruthers' description of the appearance of *Dulcibella* in *The Riddle* is as emphatic as Erskine's view of his yacht *Vixen* in the *Yachting Monthly* magazine. The former calls *Dulcibella* 'a scrubby little craft of doubtful build and distressing plainness', very much in tune with Erskine's view that 'no one could call *Vixen* beautiful'.

Looking at the photographs, one of the features was that *Vixen* had a large companion hatch and that this was the only way below decks other than through the fore-hatch into the fo'c'sle, and maybe through the round hatch aft into the lazarette. This companionway hatch gave access to *Vixen*'s sail store and the berth which would have the same purpose today as the fo'c'sle, the accommodation in modern terms being 'back to front'. This sail store gave into the saloon and from the saloon it was possible to gain access to the diminutive fo'c'sle through a sliding door in the forward bulkhead. Group Captain Frank Griffiths remembers this uncomfortable route and how the door worked from left to right, for the entrance must have been on the port side. There is a description of the same hatch in *The Riddle* in Chapter 2, describing Carruthers' first experiences on *Dulcibella*. 'The latter sentences were spoken from the fo'c'sle, whither Davies had crept through a low sliding door, like that of a rabbit-hutch, and was already busy with a kettle over a stove which I made out to be a battered and disreputable twin brother of the No. 3 Rippingille.' A further difference was the skylight. There were no skylights on *Vixen*, but *Dulcibella* had two, one letting light into the saloon and the other into the sleeping cabin. *Vixen* did not have the advantage of a lobby between the sail store and single berth and the saloon – only a bulkhead separated the two. *Dulcibella* had such a lobby to accommodate the midship side companion to the deck. Remember Clara's hurried exit when she knocked her head on 'the sharp lintel of the doorway and stumbled on the step of the ladder'. On one occasion, Erskine rather loses himself and slips back to pure *Vixen* when he describes the tow out of Bensersiel by the Imperial Navy steam-launch with von Brüning aboard. 'I brought up cigars, and we settled ourselves facing him [Davies], our backs to the wind and spray. And so we made the rest of the passage, von Brüning cuddled against me and the cabin hatch.'

The huge centre-board case, on the other hand, was common to both, as were the two bunks. Otherwise, apart from the lack of headroom, Erskine gives few details of *Vixen*'s saloon in his log but a wealth of description for *Dulcibella* in *The Riddle*. There is one interesting comment on paintwork which points to another variation.

According to the *The Riddle*, *Dulcibella*'s internal woodwork was painted white, her topsides were black and she had a skylight over the saloon and another lighting the sleeping cabin. Both 'saddened the eye with dark iron and plebeian graining.' An entry for *Vixen*'s log for 30 April 1899 makes it clear that most of the interior suffered the indignity of plebeian graining, for Erskine refers to the refit at Moody's yard at Bursledon: 'Painted as before outside, but inside the graining abolished and white and green paint substituted.'

Erskine, therefore, saw *Dulcibella* as *Vixen*, at least in part, as she was after this refit. Other than the detail of the paint, *Vixen*'s fo'c'sle and her saloon were exactly as *Dulcibella*'s, but from the saloon aft the plans were different.

Erskine did not have to look far for inspiration for in 1901 he arranged with Alan Herbert Moody to part-exchange *Vixen* for the twenty-eight-year-old, fifteen-ton yawl *Sunbeam*. The transaction took place before Erskine began to write *The Riddle* on the usually unlucky day of Friday, 13 December.

The old yawl had been built in 1873 at Beccles, Suffolk, by W. Wright, probably to the builder's design. Her last owner, W. W. Cheadle, was also an East-countryman who lived at Ipswich and was a member of the Royal Thames Yacht Club. Anxious to sell, he put the yacht in the hands of Mr Moody, who arranged to take *Vixen* from Erskine in part-exchange, confident of selling her on. *Sunbeam* was a larger yacht, being thirty-eight-feet between perpendiculars and with a beam of ten feet, a foot larger than *Dulcibella* and two feet six inches plumper than *Vixen*. Perhaps she influenced Davies, through Erskine, to adopt the yawl rig for *Dulcibella* soon after he was nearly drowned by Dollmann on the Hohenhorn bank.

But to return to *Vixen*, lying in Dover Harbour: the end of the 1897 season approached, for according to Victorian/Edwardian custom the falling of the first leaves marked the end of the yachting year. The yacht was already in commission and so there was little time between *Vixen*'s purchase and the start of the great voyage. In the yacht's log, it is clear that Erskine became the owner of *Vixen* on 1 August and sailed on the 11th. A week was spent fitting her out, perhaps with a certain amount of difficulty, for Dover was not a yachting centre in those days and there were only a couple of small yards.

Vixen had her boom shortened and her mainsail altered by Erskine but little else. From the attention given to the cooking stove in *The Riddle*, it is likely that Erskine dropped into the Army and Navy Stores in Victoria Street and carried out a Rippingille No. 3. The large dinner stove was then priced at 55 shillings, complete with all utensils. In *The Riddle* it is remembered 'as a formidable and hideous piece of ironmongery which burned petroleum in two capacious tanks, horribly prophetic of a smell of warm oil'.

Erskine did not conform with *The Riddle* in searching for rigging screws, for *Vixen*'s shrouds were secured directly to her chainplates by lanyards. *Sunbeam* would not have put the idea into his head either, for she had deadeyes. He would have visited the Minories though in search of almost anything else nautical, for Imray, the chart publishers, were at 89 East and their competitors Norie & Wilson were at 156 in the same direction. Ridsdale & Co., the nautical lamp makers, and Hawkins & Timpson, lamp and wire rope makers were there too. The journey east from his clerk's desk in the House would have been on the District underground line from Westminster to Aldgate, pulled by a steam train. The blow holes, to prevent passengers being asphyxiated, are still on the Embankment and an example of the engine may be seen at Covent Garden's London Transport Museum. With these two examples in mind, it is easy to believe the description in *The Riddle* that the ride would have been 'sulphurous'.

Oilskins would have also been available in the Minories, where the London Waterproofing Company had its headquarters at 132, though Erskine may have visited 'the villainous den in a back street' off the Minories, 'where a dirty and bejewelled Hebrew chaffered with me (beginning at 18 shillings) over two reeking orange slabs distantly resembling moieties of the human figure'.

Oilskins had developed from the tarred canvas hats, blouses and trousers that were responsible for the sailor's nickname 'tar'. The oilskin was an altogether better garment, made of very fine canvas, dressed with an oil-based waterproofer that produced a shiny finish. This was deceptive for two reasons. The coat gave off a lively smell and after long exposure to the elements would become sticky and porous. However, sailors had to rely on such clothing for some fifty years before PVC came to the rescue in the 1940s. There were instrument-makers in the Minories too and they would certainly have been able to provide Carruthers with a prismatic compass for Davies, but it would have been a proper economy to seek such an instrument, as catalogued in *The Riddle*, from a Victoria Street pawnbroker. Childers may have obtained a Short & Mason or another well-known make of the time from 'one of those showy shops which look like a jewellers but are really a pawnbrokers'.

The pocket prismatic was later superseded by the hand bearing compass. *Vixen*'s standard instrument may have come originally from *Shulah* via *Marguerite*, for that is how the latter gained her compass and it may well have been in a box. Box compasses often went from boat to boat with their owners and were secured on deck where most convenient. The universal attraction of the auxiliary engine was to make this carefree attitude more difficult after the first ten years of the new century. It is clear that *Dulcibella*, however, like *Sunbeam*, had a binnacle, though on the former it 'was of a size and prominence almost comically impressive'.

As there was no major work to be done, the principal preoccupation of fitting out and preparing for the cruise would have been victualling. *Vixen*, like *Dulcibella*, had, no doubt, her own 'medley of damp tins of varied sizes' that Carruthers described so graphically in *The Riddle* when remembering his search for lunch just after they had experienced the 'tantalising loveliness' of Ekken Sound.

It was clear, though, that the owner and crew of both *Vixen* and *Dulcibella* preferred fresh meat. Erskine had found out for himself that 'steak tastes none the worse for having been wrapped in newspaper and the slight traces of the day's news disappeared with frying in onions and potato chips'. He may not have been a good cook either, if personal experience led him to suggest Carruthers calling attention to the chops on *Dulcibella*'s stove: 'they had indeed been crying aloud for notice for some minutes, and drew a candid attention to their neglect when they appeared'.

The Childers' own pursuit of sport, if not fresh meat, was noticed when Henry and Erskine took time off to shoot partridges when in Weymouth aboard *Marguerite*. They may have borrowed guns for that occasion but Davies and Carruthers had them with them on *Dulcibella*. *Vixen* was similarly armed in August 1897 and in the end achieved the same bag as *Dulcibella*, perhaps with a Lancaster gun and even No. 4 shot, both parties being primarily after duck.

White bread would have been sought and bought when required, and was considered, along with fresh milk a bit of a luxury by the Victorian cruising Corinthian. Erskine discovered, as did Davies and Carruthers, that a big rye loaf would last ten days. It is perhaps difficult to realise the status gained by good white bread until the coming of the modern cotton-wool loaf. White bread has enjoyed popularity since the days of the Romans. Bob Ridding, an expert on the victualling of the Navy, in his study of the subject writes that the Romans coined the phrase 'to know the colour of your bread was to know your place in society'. Centuries later this was still true and professional bakers employed all sorts of artificial colourants to whiten coarse flours, including burnt alum, white lead, lime and even ground bones from the charnel houses.[16]

Baking aboard ships of the Navy had to await the advent of baking machinery introduced in the nineteenth century with the coming of iron ships. They made use of steam-ground flour, finer than that which could be obtained from between stones. Erskine was able to use his Rippingille, substituting Eno's fruit salts for baking powder, so discovering and recording in *The Riddle* that bread rolls 'would not rise much with that'.

These bread rolls would have owed life to the Rippingille, which consumed oil in large wick burners. The wick of the Rippingille required patient and devoted attention or in protest poorly burnt oil produced a cloying smell and clouds of smoke. This was part of the bouquet that met Carruthers when he followed Davies cautiously down the companion ladder to discover *Dulcibella*'s internal secrets: 'The complex odour of paraffin, past cookery, tobacco and tar saluted my nostrils.'

To this catalogue of disadvantage must be added the lack of quick heat. Jim Young, who was a partner with Claude Hapgood in what he called the 'beer money yard' at Wootton Creek, recalled that an old, single-burner Rippingille took twenty minutes to bring to the boil the small amount of water required for a cup of tea. The primus ended all that, by vapourising the same fuel under pressure before burning.

Paraffin was carried aboard in strong tin oil bottles and used for the navigation and cabin lights as well as the stove. Water, on the other hand, was carried in small, wooden breakers at that time. Claude Worth, who was six years senior to Erskine and whose first yacht *Ianthe* was a twenty-two-foot converted ship's lifeboat, remembered them well, for he had three breakers on the first of his *Terns* and she was one foot six inches shorter than *Vixen*. He recorded that they took up a great deal of room and were heavy and awkward to carry. They were all but essential though when watering ships was done from wells and pumps many steps from the shore. If the water in a couple went sour, there was at least a chance that the contents of another would remain sweet. In spite of these advantages, the problem of stowage was never satisfactorily solved and Worth replaced *Tern*'s breakers with galvanised iron tanks. Even so, it was possible to buy six-gallon, brass-bound teak water breakers from Simpson & Lawrence up until the late 1950s.

One great advantage that such awkward containers possessed was that the water was used sparingly. Washing was done wherever possible with patent marine or salt-water soap. *Vixen* must have carried bars of it, as it had been about for some time, having been invented in 1819. From the 1860s, quarter pound bars were issued free in the Royal Navy after coaling ships. Erskine and his brother Henry must have been pleased to have stocked up with a few cakes at Dover when they had to clean up after lightening *Vixen* by removing ballast. Their experience, no doubt, added colour to the account in *The Riddle* where Carruthers remembers grounding on a perfect Ararat of sand on the edge of the Rute Flat and not being able to get off without the 'horrid business of handling the pigs of lead, heavy, greasy and black. The saloon is an inferno, the deck like a collier's and ourselves like sweeps.'

It was not so much that Erskine or, indeed, Davies were particular about their appearance at sea. Remember the latter on the platform at Flensburg as described by the smart, if not dapper, Carruthers: Davies 'wore an old Norfolk jacket, muddy brown shoes, grey flannel trousers (or had they been white?) and an ordinary tweed cap.'

Erskine was not one for proper white flannels, blue reefer and engraved black buttons either. He preferred, like a number of his contemporaries, the general outdoor rig of the day– grey flannels, a flannel shirt with collar attached and a tweed jacket. He was to write to Basil Williams on 11 September 1902, talking of London in September, 'It is a very pleasant climate as one lives in flannels.' Erskine was one of the growing number who were moving away from more formal dress, especially when enjoying active sports, into what was to become almost a uniform of tweed jacket and grey trousers.

Of all the comforts, victuals and stores that went aboard *Vixen* in early August of 1897, none gave more pleasure in the succeeding weeks and months than books. Erskine carried them in ones and twos on *Marguerite*, but with *Vixen* he was able to take a small library. He was devoted to Thackeray and took aboard two of his novels – *Esmond* and *Pendennis*. They were to be the perfect companions for the voyage. They insulated Erskine from too much pleasure in his natural surroundings and from the storms and trials of autumn and winter weather in the North Sea. Every now and then the log refers to the title of the book that had captured him and shut out the magic of a quiet night among the sands or stilled within him the effects of the wild water without. Look forward to the night of 2 October off Langeoog – '3 fathoms, fine deep channel – just off a long pier. Lovely calm night. *Dinner*, white soup, steak, onions and potatoes, champagne, black coffee, cigars – Esmond.' The picture is complete.

Now for the other scene. *Vixen* is lying in the lee of the Wurster Watt, a barren sand miles from anywhere on the way to the Weser. He writes: 'A fine sail. Blew hard rest of the day with hail squalls, fine evening. Expecting swell at night, we sleep on the floor but wind went down. Agreed that the plan was comfortable but caused too great a displacement of things – Pendennis.'

Thackeray was not the only author who had such a valuable ability to transpose, for Stevenson's *St Ives* was also on the shelf. Erskine certainly enjoyed it, for he writes in his entry for 6 December, 'St Ives getting very exciting.' Books were indispensable to him and his shelf was full. He refers in the log to the presence of *Captain Cook's Voyages, the Aeneid*, Book 6, and to the tragedy *Maria Stuart* by Friedrich Schiller. There were volumes of Baedeker, to give guidance ashore and on rivers and canals. The German printer Baedeker published his first guide in the English language in 1861 and Erskine used his editions as Michelin is used today – '29th August. Followed some schuyts to Willemstad through difficult channels, where charts ceased and we navigated by Baedeker.'

Dulcibella's library is simply described in *The Riddle*: 'Across the forward bulkhead was a bookshelf crammed to overflowing with volumes of all sizes, many upside down and some coverless.' Later, the books themselves are named. These were predictable – a nautical almanack, sailing directions and 'several books on the cruises of small yachts'. E. F. Knight's *Falcon on the Baltic* would have been among them. Then there were volumes on the Navy and sea-warfare – Mahan's *Influence of Sea Power* and his *Life of Nelson*, and Brassey's *Naval Annual* of an undisclosed date. Some of these titles may have found their way on to Dulcibella's shelf by remembering the happy months with them in *Vixen*'s saloon and the others may have arrived to help the story, which must have been the case with 'the drab little book' – *A Pilot to East Coast Rivers*, because this, as indicated above, was not published until 1903.

Erskine's progression from a half-decker to *Vixen* had one disadvantage, for she needed a dinghy to allow her crew to reach the shore. E. F. Knight provided his twenty-nine-foot *Falcon* with an eleven-footer. *Vixen*'s tender was one foot shorter. Neither of the two converted lifeboats could carry their small boats on deck. Knight towed his to Copenhagen without incident. He wrote: 'We were in the habit of putting a half hundred weight of iron into her stern, to steady her when the weather was rough, with the result that she followed us as quietly as possible, not sheering wildly about and rushing furiously down on us as is the wont of dinghies under such circumstances.'

Erskine lost *Vixen*'s dinghy a few days from the end of the great cruise when the painter came adrift, but she was returned to him. *Dulcibella*'s boat was much less well behaved, for in his narrow escape from death while following Dollmann, the yacht struck the sand bank and the dinghy, 'which was towing astern, came home on her painter and down with a crash on the yacht's weather quarter'. Davies attempted to ward the boat off and had his hand nipped on the gunwhale, a cautionary tale for all yachtsmen. The boat was stove in and Davies was, therefore, unable to use it for another vital purpose amongst the sands, laying out the kedge anchor, to haul it off.

Walter Runciman, Erskine's salt-water mentor, had promised his friend a new dinghy early in 1897, but something undisclosed went wrong. Writing from *Vixen*, then at Sonderburg, in October of that year, Erskine mentions the kind offer. 'Please don't worry about the lurky! *[sic]* It was very good of you to order it and I fear the whole thing has given you a lot of bother. But by Jove it's awfully good of you to say that you are giving me another one as an Xmas present! It will come in awfully handy for the next season in *Mad Agnes*, for I don't think I shall get this boat back to England this year, a thousand thanks old chap!'[17]

The term 'lurkey' or 'lurkie' was applied particularly to small, square sterned open boats from the Orkney Islands that were provided with a standing lugsail. This may give a clue to the reason why the boat had not been delivered. She may have been lost on delivery or even still building in those far-off isles.

The day that Erskine became the owner of *Vixen*, 1 August 1897, was a Sunday. The parliamentary recess, as has been mentioned, started on the 6th the following Friday. Erskine may have made use of the excellent train service from Victoria on the L.C. & D. service or the South-Eastern Railway going from Charing Cross. It made little difference in time, for the express on both lines took an hour and fifty minutes. The eight o'clock from Victoria would have been at the Admiralty Pier, Dover, by 9.53 pm while the South-Eastern was a couple of minutes later. The slower trains all called at the town and harbour station which would have better suited Erskine for Granville Dock, where *Vixen* was secured. Granville Dock lay inside and to the west of the tidal harbour and was insulated froin the sea by a lock gate, opened a while before and a little after high water to allow vessels to enter and leave.

Erskine completed his stores and prepared to depart when the lock opened at midday on Wednesday. He was making for Boulogne and would have had a foul tide until 5 pm. The day was cloudy with heavy showers. A low hung over the Lake District; the barometer at Dover read 29.9 inches and the wind was in the west-southwest, light. *Vixen* reached over the Cap Griz Nez with Erskine at the helm. He was alone as he had been in Dover. The wind headed *Vixen*, but by five the tide was fair and he beat into Boulogne, mooring in the Avant Port about nine in the evening. The rain had cleared by then and it was a lovely night. The next day gave a promising start to what, it was confidently predicted, would be a long cruise.·

Erskine's plan was to make to the westward. He explained his original ideas in retrospect, in the letter to Runciman quoted earlier. 'I was off. I scarcely knew where. At least my plan was to make for Bordeaux, canal it through France and then spend the winter in the Mediterranean: that is the dream of my heart.' Again, he confirmed this had been his plan when he wrote to his sister, Dulcie, from *Vixen* on 8 October of that year. Writing from Brunsbüttel, at the west end of the Kaiser Wilhelm Canal, he said, 'My energy is not half exhausted yet, but the French plan, having broken down, yachting all my holiday is impossible, though I want to do it for many reasons, though I needn't say how much I miss seeing you too.'[18]

His determination to reach the shores of the Mediterranean may have been sparked off by his grandfather, the Reverend Canon Charles Childers, who had succeeded to the chaplaincy of Nice in 1843, following a little behind his brother, who died in 1830. He was to hold the post until his retirement in 1884, four decades later. Andrew Boyle, in his biography *The Riddle of Erskine Childers*, believes that the canon was 'perhaps the most powerful single influence on the brief London childhood of his grandson, Erskine'. The old man must have spoken of the attractions of the Riviera, which was beginning to provide a magnet to the owner of the salt-water palace, rather than the Corinthian yachtsman. The South of France could offer the latter, though, a considerable extension to the sailing season.

There is no doubt that the plan to go south had been fermenting for some time, as Dulcie seems to have heard of the idea before, from the tone of Erskine's letter. It was sad that Canon Charles died in February of the year before in Florence.

The plan was to go westward, along the coast of Normandy, reliving part of the cruise of *Marguerite*, past the Channel Islands, along the rock-bound and 'tide-wracked coast of North Brittany, round Ushant to south Brittany and on to the entrance of the Gironde River'. Erskine would have looked forward to that part of the cruise, for he would have been able to visit his Barton cousins at the Chateau Langoa and their vineyard at Leoville Barton, in the Medoc, on the starboard hand going in. The River Garonne would have taken him to Bordeaux and onward to Toulouse, where he would have entered the Canal du Midi to Sete, into the Gulf of Lions and eastward to Nice. This is a journey of some 1,200 miles, but Erskine's holidays were long and the next sitting of Parliament did not start until 8 February 1898.

Erskine had visited Biarritz when he was five, but had not been back. He was to write to sister Dulcie in October 1899 from Souillac, on the River Dordogne, 'I can't describe the beauties of this country; they are so utterly new and strange,'[19] so he evidently hardly knew that part in 1897.

Vixen set sail the next day for Dieppe. As the crow flies, the distance was fifty-four nautical miles. The barometer was rising, the day fair at first, but colder, the wind southwesterly, fresh. Consequently, the wind was on the nose and there was 'no place with water in it to get to that day'.

Erskine pressed on for a while. He was not yet used to *Vixen*'s peculiar ways and so, with regret, went about and returned to Boulogne. It was a fateful decision, for without that change of tack, *The Riddle of the Sands* would not have appeared. The immediate result, though, was tedious, for a succession of westerlies and bad weather were to keep him in port for eleven days. Without auxiliary power to press on regardless but blessedly free of unbreakable modern deadlines, the daily decision to stay was probably less irksome. Sky-watching and barometer-tapping were more rewarding, too, without the radio forecast. Erskine could only guess at the weather system that imprisoned him. What happened then may be a little clearer now, for we have the 1897 daily weather charts and nearly ninety years of meteorological experience by which to interpret them. 'Fronts', though, had not been thought of.

Erskine had anticipated that he might not have been able to go west. He wrote in the *Yachting Monthly* magazine in 1898 that: 'It was disappointing to have to abandon our French scheme, but cast-iron intentions are out of place in a small yacht, and the North Sea charts were already below in case of a change in plan.'

Erskine would have known Boulogne well by the time his brother Henry arrived from the Tyrol on 20 August. He did not bring any better weather with him, for the bad conditions and foul winds continued. The third member of the crew, Ivor Lloyd-Jones, arrived on the 23rd. With a full complement and after days spent waiting in port they just had to leave. Erskine wrote in the *Yachting Monthly*: 'It seemed hopeless to wait for suitable weather for going west, so we regretfully pulled out the North Sea charts and prepared to run east before the prevailing winds, in spite of the weather. We left Boulogne on the 24 August, a dirty south-west windy day and started two-reefed for Calais in a lumpy sea, though we found calmer water when Gris Nez was rounded.'

Vixen had a fine run across the mouth of the Western Scheldt and entered Holland by the Roompot Channel of the Eastern Scheldt. They struck on the forward thrust with the plate down, bending it and as a result spent the night sheltered from the wind and rain under the shore of Nord Beveland.

The wind stayed in the southwest and *Vixen* ran up the tidal canal that leads to Zierickzee, their first Dutch town and a 'pretty little place'. Zierickzee was also their first experience of Dutch boys. The log records for the 27th: 'Ashore and found everything very pretty, novel and amusing. Views changed in the evening, brisk bombardment by small boys – missiles, mud and crabs – nearly caused a riot.'

He should have taken heed of E. F. Knight's words in *Falcon on the Baltic*, for the Dutch boys had quite a reputation in those days. 'These small ruffians stood on the quay and reviled us in unknown tongues, they hurled stones at us and also bricks from a convenient stack.' Knight supposed the reason too: 'The Hollanders spoil their children, never punish them, and allow them – provided they don't play truant from school, for education is a serious business in this country – to do pretty well as they like.'[20]

Erskine was not to forget the experience and brought it into *The Riddle* when Davies described his cruise through Holland. 'Heavens! Shall I ever forget those boys! A perfect murrain of them infests Holland; they seem to have nothing in the world to do but throw stones and mud at foreign yachts.'

As they drifted up the Keeten Mastigat under Duiveland, they 'took some art photographs'. The photographer is unknown, though it may have been one of the two brothers, as the pictures are not in the Lloyd-Jones album. There are later references in the log to 'Kodaking', a phrase used then in the same way as 'Hoovering' is now. (George Eastman had invented the simple camera, which used laboratory-processed film, in 1888, and had coined the word 'Kodak'.)

They arrived in the centre of Rotterdam on Monday, 31 August. *Vixen* was slipped the next day to repair the twisted centre-plate. This was done in Zalmhaven, which Erskine thought 'the dullest place on earth'.

The canals were certainly not Davies' cup of tea and he made his feelings clear in *The Riddle*: 'We had a splendid sail to the East Sheldt but then, like fools, decided to go through Holland by canal and river. It was good fun enough navigating the estuary

– the tides and banks there are appalling – but further inland it was a wretched business, nothing but paying lock dues, bumping against schuyts and towing down stinking canals.'

Towing was undertaken on some canals by a regular *sleepboot dienst*, or towboat company, for a fixed tariff. Nearly every craft led her towline direct to the steam-tug so she could be cast off without disturbing the others in the string.

At villages, bum boats would put out and secure alongside the towed to cater for their varied needs. The tug paused when the canal opened out into a large, glassy rush- and willow-bordered mere for crews to fill their fresh water breakers and tanks from the canal itself. In the towns, though, it was generally admitted that the canal water was noisome through defective drainage, so Davies' stricture was deserved.[21]

The only way of avoiding a tow by tug, horse, or the brute strength of the crew, was to choose a route with a fair wind on the day. In the principal canals, yachts and commercial sail were able to tack against the wind and the sight of a sixty-foot commercial vessel climbing to windward would not have surprised anyone then and may be seen to this day.

Vixen left Rotterdam on 7 September and sailed with a fair wind up the Lek, reaching Lexon before the stream stopped them. The stream and lack of wind kept *Vixen* at anchor the next day and the three set to work 'spring cleaning'.

Childers, like Davies, was thorough and so 'jettisoned three pounds of steak accidentally'. Davies had thrown *Dulcibella*'s old Rippingille stove overboard and Carruthers noted in *The Riddle* that that was one of the weaknesses of his friend, 'to rejoice in throwing things overboard on the flimsiest of pretexts'. They could wait no longer and *Vixen* was towed to Vreeswijk and Erskine remembered this as 'the pleasantest part of the inland enterprise' in his article 'A Dutch Cruise' in *The Times* of 7 June 1910. He traced *Vixen*'s voyage 'through ancient and beautiful Utrecht, and from thence down the river Vecht to the Zuyder Zee at Muiden. The Vecht is very little used by traffic and has some beautiful reaches, closely resembling some familiar portions of the Upper Thames. One can tie up for the night at any one of a hundred different spots, in peaceful security under overhanging trees or by the sedge-grown banks of a broad meadow.'

Amsterdam is six miles west of Muiden and *Vixen* anchored off the station on Saturday, 11 September, in time to dine on shore. There is another cry of pain in the log: 'returning late found a dinghy oar stolen – boys again. Paddled back somehow, cursing this tireless pest and praying for a Herod to rule over this land.' Carruthers was to have the same thoughts in an echo to Davies: 'they want a Herod, with some statesmanlike views on infanticide.'

Ivor Lloyd-Jones had to leave and after a quiet Sunday at the zoo and Monday on a steamer trip to Marken, the two brothers said goodbye to their friend and set sail on Tuesday down theNorth Sea Canal to Ijmuiden, sharing the sea lock with the SS *Johannesburg* and mooring in the tide beyond. After a false start on the 15th, turning back for the weather, they set sail the next day undecided which way to go, leaving the decision to the wind. This was the second time there was a question mark over the direction of the cruise.

The attractions of making north and east were rehearsed in *The Times* sequel of 28 June 1910, headlined 'A Frisian Cruise'. Erskine had a long memory, unlike his brother, and made good use of his old log:

> *For those who have time, a taste for work in hand and a suitable craft, there remains the alternative of sailing northeast and exploring the Frisian coast, together with the chain of little islands, Dutch and German, which stretch along it like a necklace – not exactly of jewels, but of sober-hued beads – for a distance of 120 miles. As to time, progress will certainly be slow; how slow depends on a multitude of factors. It would certainly be possible to fill a month or even six weeks with pleasant exploration, especially if one added wildfowl shooting to other interests; a fortnight, perhaps, for the eastward voyage alone is the least one should allow. As for taste, one must possess innate or acquired liking for low countries and for navigating the intricate shoals which bisect their shores. One must learn to look for beauty, not in lucid blue seas and sunny wooded cliffs, but in vast, almost featureless, distances. For the mainland coast the eye must be content with a fine pencil-line of grey, dotted with a windmill or two, an occasional spire, and a rare clump of trees. Above all, one must*

> *love sand in all its manifestations; the delicate pink of the island dune in the evening glow, and all the infinitely various and subtle hues – from umber to pale straw – of dry or drying flats. Monotony of scene must be a joy in itself, and inspiration must be found in a kind of solitude which, if the spirit is not tuned to it, seems more dreary than the dreariest moorlands and the most naked mountains. Not that there is not plenty of warm, human life in Frisia; but the centres of life are far apart as communications in that strange region go.*

This was written with the benefit of hindsight but it is a marvellous summary of an experience in store and one still to be had today.

Vixen turned her long bowsprit east by north and arrived in Nieuwediep, the Dutch navy harbour, opposite Texel, the first of the Frisian islands. In real September weather, they started picking their way through the sands inside the islands, the broad yet untamed Zuyder Zee on their starboard hand, and soon they were reaching down the Inschot Channel, before squaring away for Terschelling harbour. It was an exciting moment, as he wrote in the *Yachting Monthly* magazine article: 'The mist cleared, and we were racing under scandalised sail down a narrow channel, between foam-washed sands, with a little red town before us, huddled under the white sand-hills, and crowned by a noble old light-tower.' He had something to say about charts: 'I may mention here that our charts of all these waters, though the latest Admiralty editions, were altogether unreliable for the minor channels and swatchways.' Erskine's hero, Davies, thought that the English charts were relatively useless too, though his namesake, the yachting author G. Christopher Davies, an authority on Holland and the East Coast of England, held that 'the English Admiralty chart may be relied on for the Zuyder Zee'.

This Davies, author of *Cruising in the Netherlands*,[22] was also responsible for a standard work on sailing much in vogue at the time – *Practical Boat Sailing for Amateurs*.[23] As already mentioned in the last chapter of this book he describes 'a small sea-going cruiser' with rather more draft and longer than *Vixen* but with similar interior layout and rig. Though there is no clear evidence, Erskine may have borrowed the surname 'Davies' for Arthur H. in *The Riddle of the Sands*.

A southwesterly gale kept *Vixen* in port on the 18th and as a result Erskine and Henry were to meet a man engaged in an historic, if not almost fruitless, venture. The meeting is recorded in *Vixen's* log:

> *Mr. Fletcher, Lloyd's agent, engaged in diving for treasure in the wreck of the* Lutine, *outside, asked us to lunch and was very hospitable. In the evening met a lot of skippers, pilots, etc. at his rooms. The* Lutine *was an English frigate (captured from the French) and wrecked a century ago with £2 million on board insured by Lloyd's. They have found no gold yet.*

This was not strictly true, for Fletcher and his team had scraped up a number of Spanish dollars.

J. Fletcher was an engineer and surveyor of Botolph House, Eastcheap, who had teamed up with a Mr W. K. Kinipple, an eminent harbour constructor, in order to salvage the bullion from HMS *Lutine*. *La Lutine*, a thirty-two gun frigate, was carried off by Vice-Admiral Lord Hood at the surrender of the French republican fleet at Toulon in August 1793. The 932-ton vessel had been launched fourteen years earlier and had been wrecked on 9 November 1799 when under the command of Captain Lancelot Skynner.

Whatever the reason for the loss of the *Lutine*, all but two of the crew were drowned. Locals plundered the wreck before she sank below the sands. A determined effort to salvage her was made by Lloyd's and the local foreshore owner in 1857, and in the following year some £39,203 worth of bullion and the famous bell, bearing the puzzling inscription 'St Jean 1779', were raised. Between 1800 and 1861, some £99,893 was brought up, leaving, in theory, over a million pounds on the bottom.[24]

Fletcher and Kinipple had prospects, but Fletcher's manuscript, now held at Lloyd's, shows that they were poorly rewarded for their years of effort.[25] In spite of removing the deck of the vessel on 14 July 1895 and collecting the coins and many cannon, one of which was given by Lloyd's to Queen Wilhelmina, the four years, 1894–8, produced little.

Fletcher provided Erskine, though, with a rich vein of material. He was able to describe vividly the inside of the hut at Memmert, 'where relics of the wrecked frigate abounded'. The 'balk of curved timber garnished with some massive bolts' may have been part of the wreckage that frequently appears in Fletcher's log from 11 June to 28 August 1897. *Vixen* arrived during a small pause in the operation but Childers must have seen relics, wrested by the diver Van Drimmelin and his team, that probably littered the office or buildings at Terschelling.

In *The Riddle of the Sands*, *Lutine* is disguised as the 'French frigate *Corinne*, bound from Hamburg to Havre in 1811'. She was carrying a million and a half in gold bars and was wrecked thirty-two nautical miles to the east of *Lutine*'s grave in German waters off the western end of Juist.

Erskine moved the scene of the disaster, for the benefit of the story, and so had to change the frigate's name. Being well read, he knew the romantic novel *Corinne* by Madame de Stael, a psychological study of two tormented souls. Whether the title would carry a descant on the relationship between Carruthers and Davies, audible to friends of literary weekends, may only be guessed.

The insurance history of *Corinne's* golden cargo differs from that of *Lutine*, though the sum is roughly similar. According to *The Riddle of the Sands*, the bullion became the property of Lloyd's in 1825 and remained with, but untouched by, them until 1875. The ownership then went to a couple of Hamburg firms before passing to the engineer from Bremen, Dollmann and friends.

There was a similar difference between Herr Bohme, the distinguished engineer from Bremen, and Mr Kinipple, 'the eminent harbour engineer'.[26] Kinipple wore a full white beard and not the jet black tuft of Bohme.

The meeting took place in the fishing port of West Terschelling, the name of the island's harbour, then the second largest town in the Frisian chain, bowing only to the fashionable watering place of Norderney. Erskine found it typical of the islands. 'Sand is the ruling element; it lies soft and deep in all the streets; it rises in great clusters of dunes outside, and is only solidified and tamed in the neighbourhood of habitations by being planted with the tenaciously-gripping marram-grass,' he was to write in his second *Times* article of 1910.

On 19 September began the experience that was to blossom into words of description in *The Riddle* and sound advice in his *Times* article. The sands inspired both awe and love in Erskine and he was able to work on these feelings with his pen. *Vixen* ran aground and the two brothers experienced wild weather in the open that day. It is difficult to believe that any writer has bettered the description of the torture wrought by weather on a small wooden yacht than the capture of the song of the demon horde in *The Riddle*. Though these words capture a night under the Hohenhorn Sands further east (when Davies and Carruthers take a walk on the sands), they tell of the ways of a small yacht at anchor, in wild weather, anywhere.

> *Every loose article in the boat became audibly restless. Cans clinked, cupboards rattled, lockers uttered hollow groans. Small things sidled out of dark hiding-places, and danced grotesque drunken figures on the floor, like goblins in a haunted glade. The mast whined dolorously at every heel, and the centre board hiccoughed and choked. Overhead another horde of demons seemed to have been let loose. The deck and mast were conductors which magnified every sound and made the tap-tap of every rope's end resemble the blows of a hammer, and the slapping of the halyards against the mast the rattle of a Maxim gun. The whole tumult beat time to a rhythmical chorus which became maddening.*

Vixen spent two nights anchored uncomfortably in such surroundings, viewing the tide change in wild weather from the southwest. She crossed the West Gat on the 21st, and ran in rain through the gap in the stone causeway that connects the mainland to Ameland. They 'had just reached the edge of the Friesche Gat, the next broad channel between the islands, when a black storm, that had been surging up from the northwest, struck us. We were still under the lee of the sand, and had just time to shake her up, let go the anchor, and tumble down the sail, then we were pitching and rolling in a whole gale of wind.' *Vixen* was lying under that strangely named sand, Engelsman Plaat (Englishman's Sand), so called after two English shellfishermen drowned there in 1708.[27]

The next day, *Vixen* reached Oostmahorn, a port that they were to know as well as any by the end of the cruise. The first welcome was not encouraging, judging from the log: 'Officers in uniform crept out of hovels with huge books and searched and classified us. We bought all Oostmahorn's bread and butter, and eggs, and in the evening walked two miles to Anjum, a large village where we did some shopping.' The weather kept them in port for a couple of days and they made further expeditions to Anjum where they met Visser, the innkeeper, for the first time.

Vixen would have made German waters on the 25th, had she not grounded 'five miles due south of Rottum Island, inhabited,' he wrote in the *Yachting World*, 'by one lonely farmer who's grown fabulously rich by the export of sea-birds' eggs'. They passed Borkum on the 26th. Childers was to write of this in his article 'Cruising in German Frisia' in *The Times* on 23 August 1910: 'Through the midst of the flats run the two great arms of the Ems River, enfolding the little island of Borkum, and behind it, a vast triangle of shoal ground known as the Randzel Sand.' They did not pause to visit the island, though Erskine recommended others to do so. 'There is no harbour but a notch in the sand with safe anchorage and access to the long jetty by which the island is reached. Borkum, besides being of *some importance as a strategical outpost* [author's italics] is, like all German islands in one degree or another, a summer resort for town dwellers of northern Germany; for the gently shelving foreshores facing the North Sea give admirable conditions for bathing.' Borkum was to feature greatly in the plans of others in succeeding years.

After crossing the-eastern Ems, Erskine entered the waters of *The Riddle of the Sands* for the first time. He explained the ways of these waters in his article in *Yachting Monthly* magazine. He little realised how useful this 1898 account and *Vixen*'s log was to be when he settled down to write of the goings-on in these waters four years later.

> *We now entered another great series of flats stretching over forty miles to the estuaries of the Jade and Weser rivers, where the islands end, and bounded at a distance of three to six miles from the coast by the islands of Juist, Norderney, Baltrum, Langeoog, Spiekeroog and Wangeroog. Between all of these the North Sea tide set strongly in, and curling round each of them nearly encircles them with a practicable channel, but always leaves one shallow spot, about opposite*

> *their centre, which can only be crossed if half-flood or more. The flats themselves are, for the most part, dry at low water, but a new feature becomes increasingly common as you go east in the shape of minor tidal channels, leading from the main one to a series of little ports on the mainland. Wee, miniature basins, presided over by pretty little villages, which own the dozen or so of craft which frequent them, they stand on the outfall of small streams which have been canalised, and carry a modest traffic to towns in the hinterland.*

He was not to begin to discover their importance until *Vixen*'s return over a month later. But to return to *Vixen* – for at three o'clock in the afternoon of the 26th, Erskine and Henry had reached and grounded on the shallows of the Slapershorn where the channel cuts through the Koper Sand. The original of Erskine's chart for *The Riddle of the Sands* shows the place. This section is cut from the large-scale German chart No. 64, on which he sketched the track chart of the voyage of *Dulcibella*'s dinghy from Norderney to Memmert. As they waited for the tide, Erskine read *Esmond*, while Henry made best use of the time by cutting out a chaffed section and long-splicing the grass anchor warp back to health. They made Norderney that night on a direct course, crossing the sands as the tide rose.

Norderney was their first German port and Erskine was delighted – 'Change immediate and delightful. No boys, no bothers, no customs,' he wrote in the log. He thought the town 'Bright, pretty and strangely southern looking'. He said in *The Times* that 'Norderney seems strangely out of harmony with the wild solitudes in the midst of which it stands.' His Baedeker told him that it was the most popular German sea-bathing place, with 24,000 visitors a year, not including those in the large institution built for 'scrofulous children'.

The season, in those days, lasted from 1 June to 10 October. Erskine noticed this, recording that the town was 'just going to sleep again after the summer season'. The hotel Four Seasons, where Carruthers and Davies eat 'the king of breakfasts', did not exist under that name. Erskine's imagination may have taken him to either the Kaiserhof or the Europaischer Hof. Both of these were of high standing and 'on the esplanade facing the northern beach'.

The Schwanallee was equally disguised, though there was a pond adjacent to the Napoleonschanze, or an entrenchment, constructed during the French occupation of 1810.

The little port that Erskine knew is unrecognisable today, having become one of the most highly developed of the Frisian Island harbours. Yachts now lie bow on, their sterns secured to posts at the far end of the harbour. Such an arrangement would have saved *Vixen* the indignities of the night of 27 September 1897. In his usual economic style, Erskine noted what happened in the log: 'Terrible night – boat refusing to lie properly and getting under the quay-piles; smashed the crutch thus. Finally got out two anchors into the stream fore and aft, and then slept.' He forgot all this when he wrote for the benefit of yachtsmen reading *The Times*: 'If one wishes for the luxury of lying afloat in a real harbour, here is the only opportunity which the German islands provide.'

A soldier's wind had carried them along effortlessly from one grounding to another and when Erskine decided to head for the open sea, they found the wind foul and went about. They 'ran back across the bay to the mainland side at Norddeich, where is a ferry station, which theNorderney steamers use.' He was to draw on the experiences of this day to edge and shade the climax in *The Riddle* when Carruthers drives the tug and barge ashore after managing to deceive and relieve Grimm's coxswain: 'My ruse developed in all its delicious simplicity. We were, I estimated, about half-way to Norddeich, in the Buse Tief, a channel of a navigable breadth, at the utmost, of two hundred yards at this period of the tide. Two faint lights, one above the other, twinkled far ahead.'

They were, of course, the leading lights that drew incoming vessels between the long piers. Erskine found Norddeich, the port of Norden, empty and dirty and in strange contrast to Holland. The name of the port is heard almost every minute of the day now, for the coastal station – Norddeich Radio controls the marine airways from a station two miles northeast of the port.

The ferry still sails to the islands of Norderney and Juist. The sleepiness and the dirt have disappeared under concrete. The magnificent German charts that Erskine so much admired are now available, though they could not be obtained there in his day.

The closing days of September were packed with resource. *Vixen* was in the very heart of *The Riddle* country and fickle weather and sluicing tides meant that the old lifeboat sailed over much of it. The two brothers kedged wearily out of Norddeich on the 29th, hoping for Delfzyl and Emden further up the estuary of the Ems. But *Vixen* was denied either port and in the end 'beat to the mouth of the Ems on a roaring ebb-tide'. As they went downstream, the two Corinthians may have spotted a *Panzercanonboot* of the Wespe or Wasp class. There were two divisions of these ships, the eastern section serving the Baltic, and the northern the North Sea. They crossed over from time to time. The gunboats were built at Bremen from 1875 to 1880, so were long in the tooth in Childers' day and had been pensioned off for light work such as fishery protection and harbour defence, much as von Brüning had admitted.

When Erskine came to write *The Riddle,* he had such a gunboat in his mind's eye. Her profile is identical with von Bruening's SMS *Blitz* (lightning).

Carruthers recalled that 'she is an ugly, cranky little vessel painted grey, with one funnel. Davies is contemptuous about her low freeboard forward; says he would rather go to sea in *Dulce.* He has her dimensions and armament (learnt from Brassey) at his finger ends: one hundred and forty feet by twenty-five, one 4.9 gun, one 3.4, and four maxims – an old type.'

Davies' opinion of the sea-keeping abilities of the Wespe class is shared by naval historians today. ' On the open seas they shipped a lot of water and were hardly usable in force four winds but with their flat hulls they could be readily beached on the flats at ebb tide and serve there as stationary batteries,'[28]

The vital statistics and the armament thoughtfully provided by Davies, direct from Brassey, were not, though, for the Wespe but for the Wolf class of gunboats. Wespe ships were fourteen feet seven inches longer, ten feet eleven inches broader in the beam and drew ten feet two inches, four inches more than the Wolf class. On the face of it then, *Blitz* was not a Wespe, despite appearances. But she was not a Wolf either, for better reasons. In spite of an excellent Brassey pedigree, the Wolfs could not be described by Davies or anyone as ugly, cranky or unseaworthy. They were good-looking, designed as colonial gunboats and considered eminently seaworthy.

Further, and this would have prevented Davies from making such disparaging remarks, the Wolf class were thought to sail well under their barquentine rig.[29] Von Bruening's *Blitz* must, therefore, be added to the Wasps, the Bees, the Gnats, the Adders and the Bumblebees that make up, with others, the Wespe class. There was a peculiar twist to the name.

The only *Blitz* serving with His Imperial Majesty in the period 1897–1903 was a 246-foot, third-class cruiser laid down at Kiel in 1882 and broken up in 1921. She was too large and powerful for such humble duties. A few years earlier, though, and perhaps unknown to Erskine, Lieutenant Alfred Tirpitz (later Grand Admiral and father of the new German Navy) served from 1871 on the then *Blitz*, a 142-foot Chameleon class gunboat, built of wood. This snipey, three-masted, schooner-rigged vessel was based originally on the Elbe, doing light river and harbour duties until being sent off to protect the German herring fleet sailing out of Emden. Tirpitz noticed how badly his native fishermen were treated by other North Sea nations when they went without the protection of a proper Navy. In his memoirs he recalled how, from the deck of *Blitz*, 'we saw in the most illuminating way how intimidated a great nation can become without sea-power, and how cut off we were from the riches which the sea offered us.'

Blitz, therefore, may have performed an important role, perhaps a central one, in shaping the career of a man who was to play such a vital part in deciding the course the world would take from then on.

Erskine, unaware of all this, was tacking seaward against a northerly wind, benefiting from the great push of the ebb. They tried for the Juister Balge channel that creeps along the south side of Juist; in vain, for *Vixen* was forced back and had to anchor. The log recalls that significant moment: 'Let go in 13 fathoms with a tiny dinghy anchor and 45 fathoms of warp. A tremendous tide swirled past and the anchor held well. We were in a weirdly lonely place just at the verge of the North Sea, close to a grotesquely dreary structure called the Memmert Beacon.'

The fog came down furring the outline of the lattice tripod. This was to be the first view that the two intrepid sailors were to have of Memmert and the forty-nine-foot beacon, that spider's web of rusty bars which, Carruthers remembered, 'grew into being above and around me, like the arms of a ghostly polyp'. The beacon was the only structure marked on the large-scale German chart,[30] until Erskine penned in his depot there. A building has arrived since, though, only a little to the north.[31] 'The island was one of the loneliest spits of sand that ever was,' he recalled in the *Yachting Monthly*. 'I never remember such a furious current anywhere. It hissed and foamed round us like a mountain torrent.'

Memmert, sylph-like and club-shaped at high water in 1897, has rounded out of all recognition. From being three-quarters of a mile wide at the north end then, it is now nearly two and a half miles across. Now an important nature reserve, 1,439 different sorts of insects have been counted on the island.[32] Memmert still commands the eastern and shallower entrance to the Ems in the same way that Borkum is sentinel to the western arm of that river. Together they keep watch over the approaches to the port of Emden.

Memmert's strategic position would have been plain to Erskine when he looked at the chart. In *The Riddle* he was to say that Memmert was part of the outer rampart. 'No more admirable base could be imagined; self-contained and isolated yet sheltered, accessible – better than Juist and Borkum.' He may have wondered, too, about the added significance of both arms of the Ems and the town of Emden, now that the Ems-Jade Canal was operating. In *The Riddle* he was to paraphrase the words of the Admiralty *North Sea Pilot*, vol. 4 of 1896: 'The Ems-Jade Canal is intended for both commercial and military purposes. The canal connects Emden with Wilhelmshaven.' Baedeker put it that Wilhelmshaven was 'the second war-harbour of Germany', telling readers that the naval port had been 'constructed by the Prussians in 1855–69'.

The canal though would not have accepted ships of the Wespe class, being limited to vessels of one hundred and eight feet in length, twenty feet in breadth and with a maximum draft of six and a half feet. The waterway might just have taken the 'W' class torpedo boats that Germany built between 1884 and 1893 and their smaller Vedette craft.

Erskine was to trace the course of the canal on his map. This was to form the basis of the one published eventually in *The Riddle*. He may not have known then the waterway's history and the idea behind its building.

In 1880 it was decided to cut a canal from Wilhelmshaven to Aurich, the centre of the German horse trade, and also of the *Fehn Kolonien* (or fen farmers). There was already a waterway from Aurich to Emden. In the total course between Wilhelmshaven and Emden, there were five locks, each thirty-six yards long. Two objects were to be served – the provisioning of the town of Wilhelmshaven in the time of war, and the opening up of the *Fehn* districts round Aurich. The peat farms could thus send away their peat to either Wilhelmshaven or Emden and the turf boats, which took the peat fuel and farm produce to either place, could return laden with fertilising *Schlick*, a mix of sand and clay, from the *Watten* or mud-flats. The bog dweller was said to 'make' his 'land' by digging in the *Schlick* to a depth of three or four feet after he had removed the peat.[33] The idea was a great success and this form of soil conditioning, using barges, was employed to great effect on the north coast of Harlinger Land, as will be seen later.

Thick fog and light easterlies slowed down *Vixen*'s progress. A wet wind from that direction drove them from the strange island of Memmert, and after groping and grounding, *Vixen* brought up a mile off the southern shore of the Island of Juist.

Erskine and Henry rowed ashore and 'walked over sand, taking careful courses by grounded ships with the compass in view of darkness returning. Found a brand new little budding watering place among the sand hills, empty now.' The prismatic compass was essential to their work. Erskine laid great store by 'sand tramps,' as he called them. They were part of cruising Frisian fashion, as he remembered in *The Times*.[34]

> *They gave a kind of physical exercise which is a pleasant change from the work afloat, hard enough as that work often is. There is an extraordinary exhilaration in treading the firm, wet sand with the wind blowing fresh and free over it, and no living thing near, perhaps for miles, but the wheeling gulls and there is more 'object' in such walks than in most walks that landsmen take, and greater sense of adventure and excitement. The object is generally one of three-sport with the shotgun, exploration, or foraging. The first, though it never ceases to entice, is rather visionary, as it is almost impossible to get near wildfowl on*

> *foot; the second and third are practical, and sometimes imperative, at some unusually perplexing stage of navigation, so perplexing perhaps that you have stranded in very bewilderment, it is of the greatest help to walk ahead at low water and study the lie of the banks and channels which have puzzled you so much, remembering to take a special bearing of a favourite spot for dropping anchor, if possible under the lee of a good, high bank, when the tide shall have floated you off. Then there are the foraging expeditions, which sometimes must be made in the teeth of considerable difficulties; for there is no cruising ground where calculations as to supplies are more liable to be upset by accidents of weather and navigation. A spell of fog after a spell of storm may drive one to very short rations.*

Almost every minute of those days were to be turned over, fined down and penned in that small, steady hand for Carruthers to describe the sand tramps from *Dulcibella*, whether it was the night that Davies showed him where *Dulcibella* had touched the west Hohenhorn and he had been nearly drowned in following Dollmann, or in Chapter 15, when Carruthers took the turn ashore and walked to Wangeroog with the water-breakers. In this he gave examples of two of the reasons for walking the sands.'A heavy tramp back to the yacht, nearly crushed by impedimenta. While Davies made yet another trip; I stalked some birds with a gun, and obtained what resembled a specimen of the smallest variety of jack-snipe, and small at that.'

Juist's massive steamer pier was not shown on the charts then. There was no harbour in 1897 or now. Today a small, dredged area lies to the south of the twin villages of Ostdorf and Westdorf, Erskine's 'brand new watering place': Mark Brackenbury does not recommend the island in his *Frisian Pilot* to the modern yachtsman,'except for the specialist with unlimited time', which might have described Erskine in those days.[35]

Saturday, 2 October, was almost a soldier's day. A fresh, reaching wind, full of sun and sparkle, urged them eastward, or was in the process of doing so until Erskine found himself in a *cul-de-sac* among the sands and had to go about.

The lost time and the frustration burnt that day on his mind. It may have been for this reason that Davies and Carruthers were to row *Dulcibella*'s dinghy 'blindfold' to Memmert (Chapter 21), westward down the Memmert Balje, landing on the desolate, southern end of that sand spit, not taking the shorter but shallower waters of the Juisterwattfahrwasser, close to Juist's southern shore.

They crossed over the tortured and usually uneasy waters between Juist and Norderney, past the harbour, where they had secured five nights before, and, carried by the floodtide, passed the island of Baltrum, until they lost that helping hand and were pushed back by the young ebb, off the mile-long pier that served the island of Langeoog. They did not go ashore and the night was perfect, fit for *Esmond*, or as he wrote in the *Yachting Monthly* magazine, 'a thousand spirits of whispered "peace"'. Sunday's voyage had a hiccup in it too, as they grounded yet again. Forgetting the Sabbath, Henry walked a mile over the sand to a farmhouse for milk. He did not use the pier that carried passengers from the steamer to the village further inland, to the shadow of the lighthouse. Mark Brackenbury mentions Langeoog as one of his favourite stopping places.

Henry was back by two and *Vixen*, now released by the rising tide, continued her journey, 'past a huge fleet of trading boats, something like Thames barges but with better lines and less canvas'. Erskine's seaman's eye provided an instant and accurate description of the wooden galliots, much favoured by owners in the coasting trade of Germany, Scandinavia and northern Holland. Usually from sixty to ninety feet long, they were expected to take the ground. Many had clipper bows, rounded sterns, leeboards or even a steel centre-board. A percentage carried on the mainmast a square foresail set flying with a square topsail or raffee above. They had a standing bowsprit with three or four headsails and both the gaff main and mizzen were rigged to carry topsails. The last of the commercial, wooden galliots were built in the middle 1930s; 1897 must have been the heyday of small, coastal sail. The motor, rather than the steam-engine, was to produce the eclipse of sail. In the short-haul coastal trade, steam had not caught on, as the boiler, bunkers and engine took up too much valuable cargo space. *Johannes* was a schooner rigged galliot, owned by Captain Bartels, whom Davies first met when the former helped to repair *Dulcibella*'s smashed rudder after the young Englishman had tried to follow *Medusa*, the galliot-type yacht belonging to Dollmann. *Kormoran*, the Memmert wreck-works boat, was a galliot, too. Only one of these little ships from the pages of *The Riddle* has, as far as can be discovered, her own name and proper owner: that was *Johannes* and her owner Captain Bartels. They were to meet on this cruise and again, after the book had been published, in the lock at Holtenau when Erskine was there in *Sunbeam* in 1903 and Ivor Lloyd-Jones had his camera. Erskine had a soft spot for the masters of these galliots – 'in the course of our cruise we made many friends among the skippers of these craft, most friendly, hospitable fellows we found them', he was to write in the *Yachting World*.

The weather was breaking and in heavy rain *Vixen* anchored out of the channel and under Wangeroog, the easternmost and last of the German Frisian islands. They were close enough in to dry out at half tide and so could count on a comfortable night. It was just as well, for the weather kept them in the island's embrace for two further days. There was time to explore – 'to go to the west point of the island to see an old church tower which stands right in the sea at half flood,' Erskine remembered in the log. In his article for the *Yachting Monthly* magazine, he recalled that it was 'now used for signalling purposes'. There is an historical postscript in R. M. Bowker's edition of *The Riddle of the Sands* in which he gives a history of this 177-foot tower. The structure that Erskine would have seen was the second, built in 1600. An upper floor was used as a church, but the bulk of the building did duty as a sea mark. In 1854, a violent storm and a tidal surge at the entrance to the Jade washed away the village that stood at its foot to the west, leaving the tower with more than a toe in the water, as Erskine described. The present tower, a replica, was erected in 1933.

At that time there were no fortifications, though Wangeroog commanded the western side of the Jade estuary. Erskine was to write in his 1910 *Times* article, *Cruising in Frisia*, 'far away at the head of the Jade is the great naval base of Wilhelmshaven, the dynamic centre of Germany's 20th century Weltpolitik'. He was to catch the first glimpses of this on his return a few weeks later.

On 6 October, with a fresh, east-northeasterly breeze, *Vixen* headed down the Jade until she reached the open sea. To starboard, between the Jade and the Weser, lay the Hohe Weg Sands that Davies called the 'Pike' in Chapter 14 of *The Riddle*. The banks that made up the other group of sands between the Weser and the Elbe, which he called the 'Fork', contained the Scharhörn and Hohenhorn sands and were to the south, as they made their way between the Elbe I, or outer Elbe, and the Elbe II lightships.[36] *Vixen* short-tacked up the river, helped by a roaring tide, and entered the port of Cuxhaven, 'after the finest sail of the year, very tired and hungry'.

The fourteenth-century chateau could be seen from the Elbe and represented the early strategic importance of the town, guarding the mouth of the river and the approaches to the great trading city of Hamburg and now to the Kiel Canal. The place was quiet as the summer bathers had left. Cuxhaven was at an extraordinary depth below sea level: 'Behind a gigantic dyke on the north side', Erskine wrote in *Vixen*'s log, 'stand a row of big hotels right down in a hollow, to live in which must be a severe trial to the nerves.' This feeling may have fuelled his desire to continue eastward, for on the next morning, 7 October, Erskine and Henry decided 'to go to Kiel by the Kaiser Wilhelm Ship Canal' and on to the Baltic, which he was to picture in his *Times* article as a 'new cruising ground of boundless variety and beauty'.[37]

It was dark before the tide served and so they were able to experience the confusion of signals that electric power could bring to the approaches of a port: 'a blaze of many coloured lights marked the canal entrance. We shortened sail and ran in, groping for a quay to moor to, but the darkness was made almost worse by the overhead electric dazzle. All was dead silent and seemingly deserted. Suddenly a wall loomed over the bows; we-luffed hard up, tumbled everything down, and found ourselves by a sort of floating stage to which we moored. Same silence and desertion.'

They entered the canal at Brunsbüttel, and Erskine wrote to his sister Dulcie about the 'immense canal – only just made and rather too grand for us'. Carruthers saw it in the same way in *The Riddle*: 'Broad and straight, massively embanked, lit by electricity at night till it is lighter than many a great London street; traversed by great war vessels, rich merchantmen, and humble coasters alike, it is a symbol of the new and mighty force which, controlled by the genius of statesmen and engineers, is thrusting the empire irresistibly forward to the goal of maritime greatness.'

The canal was late in coming. The idea had long been a dream. The Vikings carried their longboats across the ten miles of the Kiel watershed into the Eider lakes and down the river of the same name. This river had provided a good part of the first waterway when, in 1784, the Schleswig-Holstein Canal was built to link the Gulf of Kiel to the Eider waters. Employing these courses from six miles east of Rendsburg to Tonning, it was possible to reach the Heligoland Bight and the North Sea. The waterway saved the stormy route around Jutland, but was not practicable for vessels much over 100-tons burden or with a draft of over ten feet: Knight went this way in his *Falcon* and thought that 'few rivers can show such a succession of lovely scenes as the Eider above Rendsburg.' He noticed the schooners and ketches of about ninety tons and thought them clumsy looking but very handy. 'They turn to windward in the narrow reaches of the river as smoothly as a Thames barge will.' *Johannes* was such a vessel' and was loaded with apples when Davies met her – a cargo that Bartels, her master, hoped to sell at Tonning. 'I raced him there,' Davies boasted to Carruthers when recounting *Dulcibella*'s outward voyage, winning hands down, left him at Tonning and in three days was in the Baltic.'

Kaiser Wilhelm I laid the foundation stone for the Nord-ostsee-Kanal in 1887 and the inland route was opened by his son in 1895. 'Six crossing places allow the largest men-o-war to pass each other,' Baedeker told travellers.

For *Vixen*'s crew, 8 October was rather frustrating, for they were up at six but no tug appeared until the afternoon. There were, however, compensations, for it was on that day that Erskine first met Bartels. The log tells of the meeting.

> *S.W. gale blowing, heavy rain, and very cold. At last started, lashed alongside the Johannes schooner, bound for Kappeln in the Baltic. Skipper Bartels, a right good sort, who helped us a lot. He began by a solemn present of pears. We replied with wax matches (an everlasting source of wonder and joy to all foreigners) and a clock which wouldn't go, also hot punch, very welcome on that bitter day. His boy steered for us both and we had long yarns in our cabin.*

Karl, the boy, helped in much the same way when Davies and Carruthers made the journey in the opposite direction.

Once out of the canal, the approaches to Kiel were displayed in dramatic fashion: 'Nothing visible until suddenly mists rolled away and showed a noble fjord, edged with tree-clad, villa-dotted hills, deep blue tideless waters, all a-ripple and a-dazzle in the sun and a long line of battleships moored in the fairway where the town lay sparkling and glistening after the rain. A marvellous and magical contrast to the great expanses of the North Sea and the lonely levels of Friesland.' Erskine was using *Falcon on the Baltic* as a pilot, for he, too, anchored off Folker's Garten. Knight had noticed the men-o'-war and sailed among them in *Falcon*'s dinghy.

A visitor to Kiel in October of 1897would not have known much about the career of the one-time first officer of SMS *Blitz*, yet Rear-Admiral Alfred Tirpitz, recently appointed State Secretary of the Imperial Naval Office, was preparing to father the new Imperial battle fleet. At the age of forty-eight, he was thirteenth in the 'pecking order' of German admirals.

However, it would have been difficult to spend a week in October 1897 in the chief war harbour of Germany without being aware of the propaganda campaign of the German Colonial Society. They had organised 173 lectures, printed 140,000 pamphlets and distributed 2,000 copies of Mahan's *The Influence of Sea Power Upon History*. The society was determined, with Tirpitz, to ensure that Germany was not intimidated or cut off from the riches that the sea offered them. They realised that without political nerve and verve, the Reichstag would not vote the necessary money for the modernisation and spectacular increase in the fleet that the Kaiser so passionately wanted and which Admiral Hollmann, Tirpitz's predecessor, had failed to provide.

Erskine's German was fluent enough to follow the newspaper campaign of the German Colonial Society. His school record noted that he was consistently better at languages than mathematics and he made use of German in one of his later *Times* articles.[39]

Looking out of *Vixen*'s sliding companion hatch in the third week of October, Erskine would have seen only yesterday's warships. The Siegfried class of coast defence battleship with the strange tandem nine-and-a-half-inch forward turrets would have caught his eye then, as they did in 1903 in the Kiel Canal. Built for the protection of German harbours, they represented the old defence thinking that Tirpitz was now set to change.

A lovely day and a light southwesterly wind persuaded Erskine to leave such views and any thoughts they may have inspired, to sail northward to explore the Schleswig fjords. He was by himself, as Henry had to return to England for a spell. These early winter wanderings in the Baltic were to provide bright, sharp images and to ink in the soft background against which the opening chapters of *The Riddle of the Sands* were set. Sailing alone, on the 17th, he slipped into Schlei Fjord. It was now dark and he went aground in the narrow entrance. 'Unkedge-offable,' he wrote. The log continues, 'then walked up to the only house visible and found a jolly inn owned by the local pilot, a jolly old chap and his son, son's wife and children. Had a merry gathering round the fire. The pilot – in English – "yes, we will have a glass of beer, then we will go and push off the boat, then we will come back and have more glass beer."' Translated into *Riddle* language, the experience was very much the same, after the pilot's house was reached. The pilot was there, as was his 'buxom, bustling daughter-in-law and some rosy grandchildren'. Erskine's mind recalled and honed the experience just slightly to fit Davies and Carruthers: '"Yes, yes," he said, "all right. There is plenty ducks, but first we will drink a glass beer; then we will shift your ship, captain – she lies not good there ... Then we will drink another glass beer; then we will talk of ducks – no, then we will kill ducks – that is better. Then we will have plenty glasses beer."' A long evening followed in both cases.

A light, southerly wind and a calm, hazy day saw *Vixen* inside Flensburger Fjord and 'anchored in a calm in a little indentation opposite the Langballig Buoy, under the shade of deep woods'. *Dulcibella* reached hereabouts when the wind died in much the same way on the second night. 'Isn't this rather an open anchorage?' Carruthers was to suggest. Open or not, Erskine 'decided', or so he wrote in the log, 'that the southern Baltic was the finest yachting country I had yet seen'.

Fog and calm marred the dawn on Tuesday, 19 October – 'a day to be hurried over'. Erskine towed *Vixen* through much of the dog-leg in the fjord, anchoring in an inlet on the northern shore, a mile from Egernsund Narrows, as it is now known. Erskine called it Ekken Sound; Baedeker agreed if one 'k' was deleted.

Carruthers caught the same quick glimpse of Ekken Sound as Erskine did.

'A seductive inlet,' he recorded, 'so sailed in through a tiny slit in the hills and found

The Purpose of our voyage 'Ducks'

a big stretch of water fringed with woods in gorgeous autumn colours.' *Dulcibella* was there nearly a month before: 'we were drifting through a dainty little strait, with a peep of open water at the end of it. Cottages bordered either side, some overhanging the very water, some connecting with it by a rickety wooden staircase or a miniature landing-stage. Creepers and roses rioted over the walls and tiny porches.'

Flensburg was 'a big bright town, humming with vitality'. Erskine had shied away at first sight and anchored under the beechwoods, off Garrison Point, a mile back. He could still see the spire of the thirteenth-century church of St Nicholas and yet was free from the quays 'lined with English steamers'. The train took him to Kiel the next day and he found there a letter from Henry, saying that he would be able to rejoin *Vixen* on 3 November. Erskine had a week to discover Schleswig and 'explore up Sonderburg way'.

Early on the 23rd, in light airs, *Vixen* retraced her course down the fjord, until the cat's-paw faded and it fell dead calm. He anchored on the Krage Sands on the north side of the entrance to Flensburger Fjord. Dusk brought a fresh southeaster and persuaded him to seek shelter at Haruphav, on the other side of the Sonderburg Bight. Knight's words may have had some influence, for he, too, had anchored there in the evening, having 'had enough tumbling about for the day'. Erskine woke 'opposite a beautiful little village among the trees at an angle where the arms of the haven meet'.

Vixen moored at the north end of Sonderburg the next afternoon, 'unobserved and unmolested'. Like Davies, Erskine distanced himself from civilisation, though he loved to wander, alone in himself, ever interested in the look of past works of man and in history. He recalls for 23 October: 'Ashore and strolled over town. Wonderfully fascinating houses in the old part. The town is Danish to the core, though German since '68. The very shopkeepers spoke German with reluctance.'

The reason was underlined by the 'sight of a little monument in a clump of firs' that he spotted going north through Als Sound on Sunday. Landing, he found 'a graceful little Gothic memorial to those killed on the spot in 1864 when the Germans

Als Sound

forced a landing and conquered Als Island ... It was a monument to the memory of the dead of both nations and seemed to me singularly dignified and touching in its exquisitely peaceful surroundings.'

Davies was strangely moved by the same sight, as Carruthers remembered. 'His eyes flashed and filled with tears as he glanced , from the inscription to the path we had followed and the water beyond. "It was a landing in boats, I suppose," Davies had said – he was like a schoolboy reading of Waterloo.' The German inscription and its translation is included in *The Riddle of the Sands*, underlining Erskine's familiarity with both the language and the bloody history of that part of the world.

He would have known that in the middle of the nineteenth century, the King of Denmark had ruled over his own kingdom and the duchies of Schleswig and Holstein. The former was divided, both by language and culture, between Denmark and Germany and in this ethnic amalgam the majority of the Danish-speaking population favoured the Eider Policy, which laid down that all north of that river – Schleswig's southern boundary – should be incorporated into the Danish kingdom. The German speakers, on the other hand, preferred the affiliation of Schleswig to Holstein and to join the Confederation of German States.

Holstein was already a member of the latter and so when the Danish National Liberal Government went for the Eider Policy there was a rebellion. Prussia took a hand and the Danes lost, undertaking that they would not clasp Schleswig again, but by 1863 the Danish government decided to separate Holstein from Denmark and to annex Schleswig. Otto von Bismarck acted swiftly and Prussia and Austria declared war. The Danes were defeated at Dybbøl and the whole of Jutland occupied. The Treaty of Vienna surrendered both duchies to Prussia, pushing the boundary some forty miles to the north of the present 1920 boundary and eighty miles beyond Schleswig's Eider River, which perhaps was the reason that 'the very shopkeepers' of Sonderburg spoke German with reluctance.

Knight had visited the Arnkiel monument too, and was pleased that the obelisk was dedicated to the fallen of both sides. The English press, in 1864, was not so even-handed. They had sympathised with Denmark. Palmerston and Russell had been keen to become involved. Davies 'lighted up', when Carruthers talked of the

Danish war. 'Germany's a thundering great nation,' he said, 'I wonder if we shall ever fight her.' The Danish war caused others to wonder momentarily about German ambitions then, but England was more concerned with the intentions of the French and rather less inclined to intervene in Europe. 'We are fish' was the way that Lord Salisbury often put it.[40]

The obelisk at Arnkiel has a sister at Dybbøl, the scene of the last desperate stand of the Danes. Erskine's trip to both of these stone reminders of German action must have dominated his lonely *Vixen* days. Perhaps during those minutes at either, the seeds of doubt about German military intentions were sown, and in secret slept. In any event, he returned to Sonderburg and Dybbøl, as if on pilgrimage, aboard *Sunbeam* on 19 August 1903, four months after the publication of *The Riddle of the Sands*. Much of the town had been razed during the Prussian assault on Dybbøl.

Sonderburg played host for five days, except on the Sunday night, when much of the evening was spent at the inn at Satrup with fishermen and coffee punch. Fog held him in the port – 'Stove alight all day as the fog was dripping wet.' Knight visited the town and castle of the Dukes of Augustenburg, then a Prussian barracks. Erskine may have wandered there between writing, studying German and buying cook pots, activities carefully recorded in the log.

On 29 October, the fog lifted and *Vixen* in a fitful southeasterly tacked with difficulty through the pontoon bridge. Erskine, finding that he was headed by the wind, gave up hope of reaching Kiel and meeting his brother with the yacht, so took the wind again to Flensburg.

Henry duly reached the town by train on Wednesday, 3 November, arriving on the platform where Davies was to meet Carruthers, and, like the latter, he was loaded down with useful stores for the cruise and the yacht:

> *'Loads of guns, cartridges, etc. and a big new double oil stove, and our fine old* "Shulah *compass*". *Erskine may have sent Henry a telegram from Sonder burg during those days of misty imprisonment and Henry's day in London may well have been taken up on a sulphurous underground train in search of chandlery, visiting Lancaster's for cartridges and the Army and Navy Stores*

> *for that 'formidable and hideous piece' of replacement ironmongery.* Shulah's *box compass had done duty on* Marguerite *and may have been more readily to hand.*

Henry was 'rather seedy', and so *Vixen* remained at anchor until the 7th, when they made Haruphav. On the 8th they were under way at 5 am by moonlight, enjoying a light to fresh easterly, making best speed. *Vixen* was moored by the quay at Schleimunde by 9.30 that morning, where the two brothers met Erskine's October friend, the pilot. Erskine had been told by the fishermen of Satrup that the Schlei was a good place for wildfowl, but only the pilot was lucky enough to bag anything. It was arctic cold and Erskine and Henry saw nothing. Davies and Carruthers had a carbon-copy experience. Erskine wrote in the log that the pilot had told them that 'strangers were not allowed to shoot in the fjord but we gathered that personal considerations had much to do with this assertion.' His record of that day tailed off in disappointment, for they were both keen shots: 'anyway we decided on Holland via Kiel.'

The weather saw to it that *Vixen* was trapped in Schlei Fjord, so Erskine and Henry attempted to make the best of it by exploring the upper reaches of that long, thin gut. They squeezed through a pontoon bridge at Kappeln, glided past Arnis, to go hard aground a mile before the Flensburg-Kiel railway bridge – 'nothing to do but to take out ballast. No words to describe the exertion and the loathsomeness of this job. Filled dinghy and then a friendly boat which we hailed took all starboard ballast out and then she floated off; long before this it was a frosty, moonlight night. Lay down among the ruins, dog-tired, supped and slept.'

The experience was to help Erskine put into words the deadening, dirty, muscle-wringing task of lightening ship. Carruthers was to recall later: 'A horrid business, handling the pigs of lead, heavy, greasy and black,' after running aground south of the east spit of Langeoog. The evidence of their distress was notice d the next day when ashore again in Keppeln, the baker asked in quite a friendly way if Henry was off a coal ship. He might have just come from *Dulcibella*'s saloon, described as 'an inferno, the deck like a collier's, and ourselves like sweeps'.

The accursed fog rolled in again, keeping *Vixen* within the narrow entrance for the third day. Davies and Carruthers were to be similarly imprisoned in the same place and as a consequence the latter had his first meeting with Captain Bartels of the *Johannes*. The log on the 11th showed that Erskine and Henry had just such a get-together: 'Who should tumble down the hatchway but our old friend Bartels of the *Johannes*. He was on his way to Hamburg from Kappeln without cargo, and was fog-bound as we were. A joyous meeting, celebrated in hot rum punch.'

They escaped the Schlei the next day and had 'a very wet but jolly thrash with one tack to Kiel Fjord. Just about as much wind as she could possibly stand.' At Friedrichsort, where the channel narrows, they were 'hailed from a customs steamer'. They heaved to and were boarded by an officer who searched everything, 'a most unusual proceeding in Germany. Then demanded a table, pen and ink, embarrassing requests in view of the mess the cabin was in after our hard day's sail.' The crew of *Dulcibella* were to meet just such an officer in Bensersiel, after a similarly testing time at sea. He too 'marched down into the cabin, which was in a fearful mess and wringing wet, and producing ink, pen and a huge printed form, wanted to know our cargo, our crew, our last port, our destination, our food, stores, and everything.'

Vixen suffered further indignity by hitting a buoy, carrying away her bobstay and damaging her stern. They could have come off worse, for the harbour was 'full of warships (just before the Kiaochow affair) whose launches were tearing about everywhere'. There was reason for this activity, for two days before, on 10 November, the Kaiser had ordered Vice-Admiral Otto von Diederich's squadron, with the cruiser *Cormoran* amongst them, to seize Kiaochow, a fishing port in the Chinese province of Shantung. In *The Riddle*, the galliot *Kormoran* was the Memmert wreck-works boat.

Germany had long wanted a coaling station in the Far East. Rear-Admiral Alfred Tirpitz, as commander of the East Asian Squadron, in the spring of 1896 had poked his nose into every possible bay on the coast of China in search of just such a place. He selected Kiaochow.[41] In November of the same year, Germany's Chancellor suggested to the Kaiser that 'the Minister at Peking should be instructed to keep his eyes open for an event suitable as a cause for advance'.[42] A 'suitable event' came in

Vixen's November, for a number of Chinese bandits burnt houses and murdered the occupants of a Chinese village in Shantung, including two German Roman Catholic missionaries. The Kaiser did not hesitate and he made his order clear:

> *Plentiful atonement for this must be secured by energetic action of the fleet. The squadron must instantly proceed to Kiaochow, seize the port there, and threaten the severest repression unless the Chinese government instantly agrees to a high compensation in gold as well as a really effective pursuit and punishment of the criminals. I am fully determined to abandon, henceforth, the over-cautious policy which had been regarded by the Chinese as weakness, and to show the Chinese, with full power, and – if necessary – with brutal ruthlessness, that the German Emperor cannot be made sport of and that it is bad to have him as an enemy.*[43]

Strangely, Tirpitz was not pleased. He telegraphed the Chancellor, Prince Hohenlohe: 'Regard the action against China as unfavourable for the Navy Bill and in the proposed form very dangerous. The consequences of this sort of action must lead to serious threat of hostilities. Request by return permission for audience with Your Highness.'[44] It was too late: the ships had sailed.

Germany's action would not have been lost on Erskine or Henry, for they were two days in Kiel. Erskine would have read the newspapers, for the log recalls that they were 'ashore for comprehensive shopping of all sorts'. They may have discussed the turn of events with others. The record for 14 November reads: 'farewells to my friends there'. German actions of 1864 were being brought dramatically up to date, though on the other side of the world.

Vixen started westward, through the Kiel Canal, in a string convoy behind a tug. The warp broke and they had to 'implore a tow from passers-by, like roadside mendicants'. By evening *Vixen* was safely in a siding at Rendsburg, after passing 'through wild northwest squalls and sleet'. The yacht was anchored in the tideway of the Elbe by the next evening, 15 November.

Carruthers described a similar scene from the deck of *Dulcibella*: 'We swung close to a *glacis* of smooth, blue mud which sloped up to a weed-grown dyke; behind lay the same flat country, colourless, humid; and opposite us, two miles away, scarcely visible in the deepening twilight, ran the outline of a similar shore.'

The roaring ebb carried *Vixen* close-hauled to Cuxhaven. They tried to luff into the harbour, but in an instant were whirled past by the tide, just saved by the anchor and all the chain. St Peter's Day had closed all the shops and it was with difficulty they found water. A railway porter 'with great solemnity lifted some mysterious flagstones inside the railway station, and lying on his stomach, filled our jars laboriously from a subterranean pool. No public supply at all.' A carpenter repaired the stern, while the crew spliced, 'bought landing nets and sponge baskets of colossal size to hold meat', and counted the liquor on board – thirteen varieties – the best being Doppel Kümmel – from Flensburg. 'Excellent in cold weather.'

Vixen remained in Cuxhaven, held by repairs and a dead foul wind until 21 November. On the last day, they had hot baths in the Hansa Bad Hotel, recommended by Baedeker, and wandered to the northern point of the land. 'There were some tremendously strong forts on the point, to command the Elbe fairway.' Carruthers later made notes of them too: as *Dulcibella* was 'whirled down' on the tide, 'the shore sharpened to a point like a claw, where the innocent dyke became a long, low fort, with some great guns peeping over.' *The Naval Baedeker* of 1902 listed five forts defending Cuxhaven and the great river.[45]

The thick, unsettled weather persuaded Erskine 'to cut in across the sands behind Neuwark Island, following the boomed channels as shown in some excellent up-to-date German charts we got here'. He had not wasted his time in Cuxhaven. The unreliability of British charts of these waters was his constant complaint, ably taken up by Davies in *The Riddle* who denounced 'the prehistoric rottenness of the English charts' and praised 'the excellent quality of the German'.

The Stickers Gat route behind Neuwark was to be followed exactly by *Dulcibella*. Henry Childers, unlike Carruthers, had seen the sands before, as he had been Erskine's companion on the outward voyage. Carruthers called the scene that met them 'the desert', though he agreed that it was not entirely featureless. The colours varied 'from light fawn, where the highest levels had dried in the wind, to brown or deep violet where it was still wet, slate-grey where the patches of mud soiled its clean bosom. Here and there were pools of water, smitten into ripples by the impotent wind; here and there it was speckled by shells and seaweed.' The view has not changed much over time and this passage in *The Riddle* is still quoted by those who wish to describe the 'sea of mud'.

This amphibiland, between the Elbe and the Weser, was the Fork of *The Riddle.* Beyond and west lay the Hohenhorn Sands. *Vixen* crept past their shelter on 22 November, short of water in both senses – salt and sweet – grounding and kedging with no result, before setting a good example for the two that were to follow by going for a long walk. They spotted the lie of the channels and unknowingly captured a negative that was to be developed in *The Riddle*, a picture of Dollmann's deceit.

In *The Riddle* and in that place, Carruthers remembered how they had set off 'with a long, stooping stride in the teeth of the wind, and straight towards the roar of the

Aground on the Hohenhorn

breakers on the farther side of the sand'. A line of Matthew Arnold's *Dover Beach* ran through his head. He kept the last line and took courage.

But now I only hear
Its melancholy, long, withdrawing roar,
Retreating, to the breath
Of the night-wind, down the vast edges drear
And naked shingles of the world.

These close-hauled, Arnold-type days were all bumping, rolling gunnel under and spending nights listening to the tremulous song of the demon horde, so well captured in *The Riddle*. The night of the 23rd may have been the inspiration. Earlier in the evening, *Vixen*'s crew had replenished their water-breakers from a schooner anchored nearby in return for cigars. At midnight and high water, the full force of the westerly hit the anchored yacht, 'Henry was flung out of bed. Lockers burst open and floor paved with honey, flour, broken glass and petroleum.'

'The furious squalls' continued but the wind went round to the north and they had to get out. At a 'tearing rate', with a beam wind, *Vixen* cleared the Fork, and anchored amongst a fleet of boats behind the edge of the Wurster Watt sand, in the Weser tide. To the east, between that river and the Jade, lay the Pike.

Vixen took a day to pass by this sharp spike of sand. She had managed the Fork in three days, and so in a total of four Erskine and Henry had crossed the sands between the Elbe and the Jade. The same journey took Davies and Carruthers ten. The crew of *Vixen* had quickened the hours of daylight and darkness spent 'sailing or anchored, aground or afloat, in rain and shine, wind and calm' that the crew of *Dulcibella* had used to study the bed of estuaries and to practise the threading of the network of channels, holding no communication with the land and rarely approaching it. *Vixen*, in her short passage, had plenty of 'wild autumnal' weather. Both yachts making for home would have had a desperate battle against the continuous southwesterlies of that time of the year.

In crossing the Fork and the Pike, Erskine and Henry were able to see for themselves that 'the whole region would in war be an ideal hunting ground for small, freelance marauders'. They saw how the tidal channels that threaded their way between 'the three sea-roads through the sands to Hamburg, Bremen and Wilhelmshaven were indeed like "highways" piercing the mountainous district by defiles, where a handful of desperate men can arrest an army,' to anticipate Davies and his channel theory.

Erskine made his landfall Wangeroog, on the other side of the Jade estuary.

In 1897 the island was a guardian without arms or armour for the growing naval port of Wilhelmshaven. Wangeroog, with its strange church tower, was familiar, for Erskine and Henry had spent three early October days there on the outward voyage. The shopkeeper gave them a warm welcome and, soon after, they almost 'lost' *Vixen*. As was now traditional, they 'ran her right in till she grounded a mile off the village and let her dry out'. They forgot, in their pleasure at having had done 'with what was the only difficult part of the return voyage', to guard against the returning tide by putting an anchor out, or against the approach of nightfall by lighting the lamp. The crew had to 'separate and search' and they found her a long way from where they thought she ought to be. 'Relief' was the way Erskine put it in the log.

The crew of *Dulcibella* were to have an unpleasant shock on the shores of Wangeroog too, for it was there, on the night of 15 October a few years later, that Carruthers discovered an intruder in the act of descending *Dulcibella*'s companion-way. The trespasser, later identified as Herr Grimm, had taken the precaution of blowing out the riding-light before exploring further. The effect of a blackout was, therefore, only too well known to Erskine.

To their 'profound disgust', the wind had backed to the southwest and the glass had fallen heavily. The channel south of Wangeroog bore north of west and *Vixen*, with two reefs down, lay close-hauled, on the port tack, with the tide under her, beating across the sea channel to Spiekeroog, 'in a drenching sea'. Taking advantage of the tide, they took long legs over sands, sounding continuously with the lead, eventually running aground opposite Neuharlingersiel: 'Blew a hard gale in the night with snow, cabin quite warm with both lamps of stove alight and curtain up, heavy roll on the weather tide.'

The next morning, 27 November, in thick fog and when there was water enough, they groped their way into Neuharlingersiel, warping into 'the tiny little basin set in a ring of cottages'. The constant use of the stove for heating and cooking, as well as the spillage, must have meant that stocks were low. The log agrees: 'Bought petroleum and thirty rolls and five pounds of sugar. Customs came along – chiefly for a drink.' The rule held good then, as now, that any beadledom and bumbledom in the revenue service was less on show on wooden piers than stone quays, but then all the people of Neuharlingersiel made a good impression: 'pleasant people', he wrote in *Vixen's* log.

They are like that today. The little port is the least affected of all the 'siels by the continuous seaward reclamation of the shore. The small town looks much the same as it did in Childers' day. Many of the old buildings remain, perhaps brighter and more prosperous now. A lifeboat station is still there today. The twin *Tiefs*, or canals, wander inland, one just a dribble by the time it reaches the Wittmunder Canal, the other holding but a few drops and ducks when it reaches the Wittmunder Tief. Both arrive at the sea through the old sluice at Neuharlingersiel. It is not surprising that the little port was selected as one of the locations for the filming of *The Riddle*.

The two brothers had to press on, braving a fresh to strong southwesterly when the tide gave enough water for *Vixen* to pass over the sands. Hesitation might have meant even worse weather, for the days of ice were not far off. *Vixen* had another 'long, dead beat along the island (Langeoog), tacking with the lead over the sands in company with six loaded boats. Wind stronger and rain.'

They took in two reefs at three and later moored with two anchors under the mainland shore as the glass was falling 'with frightful rapidity' – one and a half inches in twenty-four hours. Erskine wrote in his log: 'blew a heavy gale in night'.

When the light came on the morning of the 29th, the wind was still in the same direction but had abated. It was very thick and the rain was still with them. They determined to 'seek shelter at Bensersiel, a little place exactly on the lines of Neuharlingersiel, about four miles away on the mainland shore, approached by a boomed high water channel'. Retrieving one of the anchors proved a fearful job, but in the end they managed to break it out, to find one of the flukes bent.

Davies and Carruthers were not so lucky, for the latter lost control of the chain.

Unlike *Vixen*, they had the benefit of a winch, but the chain jumped the drum and thirty to forty fathoms went overboard; it was buoyed, though, so all was not lost. *Vixen* and *Dulcibella* experienced the same conditions on that wild day, so let *Vixen*'s log tell the story.

> *Groped three-reefed to the Bensersiel channel and anchored outside for water. Wind grew to an even worse gale with heavy rain and hurricane look in the sky. A waterspout passed us at a distance of about 400 yards. We were in the centre of a cyclone, we supposed, about 11, for the wind suddenly veered to the northeast and blew a hurricane, making our anchorage and Bensersiel a lee shore. It was half flood and we decided to start, but how to get up anchor. Couldn't get in a link, as it was. In view of slipping it we buoyed it ready; then got up sail three reefed and tried to sail it out of the ground. Just giving it up when it came away and we got it up. Then bore away for Bensersiel. Got into the channel but found the booms almost covered by an abnormally high tide and very hard to see. Henry stood forward and waved directions, while Erskine steered. Soon got into breakers and found it a devil of a situation. Fearful work with the tiller under so much sail. One or two heavy gybes at turns of the channel. When close in shore, sea less bad – missed booms altogether and grounded but blew off again. Whole population on the beach yelling. Tide so high that all clues were obscured. Henry conned her skilfully on and we were soon tearing into the mouth of the 'harbour', about 15 feet wide at about 7 knots. It was a tiny basin with not even room to round up. Tried to get sail down but peak jammed: let go anchor with a run, luffed and just brought up in time with the bowsprit over the quayside and received bewildered congratulations of the people who seemed to think we had fallen from the sky.*

They thought that Davies and Carruthers had come from there too, when they entered in the same way.

Erskine and Henry felt the general welcome was tinged with 'a slight current of disappointment connected with salvage operations which had at one time appeared probable!' The customs man was hospitable, unlike the gentleman that Davies and Carruthers were to meet, for he was the spit image of the tedious officer who had joined them in the narrows of Kiel Fjord. Even he was to thaw and become 'human, talkative, and thirsty'.

The harbour was not busy. 'The crew of the Langeoog post-boat were also very friendly – stowed our sails and asked us to pay them a visit.' They may well have been the twins, the most 'benignant giants' who were to ask Davies and Carruthers 'aboard the post-boat galliot for a chat'. *Vixen*'s log does not tell of any other vessels in the port and does not mention the presence of *Kormoran*, the Memmert work-boat that *Dulcibella's* crew spotted.

The Benser Tief entered the harbour through a lock. As it winds south, the waterway joins the Kloster Tief and then the Esens-Wittmunder Canal, to arrive at neither Esens nor Wittmund.

Carruthers was to discuss the progress of the Esens-Wittmunder link with a Gasthaus owner at Esens and the latter confirmed that the work was still under way, though he did not believe in such new-fangled schemes. He was right, for the canal never reached Wittmund. The waterway's principal purpose was to carry peat dug from that low-lying district to Esens and Bensersiel for fuel. Sand was dredged from the harbour and returned to the excavated land for soil conditioning in a seemingly never-ending two-way trade. This was part of the purpose of the more strategic Ems-Jade Canal to the south, as has been described.

The barges of the sort shown on the postcard could carry forty to fifty tons of peat or other goods and so laden used to be towed out to the islands to supply their need of fuel, bricks and farm produce, bringing back sand and *Schlick* for use on the land. There was a need for these dumb vessels to be able to cope with 'the vicious surf' between the islands in poor weather. A marked forward sheer helped, as Carruthers noted when he inspected the barges on the banks of the Benser Tief.

Erskine would have learnt about such barge work from the harbourmaster, or at the inn, or from the post-boat's crew. He may have also seen lighters coming down the Benser Tief 'with bricks and produce from the interior' to be towed to the islands, as mentioned in *The Riddle*.

There is rather more mystery about Erskine's intimate knowledge of the geography of the land around Esens. The commercial director of the town in 1981, Herr Hardo Sziedat, explained that when *The Riddle* came out in German people recognised the names of the local characters, for the families were still to be found in the district. He went on to say that there had been a sawmill on the banks of the Benser Tief, south of the main road bridge on the Dornum road, and that everything described by Carruthers had been there, except for the barge-building yard. It was clear, he continued, that the author of *The Riddle* was well acquainted with that small part of Harlingerland.

From *Vixen*'s log, it is apparent that Erskine was only there for one full and two part days, having entered port in a flurry about mid-day on Monday, 29 November, leaving after four o'clock on Wednesday, 1 December. Erskine would have had little time for exploration on the Monday, by the time he had squared up, dried out and been entertained by the customs officer to tea and at the hotel bar. The next day was almost as social, judging from the log: 'Stayed in port. Rain and wind. Carpenter fixed post and made us a new crutch. Visited on board the post-boat. Cleanings and repairings. Customs man dined with us.'

Erskine could have walked into Esens on the Tuesday, just under two and a half miles from the harbour, taken the south high road, glancing at the station on his right, going over the level crossing and taking the first footpath, again to the right, that leads southwest into what is now Aurich State Forest, and on to the Kloster Tief, along the bank to Carruther's bridge, into Esens and back to Bensersiel on the main road, a distance of about nine miles in all. With his limp, he could have managed the tramp in three hours, especially with a good ordnance map.

Erskine certainly possessed such a map, to a scale of 1:100,000, printed in 1895, with small corrections to 1896, so very up to date. The fine condition of the sheet even today indicates though that it was bought as an *aide-memoire* when writing *The Riddle*, and kept in the desk drawer rather than in the back pocket of a pair of grey flannels during the beginnings of a Frisian winter. The railway line through Dornum to Esens, Wittmund and eventually to Wilhelmshaven, built in 1883, has been outlined by Erskine in red and the' principal places in the story similarly highlighted.

If any further proof is needed, the top margin is marked '(Appendix No. 4) – (Map) to illustrate the "siels" (Chap. 25)' – an instruction ignored by the original publishers, Smith Elder, and their successors, for the map has not appeared before.

The best opportunity to look at Esens and the wanderings of the Benser Tief was to come on Wednesday. The log explains that there was 'no water to get out 'til afternoon so shopped, etc.' It is more than probable that this meant a short walk into Esens for supplies, just as Erskine and Henry had visited Anjum from the port of Oostmahorn on the outward voyage.

When Erskine and Henry arrived back at the yacht, they found enough water but a northeasterly wind blowing straight through the narrow piers. Commander von Brüning was not there in his steam-launch to pluck them into the eye of the wind, but the strenuous efforts of two men 'hurriedly chartered' for the same purpose may have put the advantages of such a tow in Erskine's mind: 'It was a long, tiresome business against a fresh head wind and we grounded several times but the men worked like niggers and at last we were in the open and they left us in their boat.'

Vixen sailed blindly on that night for Langeoog but gave up when the lead found deeper water and, in the words of the log: 'let go having not an idea where we were'. They discovered when light came that they were off the west end of the island and so hurried before a strong east-northeasterly wind across the sea entrance to the shelter of Baltrum, bumping across a watershed made shallower and less easy to cross by the continuous northeasterlies. Henry took a pot-shot at a seal on the way and *Dulcibella*'s crew were to do the same, equally unsuccessfully. *Vixen* anchored near a loaded coaster and the 'very civil skipper' suggested that they lay alongside. It may well be that she was, or became, immortalised as *Kormoran*, later the Memmert work-boat.

On the run to Norderney, Henry sat on the bowsprit to reduce the draft aft caused by the false keel. They 'saw a lot of ducks quite near but no leisure to shoot'. Mallard, wigeon, teal, pintail, shoveller and the fishy-tasting Eider abound in these waters in winter.

Vixen ran aground again just off Norderney pier. The two were recognised, for their memorable arrival at Neuharlingersiel had been headlines in the local newspaper. The town was empty and lifeless, though meat could be purchased. Erskine could hardly wait to leave, for the urge to press on was now strong. *Vixen* reached across to Norddeich, arriving as darkness fell. Norddeich was a step in the right direction when crossing the Ems south of Borkum.

The sands of *The Riddle* were now astern.

The evening of 4 December saw *Vixen* aground in the shelter of the Dutch island of Rottum. At the close of the 5th, they dried out on 'a perfect Ararat of sand', with only a couple of miles made good. On the 6th, headed by the wind and stranded by the tide, now short of water, oil and provisions, Erskine's only consolation was his book: 'St Ives getting very exciting'.

Tuesday, 7 December, brought some relief and they enjoyed a fine sail on a lovely day, tacking against a fresh southwesterly. But needless to say not for long, as they grounded yet again, this time two miles off the village of Pieterburen. Henry managed to shoot 'a bird resembling a small example of the smallest variety of small jack-snipe' (more probably a dunlin), which they had for dinner that evening, 'with due honour'. Carruthers had the same experience, for he stalked just such a bird, pleased with his success as it gave substance to the ruse that *Dulcibella* was a salt-water shooting-box.

Vixen suffered that evening. A gale blew up from the southwest, accompanied by heavy rain, but Erskine noted the next day that 'the boat seemed none the worse for her racketing and never made a drop of water.' The lifeboat hull took such a thumping in her stride. Worse things had happened in her youth, for she had been wracked, twisted and bumped through a hole in the chalk cliff and dragged over lumps of hard rock into the sea at Kingsgate, only to return, manhandled back to safety on wild and unforgiving nights.

Oostmahorn lies just over ten nautical miles to the west, tucked into the great open, sand-choked bay of the Lauwer Zee. Erskine did not relish the idea of returning; he had vowed never to go there again after a disagreeable meeting with the customs and a rowdy train of boys who had followed him to Anjum, but there was no choice; they were virtually out of stove oil and drinking water. The bread bin was all but empty and without water or fuel they were unable to bake. The weather did not leave them alone either, for 'a mile from the piers a heavy black-squall struck us with a torrent of rain and we had to scandalise and stumble in anyhow.'

Vixen left Oostmahorn on the Friday morning at nine, and by one o'clock had again sailed through the gap in the stone breakwater, as the log and the 1893 Admiralty chart called it.[46] The wall of stone was built as a causeway by the island's monks and the gap was made after they lost interest in the crossing.[47] Another survival of later days is the Ameland surf lifeboat station on the island's north side, where the boat is still launched by horses.

Vixen went astray and grounded, following a now long tradition, and 'in the evening the usual gale got up and we had another terrific bumping, in rising.' The dinghy was missing in the morning and Erskine speculated that 'one of us must have let go the painter in mistake for another rope, when setting sails in the dark and storm'. Henry and he reckoned that it must have 'blown to Ameland island three or four miles to leeward', and so they made for Nes, the island's capital, homing on the huge, square clock tower put up in 1732.

Erskine landed 'among a crowd of natives and shouted for someone who spoke English. A diffident ex-sailorman was pushed out and proffered his few words.' He turned out to be the inn-keeper and was most helpful, for after they left, the dinghy was found and he arranged for its despatch to Terschelling.

Sunday, the 12th, was spent, in the absence of news of the missing lurkie, listening to the Amelanders singing hymns in the street and, as was so often Erskine's habit, in writing letters. Though it was the Sabbath, he was able to obtain screws to repair the loose lower rudder pintle. It was evening before the boat dried out so the work had to be done 'in the dark on the slushy mud by the lantern dimly burning and (by a fatality) continually going out. The screws had broken in the holes and we couldn't punch them out. A beastly job altogether.' *Dulcibella* was to have the same problems after her experience on the Hohenhorn Sands. The Ameland mud was particularly sticky, for Erskine notes that he had 'to get the jib halyards onto the chain to get the anchor up, though no wind'.

Monday was lovely, the wind south-southwest and fresh. There was a little delay at a shoal place but otherwise they had a 'long beat against tide and wind along the island', reaching the sea channel between Ameland and Terschelling which they crossed, having to anchor suddenly as fog rolled up. It lasted little more than three-quarters of an hour. They progressed from beacon to beacon with Henry on the bowsprit end, keeping the heel of the keel away from the sand. *Vixen* was seven miles from the town of Terschelling when they finally struck. The log, in three short sentences, captures the cosy world down below of the confident, small-boat sailor. 'Threw out kedge and spent a pleasant evening reading Schiller *[Maria Stuart]*. Usual gale at night, with heavy rain but this time a comfortable berth. Glass falling heavily.'

They had a 'splendid beam-wind sail to Terschelling' and entered harbour 'gradually shortening sail to bear poles and ran gently into a snug berth by the quay', where they received a welcome from the crowd. The harbour was filled with Zuyder Zee smacks that were weather-bound. Mr Fletcher had left, the salvage season now well over, but he asked Herr Schroo, the British Agent and 'a man of note in the island, to look us up and give us help'.

Erskine and Henry 'decided to lay up the boat there for the winter and go home for Christmas'. Herr Schroo offered to store all *Vixen*'s gear and equipment in his own house for no reward and to keep an eye on the boat in the harbour. And so it was that after 'skinning the boat and transferring ballast to Schroo's, clearing and cleaning the hull thoroughly', they dined with their benefactor and slept at a 'very comfortable hotel'.

They were on the post-steamer by six in the morning and reached England via Harlingen, Stavoren, Amsterdam and the night boat from The Hook of Holland. The cruise was not quite over, for the last entry for Tuesday, 16 December 1897, reads: 'Befogged outside Harwich, 16 hours, no bread. London next morning a day late.'

In his article for *The Times* on cruising in German Frisia[48] Erskine commented, 'Small boats do better to contemplate than to mingle in Imperial traffics.' He was advising the use of the quieter channels behind the islands to 'the rushing, murky waters of the Elbe fairway'. He had contemplated from the deck of *Vixen* 'Imperial traffics' and he was anxious about what he saw.

He was back at his desk on 16 December, one day adrift. The House did not sit until well into the New Year, the new session starting on 8 February 1898. Erskine seized on the short Easter break in this session to bring *Vixen* back from her winter quarters on the island of Terschelling.

He took with him Albert Rice, a paid hand from Burnham. They arrived to find the yacht 'all ready for sea but shocking bad fit-out – mast black, paint dull outside and evanescent inside'. The word fits the condition perfectly, for evanescent means 'liable to vanish or pass away like vapour'. The painter had a light touch.

If *Vixen* was looking different, the weather was not, for they were unable to leave for England until 12 April. They had a good passage to Den Helder and then took the North Holland Canal to Amsterdam. At last the log rejoices:

> *Dover in prospect – About 8 pm towed with dinghy between piers and moored to a buoy in the tidal harbour. Illegally went ashore at once to look up the trains but happily just returned before the Customs officer came on board; he cleared us and we went to bed, well satisfied with the cruise.' Erskine had every right to feel so, for he was at his office punctually at eleven, leaving 'Rice at Dover to paint and varnish anew in the Granville Dock.*

Vixen arrived back at Dover on 17 April, set for immortality.

Chapter 5

THE MAKING OF AN AUTHOR

Vixen remained in home waters for the remainder of her days. At the end of April, Erskine introduced her to the waters that *Marguerite* had known so well. He called the Thames Estuary 'the Londoner's cruising ground' and had great affection for the barge sea, recalling the Essex coast later in an article for *The Times*.[1]

> *A spirit of melancholy reigns over a greater part of the Essex coasts. The charm is the charm of a low and lonely country where the view is bounded by a delicate fringe of trees, by a few red farm buildings, or a distant church spire; where vast and desolate flats, screamed over by wild-fowl, are slowly laid bare as the tide falls and the ribbons of navigable water shrink into smaller and smaller dimensions. The wild reaches of the Blackwater, Mersea Quarters, the bleak Foulness Peninsula, the Colne, the Crouch, and the many tortuous ramifications of the Roach, all suggest sober hues, infinitely wide horizons, and water dulled to a neutral hue by contact with the great Thames Estuary.*

He did not stay there long though, leaving the Thames on a Whitsuntide cruise with William Le Fanu. They were delayed by the weather in Newhaven and in search of adventure rowed *Vixen*'s heavy dinghy to Lewes to sup; rowing back at 'a great pace', no doubt with the tide.

On they went and William dined with his brother, Hugh, on board the almost brand-new majestic class battleship *Illustrious*. Erskine was anxious to join them but was unable to find a safe berth in Gosport, so he stayed aboard *Vixen*.

Vixen became a Solent boat and seldom left the waters of the Wight.

Comparing these to the Thames Estuary and the east coast rivers, Erskine remarked that the southern cruising ground was 'a gayer spirit and the scenery far more varied. Cliffs, hills, or rolling downs generally provide a background, more or less distant, to every view. There are rocky coves and sandy beaches, as well as secluded tidal creeks and great natural harbours. There is one veritable forest beside a quantity of rich woodland. The sun glances on blue, if not on translucently blue water, and on livelier land colours; navigation is far more varied and interesting, and havens far more numerous.' [2]

In these two short descriptions, his eye had dissected the view from the sea and his pen recorded the qualities of the two principal and popular cruising grounds within steam reach of those who lived and worked in the capital. Three-quarters of a century on, the descriptions still hold good.

Erskine kept *Vixen* at Picketts Yard, Southampton, in the tradition of *Marguerite*, again using the Crown Hotel for his breakfast before catching the 8.48 to London. He would weekend by the 4.55 pm train on the Friday, perhaps anchoring in Ashlett Creek, near the head of the Southampton Water, for the night. His companions were John Horsbrugh-Porter, later Sir John and senior clerk in the House of Commons; an unidentifiable 'Turner' (without a Christian name); J. H. Garland, an American who lived on Broadway and owned a steam yacht; Alfred Hull, later Sir Alfred, who retired as chief assistant solicitor at the Treasury and was to become, after Erskine's death, chairman of the Northern Ireland Civil Service Committee; and, of course, William Le Fanu.

Vixen's Solent summer ended early. Erskine devoted the weekend of 10 August to putting the yacht to bed and sailed from Picketts Yard to the Hamble, where he 'landed to interview Moody about laying up the boat, arranged terms and started laying up gear,' including the removal, once again, of all the ballast.

The House rose on 12 August, the day *Vixen* was pulled from the water. It was an early lay-up, especially, as he wrote to his friend, Walter Runciman, 'All this year

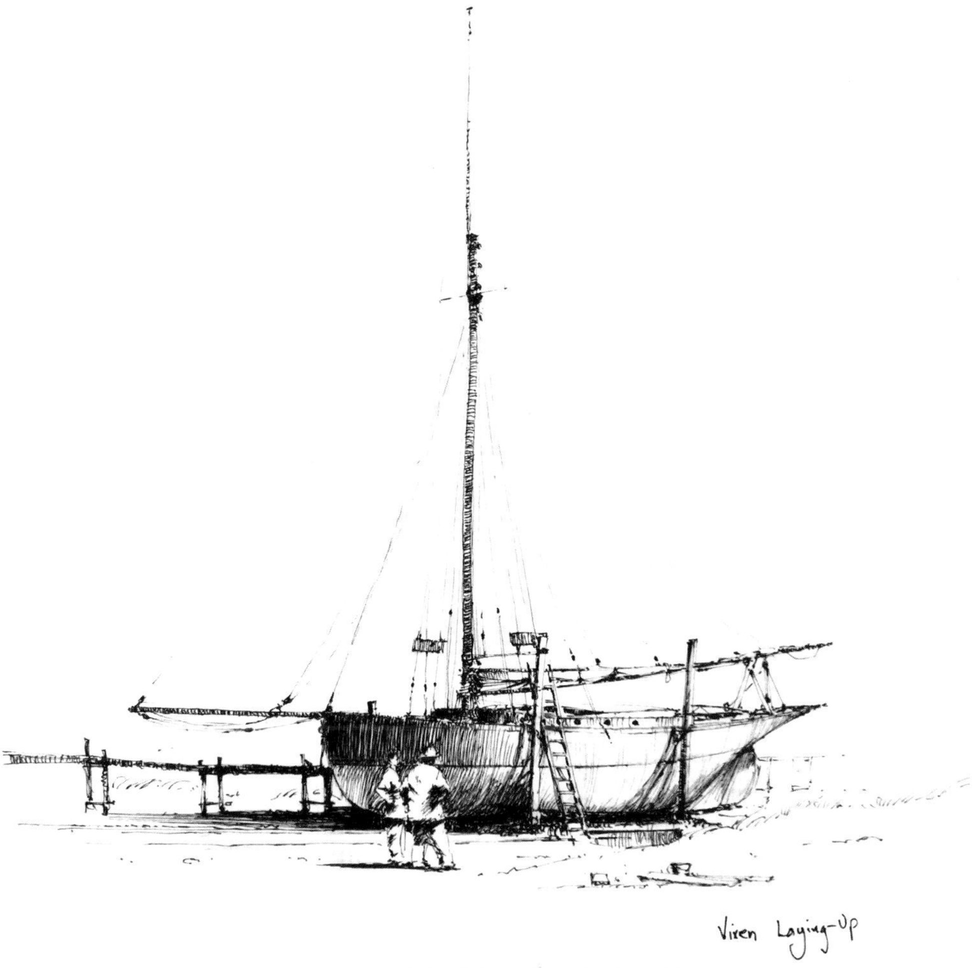

Vixen laying-up at Moody's Yard on the Hamble River

I have had the sea-thirst on me.' Because of this, he had arranged, through his friend Runcy, to go by steamer to the West Indies. It was a way of quenching the sea-thirst and certainly increased his sea time for the year. This was the original object of the 1897 voyage – to follow the sun as the English summer drew to a close and to go to seas where the weather was kinder to the Corinthian sailor.

Erskine left from Liverpool aboard 'a small and very slow boat' – SS *West Indian*, bound for Trinidad. He wrote of his experiences in a series of letters to his sisters in which he managed to capture the flavour of all about him in a few words. It was this ability to entertain his sisters, and no doubt their friends, that added power to his pen. The growing mastery had been polished by log keeping and writing of the doings of *Marguerite* in the *Cruising Club Journal.* His economy of language did not hinder the translation of eye or his powers of description. The 'Bicycle Ride Across Ireland' (see Appendix, p. 204) had been a start in this, just as *Shulah* and *Marguerite* had tutored the skills needed for the proper management of small boats.

The letters home from the West Indies were to be succeeded by letters from other parts of the world. A collection of these from another continent was to make him a successful author.

The West Indian adventure lasted from October to early December. In a letter to 'Dearest Girls' (his sisters), he painted a picture in words of his companions.[3]

> *But I haven't introduced all the characters to you yet. There is Mrs McCarthy, a most good-natured little party with perhaps a shade too rich a 'County Cork' accent: and Miss M., golden-haired, eighteen or thereabouts, and a very good sort with no rot about her. We all got on very well together and often read aloud – Martin Chuzzlewit and Kipling, chess, etc.*

Erskine enjoyed Kipling. He used to read *The Anchor Song* and others in a nautical vein, to the red-haired Welsh captain, when not discussing the politics of the moment and 'giving him a fine, sound imperial policy on the Cretan, Egyptian, Armenian and other questions: We did the Dreyfus Affair last night.' That was a matter of the day. Alfred Dreyfus, a French Army officer of Jewish background, was accused of spying for Germany and sentenced to life imprisonment on Devil's Island. Emile Zola and others campaigned for his release, but they had to wait until 1904 before the convictions were quashed.

Erskine went on: 'I always find seafaring men very interesting – their minds are clear, broad and tolerant. Having lived at large all their life and in all climes and among all races they have no narrow grooves in their mind and have, I think, an extraordinary power to "see life steadily and see it whole".' He may have extended this to the purser: 'A dandified youth of twenty who sets up for culture, having read *all*

Marie Corelli's novels: he is really a very nice young chap and supplies me with an inexhaustible supply of unconscious amusement.'

The ship barely made five knots with foul weather on the bow. 'I have offered to race her in *Vixen*, but I think the Captain is afraid,' he wrote with a smile to his three sisters. Sybil was then twenty-seven, Dulcie twenty-five and Constance twenty-three. They had left the shelter of Glendalough and were preparing to live with Erskine in a new flat, at 16 Cheyne Gardens.

The SS *West Indian* wheezed to the harbour of Barbados, delayed by the 'vagaries of a feed pump'. The old ship then limped on to Trinidad. From that island, within sight of the shores of South America, Erskine's purpose for the trip was fulfilled – or almost fulfilled – by a voyage under sail to Grenada in 'one of the little negro-manned sailing vessels which ply a humble and precarious trade between the islands'. Erskine had wanted to charter one of these boats for his own use and had discussed this with Runcy, but it was not to be, so he made the best of the inter-island trader *Faith*, enjoying the dog house, or kennel as he called it, as his cabin. Many years later and for the benefit of his *Times* readers, he remembered the scene:[4]

> *In a universal chatter and laughter, we had our various meals by the light of the moon, while* Faith *yawed unsteadily through half the points of the compass. Someone was giving casual attention to the helm; someone else was hovering wistfully about the side lights, which seemed to be the victims of an intermittent disorder; but the general impression to my eye was that of a party of children out for a frolic, without any question of a serious commercial enterprise. Before long, showers began to fall, and I resorted to the 'dog-house' for refuge. Once inside, in spite of an uncomfortable sensation of being irrevocably sealed up, I was soon dozing.*

Erskine had hoped that his brother Henry would join him in Trinidad for the voyage under West Indian canvas, but he did not arrive, going to British Columbia instead, joining the ''98 Gold Rush'.[5]

To the girls he wrote, 'This is a wonderful land and I see stranger things every day.'[6]

Hospitality was boundless but viewed from Government House, where he had been bidden by introduction, 'It is too grand and respectable and you have to wear stick-up collars which in the tropics are absurd.' Kipling helped, 'if you would like to realise these places', and Erskine quoted:

To the cool of our deep verandas,
To the blaze of our jewelled main,
To the night, to the palms in the moonlight,
And the firefly in the cane.

He added another line in a postscript to his sisters: 'On from island unto island to the gateways of the day'. His friend Basil Williams thought this indicated 'the love of adventure always latent in his nature'.[7]

The House returned on 7 February and the session ended on 28 March. He was back at the table in good time.

Vixen beckoned and on the 30th Erskine took the train to Southampton and on to Bursledon by trap, where he discovered that '*Vixen* had been fitted out by Moody very well. Painted as before outside, but inside the graining abolished and white and green paint substituted. Centre-plate case effectively caulked. A new medium jib and new topsail and new crosstrees and new halyards. All ready for sea when I arrived.' It may be that Erskine took the opportunity to have the false keel removed at this time, though this could have been done at the end of 1899, before the yacht was measured by the Registrar of British Ships.

Frank Cowper, the author of *Sailing Tours,* a much-valued pilot aboard both *Marguerite* and *Vixen,* was at Moody's too, fitting out his yacht *Undine.* They had met before and he went down the river as far as Hamble aboard *Vixen,* returning by dinghy.

Erskine's companion on that spring cruise, in the closing year of the century, was a man who was to suggest a scheme that was later included in and gained force through *The Riddle.*

Herbert Warington-Smyth was a natural friend for they enjoyed the world alike. Herbert had been at Trinity and was a member of the Cruising Club. In May of that year Erskine had been invited to serve on their committee. Herbert adored the sea and later wrote that 'Small-boat sailing is not a mere thought. It is a Way of Life. It is not a game which can be gauged by the multitude, written up by the press and paid for in an afternoon.'[8]

Erskine and Herbert shared the same adventurous and pioneering streak. The latter went to Indo-China soon after leaving Trinity and published an account of his experiences in two books, *Journeying on the Upper Me Kong* (1895) and *Five Years in Siam* (1899). Erskine would have counted himself lucky to have shared *Vixen*, in the space of twenty-four hours, with both Frank Cowper and Herbert Warington-Smyth.

Herbert was keen to discuss with his friend the rebirth of the Royal Naval Artillery Volunteers, or a new form of volunteer service, following what he and others thought was a disgraceful betrayal when they were disbanded in 1891. To Herbert this was nothing less than a crusade and it was not long before Erskine shared the same view. There should be a place for anyone who knew Britain's coasts like a book to be made best use of in a naval reserve. Herbert's interests were more obviously deep in the land. He had graduated from the post of mineral adviser to the Office of Woods, the forerunner of the Forestry Commission, became the director-general of the Department of Mines, Siam, and then the secretary to the Siamese delegation in London.

Fog enveloped them as *Vixen* groped her way into Newtown on the north coast of the Isle of Wight. It is a place of tales, many true but, blessedly, more pure legend.

Herbert remembered the *Vixen* weekend long after, and wrote to the *Yachting Monthly* in 1932 that he particularly recalled the centre-board: 'it was a terrible. weight, but Childers thought nothing of it.'[9]

Beaulieu was another favoured place and Erskine and Smyth went there too on this idyllic weekend. Erskine walked to Exbury village, through beautiful woods, to telegram Le Fanu, but 'it was Sunday and the place utterly deserted, so I had to pencil it on a dirty scrap of paper, folded round a shilling and drop it in the letterbox'. They dined that evening on *Saunterer*, belonging then to John Simpson, a fellow member of the Cruising Club, and afloat to this day.

The telegram reached its destination and William Le Fanu joined at Gosport. He took his best series of photographs on 30 April and so provided a fine black and white record of *Vixen* at the end of her short career under Erskine's flag. Perhaps it is fitting that the log ends that weekend.

Clouds were gathering over South Africa. The shooting of Tom Edgar, a British subject, by the Boer police at the end of 1898 intensified feeling among the British, both in South Africa and at home. Milner demanded the franchise of the Uitlanders. He thought that firmness would convince, but Kruger had bought cannon from Germany with the reparations given by Britain for the Jameson Raid and was not going to hand his country over to the British settlers by the ballot box. On 9 November, he issued an ultimatum which Britain could not accept. War was then inevitable.

Parliament was recalled for a short session between 17 and 24 October and immediately after this Erskine and William Le Fanu took off for France on a bicycling holiday. They, like the majority of the country, were outraged by what was going on, but took the view that it would not affect them personally.

If there ever was a calm before a storm in anyone's life, it was Erskine's short bicycle ride in France. He wrote to Dulcie from the Hotel de Lion d'Or, Souillac, on 28 October, a hundred or so miles north of where the Canal du Midi cuts through southwestern France. For Dulcie's benefit, he was glorying in the sight of Domme overlooking the river:

> *Imagine a hill about 300 ft high, almost sheer on all sides and positively overhanging on the riverside and on the top, compact in grey ramparts a lovely old town, each street a perfect vista of ancient carved window porches and chimneys, with flowers and vines edging it and dark sunburnt women knitting in the sun and brown children playing. It was stunning and well worth the fearful climb; such a glorious view over the Dordogne Valley. Dejeuner at an inn and then on again by a small mountain by-road (always perfect like a billiard table for riding) across the Dordogne and threading thickly wooded glens, often suddenly coming on a 13th century village with super façades over its pig styes and carved attic windows, and so up the valley, but high above it to*

> *a strange region of these precipitous limestone heights again, to Souillac, a little town actually rather commonplace for this part of the world.*

Again, it was a collage, a letter to be added to when time permitted. Erskine had an eye for windows, porches and façades, developed from the days of *Marguerite* and the visit to Courseulles.

He could not shut out the wider world. Worries had intruded into the world of *Vixen* at Kiel and more evidently this time, for in the final paragraph he added: 'We get belated news (and it reads bad) of war through the reptile press of this country which is venomously hostile to us, though the people we meet are, of course, very nice to us.' On the 31st, he wrote to his great-aunt Flora Priestley in much the same way, of cathedral columns, water lilies, cabbage beds and statues, of landlords in blue smocks and the 'whisper of pretty little trout streams like the Annamoe'. His thoughts were never far from Glendalough, though he went on: 'we are anxious about the Transvaal, but find that the papers give a good deal of news here, of course venomously hostile. I am collecting cartoons on the subject and have one or two very choice ones.' If any further key is needed to his mood, his postscript on a postcard of 2 November to the girls, provides the underline: 'Much depressed by this terrible news from the Natal.'

Their return to England brought no better tidings – rather the reverse. In that 'Black Week' of December 1899, General Lord Methuen was defeated at Magersfontein and General Gatacre at Stormberg. General Sir Redvers Buller, who came out as commander-in-chief, failed to relieve Ladysmith and lost eleven guns at his defeat at Colenso.

Erskine, troubled, went to Glendalough, as usual, for Christmas and soon after received a letter from Basil Williams suggesting that he volunteer. Basil was already a member of the Honourable Artillery Company (HAC) and they had formed an emergency reserve, the CIV, the City of London Imperial Volunteers. Erskine signed on at Armoury House on 5 January 1900, giving his age as twenty-nine years, six months, and his address (the new one) as 20 Carlyle Mansions, London SW1.'[10] It was not easy to obtain a place in the CIV, as the battery was already at full strength, but through determination Erskine managed to become a trooper, joining the same section as Basil Williams. Men were urgently required in South Africa, for the Boers could put more than 50,000 men in the field and Britain had less than half that and had already lost men and materials. Guns and gunners were in particular demand and so, with under a month's training, the battery embarked on the trooper SS *Montford* at London's Albert Docks, reaching Cape Town on 27 February 1900. The new commander-in-chief, Field Marshal Lord Roberts, had arrived there on 10 January and Ladysmith was relieved the day after SS *Montford* docked. However, much work remained to be done.

Basil Williams remembered his bombardier friend and the South African days in his sketch, written as a tribute after Erskine's death.

> *It was nine months or so, when we were almost inseparable companions, that I came fully to realise the nobility and sweetness of his nature, his absolute disregard for himself and at the same time his dogged perseverance in carrying out the job to which he had set his hand. At first he was not considered a very promising soldier, for he not only had to wear glasses – in those days an almost unheard of singularity in one of the rank and file – but he also had a limp in one leg which was liable to bad pains, due to a severe attack of sciatica contracted on a holiday in the west of Ireland; nor, though used to a country life, had he ever had practice in the care of horses, his chief occupation as an artillery driver.*[11]

Mafeking was relieved on 17 May; Roberts entered Johannesburg on the 28th, and chased Kruger from Pretoria on 5 June. The tide had changed.

The CIV were engaged in another part of the campaign, as Williams remembered:

> *When we got up country and were engaged in the more serious work of chasing the elusive De Wet, and rust was allowed to gather on harness, spurs and leg irons, we still managed on most nights to doss out together under the clear South African sky; and there are few better tests of a man's real nature than to*

> *be doing so for months together, as I was able to do with Childers. Both of us, who came out as hide-bound Tories, began to tend towards more liberal ideas, partly from the jolly democratic company we were in, but chiefly, I think, from our own endless discussions on politics and life generally.*

Politics occasionally surfaced in Erskine's own diary and show this change. While at Bethlehem in July he wrote:

> *Many of the farmhouses are smoking ruins, the enemy, after annexation, being rebels according to the law, and not belligerents; but it seems to me that such a policy is to use a legal fiction for an oppressive end, for it is quite clear that this part of the Orange River colony has never been conquered.*

A note at the bottom of the page qualified what he had just written:

> *I leave this as I wrote it, but drivers are not politicians, and doubtless there are special circumstances, such as treachery, concealed arms or sniping to justify what at the best must be a doubtful policy; for a burnt farm means a desperate farmer.*

Perhaps remembering his days on the German coast, he noted that 'The remains we found in the gun emplacement at Slabbert's Nek were those of Lieutenant Muller, a German artillerist.' He later recorded: 'A very large proportion of the Boer force were foreigners – French, Germans, Dutch, Russians, Norwegians.'

Erskine's active service and the few half-political thoughts that were allowed to escape in his diary came to an end on 24 August. He had suffered a veldt-sore on the sole of his foot and was sent back to the tented Imperial Yeomanry Hospital in Pretoria where a fortnight later, totally unexpectedly, he met his brother Henry, who had joined Strathcona's Horse, and having been wounded in the foot was convalescing within sight.

Erskine left Cape Town on the *Aurania* with his battery on 8 October 1900.

He wrote in his diary during the return voyage via St Vincent that 'We can fairly claim to have proved, or helped to prove, that Volunteer Artillery can be of use in war; though how much skill and labour is involved in its sudden mobilisation only the few able men who organised ours in January last can know.' He must have recalled his long talks with Herbert Warington-Smyth about the need for a volunteer force. The CIV battery was proof enough of the effectiveness of the idea. General Lord Roberts, his commander-in-chief, had similar views and was to be forceful in support of the need for properly organised and trained volunteers to supplement the regulars in both the Army and Navy.

Lord Roberts returned to England in the autumn too. It was generally believed that the war was over. Two Boer republics were in British hands and their presidents had fled. The British government little realised at that time the way commanders like De Wet could continue the fight with lightning strikes. They knew the ground and were still well supplied. Erskine, though, understood only too well and Davies was to suggest the probable success of such tactics in the salt-water world behind the Frisian Islands. He admired De Wet's unbending determination.

A hero's welcome awaited the CIV in London, but it was a proposal of a different sort that was to launch Erskine as a celebrated author. Reginald Smith, senior partner in Smith Elder & Co., the publishers, was waiting for him when the trooper docked at Southampton on 5 November.

Erskine's diary had been sent home in instalments and passed round the family and selected friends. His sisters had developed this method of spreading family news over the years. Letters written uncomfortably on the bottom boards of *Mad Agnes*, on *Vixen*'s table secured to the centre-board case, through his bicycling days in France, to blood-letting on the sands of the veldt, were written in paragraphs, separated by time and posted whenever the opportunity arrived. Churchill developed his capture of events with despatches to the daily newspapers. In Childers' case they were for the benefit of his family, but he was as keen to satisfy his readers as Churchill was the subscribers of the *Daily Telegraph* or *Mail*. Erskine took every opportunity. His lines were written by the light of his storm-lantern, in the shade of gun limber, or the sparse protection of the African bush. Basil Williams writes that he even managed to write a few in the middle of battle. Perhaps that was when he wrote of his thoughts under fire: 'I never can connect shells and bullets with a malicious sender, nor do I bear any grudge against the people I am helping to kill.'

It was this directness, the bright pictures that he painted in words with highlights and shadows, that were so easy to read aloud and which enabled the reader to imagine that he was there, alongside the British soldier in his pain or triumph. Reginald Smith could see this and proposed that he make the diary into a book. Erskine wasted no time.

In the Ranks of the CIV became a best-seller and led to Erskine being invited to write, with Basil Williams, the official account of the Honourable Artillery Company's part in the campaign. Much later, under Leo Amery, his brother's friend, he was responsible for the fifth volume of *The Times History of the War in South Africa*.

Erskine did not allow his success with the pen to prevent him from returning to the clerks' table in the House of Commons. Basil Williams also came back and they took with them their newfound outlook, the liberal tendency that had been born and nurtured by their recent experiences together. They would have been disappointed at the poor showing of the Liberal Party at 'the Khaki Election', which returned Lord Salisbury as Prime Minister. The name came from the new colour of Army uniform that was adopted after the Boers made a bullseye out of the old red cloth.

In a letter to Basil Williams of 5 January 1901, he writes, 'I have been irritated and disgusted by the press and other ignorant persons towards the Boers. It was worth going out there if only to learn to respect them. Otherwise the excesses of the anti-boers would have made me a pro-boer, I believe!'[12]

Erskine would have also noticed that the reported Anglophobia in Germany throughout the Boer War was producing its own reaction in London. Anti-German feeling was rising. He reported on the anti-British feeling in France before going to Africa, but if he had stepped through the doors of the Athenaeum Club on his return, he would have seen a display of anti-British feeling cut from the continental press.[13]

The first few days of 1901 saw a return to better relations between Germany and Britain. The Kaiser did a great deal to improve matters by spending some time with his grandmother in her last hours. Soon after her death in January, the press took up the anti-German cry again. 'Calchas' Q. L. Gavin) in the *Fortnightly Review* for that month saw the growing menace of the German fleet and called for a naval base on Britain's North Sea coast as a precaution. Others were beginning to suggest the possibility of invasion of England by Germany.[14]

Erskine was in Scotland, or North Britain as it was then known by the Post Office, on 8 January and wrote to his great-aunt Flora Priestley, then at Rapallo, from the Inveran Hotel at Invershin, Sutherland. This letter gave the first news of *The Riddle of the Sands*. Erskine and William Le Fanu were shooting with the Thompsons. Mrs Thompson was a Smith, the daughter of W. H. Smith, and a close relation of Reginald. He did not post the letter until he reached his home village of Annamoe on 11 January and it took four days to reach Italy.

Erskine says: 'I haven't begun that book yet! I forgot before coming away to get the diary of that cruise from the flat. An idea has struck me that a story of which I have the germ might be worked into it as a setting. Do you think that that would be a good plan – supposing of course the story was a possible one?' Flora knew all about the epic cruise, so was in a good position to advise. He ended his letter by mentioning that 'there is a third edition of "In the Ranks" and a lot of reviews, none bad, except *The Standard* – "tedious" – and some very good.'[15]

The surviving manuscript of *The Riddle of the Sands* starts on 13 December 1901. There may have been earlier attempts as the copy is unusually neat with few scratchings out, but then all Erskine's writings were like that. He wrote in a fine, small hand, executed with a narrow nib which occasionally sent a burst of ink across the page. Clearly he thought, then wrote, rather than writing and thinking at the same time.

Erskine went from Scotland to Glendalough and then on to the Rectory at Athy, Co. Kildare. He had heard the rumour that another battery of the CIV was to be formed and he expressed his worries in a letter to Basil Williams on 19 January 1901, showing an unsettled frame of mind:

> *There have been allusions to activity on the part of the H.A.C. but nothing definite. I have been for some time growing more and more depressed and irritated about the whole thing, fervently wishing we had never come home and cursing the short-sightedness of those who sent us. For my own part I should be happy to take the veldt again, at any rate if you would come too, but for many reasons it's very difficult now. We have come back and been discharged. Would Milman* [A. J. S. Milman, Clerk of the House of Commons] *give us leave? Besides that, it's rather a cruel thing to break all one's ties again after reforming them, yet it is exasperating to think that we belong to a pampered class in the Army who came home in the very middle of the trouble, especially with Bryn Roberts* [Liberal MP] *about. My brother too is there with no likelihood of leaving. I don't know what you think, but on the whole I don't think I should ask leave to go again unless the battery was formed again with an appeal to old members to rejoin; anything short of that would scarcely justify one. If you hear anything of such an event could you send me a card to Annamoe, Greystones (because that sec. is such a hopeless ass).*[16]

Erskine was back a little late for the sitting of the House which had commenced on 23 January and which lasted until the beginning of April. Perhaps to rid himself of these flutters of uncertainty and bouts of depression, he turned again to his boat. *Vixen* had been laid up at Moody's yard for over a year and the rigours of the veldt may have made him less keen to bow before that inconveniently large piece of furniture, the centre-board, or again hump out those small pigs of lead when hopelessly aground or before putting the yacht to bed. The one thing that military service teaches beyond all else is that any fool can be uncomfortable and that steps should be taken accordingly. He may have considered alterations to improve the comfort below when he went to see the yacht in April. He may have been in this frame of mind when Moody showed him the ageing *Sunbeam*, then twenty-seven years old.

Erskine, much attracted to the old yacht, formed a syndicate to buy her with William Le Fanu and Alfred Dennis; the latter had been with him on *Vixen* and was a fellow member of the Savile. They all lived in Carlyle Mansions, Erskine at 20 and Basil and Alfred at 23. By that time all were members of the Cruising Club. Alexander Moody's firm, as part of the deal, agreed to purchase *Dulcibella* (the former *Vixen*).

The old cutter is so much a part of the story behind *The Riddle* and there has been so much speculation, both over her past and particularly the days after Childers disposed of her, that it is worth looking briefly at what happened to the yacht after the spring of 1901. Remember, Childers renamed the yacht *Dulcibella* after she was registered as *Vixen* in 1899.

Alexander Moody wrote that his firm carried out alterations to *Dulcibella* and removed her iron drop keel before selling her to Mr George Newbury for, it is believed, £12.00. Newbury used her at Hill Head Haven at weekends as a houseboat. He built a gazebo on her coach-roof and was often seen enjoying a cup of tea and sea peace. He was a pillar of the local nonconformist church, living then at Salisbury Green, off Holly Hill Lane. News of the yacht's sad fate reached the Registrar of British Ships on 27 November 1906, and with meticulous care the entry was endorsed: 'Closed – Vessel converted into a houseboat and registry no longer required. Advice received from the unregistered owner. Sale confirmed by the registered owner. Certificate of registry delivered up and cancelled.' As far as the Registrar was concerned that was that.

Dulcibella returned to the Hamble after a few years and was laid up on the mud on the east side of the river half a mile below Bursledon. Commander E. Eldred saw her there and in his article for the April 1924 number of the *Yachting Monthly* – 'The Derelicts of the Hamble River' – he wrote:

> *A little below the 'New Hope' on a patch of reedy marsh and hauled up as high as possible, is the hull of a small yacht burdened with a most preposterous and cumbersome superstructure, a home-made-looking erection of the roughest carpentry. This derelict is more or less vaguely reputed to be 'Dulcibella', the vessel figuring in that very popular story: 'The Riddle of the Sands', by Erskine Childers. I have before me at this moment, a letter written by Mr. Erskine*

The last of *Dulcibella*, ex-*Vixen*

> *Childers not long before his execution confirming this as true, and adding that he bought her in 1897 under the name of the 'Vixen'. She was very strongly built, having been a lifeboat with three skins of teak. In 1900 [actually 1901] she was sold to a stranger for £12. Perhaps she should not be numbered with the derelicts, being still to some degree habitable. I have seen vessels stranded on this marsh, one would think finally, and yet hauled off and fitted out, presenting a very different picture a few months later.*

Commander Eldred was to be proved right, for *Dulcibella* was hauled off. She was bought in 1932 by Claude 'Happy' Hapgood. In November of that year she was taken to Wootton Creek on the Isle of Wight where he and Jim Young had their 'beer money yard'. The phrase belonged to Jim Young for both partners used to work during the summer – Claude Hapgood as a yachting correspondent for the *Daily Telegraph* covering the eight-metre and smaller classes and Jim Young as a yacht skipper. They relied on boat-building and repair work for winter employment. Apparently Claude Hapgood used to pull from his pocket a copy of *The Riddle of the Sands* at lunch-time and gradually they worked their way through the book, Claude Hapgood reading extracts between sandwiches.

No wonder he was anxious to be the owner of *Dulcibella*. He recorded in *Yachting*

World of 26 May 1933 how he bought the houseboat from Mr Moody, who again acted as agent. On his way back to Wootton, 'Happy' went on:

> *Full of hot tea and buns, I lay back in the car enroute for South Sea Pier and the gentle motion sent me off to sleep, and in my dreams I wondered what I should do with her. The first vision pictured her fitting out as a privateer, and we started off, under full sail, to engage the model of the 'Victory' in Portsmouth Harbour. Then I saw her on a plinth in Trafalgar Square. I was just about to be presented with a knighthood as a fitting reward for saving her for the nation, when I felt somebody prod me in the ribs, and a voice shouted in my ear: 'Are you going to catch the boat back to Ryde or sleep in the car all night?'*

Returning to reality, Claude Hapgood towed the yacht to Wootton Creek the following weekend and noted that she 'did not leak a cupful'.

The yard was busy, little work was done to *Dulcibella* and she remained beside the slip. Quite a number of people used to come to pay their respects. Donal Dunne, the artist, painted her and recently made an etching of the watercolour. The correspondent of the *Portsmouth Evening News* wrote on 12 May 1933 that 'her hull is leprous with flaking paint, her deck-boards are bleaching silver-grey, her cabin portholes are cracked and smashed. Her name is the *Dulcibella* – a name linked with one of the strangest adventures twentieth century Europe has known.'

It was becoming clear to those who visited her that if something were not done soon there would be little enough to remember, photograph or record.

So, in 1937, the Dulcibella Memorial Committee was set up chaired by James Rogers of Ryde, together with W. Hodgkinson as vice-chairman, C. J. Evans as treasurer and C. H. Gibson as secretary. A subscription list was opened on 16 November that year. Some strange proposals were put forward. One suggested that the yacht should be cut in half, so that the bow and stern could be upended to act as shelters on the sea front at Ryde. However, the plan adopted was that she should be restored and placed on a plinth. Molly Childers, Erskine's widow, recalled that Mr Rogers' committee suggested that she should be displayed at Ryde on 'the tip of a narrow triangle of land with roads on each side – not far from the shore'. The *Evening News* reported later, though, that 'although several councillors were on the committee, Ryde Borough Council cold-shouldered a proposition that they should take the yacht under their wing.'[18]

Happy Hapgood did little work on the yacht either. Dick Stower, a partner in Laurent Giles & Partners and a kinsman of Happy's, who was responsible for the 1979 film version of *Dulcibella*, created from the Royal National Lifeboat Institution Brook lifeboat, *Susan Ashley*, remembered why. '"Happy" had a mania for buying old "tore-outs": the mud berths, which were plentiful around the yard, were full of old yachts in various stages of decomposition, which he had bought usually for a "song" with some vague idea of "doing up". The *Dulcibella* was beyond all doubt Happy's most prized possession, and he had great plans for her, but somehow or another, as with all his old wrecks, he never got round to it.'[19]

Happy did not spend much on her but he had only paid £3.00 for the near derelict to begin with and sold the lead pigs for £4.00. He sold the yard toTed Watson, who lived on the old 'plank on edge' racing yacht *Valkyrie*. *Dulcibella* was part of the 'good will'. Ted Watson remembered that she was a great nuisance and thought of burning her. He was grateful when the Dulcibella Committee came along to save her.[20] Molly Childers suggested names of people who might give money for the restoration work, including her family and friends, and small amounts began to flow in.

However, in April 1938, Herbert Hanson, the honorary secretary of the Cruising Association, and a well-known yachtsman, wrote an article in the Club's *Bulletin*, stating that *Dulcibella*, purchased on behalf of the fund, was a counterfeit, so casting doubt on Claude Hapgood's well-founded claim that his *Dulcibella* was Erskine Childers' 1897 *Vixen*, the yacht behind *The Riddle of the Sands*.

The article caused the funds to dry up immediately. The total had reached £45. The secretary of the Dulcibella Committee wrote to Molly Childers that 'our plan to get public subscriptions was frustrated by reasons of the identity of the boat having been challenged by a gentleman, influential in yachting matters, and although we secured proof, the war came and prevented anything being done to accomplish our objectives.'[21]

The proof Gibson referred to was obtained on 25 May 1938 from a 'Statutory Declaration by Alexander Moody relating to the identity of the yacht *Dulcibella*', given before Stanley Allen, a commissioner of oaths, at Moody's Yard, Swanwick Shore. Alexander Moody traced the history of the yacht, as he knew it, and ended with:

> *There is no doubt that the yacht now known as 'Dulcibella' at the late Mr. Claude Hapgood's yard at Wootton Creek, Isle of Wight was formerly Mr. Erskine Childers' 'Vixen' and that a few years ago my firm broke up her dinghy which had the name 'Vixen' quite plainly cut in the transom and I make this solemn declaration conscientiously believing the same to be true and by virtue of the provisions of the Statutory Declarations Act, 1835.*

That should have settled the matter, *Dulcibella* could not stay at Wootton after Hapgood's death, so she was in need of a safe berth. One was offered by the Lymington Slipway and Engineering Company. The directors, Alderman Jack Beagley, one-time mayor of Lymington, C. E. Linaker and Osmond Hill, heard of *Dulcibella*'s plight and came to the rescue. They had the Bridge Yard up the Lymington River, near the causeway. Hill and Linaker went to Wootton in August 1939 in the yard launch, a twenty-six-foot lifeboat powered by an old Morris car engine, to collect her. She nearly foundered on the return voyage and they had to beach her in Osborne Bay, just off Queen Victoria's bathing hut.

Returning the following day with the foreman shipwright, A. A. Raines, they were met by an old colonel. 'He moaned on about the fact the beach was private,' Raines remembered, 'but he cheered up and took an interest in the salvage operation when he learnt the identity of the wreck.' Raines managed to repair the nine-inch hole in her bottom with canvas, battens and grease and he and the boy Wheeler, whom he had taken along as a mate, remained aboard to pump, though little water came in, for the voyage to Lymington.[22]

The yard were to renew the decks, fit out the interior and re-rig her to look as near as possible as she had in her sailing days. She was to be restored 'to the appearance of the boat as she was when Erskine Childers knew her', *Portsmouth Evening News* told their readers on 11 August 1939. The Dulcibella Memorial Society undertook to pay the berth rent.

The Second World War came on 3 September and C. H. Gibson remembered that 'labour shortage and restrictions made preservation of the boat out of the question, that point had been accepted by the Committee and further, an article in the *Portsmouth Evening News* failed to get a solitary enquiry.'[23] Group Captain F. C. Griffiths was stationed at RAF Christchurch in March 1942. He had read *The Riddle* in 1920 and was reminded of it by a short piece about *Dulcibella* being at Lymington in the *Evening Standard* of 21 August 1939. His account of what followed is worth repeating, for it demonstrates the interest that those devoted to *The Riddle* often feel when discovering a reminder of their favourite book.

> *Being stationed at RAF Christchurch in March 1942, I visited Lymington to try and find her. At the first yard I called at, the one nearest the Toll Bridge, I struck lucky. An ancient mariner with a broad Dorset accent told me that I'd find 'Dulcibella' 'where the bomb dropped'. She was easy to find. A ten-tonner alongside her had had her counter blown clean off, but 'Dulcibella', apart from having her cover blown off, was virtually unscathed.*
>
> *It was a tremendous thrill climbing aboard her. You felt that, even if the whole of 'The Riddle' isn't true, standing there on what remained of her deck I had no difficulty in visualising Davies and Carruthers in Ekken Sound ... 'down this exquisite sea lane we glided till it ended in a broad mere, where our sails, which had been shivering and complaining, filled into contented silence'. I was brought back to reality by the sound of the air raid siren and in the miserable March weather, in fading light, I examined the inside. The forepeak, with the sliding door on the starboard side [he afterwards said it must have been port] was exactly as described in the book. The rest of her accommodation was fairly well gutted. She had no floors and the massive keelson was exposed. The filled in slot where the centre-board had been was of a size which inferred that it must have been 'beastly heavy'.*[24]

Doug Baverstock, the Royal Lymington Yacht Club boatman, who was employed at the Bridge Yard when *Dulcibella* was there, remembered that she started to 'sit down' during the War, that is to say her fastenings had begun to go and her bilges had slumped a little over her keel.

The proprietors sold the yard to Ian Carr when he left the Army after the war. He started to build the Lymington Slipway five-tanners at the end of the 1940s. Carr was contacted by Douglas Dixon, the author of *The King's Sailing Master*, as the latter had begun to take an interest in the preservation of *Dulcibella* in 1948. Carr's attitude was plain, and Commander Dixon quoted this in a letter to the *Yachting Monthly* in March 1948. 'Ian Carr states,' he wrote, 'that *Dulcibella* is in his yard. In fact she has become somewhat of an embarrassment to me. There is enough junk lying about in shipyards as it is, and to the average visitor *Dulcibella* in her present state looks little more than that.' Dixon went on, 'I do trust that this may now catch the eye of the pre-war Dulcibella Memorial Committee.' It did and a despairing Gibson wrote to the *Portsmouth Evening News:*

> *The next few days will decide the fate of Erskine Childers' famous yacht 'Dulcibella', heroine of 'The Riddle of the Sands'. The storage space at Lymington, where she has been laid up for about ten years, will be no longer available after August the 13th and unless another berth is offered by then, she is to be broken up. The Dulcibella Memorial Committee, which is trying to preserve the yacht, hope that some such offer may be forthcoming in time.*

It was not.

Ben Boxall, who used to own the Lymington Sail and Tent Company, held that soon after this, *Dulcibella* was cremated in the steam box used for bending frames and planks of yachts and that her iron keel still lies somewhere buried in the wasteland adjacent.[25]

Vixen, now *Dulcibella*, had lasted sixty-eight years. She had begun her life serving sailors in peril and had ended her days fuelling a steam box that others might go to sea.

Herbert Hanson, who muddied the water before the war, had another go just

Soundings

after, questioning the yacht's credentials in a letter, this time to the *Yachting Monthly*. In March 1945 he said, 'Belgian yachtsmen emphatically assert, on evidence of eye-witnesses, that *Vixen I* was lost on her voyage in 1898.' He infers that Happy Hapgood's historic yacht was *Vixen II*. He, of course, did not know at that time that *Vixen*'s log had survived and that Erskine had had a relatively pleasant, though foggy, sail from Terschelling to Dover.

Hanson was worried about draft and other measurements, and had profile and deck plans taken off in 1938, which he published with his letter to the *Yachting Monthly*. He had not thought, though, of the possibility of a false keel, removed before the yacht was measured by the Registrar of British Ships and certainly before his plans were drawn. R. M. Bowker repeats these doubts in his *Unique Edition of The Riddle of the Sands*.[26] Again, he had not known of the account of the 1898 voyage. Most of Bowker's queries have been answered too, but he has a point over ballast. Erskine wrote in the *Yachting Monthly* magazine of 1898 that 'Her ballast is three tons of lead.' Bowker argues, 'According to my very rough calculation, allowing the whole of the rest of the boat with mast, spars, sails, gear and heavy centre-board to weigh two tons, she would have sunk while heeling. Surely Childers could not make such a huge mistake.' Erskine certainly heaved the ballast about on many occasions and it could be argued that he exaggerated its weight. We will never know, for Happy Hapgood sold it.

Erskine was to know little of *Dulcibella*'s days after he disposed of her, though many years afterwards he showed his wife Molly the houseboat as she lay disfigured on the Hamble sedge. *Asgard*, the yacht he received as a wedding present from his father-in-law, had a mooring just off her Hamble resting place.

✦ ✦ ✦ ✦

The syndicate's first cruise on *Sunbeam* was to Poole towards the end of July 1901. Two of his sisters joined the party which, from a series of Le Fanu photographs, seemed to be one of those carefree Edwardian long weekends. Both girls were dressed in blue sailor tops with long serge skirts and the men in flannel shirts and tweeds, looking a touch smarter than Davies.

Bombardier Williams was not with them, for he had returned to South Africa. One of Lord Milner's private secretaries had persuaded Basil to leave the clerk's table and to join the 'Kindergarten', a collection of bright young men from England who joined the new administration there. Erskine knew he would miss him, for when he heard he might be going he had written, 'We two seem to have something in common which I don't find in the rest, the something that made us snatch at troop ship squalors in preference to the cigarette-smoking, gossiping, bottom-warming, Bradshaw-studying, life at Westminster. It is easy to say that you can do other work as well, but *it is*, as you say, demoralising.'[27]

The 'other work' in Childers' case was the new book. He was well into his stride early into 1902. In a letter to Basil Williams dated 13 February, he observes, 'There are no committees for me yet, and I spend all my time in writing. I wonder sometimes how I didn't die of boredom without it in other sessions.'[28]

On 13 February he reported progress. 'I am writing hard and hope to finish my book in about a month and chuck it at Reginald's head. I expect he'll chuck it back but I hope not.'[29] It was a vain hope on both counts.

He mentioned in the same letter that he wished Basil would meet Herbert Warington-Smyth, who had gone to South Africa, and that Le Fanu, Rupert Colomb, his cousin Hugo Childers and he were going yachting at Easter. It was not all grind.

Rupert Colomb came from Co. Kerry and was a keen small-boat sailor, owning the Fife rater *Stormy Petrel*, which he kept near his home at Kenmare. Of greater moment to Erskine though, at that time, was Rupert's father, Sir John Colomb, the writer on Imperial defence and at that time Member of Parliament for Great Yarmouth. Vice-Admiral Philip Colomb, Sir John's elder brother, was known as 'Column and a Half', because he was always writing to *The Times*. Philip was a great advocate of the necessity of military preparation, and of an Army for garrison at home, for field defence and for expeditions; but he insisted as strongly that 'in the face of a Navy of sufficient strength, properly organised, any attempt to invade these islands must be very limited.'[30]

Erskine would have been able to test some of the ideas behind the new book on Rupert and to seek advice, if any were needed, from Sir John when he was in the House. Progress, possibly because of this, was slow. He reported to Basil on 24 March, 'I am writing pretty steadily again after a longish gap caused by neuralgia.' He concluded, 'Am going down to the Denbighs on Saturday. I hope to learn something authoritative about the War-Office's intention towards the Volunteers.'[31] His own service in South Africa and Herbert Warington-Smyth's remarks were in the forefront of his mind as he wrote his book. He was pleased to learn that Basil and Herbert had met.

> *On 24 April, Erskine gave sad news about the pace of his writing. Basil had, he wrote, 'a right to be sceptical if I talk about being busy. I have been, though, very; trying to finish the book I told you about, I came to the conclusion that it was dragging and I was getting stale and also that the subject was one of interest of the moment but might become out of date, so for the last three weeks I have been giving all my spare time to it and stoking myself with grape nuts and phosphorine to that end!' He complained, 'Much looms ahead still. Also I have had, strange to say, a great deal to do here, under the strange system which gives some juniors more committees than they can properly attend to.'*[32]

The war in South Africa came to an end, to all intents and purposes, on Saturday, 31 May, in the great marquee at Vereeniging as the Boer delegates met for the final time to decide whether they could swallow the British terms for surrender. De Wet had believed that military resistance was still possible but even he accepted the terms, and so by a majority of fifty-five to six, the war was over.[33] Erskine may well have been on *Sunbeam* the weekend that pen was put to paper in the southern hemisphere. He was pleased and relieved, 'How I thanked heaven, the war was over,' Erskine wrote to Basil in June.[34] Basil was curious about the new book and asked what it was about and in his letter of 12 June Erskine gives a clue:

> *Oh, about my book which you say I have told you nothing about. It is a yachting story, with a purpose, suggested by a cruise I once took in German waters. I discover a scheme of invasion directed against England. I find it*

> *horribly difficult as being in the nature of a detective story there is no sensation, only what is meant to be convincing fact. I was weak enough to 'spatchcock' a girl into it and now find her a horrible nuisance. I have not approached Reginald yet.*[35]

The girl did not appear in the original manuscript and was entirely the idea of Reginald Smith, Erskine's publisher. Erskine found inspiration for her while on holiday in Galway.

Reginald Smith did not appear to be too anxious, for in Erskine's next letter, written at the end of August 1902, he told Basil, 'My sisters are in Ireland and I am camping in the flat trying to finish my book. I have rather over-worked at it, I'm afraid and I don't feel very fit. Reginald Smith has promised to read it when it's done but I don't feel very hopeful about it.'[36] There are occasional changes in handwriting in the surviving manuscript. Perhaps one of the sisters returned to help.

He found time to go sailing in *Sunbeam* for a fortnight and watched the Coronation Naval Review from her deck. Life at Westminster was full, as he had taken over the clerkship of the National Expenditure Committee.[37] It was with a feeling of exhausted relief that he wrote from the Grand Hotel, St Moritz, on 14 January 1903: 'We have been more than three weeks now among the snows and I am all right again, though I was fagged out when I left town. I finished my book before I left and Reginald is now considering it.'

The last days of 1902 and the first flush of the New Year had been hectic.

Erskine was working on the last pages of his new book when the 'HAC in South Africa' came up again. There had been difficulties and it was finally decided to explore the idea of publishing privately. Lord Denbigh, Captain Budworth, his battery captain and adjutant, and others had urged him to produce a short, concise account of the doings of the regiment in South Africa, based on Basil Williams' manuscript. In the meantime, the exercise books containing *The Riddle* were sent off to the Peter Jones Typing Agency and Erskine worked to have the HAC book out by April, in between tobogganing and curling at St Moritz and his normal duties at the House. These plans were upset by Reginald Smith, who demanded 'a drastic revision of the book I sent him which displeased him in many respects. In some points he was right, I know,' he wrote to Basil, 'but in others I held wrong, and I have concocted a compromise which I think he will swallow. The whole thing was rather a disappointment. I had over-worked at it, the fact was, and lost proportion. I think it will be out pretty soon.'[38]

Reginald Smith had put his blue pencil through a good deal of salty description, seen by comparing the surviving manuscript with the published edition of *The Riddle*. Thirteen of the manuscript exercise books survived and are among the papers at Trinity College, Dublin. These are numbered one to fifteen, with two missing. The collection covers forty per cent of the final book, coming to an end soon after the start of Chapter 15. The gap in the manuscript appears in *The Riddle* Chapters 9 to 12.

Not all the changes were large. In the book, when Carruthers was marooned in London, he missed staying with Lady Ashleigh at Morven Lodge. In the manuscript, he declined the same invitation from a Lady Atherton at Braemar Lodge. It may be that Reginald felt Braemar was a little close to Balmoral for good taste.

Longer passages were cut and generations of readers have missed such descriptions as that of *Vixen*'s fo'c'sle as a consequence. The passage described Carruthers' early initiation. It was after lunch and the quick look into Ekken Fjord.

> *'I'll wash up,' I announced, steeling my soul for the ordeal. And down I went, with enthusiastic directions about waste, buckets, and clothes following me. The scullery, it seemed, was the fo'c'sle and I nearly lost heart over the passage to it. Happily it had a round hatch of its own cut into the deck, for it was confined to the last degree and I at once knew by the presence of the stove and an immense shiny oil-can that I had discovered the sources of the paraffin odour. It was the home too of the anchor-chain which lay on the floor in a heap of rusty coils, one of which rose sluggishly through the hawse pipe overhead and swayed and moaned in a depressing manner. Other larger objects, such as spare anchors, and in particular a great water-cask in the angle of the peak, loomed in the half light. I sternly repressed all critical tendencies, collected my plant, crouched on*

> *a pile of chain and washed up, proving the mystic properties of cotton-waste as a substitute, where grease is concerned, to water, and realising among other better truths that to clean a knife without dirtying oneself is the idle dream of a selfish man.*

Erskine's struggle with *The Riddle* was producing after-effects and he was showing signs of wanting to be done with it and on with the new work. 'I'm getting on fairly well with the HAC book and today read something which quickens my zeal.' Apparently Major-General A. H. Paget of the 20th Brigade had 'praised the high efficiency of the CIV battery'.[39]

He was now full of enthusiasm for his old regiment, in which he had continued to play a part, both at camp and drill nights, and had now decided, with a certain amount of reluctance, to go to America at the invitation of the Boston Branch of the HAC. He had written to Basil a little earlier: 'I dread the round of drinking and feasting which is inevitable, especially as I am a tee-totaller.'[40]

Erskine was still in the midst of the HAC book when he wrote to Basil on 1 May 1903.[41] Using the title of the book for the first time, he wrote, 'My other book, the "Riddle of the Sands", will be out shortly and I will send you a copy. Publication has not had the smooth progress that the CIV book had. I had to wage battles with Reginald over maps, etc. and at the eleventh hour he has tried to wreck it by advertising it as a "novel" but by quiet persistent opposition I have managed to effect a good deal.'

Erskine had worked to include a more detailed and attractively illustrated map of the Ems and Norderney and a German ordnance survey of the Esens region.[42] From the instructions in red ink on the latter, it appears that his idea was to place the two maps and two charts, making six in all, in the Appendix (referred to on p. 185). The publisher felt that too many maps made the book a 'serious read', reducing its appeal and consequently a significant slice of his market.

The draft advertisement showed the book to have been *written* by Erskine Childers, author of *In the Ranks of the CIV*, rather than *edited* by Erskine. This characterisation as editor gave a greater impact to the account, to its message and to the background of the story, drawn, as it was, from between the faded mauve covers of *Vixen's* log. The error was corrected and *The Spectator*, among other weeklies, gave prior publicity to the forthcoming book in their issue of 23 May 1903.

A RECORD OF SECRET SERVICE RECENTLY ACHIEVED.

ON MAY 27TH – With 2 Maps and 2 Charts, crown 5vo, 6s.

THE RIDDLE OF THE SANDS

EDITED BY ERSKINE CHANDLERS

Author of 'In the Ranks of the CIV'

An account of the Cruise of the Yacht 'Dulcibella' being a page hitherto unwritten, but of vital interest to all Englishmen, in the recent history of our relations with Germany.

Thirty or so reviews appeared in quick succession from the pages of the *Daily Telegraph* on 5 June 1903 to *The Guardian* on 21 October and the *Westminster Gazette* of 22 January 1904. Erskine collected them all through the General Press Cuttings Agency Ltd. He must have been rather surprised at the splendid reception after the rather painful birth. 'A novel of unusual merit in certain respects, which will appeal most of all to yachtsmen,' said the *Telegraph* (5 June), forgetting that it was not meant to be a novel. *The Scotsman* (11 July) puts the matter right: 'One hesitates to class it in the category of fiction.' The *Academy Literature* (26 June) agrees: 'The book rings curiously true.' *The Northern Whig* (27 June) is perfectly clear in its view. 'Mr. Childers writes with restraint and vraisemblance that almost compels the belief in his narrative as a statement of cold fact.'

The cold fact was that the book was a warning and this is taken up by the *Telegraph*: 'It is a novel with a purpose written round the idea of a possible invasion of England by Germany. The author thinks that the troops for such a purpose would be collected behind the screen of the East Frisian islands, between the Ems and the Weser, and that a great part might be played among the shallows and mud banks of that region by light boats – guerillas of the sea.'

The *Liverpool Courier* (25 June) produces the most thoughtful of all the reviews:

> *Was it not Moltke who said it might be easy to land an army in Britain, but the difficulty would be in getting it out again? The grim old strategist's warning does not cover the whole matter, however, for the mere landing of troops on our shores might cripple us in such a way as to render us vulnerable to attack in other directions. In any case the problem of invading our tight little island had fascinated the military dreamer long before the days of Napoleon or Moltke. It has now become a sort of war game with our continental friends and though there can hardly be any doubt that both France and Germany have put ideas in their pigeon holes, attaching to each must be more than one of those 'ifs' upon which the best laid schemes of mice and men so often depend.*

The *Courier* agreed that 'It is difficult to say how much of Mr Childers' present work is fiction and how much fact.'

The sombre message was highlighted in the *Daily Chronicle* (25 August):

> *That serious purpose is to point out to his fellow countrymen a peril to England which lurks in the shallow estuaries and river mouths, masked effectively by any number of small islands, on that portion of the German coast which is washed by the North Sea.*

All this news *The Times* (14 August) thought 'may be highly important, and the revelation may be useful to the Admiralty and the War Office'.

The *News Chronicle* (25 August) noted that 'The author would seem to be as profoundly distrustful of the Admiralty as are most sensible persons of the War Office.' It quotes Davies on volunteers, a point followed up by *The Standard* (24 July):

> *In an ably written epilogue to the book, [the author says] that we have a magnificent Navy but a restricted one; that it is not built or manned methodically, and that there is 'an utterly inadequate reserve of men, all classes of which would be absorbed at the very outset, without a vestige of preparation or the enrolment of volunteers'.* Public Opinion *(26 June) was more forceful*

> *and ended its review: 'Is it not becoming patent that the time has come for training all Englishmen systematically, either for the sea or for the rifle?'*

Reginald Smith was right about maps as far as the reviewer of *The Times* was concerned: 'A recent novelist, in hints to his brethren, observes the indispensable quality of dullness can be obtained by the use of a map.'

However, he went on to agree that 'the book can only be read by the aid of large maps, railway guides and special information about things nautical.' The last point encouraged the *Telegraph* to emphasise that the book 'is primarily for yachtsmen and it ought to find a place in every yacht's library.' The *Spectator* (1 August) took a rather unexpected line on this: 'We are not sure of Mr. Childers' proficiency as a seaman and have our doubts as to whether he is as much at home with all the technicalities of navigation as he professes to be. Could a 7-ton yacht be manned in half-a-gale by a single seaman, however expert, and would it be safe in any circumstances to leave the tiller in order to shorten sail?'

Reginald Smith was wrong to insist on 'spatchcocking a girl' into the story, as far as the *Daily Chronicle* (25 August) was concerned: 'We regret that Mr. Childers should have so far surrendered to what he believes to be the demands of novel readers as to insert the usual conventional "love-interest". It was not wanted here a bit.'

The Times felt that the girl's part lacked credibility. 'The Germans are a practical people, and would not permit a professional traitor to drag a pretty daughter about through his muddy courses. Charles II remarked that being a woman, Christina of Sweden could not safely be entrusted with a secret, and the Germans must be aware of that feminine peculiarity.'

It would certainly have been peculiar if Erskine had not been pleased with one particular comparison. In *The Queen* (4 July), their reviewer held that 'The book, in spite of much nautical phraseology, confusing enough to the landsman, has a curious fascination, due in part to the extremely vivid writing, which occasionally recalls Stevenson.' He might not have been quite as pleased with the *St James Gazette:* 'It is true that from the moment we are put in possession of the yachtsman's suspicions of German treachery we are often reminded of Tom Sawyer and his noble attempts to emancipate an already free nigger. Davies and Carruthers appear as likely to bring their efforts to a ridiculous ending as did Mark Twain's immortal hero but our lively anticipation of a fiasco – which never ensues – only enhances enjoyment of the book, which is a breezy and thoroughly entertaining romance.' Whether *The Riddle of the Sands* was 'cold fact' or a 'thoroughly entertaining romance', Reginald Smith must have had limited confidence in the success of the book, for his firm's order for the first printing was only 1.250 copies.[43] It is difficult enough to find a first edition today.

The reviews ensured success and the early publishing history reflects a growing popularity. While under the control of Smith Elder & Co, the book was reprinted in September and December of 1903, in May and December of 1904, in December 1905, July 1907, October 1908, December 1910, April 1913 and June 1915. The cheap edition sold several hundred thousand copies. Reginald Smith died in 1916 and the firm was taken over by John Murray. Smith Elder were publishers of Charlotte Bronte, Thackeray, Trollope, Meredith, Browning and the explorer Captain Robert Falcon Scott. Reginald Smith had paid Erskine quite a compliment by greeting him on Guy Fawkes Day 1900 on the dockside at Southampton. Erskine had responded not only by giving the publishing house a household name but by chipping a question mark in the rock of Imperial Defence Policy with his second book.

The queries and comments of the reviewers of *The Riddle of the Sands* were matched by the curiosity of his friends and those who worked with him in the House. His companions at the clerks' table had noticed his preoccupation with his book, though his natural reticence would have deflated any idea that something remarkable was about to happen. After all, he doubted it himself.

Legend has it that after seeing the reviews the Liberal leader, Sir Henry Campbell-Bannerman, called Erskine to his office in the House of Commons and asked him whether the invasion story were true. Lord Rosebery also buttonholed him, as Erskine mentioned in a letter to Basil Williams.[44] Rosebery 'wanted to know how much was fact and talked delightfully on various subjects suggested by the book, urged me to write again and was most kind and encouraging. As a fact I invented the whole thing, building it, though, on careful observation of my own on the German coast but I have since had the most remarkable confirmation of the ideas in it. Source confidential of course and details too – but I think there is no doubt that my method of invasion – in general principle – had been worked out by the Germans.'

Erskine was as forthcoming in reply to a letter to Mrs Probyn, to whom he wrote from the University Club, Boston, on 17 October 1903:

> *It was good of you to take a real interest in that rather imprudent 'fake'* The Riddle of the Sands *– though that perhaps is too strong a phrase for it! Because it was really written with a very sincere purpose and is all based on fact, even though the story is fictitious. I mean that the thing might happen, the charts and all local details are absolutely correct and nothing in the invasion theory is extravagant. Beyond that I only depend on hints and rumours from the German technical press, but most of all, my personal knowledge of that coast for I and Henry did make the very cruise in the boat described (or smaller still) and I firmly believe that my warning is sound and needed, and I have had the most remarkable confirmation of this since the book was published, though I cannot give details as the matter is highly confidential.*[45]

The possibility of a German invasion by tugs and barges was clearly the most important message of the book but readers were also keen to fit faces to Davies and Carruthers, for they carried the story forward in a most realistic way, bringing the happenings on board *Vixen* out of the page, as a paper theatre coming alive. Books with persuasive plans for invasion had been forwarded by publishers and reviewers as awful warnings before. General Sir George Chesney had written the popular novel *The Battle of Dorking* in 1871, arguing the case for military improvements.[46] Less well known, P. L. Stevenson had written of a potential naval disaster in his slim volume of 1898, *How the Jubilee Fleet Escaped Destruction and The Battle of Ushant.*[47]

The principal characters in these books were not nearly as well formed as those in *The Riddle.* John Buchan, reviewing a later edition of *The Riddle,* wrote (after describing it as 'the best adventure published in the last quarter of a century'), 'As for the characters, I think they are the most fully realised of any adventure story I have met, and the atmosphere of grey northern skies and miles of yeasty water and wet sands is as masterly reproduced as in any story of Conrad's.'

Who were Davies and Carruthers? Readers have puzzled over their identity ever since the book came out. It is generally thought that Davies was essentially Erskine, or as Erskine saw himself to be at that time. He was certainly an adventurer and a fine seaman, but there were other similarities. Davies was not careful about his personal appearance and nor was Erskine, though he did not carry such disregard to the same degree. Davies was methodical, as was his creator. Davies' political views were those which Erskine had held and had thought were best for the country when he put pen to paper.

Norman Donaldson, in his introduction to the American Dover edition of *The Riddle of the Sands,* sums up the singular likeness. 'It is Davies,' he says, 'exhibited in a cool, even unsympathetic light, who represents the author. Childers, in fact, permits us to see him as others only gradually learned to know him – awkward and gentle, but single-minded and implacable. This rare ability to view himself objectively was in itself an interesting facet of his character. Carruthers depicts Davies as 'resourceful, skilful, and alert, but liable to lapse into a certain amateurish vagueness, half irritating and half amusing'. This is paralleled by O'Donovan's James O'Donovan, an IRA Department Director] description of Childers' 'doddering, drooping absent-mindedness' when wandering in Cork and even when inspecting the front line under the very barrels of the enemy guns.[48]

We must leave it to the man who knew Erskine as well as any at that time to have the last word on Davies. Ivor Lloyd-Jones wrote in his 'Appreciation of Erskine Childers' in the *Haileyburian:*

> *Davies in 'The Riddle of the Sands' is every bit Erskine Childers, though I am sure he was utterly unconscious how true a portrait of himself he had drawn. The honesty, fearlessness and the unsuspicious shrewdness, the effervescent humour, the gentle courtesy are trades that identify him at once.*

The identity of Carruthers is rather more difficult. The two obvious candidates are Henry Childers, Erskine's brother, and Ivor Lloyd-Jones. They had both, after all, been his companions during the 1897 voyage. But there are others who claim attention. Admiral Sir Edward Charlton and Brigadier Gordon Shephard have been put forward as the original Carruthers. The admiral and the brigadier had sailed with Erskine at different times, but after the book was in the shops.

Gordon Shephard, at any rate, is easily eliminated, for he was born in 1885, would have been only twelve in 1897 and eighteen when the book was published. Further, Erskine and he first met on 13 August 1909, as Shephard recorded in his memoirs:

> *August 13, 1909 – I dined yesterday with a great yachtsman, a clerk in the House of Lords, but nevertheless a good radical. He strongly recommended me to go to the Texel and work south to Flushing or only to The Hook and then back. His name is Childers.*[49]

Admiral Charlton, on the other hand, was five years older than Erskine, and was no doubt the mysterious torpedo lieutenant mentioned in a letter to the *Yachting Monthly* of March 1939, signed by 'Flag Yellow'.

> *One story is that a 'junior' from the Foreign Office and a Naval Torpedo Lieutenant were the crew of some yacht which made certain alarming discoveries. On return home both made official reports on these matters. Some time later, believing that little or no interest had been taken in them, and being imbued with the extreme importance of their discoveries, they persuaded Erskine Childers to edit the book which became so famous.*

It seems pretty certain that the latter used his Baltic cruise to provide a framework.

The then Captain Charlton had sailed with Erskine, for he was one of the crew of *Sunbeam* in 1903, but in the summer following the publication of *The Riddle.* He had joined the yacht with Ivor Lloyd-Jones and William Le Fanu at Kiel on 15 August, completing the major half of the 1,867-mile cruise that concentrated on the Baltic, but they missed out the German Frisian islands.

Captain Charlton was a man of splendid physique, according to his confidential report[50] and had been at the Torpedo School, HMS *Vernon,* Portsmouth, from July 1901 to January 1903 – just the time that Erskine was writing *The Riddle.* Erskine and he may have met while sailing in the Solent, as Charlton was a keen yachtsman.

Herbert E. Julyan, the yacht-broker, was in no doubt that Charlton was Carruthers and says so in his book *Sixty Years of Yachts.*[51] Julyan had been asked by Stuart Garnet in 1914 to meet Admiral Charlton. 'He told me that this gentleman was "Carruthers" of *The Riddle of the Sands*,' Julyan wrote.

Charlton was an unlikely Carruthers, but he may well have helped Erskine polish some of the ideas so well expressed by Davies. The 'channel theory' may have been tried on the naval officer. Remember how Davies, in Chapter 8, had explained to Carruthers 'that in a war a lot might depend on these [channels] both in defence and attack, for there is plenty of water in them at the right tide for patrol boats and small torpedo craft, though I can see they take a lot of knowing. Now say we were at war with Germany: both sides could use them as links between the three estuaries; and to take our own case, a small torpedo-boat (not a destroyer, mind you) could, on a dark night, cut clean through from the Jade to the Elbe and play the deuce with the shipping there.'

Charlton would have confirmed the capability of the torpedo boats for he had been in command of numbers 77 and 82 in the summer manoeuvres of 1889 and 1890. Edward Charlton, like Captain Arthur Barrow, whom Erskine had seen in Portsmouth in 1896 and who had been assistant director of Naval Intelligence, could have provided valuable background. They may have felt as Davies did in Chapter 9 that 'those Admiralty chaps want waking up', referring more to the civil than the naval side.

However, let us return to the main contenders for the part of Carruthers.

Brother Henry was alone with Erskine on *Vixen* for most of the epic voyage. Henry was not unlike Erskine in some ways, though he was certainly not the foil that Carruthers was to Davies. His son, Professor Walter Childers, remembers his father as 'kind, self-effacing, stubborn and a man who found difficulty in communicating, even with those close to him.'[52]

Osmond Hill of Lymington, who tried to save *Vixen*, was convinced that Henry was the model for Carruthers. He wrote to Dulcie Philpot, Erskine's sister, on 23 August 1939: 'I know that Carruthers was the author's brother and wish it were possible to meet him as I would like above everything to hear from first-hand details of that famous cruise.'

Ivor Lloyd-Jones is the other claimant. Douglas Dixon, the author of many yachting books, met Ivor Lloyd-Jones, and wrote in the *Yachting Monthly* of May 1939 that 'If there was a flesh and blood "Carruthers" then there seems little doubt that he is Ivor G. Lloyd-Jones.' W. F. Brooke-Smith had as good a reason for holding the same view, for he had been Lloyd-Jones' pupil. 'I was taught German by one of Childers' great personal friends who was reputed to be the original Carruthers.'[53] Ivor Lloyd-Jones was a schoolmaster most of his life and had experienced feelings that would have come easily to Carruthers when first introduced to small-boat sailing: 'I was exhausted, cold, wet, hungry, miserable and terrified.'[54]

Ivor left *Vixen* at Amsterdam and there is no record of his sailing with Erskine until he joined *Sunbeam* on 15 August 1903 – that is, unless Erskine brought him back earlier as Carruthers aboard *Dulcibella*.

There is no real reason, though, why Erskine should have modelled his two principal characters on his friends. The Preface leads the reader into this likely-looking snare, as Hammond Innes pointed out in a letter to the *Yachting Monthly* of July 1974: 'To take the author's Preface seriously is to ignore a common practice of the period. The use of a club conversation or other opening gambit to give verisimilitude to fiction – Buchan did it, so did Rider Haggard, Conan Doyle, Lord Dunsany and others.' The characters of Davies and Carruthers may have been built up in the way of the Victorian game of 'Head, Body and Legs' – parts taken from the office, from friends outside, from life that passed by to be fitted together with neat flicks of the pen. Arthur H. Davies may owe his name to the yachting author G. Christopher Davies and Carruthers to the caricaturist, assistant editor of the *Westminster Gazette* and parliamentary expert, Francis Carruthers Gould. But again, like much of the matching that has gone before, this is pure speculation.

PART THREE

The Invasion of England

Chapter 6

BOLT FROM THE BLUE

There was plenty of speculation in the air following the publication of *The Riddle*. Members of Parliament with east-coast constituencies, particularly those bordering the Thames Estuary and the Wash, the favoured invasion sites, were full of surmise. They pressed their views on the government and as a result Lord Selborne, the First Lord of the Admiralty, wrote a note to the director of Naval Intelligence, Prince Louis of Battenberg, receiving on 23 February 1904 this reply:

> *I have read the novel you mention. As a* novel *it is excellent, as a* Warplan *it is rubbish. It is a scheme of invasion, to be put into execution the instant war breaks out and without reference to the Royal Navy. Apart from the unsoundness of the* principle, *the details are absurd. At any rate, if Germany wished* to invade *us, there are other and simpler means than these here suggested; of embarking the military forces and transporting them – or rather attempting to.* The Hydrographer concurs.[1]

The hydrographer, Rear Admiral Sir William Wharton, would not have been too pleased by Davies' view on the 'prehistoric rottenness of the English charts'. The reply did not satisfy Lord Selborne either, who wrote again on 27 April to Prince Louis:

> *I have several times spoken to you about a book called 'The Riddle of the Sands', and I think you told me that, although you had not read it yourself, it had been examined*

in your Department. I have no more than merely glanced at it and therefore do not profess to have any opinion on it, but it is very remarkable how many people have been struck by it and who constantly come to me about it. The last person who did so was Sir William White [renowned naval architect and assistant controller of the Navy], who was immensely impressed by it. I do not know which of your officers examined the book for you or whether his examination of it was cursory or thorough. Unless the book was examined by an officer in whom you have complete confidence and in a very complete manner, I shall be greatly obliged if you will again have it examined most thoroughly and by an officer on whose judgement you can absolutely rely.

Lord Selborne had served as assistant private secretary to Erskine's cousin, Hugh Childers, when he held the posts of Secretary of State for War and Chancellor of the Exchequer, between the years of 1882 and 1885. Though Selborne professed that he had not read *The Riddle of the Sands*, his curiosity may have extended to the author. He would have discovered Erskine's growing reputation both inside and outside the House.

The First Lord's added interest in the book was due, though, not to the reputation of the author but more to concern at the turn of events at the time of publication. The book acted as a focus and those who may have considered the idea of invasion casually now fastened on to it as a real possibility. The threat was not, of course, new, for invasion had been much feared in 1888; Palmerston had built his forts in the 1860s and the Martello towers had sprouted because of the ambitions of the first Napoleon, whose mouldering stone preparations Erskine had seen in Boulogne.

The Boer War had ended, for a time, any new British complacency. The country was beginning to realise how sorely the emergency in southern Africa had tested British might. In March 1900, the lowest point in British preparedness, only a cavalry brigade, a brigade of guards and an infantry division[2] remained in the country to give any sort of professional resistance to an enemy that managed to evade the Royal Navy. The threat was not seen as coming from Germany, but from a more traditional direction – France. The French were not averse to settling old scores. Captain Houette, of the French Navy, gloried in the idea and was quoted in *Public*

Opinion, under the headline, 'How to Attack England', of 6 April 1900:

> *At the present moment, between Havre and Dunkirk, we have enough fishing vessels and tugs to put 90,000 men across, given sixteen hours free from molestation, with artillery, baggage, munitions, and four days' provisions. Who can say that the sixteen hours will never be found, even at the sacrifice of our whole fleet? I need not make any eulogy of the* personnel *of the Navy. Give us numerous and powerful vessels, and I assure you we will write some glorious pages in the history of France.*[3]

The French were seen by the British press as adept at bicycling, in the forefront of the development of the motor car (both useful for swift access to London in war), and already across the Channel in all sorts of peaceful guises, capable of organised mayhem, given the word. It was not all press speculation either, for France did have plans to invade and had been developing schemes for a few years. In June 1897, their general staff worked out that they had fifteen days after the outbreak of war to land on British soil before the overwhelming strength of the British fleet would prevent such a plan. They aimed to organise things so that they would be capable of landing in Britain on the ninth day of mobilisation. Newhaven was selected as the best place. The invasion force would have a short crossing and there was plenty of livestock on the sunny side of the South Downs for further supplies of meat and horse transport. Brighton would be an immediate objective for the cavalry and another mounted force would fan out to protect the bridgehead, the main force passing through, bent on reaching London. Sixty thousand men would be employed, including some cyclists, and the transports would achieve their objectives and return to France in thirty-six hours.[4]

France continued to think on these lines, to update and to polish the invasion plans, especially after the Fashoda incident in 1898. Full-scale exercises were held in 1901, during which troops practised bicycling ashore. Plans continued to be studied until 1907, three years after the signing of the Entente Cordiale in April 1904. Old habits died hard.

French ambitions and capabilities were officially recognised. Lieutenant Colonel

William Robertson, later Chief of the Imperial General Staff, produced a paper summarising the dangers from across the Channel. He showed that France had '3,300,000 trained men at her disposal, well armed and well led and amply supplied with transport and war material of all kinds'. He noted that twenty-six of their ports were connected by rail and several by canal and that seven of the northern ports, Dunkirk, Calais, Boulogne, Dieppe, Havre, St Malo and Brest, had first-class facilities for the despatch of an expeditionary force, and many smaller ports would make second- or third-class bases.[5]

The Prime Minister, Lord Salisbury, had been reluctant to enter the invasion argument, which was perhaps not surprising for a man who had described his government's foreign policy as 'to drift lazily downstream, occasionally putting out a boat hook to avoid collision'. Speaking in May 1900 – some time before the Robertson paper – he recognised the dangers across the Channel and proposed improvements to home defence by the provision of large training areas, armouries, rifle ranges and drill halls for an Army volunteer force. *The Times* of 10 May reported the Prime Minister as arguing that 'when every Englishman knew how to use his horse, his bicycle, his motor car and his rifle for home defence, Continental nations would no longer study in their military colleges the mode of invading England, and we should be safe from all dangers.'

There were two schools of thought on how safety 'from all dangers' might be achieved and the real collision, which would take more than a 'boat hook' to avoid, was the encounter between these two groups.

The 'Blue Water' school emphasised the essential value to Britain, in the imperial age, of a strong navy. The establishment and continuation of command of the sea by a powerful British battle fleet, able to overcome a power, or combination of powers, was their answer to Britain's defence both at home and abroad. They believed in Mahan's ideas, so well put in *The Influence of Sea Power Upon History*, where he argued the overriding historical importance of sea power – both military and commercial – to achieve national supremacy. Paraphrasing Mahan, Marder wrote: 'Invasion would never be attempted, history had taught, until the enemy had established control of the sea and his communications were secure. To assign to the army a co-responsibility with the navy for the defence of the United Kingdom was to misconceive the fundamental principles of the problem.

Money spent on "earth, stone, iron walls" and a large army for home defence was for the most part money wasted.'[6]

Mahan's principal acolytes in Britain were Sir John Colomb, Admiral Philip Colomb, Sir Charles Dilke and Spencer Wilkinson. Sir John Colomb said rather extravagantly that an army of ten million men would be useless to Great Britain unless she could also hold undisputed command of the sea. Admiral Colomb held that without this command, invasion would be comparatively easy but unnecessary, for all the objects of war could be gained without it: 'Their enemies had only to sit still and starve them out.'[7] Spencer Wilkinson formed the Navy League to give mass support to the concept of a powerful Navy. Alfred Harmsworth's *Daily Mail*, the first mass-circulation newspaper, supported the navalist or Blue Water cause.

Admiral Lord Walter Kerr, whose flagship HMS *Majestic* Erskine and Ivor Lloyd-Jones had visited in 1896, observed that 'the many difficulties are not realised by those who are possessed by the invasion scare, and who have not practical knowledge of sea incidents. Unless our Navy was quite wiped out in home waters, the risk to an invading force would be enormous, and I suspect this is fully realised across the channel.'[8]

The 'risks' were not accepted or 'fully realised' by the opposing 'Bolt from the Blue' school of thought, whose leader was Field Marshal Earl Roberts. The Army, worried and dispirited after their experiences in South Africa and jealous of calls for more money for ships and their crews, pointed to the danger of surprise attack from across the sea, a 'bolt from the blue', which could go under the Navy's guard. They saw that 100,000 to 150,000 men might be brought to the shores of southern and eastern England with few regulars or organised volunteers ready to meet them on the beaches.

William Cairns, a supporter of Lord Roberts, imagined the scene if the Blue Water school were wrong and the Navy were not in the right place at the right time.[9] He saw 'a great fleet of transports, herded by torpedo craft and warships, closing with the British coast in the dark hours of the morning. I can see,' he went on, 'swift launches, towing boats crammed with infantry through the smooth water into the shadow of the cliffs, and then returning empty to transports for fresh loads. I can follow, in my mind's eye, the infantry as they quickly push a little way inland, seizing the nearest farms and cottages, placing the terrified inmates under guard and pouncing upon any wayfarer who might give the alarm. Ere the sun was well over the horizon many thousand men and many guns would be on shore, thousands more would be following them with the utmost speed, while London, the heart of the Empire, would be slowly awakening from its slumbers to find every telegraphic wire cut, many railways blocked, unconscious of the enemy already firmly established on British territory.'

Erskine was still in South Africa when Cairns conjured up this picture of waiting disaster. Again, the French were seen as the invaders.

Salisbury's call for volunteer warriors was taken up by the new commander-in-chief, Lord Roberts, who wanted better training and equipment for the volunteers. Rifle clubs had spread across the face of England, fanned by a wave of public concern. Sir John Brodrick, the Secretary of State for War, encouraged ideas on security from one and all. He received 'coal scuttles full of letters and even confidential postcards' as to how best to protect England's shores from invasion.[10]

Argument between the two schools rumbled on and with it a growing criticism of the state of the Royal Navy. Many were worried that the senior service would be found wanting in the same way as the Army in South Africa. At the beginning of this period of self-examination, in the closing months of 1900, Hugh Arnold Forster became Secretary to the Admiralty, under the recently appointed First Lord, the Earl of Selborne. These two able men were later to count on the advice of Admiral Sir John (Jackie) Fisher, then Commander-in-Chief Mediterranean Station, and in combination to breathe new life into the ailing service, but for the first two years of the century the public watched, sometimes impatiently, as the Blue Water and the Bolt from the Blue factions argued in the press and in Parliament. 'The Blue Funk' school was Jackie Fisher's label for the latter and *Brassey's Naval Annual* of 1902 agreed with this spirit. In a major article, 'The Invasion of England',[11] the author, John Leyland,[12] concluded: 'Our home forces must be constituted as the base and feeder of the foreign service troops, and there must be no vast outlay, either on men or inland works for defence of these isles, the fleet being made supreme.' He continued with a certain logic on his side:

> *It is an obvious consideration that however powerful may be the forces we maintain in readiness for foreign service, they cannot be despatched from our shores until the fleet has made the sea secure for their transport. Thus – if we admit, for the sake of argument, the possibility of a naval catastrophe, there will always be plenty of trained men in the United Kingdom. In that same hour in which the fleet makes it possible for them to leave our shores, no chance of a violation of the Kingdom by invasion will remain. The true lesson of this enquiry is, therefore, that a sufficient and efficient navy is the essential factor in national as in imperial defence; and that, recognising this cardinal principle, we are able to formulate a sound military policy, and to direct national efforts and resources to this true and direct end.*

Erskine, who studied Brassey, would have seen the article but he would not have shared the views of John Leyland, being nearer perhaps to those of his old commander-in-chief of the Army, Field Marshal Viscount Wolseley, who said that 'Everybody whose intelligence is above the ordinary intelligence of a schoolboy must know that this country is open to invasion.' *The National Review* of May and June 1902 had also cast a critical eye at Emden and the development of the docks 'capable of embarking 300,000 men.'[13]

The Riddle was well under way as this battle of words continued and Erskine was still struggling with the manuscript when Arnold Forster visited Germany in August 1902 and saw for himself the progress of their naval and military development. He was very much impressed and on his return wrote, 'It is necessary to contemplate the possibility of an attempted landing on the East Coast.' Arnold Forster did not mince words and saw the danger as immediate.[14]

A few voices in the Admiralty had bracketed Germany and invasion before. They had taken rather more note than most of an early article, 'German Naval Policy and

Strategy', by Captain Baron von Lüttwitz that appeared in the *Militär-Wochenblatt* on 15 and 18 January 1896. The piece was reprinted in English in both the *Royal United Services Journal* of February 1896 and W. T. Stead's influential monthly *Review of Reviews* in March of the next year, Stead quoting a good deal of it word for word. Under the subheading 'To Cover the Invasion of England', Lüttwitz wrote: 'Our own good right hand and a strong fleet can alone help us! This will have to protect our Baltic harbours and seek out the hostile fleets, while our fleet of transports is crossing over to the island kingdom.'[15] Lüttwitz praised Napoleon's own preparations and mentioned approvingly the troop boats that were 'specially designed for their [soldiers'] transport being capable of being rowed or sailed, while they only drew six or seven feet of water, and were keelless, to enable a landing to be effected even at ebb tide.'[16]

Even the run up to Tirpitz's first German Navy Law in 1897, that Erskine had seen while at Kiel in October of that year, left the average Englishman cold. 'A sizeable section of English opinion saw no danger in the programme,' Arthur Marder observed.[17] Arnold Forster's visit to Germany changed all that as far as the official mind was concerned and early in 1903 the government was persuaded to set up two commissions, the Royal Commission on Militia and Volunteers, under the Duke of Norfolk, and the Committee of Imperial Defence, first under the Duke of Devonshire and then under Arthur Balfour, the Prime Minister. The Committee of Imperial Defence (CID) took over from the old Defence Committee of the Cabinet and was set up to look at particular problems needing the views and, more importantly, the co-operation of both the Army and Navy, so as to provide the Cabinet with proper advice on specific defence problems. The first matter they looked into was that of home defence. They were required to 'report on the possibility of serious invasion'.

Erskine had argued for just such a body in the Epilogue of *The Riddle of the Sands*. The final manuscript was sent to Reginald Smith nearly two months before the Prime Minister set up the committee, on 5 March 1903. Erskine had written, 'We have a small Army, dispersed over the whole globe, and administered on a gravely defective system. We have no settled theory of national defence, and no competent authority whose business is to give us one.' Referring to the wrangle between the two schools, he continued: 'The matter is still at the stage of civilian controversy. Co-operation between the Army and the Navy is not studied and practised; much less do there exist any plans, worthy of the name, for the repulse of an invasion, or any readiness worth considering for the prompt equipment and direction of our home forces to meet a sudden emergency.'

The hurriedly added postscript to *The Riddle*, written in March, before the book was published in May, paid some sort of tribute to the creation of the CID. 'A Committee of National Defence has been set up, and the welcome given to it was a truly extraordinary comment on the apathy and confusion which it is designed to supplant.'

Erskine would have been pleased at the diligent way Arthur Balfour attempted and, in part, succeeded, inside the committee at least, in bringing together the Army and Navy factions and, to an extent, the two schools. Arthur Balfour's report on the possibilities of invasion, marked 'Confidential', was published for the benefit of the Cabinet on 11 November 1903. The French were still assumed to be the invaders – even after Arnold Forster's visit to Germany and other events, including the focusing of attention on Germany after the publication of *The Riddle*. Marder suggests that the French were selected so as not to offend Germany.[18]

It is known too that the Committee of Imperial Defence had, in April, the advantage of a translation of the German naval magazine, *Marine Rundschau*, or 'Naval Review'. The magazine, believed to reflect the views of the German naval general staff, discussed in detail stages of an invasion of England and effectively demolished the practicality of such an idea. The anonymous author went to some length to deny any idea that the Navy Law programme was any threat to England.[19] H. R. Moon suggests that there is strong circumstantial evidence to suggest that Battenberg, the Director of Naval Intelligence and a member of the committee, brought this magazine article to the attention of the committee, as it 'so persuasively echoed his own case against the invasion contingency'.

In October 1903, Battenberg held that 'The establishment of submarine stations along the south coast of England ought to go a long way towards dispelling the ever-recurring fears of invasion so dear to the "old women of both sexes" mentioned by

Lord St Vincent.'[20] He was referring to a French threat and reinforced his views on the role of the submarine by emphasising that Britain's supposed enemies thought the invasion of their own shores would be 'the act of a lunatic' for the same reason.[21] Battenberg continued to hold strong views about the impossibility of invasion, as already seen from his letter to Lord Selbome of 23 February 1904, when he dismissed the 'scheme of invasion' suggested by *The Riddle*. Fisher, who also had the Prime Minister's ear, agreed. At the 1903 Royal Academy dinner he spoke of changes in warfare at sea wrought by the submarine and wireless telegraphy: 'Is there the slightest fear of invasion with them, even for the most extreme pessimist?'[22]

The preamble to the Draft Report on the Possibility of Serious Invasion makes it clear that the going was not always smooth. 'This committee did most excellent work; but it *did not* reconcile the views of the soldiers and the sailors. The former held, as they have always held, that our fleet affords us no certain or adequate protection.' 'The sailors, on the other hand,' the report continued, 'held that this danger is illusory. If the British fleet is destroyed, if we are so utterly reduced as to be permanently driven even out of our home waters, then it would be scarcely worth while for our enemies to incur the cost and risk of an invasion.' The words might have been written by Admiral Philip Colomb.

The report defined what was meant by invasion and decided to look at the worst possible situation. They assumed that 'the occupation of London must be the first object of any expedition bent on "serious" invasion.' The committee sought advice on how few troops might achieve this object, given that the enemy was prepared 'to sacrifice the whole expeditionary force in the case of a not improbable failure' and that 'our forces for home defence are reduced to the lowest level actually reached during the late South African War.' To paint an even blacker picture, the committee supposed that 'after denuding ourselves to the utmost of organised forces in an overseas struggle with one power, another power joins the fray and endeavours to strike a sudden blow at shores no longer protected by a regular army.' The report filled in the detail by disclosing the extent of the low point reached in March 1900 with figures. They calculated that there had been at that time in the country about 17,000 organised regular troops, with only four batteries of horse artillery, twenty-two field artillery and two companies of field engineers in support. They continued: 'In addition to these fragments of the regular Army, we had 60,000 militia, 6,000 yeomanry and 225,000 volunteers; out of a total force thus constituted, 141,000 men were required to garrison our defended ports; and the remainder could hardly have been sufficiently organised and provided with transport to make them formidable in the field under some weeks of strenuous effort.'

Given this meagre figure of defenders, the committee went on to decide how few troops a foreign power would need to attempt an invasion. They came up with the figure of 70,000 men, 'including a relatively small proportion of both cavalry (say one brigade) and of guns (say twenty-five 6-gun batteries), with no more transport than would be required for the ammunition reserve, and no more food than could be carried in the men's knapsacks.'

Balfour's team then looked at the defence provided by the Royal Navy and, before going into any detail, they permitted themselves a swift look at the possible threat from Germany. The committee concluded that if the fleet was able to deal 'with an invasion across the Channel it can assuredly deal with one that has to traverse the North Sea.'

They then returned to the supposed French threat, again assuming the worst. They continued: 'To make, therefore, the possibility of serious invasion worth discussing, we must assume either a great blunder or a great disaster. The British battle fleet must have either strayed into regions so remote from home waters as to leave these for a sufficient time open to the enemy, or it must have been beaten, and driven into port.' They compared possibilities taken from history with modern opportunities and concluded that 'substitution of steam for wind is probably, on balance, in favour of the defence.' Echoing the advice of Fisher and Battenberg, they decided that 'the whole problem of landing large bodies of troops on a hostile shore has been revolutionised by the invention of the torpedo and the submarine.' They considered that 'the torpedo boat can only be driven from the sea by a torpedo boat larger and swifter than itself; and the submarine cannot be driven from the sea at all,' so they concluded that 'even if our battle fleet were absent from the Channel or beaten, and the enemies' battle fleet swept it, like van Tromp's, from end to end, this might hamper, but could not drive into port, our superior force of cruisers, and would affect our torpedo boats and submarines chiefly by supplying them with additional objects of attack.'

The French invasion force would have a particularly difficult task. 'We may assume, at least for the sake of argument, that the 70,000 men, 150 guns and 14,000 horses destined for the expedition can be concentrated at the port or ports of embarkation without difficulty or publicity but no similar assumptions can be made about the transports required to convey them over the Channel.' The experts concluded that 210,000 tons of shipping would be required and that as 'not more than half this amount of French shipping between Dunkirque [their spelling] and Brest, including small ships as well as large ones, sailing ships as well as steamers, could be found on any one day,' the necessary transport could only be provided by 'simultaneously seizing every British vessel lying in the northern ports of France'. Such action would give full notice to the British of the impending French design.

The ships would then be moved to the port or ports most suitable for embarkation and Cherbourg was selected as likely, but would only accommodate about 200,000 tons of closely packed shipping. The other 10,000 tons, with the men-of-war, would have to be found accommodation somewhere. The committee did not try and answer where this might be.

The report went on to say that the ships would have to be unloaded, 'fitted to accommodate 14,000 horses, and to carry the 500 additional boats and horse-flats absolutely necessary for disembarkation'. Those advising estimated that six days would have elapsed before men, guns and horses were safe on board. The French would have to face the fact that by this time 'every British vessel from Gibraltar to the North Sea would have had time to take up the station assigned to it, and every tug from Sheerness to Plymouth could be supplied with extemporised armament and a crew qualified to use it.'

The committee felt that they had to state at this stage that they could not see how it was possible for the force, even allowing an escort of battleships, cruisers and destroyers, to cross the Channel from Cherbourg to the British coast without serious loss, even though the defenders were without battleships but possessed great superiority in smaller ships, including torpedo craft and submarines.

The weather would clearly play an important part and could wreck the entire operation. Assuming it was perfect, the committee could not see how a fleet strong in battleships could give protection to 200 transports through twenty-four hours when the sea was crowded with hostile cruisers and torpedo craft. 'History has no record,' the report stated, 'of what would happen to an army of 70,000 men close packed in improvised transports if even two or three torpedo boats got among them – to say nothing of a whole flotilla – that the confusion, horror, and the destruction would exceed anything which we can easily imagine in cold blood, seems certain. Fortunately, as the committee hold, no invading army is likely, in existing conditions, to run the risk.'[23]

Arthur Balfour and his committee had come down in favour of the Blue Water school. The Navy was officially given the task of defending Britain from invasion and, provided they took the right steps, they would be capable of accepting the nation's trust. Fisher had fed Balfour with memoranda and in so doing had influenced the conclusions. He was now to be given the chance of fitting the service to the role that it felt it had enjoyed since the days of Nelson, but might have lost if the report had come to a different set of conclusions.

Lord Roberts, of the Bolt from the Blue school, was not entirely disappointed, for Balfour had confirmed the Regular Army's role as primarily concerned with the defence of the empire. He was pleased with the outcome of the Commission on the Militia and Volunteers, for they reported in favour of regenerating and modernising the auxiliary forces.

The constant battle between the Army and the Navy had been contained by the Committee of Imperial Defence, even if they had pointed a finger at France rather than Germany in their first task of assessing the state of home defence. The invasion controversy was to continue, though. Erskine need not have worried that 'the subject [of his book] was one of interest of the moment that might become out of date'.

The Postscript to *The Riddle* noted progress over three other matters that he felt were of particular and immediate concern in earlier pages. Erskine had written in the Epilogue, 'We have no North Sea naval base, no North Sea fleet, and no North

The German Invasion Fleet

Sea policy.' He corrected this before publication by adding in the Postscript that a 'site on the Forth has been selected for a new North Sea naval base – an excellent if tardy decision; for ten years or so must elapse before the existing anchorage becomes in any sense a "base".' The Prime Minister had announced in the Commons on 5 March 1903, two months before the publication of *The Riddle*, that 'it was the intention of the government to establish a new home port for the Navy in the Firth of Forth,' adding that this 'should allay certain recent alarms, but will also show that those alarms were both superfluous and belated,' as the matter had been under consideration for some time.

Erskine had not been alone in feeling coldly naked looking across the North Sea to Germany. The British ambassador in Berlin, Sir Frank Lascelles, and the naval attaché had advised Lord Selborne early in 1902 that the Kaiser's new high-seas fleet was being built with Britain in mind. The Prime Minister, as a consequence, had met Lord Lansdowne, the Foreign Secretary, Joseph Chamberlain, the Financial

Secretary of the Treasury, and Lord Selborne, First Lord, and had decided to purchase secretly the necessary land for a North Sea base. They were urged on by Admiral Sir Reginald Custance, the director of Naval Intelligence who, with Admiral Lord Walter Kerr, now the senior naval Lord of Admiralty, had seen Germany as a serious naval threat for some time. The existing naval dockyards of Chatham, Portsmouth and Devonport had been built, after all, to face the Dutch and French – not the Germans.

Balfour was tactful and reported to Parliament that the idea had come from the Goschen Committee that 'the growth of the Navy would shortly make it impossible for existing ports to accommodate all the ships, and recommended the formation of another naval establishment,'[24] and they had recommended Rosyth. Indeed, negotiations with Lord Linlithgow for the purchase of 1,200 acres of land and forty-eight acres of foreshore had all but been agreed by the time the Prime Minister made his announcement to Parliament.

Erskine had been realistic and not too gloomy about the time that it would take to see the new base and dockyard playing a useful part in the defence of the nation, for progress was painfully slow. Tenders were not accepted until 1909 and King George V did not open Rosyth until 8 June 1915 – some twelve years after the announcement.

Part of the reason for this was said to be the opposition of Jackie Fisher, for he preferred Cromarty to Rosyth, as he considered the former strategically better placed and Rosyth to be an unsafe anchorage. He thought the Forth railway bridge, 'that beastly bridge', enough of a target as it was and 'if blown up, would make egress risky without examination.'[25]

Erskine may have been thinking of the Cromarty Firth and Invergordon himself. He had stayed, after all, at the Inveran Hotel, by Invershin, just before he sat down to write the first words of *The Riddle*. On the train north, he would have rattled across 'that beastly bridge', on his way to Inverness, and then skirted along the north shore of the Cromarty Firth in sight of the great naval anchorage at Invergordon, reaching the southern shores of the shallow and sand-choked Dornoch Firth, before alighting at the halt at Invershin.

'We're done for now.'

As for Erskine's allied plea for a North Sea fleet, the Admiralty's move towards an effective force in home waters is acknowledged in the Postscript as 'another good measure,' followed by the rider, 'but it should be remembered that its ships are not modern, or in the least capable of meeting the principal German squadron.'

Erskine's welcome was sparked off by the Admiralty announcement of 20 February 1903, just before they pinpointed Rosyth as a North Sea base. They said they were to strengthen the Home Fleet but were to do this by adding ships from the Reserve and increasing training rather than building anew. The new vessels, six Royal Sovereign and two Duncan class battleships, came in the spring of 1904. The major fleet switch and reorganisation followed the appointment of that Blue Water whirlwind, Jackie Fisher, as First Sea Lord in October 1904. Under his schemes, three-quarters of Britain's battleships would be available against Germany. Marder neatly points out that Fisher was fond of quoting Nelson's favourite phrase, 'The battle ground should be the drill ground.'[26] By moving his ships into home waters, Fisher was to achieve just this.

Davies, in *The Riddle*, had argued for volunteers to be trained likewise in home waters. He had pressed for 'intelligent irregulars,' in 'mosquitoes with stings – swarms of them, patrol boats, scout boats, torpedo boats'; who would produce offensive defence in the estuaries and behind the banks and shoals of England – 'the Mersey estuary, the Dee, the Severn, the Wash and best of all, the Thames, with all the Kent, Essex and Suffolk banks round it.' These ideas were picked up with approval in the *Daily Telegraph* review of the book.

Herbert Warington-Smyth had continued to campaign for a volunteer reserve for the Royal Navy. He would have told Erskine that two years before the book came out, Arnold Forster, then parliamentary secretary to the First Lord of the Admiralty, had summoned him and explained the government's interest in a new volunteer force. The parliamentary secretary wanted to know the numbers and types of volunteers that were likely to come forward. He was interested in discovering the right centres, if there was likely to be any opposition from local authorities and whether, particularly, the volunteers would be willing to serve with the fleet or overseas.

The National Volunteer Committee promoting the cause had already been set up, so the answers were not too difficult to find. This body included Herbert Warington-Smyth (as secretary), C. E. H. Chadwyck-Healy, KC, owner of the 247-ton steam-yacht *Isa*, and the energetic Marquess of Graham (chairman), who then had the twenty-five-ton steamer *Violet*. The first two were members, with Erskine, of the Royal Cruising Club. Members of this club played a recognisable part in the birth of the 'wavy navy'. The committee, so encouraged, gathered supporters up and down the land and the press, too, were generally enthusiastic. The 'proper' Navy was a little sceptical though, with the notable exception of Admiral Lord Charles Beresford. He wrote: 'the regulars will be proud to have them [the volunteers] as comrades,' and cited the 'splendid energy and patriotism of British and Colonial volunteers in the South African War'.

The government's own Manning Committee, to which Erskine refers in his

Postscript, was officially known as the Naval Reserves Committee and was set up in 1902 under the chairmanship of Sir Edward Grey.

If senior naval officers had doubts, Arnold Forster had none. He shared Erskine's view and wanted the volunteers to have a private navy of their own with small ships for reconnaissance and scouting. The author of *The Riddle* could not have put the case for a volunteer naval reserve better than the parliamentary secretary to the First Lord of the Admiralty.

'My view is,' he declared,

> *...that we are not utilising the one great resource which no nation has to the same extent as we have ... that is the enormous number of men who follow the sea for the pleasure of following the sea.... There are hundreds – I should say thousands- of men who are always on the sea whenever they can get away. I know many men who can sail a 10-ton boat from the Lizard to the Chapman in any weather you like; who know every harbour along the coast, who know every buoy, who know- what is more than most bluejackets know- which way the wind is blowing, which way the tide is running, and who are in every respect as good as any professional sailors in knowledge of the sea.*[27]

The Naval Reserves Committee reported in favour and in June 1903, a month after the publication of *The Riddle*, the Naval Forces Act 1903 was passed and the Admiralty was authorised to 'raise and maintain a force to be called the Royal Naval Volunteer Reserve'. There was now a chance for 'the hundreds of chaps who know our coasts like a book,' as Davies pointed out in *The Riddle*, 'to form a splendid naval reserve'. Chadwyck-Healy was responsible for the name.

The Preface to *The Riddle* lifted the book from the realm of fiction by putting a large question-mark in the mind of the reader. He was invited to ask, 'Could this story be true?' The Epilogue summarised the questions gleaned from the story that the reader should now ask of a wider audience and eventually of government. The Postscript showed that these questions were very much to the point and had been accepted as such, at any rate in part, by those who *should* know. Such successful persuading before the book was even published complements that feeling of truth. Add to this a rattling good yarn, to adopt a phrase of the day, and the package is neatly complete. The message was, therefore, easily delivered and scored a bullseye with Selborne, Rosebery, Campbell-Bannerman and Sir William White.

Erskine's place at the clerks' table may have ensured a proper aim, but there is not and has never been a suggestion that he used information gained there improperly. His letters to Great Aunt Flora Priestley of 8 January 1901, to Basil Williams of 12 June 1902 and that penned after publication to Mrs Probyn of 17 October 1903 show that the inspiration and the fabric of ideas are his and his alone. He had, however, access in the House of Commons Library to the German technical publications, such as the German magazine *Deutsche Rundschau,* and as he wrote in that last letter, 'I only depend on hints and rumours from the German technical press.' The 'remarkable confirmation' of his ideas, mentioned in the same letter, came afterwards and he quite properly would not divulge this information, 'as the matter is highly confidential'.

Chapter 7

OPERATIONS AGAINST ENGLAND

So what was going on across the North Sea? What did Erskine see on his voyage of 1897 that was not described in his logs or letters and has, so far, remained unnoticed? More importantly, what were the Germans up to that gave 'the most remarkable confirmation' of the ideas that formed the principal plot of *The Riddle*? We now have to look from the German side of things and go back a bit.

Lüttwitz's article on the 'Invasion of England' had been published in Germany just after the Kaiser sent his famous telegram to President Kruger on 3 January 1896 and the quick response by the British on the 7th of that month, creating a flying squadron of Royal Navy ships to go, at short notice, to any part of the world. On learning of this, the German Navy realised, for the first time, that Britain might one day be their enemy and that plans must be prepared for this eventuality.[1] Admiral (at one time Lieutenant-General) Albert von Stosch, who had sent SMS *Blitz* on fishery-protection duties, saw the point only too clearly and wrote to her one-time first officer, now Admiral Tirpitz, on 12 February:

> *The fury of the English against us, which found expression in the events of the Transvaal-Telegramme, has its real explanation in Germany's competition on the world market. ... Since the foreign policy of England is determined exclusively by commercial interests, we must henceforth reckon with the opposition of that island people. ... As a result, I have been considering the question, how can we wage a naval war against England with any hope of success?*[2]

The official thinking-cap on this subject was worn by Rear-Admiral Otto von Diederichs, chief of staff at the High Command, and his first paper of 5 March 1896 on the chances of success against Britain was not encouraging. He saw the British fleet as all-powerful, while Germany's lingered at sixth in the world league table. He imagined his country ringed by British sea-going steel and her overseas trade choked. The only chance, and a desperate one, lay in attempting a 'Bolt from the Blue', an attack on the Royal Navy Reserve Fleet at the Nore, in the Thames Estuary.[3]

Diederichs was not the first of Wilhelm's officers, though, to produce an operational plan against England in 1896. That honour should go to Korvette-Kapitän August von Heeringen, who became one of Tirpitz's aides.[4]

Admiral Eduard von Knorr, Chief of the High Command of the Imperial Navy, wrote his own memorandum on the subject on 24 April 1897 and his thoughts, given here in full, shine a light on German thinking at that time and for a while to come:

Germany at War with England

A lasting effect cannot be achieved by a small fleet aiming to destroy a larger fleet.

However, as in the war against France, we could be successful against a part of the English fleet, i.e. achieve a partial victory, if the situation is exploited immediately.

I am of the firm opinion that in a war against England alone this situation would be most advantageous to us immediately after the declaration of war, rather than later when we might be blockaded. Such an attack would most likely be possible only as long as the enemy was not fully armed and if operations on his part had not yet commenced. If the latter were the case, an attack against England could not be considered as her might is so great that she is able to blockade our ports, despite the demands in terms of men and materials this makes on her, and can carry it out in relays and with a feeling of security. If, during the further course of the war, we are then reduced to defending our ports, a large-scale attack would not be possible, and therefore we should take advantage of the opportunity offered at the beginning. As far as the .question of whether this war should be conducted ruthlessly or whether it should be viewed as a hopeless venture, is concerned, I am left in no doubt whatsoever that the greater our ruthlessness, and the greater the sense of shock felt in England and in English shipping, the better for us, for England will in any case make it a guiding principle of her action to destroy our maritime and trade positions, irrespective of whether we act ruthlessly or not..

Therefore I am disposed towards ruthless action against English shipping with any means justifying the destruction of ships – but at the same time I am against the destruction of ports, because I cannot see the effectiveness of this in the principal aim of damaging English ships. It is therefore useless.

I would come to the opposite decision if, but this is scarcely conceivable, England were to declare herself prepared to spare our merchant fleet.

As we can count on the success of our initial attack, I repeat my previously expressed view that the working-out of a plan of war, as well as all preparations should be taken in hand.

As far as the plan is concerned, I would like to believe that the installation of the first squadrons near Dover, the entry of ships into the Thames for a short time, the damage caused to English shipping, and the laying of mines outside Chatham and in the Thames on retreating, will cause the English fleet to face ours as soon as it can arrive from Spithead.

With this, I request the Chief of Staff to have the basis of the plan and the preparations set out and submitted in a form suitable for a direct report.[5]

On 3 May 1897, Admiral von Knorr had an audience with the Kaiser to consider plans in the event of war with France. As the session drew to a close, the emperor asked von Knorr for a similar study in case of war with England, perhaps prompted by the thoughts in the memorandum quoted above.

The outline operational plan took just over a month to prepare and was presented to Wilhelm on the 31st of the same month. Von Knorr had followed Diederichs' idea of a 'bolt from the blue' against the Reserve fleet, followed, if possible, by the rapid deployment of an invasion force before the Royal Navy's Mediterranean fleet was able to return. The estuary of the Schelde was suggested as a most suitable point for launching the invasion. Dutch and Belgian agreement would have to be secured by political pressure or military threat, or, if that failed, by force.

The Kaiser approved these skeleton plans. He wanted to know where the invading force was to land, the number of troops to be employed, their units, the transport required and how they would be supplied once on England's shore.

Korvetten-Kapitän Ludwig Schröder, head of Section AIIIa, was ordered to draw up detailed plans. By November 1897, they were ready and in a handwritten draft from Berlin, dated the 12th of the month, marked 'Very Secret, Hand to Hand only', he spelt out his ideas. The title was descriptive 'Memorandum, An Operation Against Antwerp'. Schröder agreed that this Belgian port and the estuary of the Schelde were the key to the invasion of England. His plan employed *seven* ships of 5000 tons each (rather than Davies' *seven* siels) with their escorts, leaving the three great German estuaries of the Jade, Weser and Elbe and making for a rendezvous off the Schelde. *Seven* landing places had been selected, for Antwerp and six strong points on the neutral Dutch and Belgian shores were to be attacked and secured, while at the same time the German Army would support these landings with three flying columns, making best speed for Breda and Antwerp. The invasion of England would follow the success of the first part of the operation. The neutrality of Belgium and Holland was not considered to be worth much thought or argument.

'We must consider, first of all,' Schröder wrote, 'that in a war between Germany and England our national wealth, the welfare of the German people, yes, perhaps our very existence as a state, would be at stake. In the face of such considerations, clinging to artificially constructed clauses of international law would be far more reprehensible from an ethical point of view than merely bending the law because circumstances force us to do so. If the life of a nation is at stake, disregarding the neutrality of Belgium and The Netherlands need not dismay us.'

He went on to argue that the English government had done the same at Copenhagen in 1807.[6] The simile was still relevant, for the idea of being 'Copenhagened' was to become the Kaiser's recurring bad dream. He and Tirpitz were able to picture the Royal Navy acting swiftly and without warning, sending the Imperial fleet to the bottom before it became a major lever in world politics.

Schröder's plan for the invasion of the Low Countries was dictated by a need to shorten the sea journey to England for the invasion itself and to ease the problem of supply once the troops had landed. He argued that:

> *... such a victory over England cannot be won by the fleet alone, thus one must consider the difference between the distance from the German North Sea and that from the mouth of the Maas or the estuary of the Schelde to the English east coast. From Wilhelmshaven to the coast of Norfolk at Great Yarmouth, the distance is approximately 270 sea miles. A transport convoy doing ten to twelve knots per hour, would need at least twenty-four hours to make the journey. The distance from Vlissingen to Dover or to Sheerness, both useful points for large-scale troop landings, is approximately 80–85 sea miles; in other words less than one-third of the time would be required.*
>
> *The distance from Ostend or Nieuwport is even less, only 60 sea miles, but because of the military and hydrographic conditions of these ports, they would be less suitable.*

Schröder's thoughts joined the plans and schemes of others considering the possibilities of invading England initiated by Heeringen's plan, von Diederichs' first memorandum of 1896 and the Kaiser's favourable reception of von Knorr's ideas fifteen months later.

The summer, autumn and winter of 1897 were the seasons of great political and military scheming in Germany. She was restless in her European bed and wished to turn over. In preparing to do so, she did not mind pulling the clothes off her continental partners. Erskine, able to read the German newspapers and periodicals, and thriving on the printed word, was in a good position to savour what he read and saw. His visits to Kiel in October and November 1897 have already been described. History now shows that June was the most significant month in that fundamentally important year. Erskine witnessed the first results by watching the wake of that month's passing.

Admiral Tirpitz took up his appointment as Secretary of State of the Imperial

Naval Office early in June and on the 15th presented to the Kaiser his memorandum 'General Considerations on the Constitution of our Fleet According to Ship Classes and Designs.' The report was the basis of the first Navy Bill of 1898. Within this technical report lay, in the words of Jonathan Steinberg, 'a fully developed strategy for the German Navy ... which can be said without exaggeration to have changed the course of modem history.'[7]

The admiral's ideas were not buried very deep, for in paragraphs 2–4 he wrote:

2. For Germany the most dangerous naval enemy at the present time is England. It is also the enemy against which we most urgently require a certain measure of naval force as a political power factor.
3. Commerce raiding and trans-Atlantic war against England is so hopeless, because of the shortage of bases on our side and the superfluity on England's side, that we must ignore this type of war against England in our plans for the constitution of our fleet.
4. Our fleet must be so constructed that it can unfold its greatest military potential between Heligoland and the Thames.[8]

In the same epic month and only two days later, Bernhard von Bülow, German ambassador in Rome, was made State Secretary of the Foreign Ministry, succeeding to a post once occupied by his father under Bismarck.

Bülow and Tirpitz were a team well suited to the Kaiser, but dangerous to the world. Steinberg put his finger on the reason why: 'Their partnership was to prove fatal and unequal, because, unlike Tirpitz, Bülow had no inner strength. Where Tirpitz's glossy surface masked a will of iron, lamed though it may be by emotional instability, Bülow's glittering exterior concealed an utter lack of force and purpose. In foreign affairs it was the admiral who had the ideas, while the diplomat had only the manners.'[9]

Bülow was bad for the Kaiser, too, as Albert Ballin, the emperor's close friend and the managing director of the Hamburg-America Line, was to admit later. 'Bülow,' he said, 'is a misfortune for us and is destroying the Emperor completely ... by saying nothing but the most flattering rubbish and thus bringing His Majesty to a boundless over-estimation of himself.'[10]

Bülow supported Wilhelm's policy of 'a place in the sun' for Germany amongst the other world powers. Tirpitz, with his 'risk theory' provided the means of achieving that favoured position. The ideas were embodied in the paragraphs just quoted. The vastly increased number of battleships would provide the antidote to being 'Copenhagened' and the lever to persuade other powers to join Germany in an alliance and so achieve the economic and military warmth desired, or to move over so that Germany might enjoy that position by herself. The fleet, the political lever, had to be in the North Sea, both to be a threat to Britain and to provide protection for her naval war ports.

The Gunboat 'Blitz'

But to return to plans for the invasion of England, the general staff had been asked by Admiral von Knorr on 2 June for their comments and co-operation in developing the outline plan presented to the Kaiser on 31 May. The Army had to provide some of the answers to the Kaiser's specific questions and to say whether they required the Imperial Navy to guarantee the invading troops an unbroken lifeline, which von Knorr's staff advised might be difficult.

Some of the general staff began to have doubts that the Schröder plan was the best way of achieving an invasion of England. The political implications had been too airily cast aside. The crossing into Belgium would be against the 1839 treaty and France might well react unfavourably. The sea crossing from Antwerp was shorter but the element of surprise in the leap across the North Sea to the English coast might well be lost in the process of invading the Low Countries.[11]

The chief of the general staff, Graf Alfred von Schlieffen, did not reply to Admiral von Knorr until 14 December 1897 and he was not particularly encouraging. Schlieffen saw that 'England's power is based on its fleet,' and so the fleet had to be destroyed or removed. He realised that the Imperial German Navy could not achieve this, though their ships could be 'prepared more quickly, are better equipped for battle and more skilfully commanded'. The only hope, therefore, was to defeat the Reserve fleet on the fifth day, leaving ten days before powerful British reinforcements could return. During this period it was vital that the invading German Army should achieve 'great successes against the enemy'. He added dramatically that 'the German must kneel on the breast of his downed opponent until the latter begs for mercy, for peace at any price. This price can consist of nothing else less than the surrender of the English fleet.' He conceded that this 'would require more than a little effort', and 'a very large invasion force would be needed.' He did not like the idea of using Dutch or Belgian ports. Flushing might have done, but it only had one rail link to Germany.

Answering the questions posed by the Kaiser and trying at the same time to satisfy von Knorr's particular concern about the need to keep supply lines to the invading forces open, Schlieffen answered that following the sea battle in the North Sea or Thames Estuary, the troops should be landed on the north shore of the latter. He advised that the troops should embark at *seven* German ports and explained, 'I have in mind Emden, Wilhelmshaven, Bremerhaven, Cuxhaven, the Kiel Canal, Hamburg and Kiel.' He did not name the units or the exact number of soldiers, answering that 'the transport vessels must be capable of carrying as many troops as possible. It would be an irredeemable error to leave even one battalion behind which could have been transported. The number of troops is to be limited only by the number of vessels available, and by the efficiency of the railways.' He recommended further study on which ports were to be used for embarkation and the number of vessels available. On the vital point of communications with the invading force after landing,

Arriving at Kiel

he rather huffed and puffed: 'After the landing has taken place, communications with Germany may only be interrupted for a short time. If the Navy is unable to maintain these links, the enemy power is to be defeated as quickly as possible by a massive deployment of strength, and in this way the opponent is to be forced to make peace.'[12]

There is no doubt that Schlieffen's reply had a sobering effect on Admiral von Knorr and his staff but the planning of offensive operations against Great Britain went on.[13]

There were three further factors that damped down the earlier enthusiasm.[14] The first was Queen Victoria's Diamond Jubilee Review of 1897, which added to the Channel fleet. The second was the Kaiser's adventure at Kiaochow, the first flowering of Bülow's *Weltpolitik*,which not only depleted German naval strength in the North Sea but demonstrated only too clearly that even the despatch of five ships and 717 marines could be a painfully slow and public business. The third factor was the most powerful of all, the rooted objection by Admiral Tirpitz to anything that would cause trouble until the Kaiser's battle fleet was a proper match for the Royal Navy. He thought that von Knorr had been irresponsible in encouraging Wilhelm towards any plans against England. Prince Hohenlohe, the Reich's chancellor, records in his diary for October 1898 the robust reply of Admiral Tirpitz when he was asked his opinion of the Schröder plan: 'The idea of an invasion of England is insane. Even if we succeed in landing two Army corps in England it would not help us, for two corps would not be strong enough to hold their positions in England without support from home. Tirpitz concludes that all hostile activity towards England must wait until we have a fleet as strong as the English.'[15]

The Kaiser and von Knorr continued to foster invasion plans in the early months of 1898 and there was an idea to despatch the training ship SMS *Olga* to survey the coast from the Thames northward to the Humber, but she did not sail.[16] At about the same period the training ship SMS *Stein* was enabled to stay a little longer in Antwerp to assess its capabilities. The idea of using the Low Countries was not dead.[17]

Professor Ivo Lambi points out though that on 26 May 1898 von Knorr ruled that work on the offensive operations plan against Britain should cease but the study of procurement of steamers for the invasion force continue. On 12 September 1898, he initialled a document that was circulating internally, emphasising that the previous studies had revealed that in the case of sudden mobilisation in the spring of 1898 there would have been available in German harbours 145 steam-ships, sufficient for the transportation of two and a half army corps to England, but insufficient for the transport for the six to eight army corps required for a successful invasion.

It was stated that the merchant marine was capable of transporting the larger force, but the preparations for it could not be kept secret and such an embarkation could not occur in the beginning of the war. The document also dealt with a possible joint Franco-German landing on the British coast.[18]

The stop/go policy continued, with both the Navy and Army staff undertaking their own studies of invasion beaches and embarkation ports. On 17 November 1898, von Knorr's staff reported on a number of alternative landing sites. These were to the south or north of Flamborough Head, Bridlington or Filey bays – depending on weather; the Humber estuary, southeast of Grimsby; the Southwold coast as far north as Lowestoft or Yarmouth, and, finally, a stretch just to the south, from Orfordness to Southwold.

When von Schlieffen was consulted, he reminded the Navy that his primary concerns were to limit the distance across the sea and to be close to a primary target such as London. Taking both these into consideration, he thought that the stretch of beach from Great Yarmouth to Aldeburgh showed the greatest promise.[19] H. R. Moon records that 'this was later to become the stretch of coast where British defence planners thought a German invasion most likely during the First World War.'[20] Erskine had pointed his best finger at the north shore of the Wash.

Professor Lambi writes that on 28 October 1898, Admiral von Knorr reported to Wilhelm about the preparations for a landing in England, admitting, however, that they only had theoretical significance for the time being, and on 10 January 1899 he wrote to von Schlieffen that without allies Germany could not achieve a temporary mastery of the North Sea, which was a prerequisite for an invasion. This was very much in line with the strong arguments put forward by Tirpitz.

This short summary shows that in the period between 1896 and 1899 Germany had seriously considered operational plans for invading Britain. At that time they had not thought of using barges for transporting troops; all their plans employed steamers. But, like Erskine, one of the blueprints foresaw the use of seven embarkation ports. The general staff, though, because they were using commercial deep-draft vessels selected ports with major facilities rather than the seven 'siels', or 'potty little places', as Davies called them.

The German plans emphasised the importance of the railways, as had the 'interesting document somewhat damaged by fire that Carruthers rescued'. The latter stressed that, 'landwards, the loop of railway round the Frisian peninsula would form the line of communication in rear of the seven streams.'

The loop from Emden, in the west, through Norden, Esens and Wittmund to Jever, was opened on 15 June 1883. Carruthers had travelled from Norddeich on the 1892 link to Norden and thence on the Esens line. The railway from Jever to Carolinensiel was opened in 1888. The Jever to Wilhelmshaven line had opened seventeen years previously.[21]

The coastal railway that linked Emden to Wilhelmshaven was, therefore, built in the time of the Kaiser's grandfather, Wilhelm I, when Bismarck was busy with internal affairs. In that year he passed his sickness insurance law Europe's first comprehensive social security scheme. Prince Wilhelm, at the age of twenty-nine, was not thinking of invading his mother's country either. He was promoted to colonel a month after the line was opened.

The principal purpose of the Emden to Wilhelmshaven railway was to serve the industrial town of Norden and the fertile districts of Harlingerland with their centre at Esens, as well as providing, in the same way as the three-year old Emden to Wilhelmshaven canal, a method of supplying the war port with food in hostile times.

The railway may not have been built for adventures against Germany's neighbours, but it was a useful asset for offence as well as defence. A scheme employing the railway, the canals and the seven siels for offensive purposes could have been achieved in greater secrecy than one using von Schlieffen's seven major ports, especially if any activity spotted could be put down to defensive manoeuvres, as suggested in the Epilogue of *The Riddle of the Sands.* The siels, though, were not fit for large troop-carrying steamers.

In March 1900, at the nadir of British fortunes in South Africa, General

Colmar Freiherr von der Goltz, one of Germany's best military thinkers, then Inspector-General of the Engineer and Combat Corps, wrote an article for *Deutsche Rundschau,* the German review. In this far-seeing contribution, entitled 'Seemacht und Landkrieg' (Sea Power and Land War), he set out Germany's position then against the background of world military history. He, like Mahan, saw the control of the sea being decisive in a long struggle. He, like Tirpitz, found that though Germany had made remarkable strides in both her naval and commercial shipbuilding programmes, she was not yet a match for the combined French and Russian fleets. Looking west, he wrote, 'at sea we are certainly at present almost unarmed, although we do possess arms which could hurt England.' He found that 'England's maritime superiority is, at present, a depressing fact and will always remain one', but he did see light, for the *Morning Post* had published a summary of the distribution of the English fleet. 'The surprise was to see how small, by comparison with the generous treatment given to foreign stations, are the units remaining on the English coast.' He saw this as England's Achilles heel and cited the emergency in South Africa as creating further danger for Britain. 'A brave enemy', he held, 'would, without doubt, use such a moment of weakness for taking action.' He went on to say that landings on the English coast should not be banished to the realms of fairy tale: 'The distance to get there from the continent is short enough to be overcome, if an energetic admiral succeeds through good gunnery and brave action in gaining control, for a time, of the North Sea.' It seemed to him an absurdity to say that a nation of fifty-five million should be permanently without defence against a nation of only forty million. He saw that Britain's riches were helped by being surrounded by sea, but Germany's main commercial centres were at the mouths of important rivers serving a big hinterland – a resource that could be developed even faster 'when the system of inland canals, the construction of which has commenced, is complete.' Davies said much the same in *The Riddle.*

The General did not develop his invasion ideas further for public consumption. He felt that this would be 'going too far.' He was not, however, so reticent in private, for he despatched his plans for invading England, using sea-going barges and tugs, shortly after the article appeared in print.

The German Admiralty staff commented respectfully on the plan in a memorandum of 30 May 1900.[22] They saw the advantage of using shallow draft lighters. 'It is possible', they observed, 'under favourable conditions to land direct from them without the help of boats, etc.' However, they pointed out more soberly that that was in ideal circumstances, for normally the lighters could not be towed into shallow water by tugs or launches as these vessels drew more, and so would have to be dragged in by rowing boats or ropes.

They saw difficulties, too, in crossing the North Sea behind a tug because of the 'uncertainty' of the hawser and the problems in controlling such a fleet.

They estimated that it would require eighty-five 1,000-ton sea-going lighters and eighty-five tugs to move a mobile division. They thought that a similar fleet of steamers could carry two and a half army corps. They were gloomy as well about von der Goltz's chances of success even if he did reach the other side without proper command of the sea, and sceptical that the conversion of barges, or for that matter steamers, could be carried out without attracting attention. On the other hand, they were sure that speed was the only way of achieving success and that the vanguard division should therefore be sent over in the large transatlantic liners available in Hamburg and Bremerhaven and already 'equipped for the transport of human beings and horses.'

They calculated that six steamers of the class of the 11,000-ton *Bulgaria* could 'get a division to the objective in practically any weather' at a speed of thirteen to fourteen knots, while 170 lighters and tugs would be needed to achieve the same result in favourable conditions and would take two to three times as long.

The Admiralty staff, though, congratulated the Inspectorate for thinking of sea-going lighters and for producing so much valuable information on their use. They ended with a recommendation that could have come straight out of *The Riddle*. 'It is only possible to support the proposal if the Inspectorate carries out next autumn the proposed test of the sea transport of troops in a sea-going lighter, making full use of the hold space in a barge already loaded with stores [horses, weapons, ammunition and kit].'

Erskine may have read von der Goltz's article in an old copy of *Deutsche Rundschau* before setting pen to paper and building on the message it contained. After all, he mentioned in his letter to Mrs Probyn, already quoted, that he depended 'on hints and rumours from the German technical press.' He was in South Africa when the article first appeared.

It seems unlikely that he would have stumbled upon von der Goltz's actual plan or heard of its receipt by the Imperial Admiralty before he wrote the book, but he may have caught a suggestion of it after *The Riddle* was published. This may account for the remarkable and highly confidential 'confirmation' to which he refers in the same letter.

Similarly, he may have heard later of the plan forwarded by August Heeringen on 12 April 1902.[23] Heeringen was the first to produce an operational plan against Britain, as early as 1896. He now suggested that the invading German forces embark from the Elbe, from Danish harbours and Dutch ports, after the 'friendly occupation' of Holland and Belgium. The idea could have been intercepted later by Erskine, but this is pure speculation, for he never revealed the source of the 'remarkable confirmation'.

PART FOUR

A Strange Conclusion

Chapter 8

THE CHILDERS' PLAN

The Childers' Plan

The *Westminster Gazette* of 22 January 1904 was not surprised by all this plotting by the Kaiser and his men. The paper took the opportunity given by the publication of a new impression of *The Riddle of the Sands* to ask, in bold type, 'THE INVASION OF ENGLAND BY GERMANY. IS IT PRACTICABLE?', with the subtitle 'The Plans of German Strategists'. The correspondent gave the broader answer in the first paragraph:

> *Practically it comes to this – that in the opinion of some of the most eminent soldiers in Europe the invasion of Great Britain from overseas is, in certain circumstances, a practicable undertaking, and that this opinion is so far from being a mere theory the practical provision for giving effect to it is actually among the elaborate secret arrangements which the German government has made in view of eventualities in European politics.*

The correspondent was at pains to avoid pouring anything inflammable on the smouldering fire of Anglo-German antagonism:

> *The German government have a perfect right, even a duty, to take any measures or lay any plans for attack or defence which it thinks necessary for its own strength or safety, and is not exposed to any charge of unfriendliness in so doing. It must also desire, if it can, to keep its plans secret, so that if they were ever put into execution they might have the force of surprise. On the other hand, it is equally our right to discover these plans if we can, to discuss them, and, if possible, to dispose of our forces that they may be effectively neutralised in advance.*

Erskine took the same care. He was anxious to alert the country to the dangers posed by Germany but not to inflame his countrymen in any way against their North Sea neighbour. Davies was shown to be an admirer of both Germany and the Kaiser, though necessarily wary of both. 'Germany's a thundering great nation,' he told Carruthers, adding, 'I wonder if we shall ever fight her.' Davies is revealed as understanding the German predicament, worried about the implications for his own country, yet able to appreciate the Kaiser's leadership without approving of his intentions. 'What I'm concerned with is their sea power. It's a new thing with them, but it's going strong, and that Emperor of theirs is running it for all it's worth. He's a splendid chap, and anyone can see he's right. They've got no colonies to speak of, and must have them, like us. They can't get them and keep them, and they can't protect their huge commerce without naval strength. The command of the sea is the thing nowadays, isn't it?' He admitted that his views had come straight from Mahan.

Erskine's underlying theme in *The Riddle of the Sands* was Britain's unpreparedness. Molly Childers, Erskine's widow, highlighted this in a letter to Frank Sidgwick in November 1938: 'At the time he believed that preparedness for war prevented war, a belief that he revised later with regret that he had ever preached the doctrine.'[1] Molly said much the same in a note first published in an edition of *The Riddle* seven years previously and included in many subsequent impressions.

The message that came across most clearly was of course the possibility of the invasion of England by Germany. The *Westminster Gazette* correspondent admitted, 'the problem of invasion has been exhaustively explored as regards France, but it is seldom, if ever, spoken of as regards Germany.'

German strategists, he went on, including von Moltke and several mentioned in the previous chapter, did not hesitate to declare their opinion publicly, 'that the invasion of England, so far from being a practical impossibility, might be successfully accomplished if certain conditions were secured.' It was not unreasonable to assume that the official pigeon-holes of the general staff may be found to contain 'more or less elaborated schemes for an invasion'. How right he was.

The *Westminster Gazette* correspondent had read, like Erskine, of the possibility of invasion in German publications. He quite understood how attention might be 'awakened here as to the nature of the schemes which might have been devised to bring to bear upon these islands the enormous military power of the German Empire'.

The *Westminster Gazette's* strategist summarises the advantages of the scheme of invasion that Erskine brings to life. Secrecy would be better guaranteed by the use of the 'small and little used harbours of East Friesland. The mainland is sparsely populated, the ports are obscure and of little commercial value, they are difficult to approach through channels threading the great sand banks which lie between the mainland and the east Frisian islands.' He makes the same mistake about the original purpose of the railway system, for he continues, 'Yet in this uncompromising and unproductive region, the Germans have constructed a great system of railways, giving easy access to these small ports, and enabling large numbers of men and great quantities of war material to be rapidly brought to six or seven points of embarkation.'

He could quite see that if the British fleet were crippled, 'the passage ought to be successfully accomplished to our coast.' He also approved of the probable landing place suggested in *The Riddle* as East Holland on the north side of the Wash, as it was the nearest place to the shores of Germany and can be reached by a simple deep-sea passage, and 'with the light draught flotilla of transports described, the landing of the advance force ought to be rapidly effected.' He saw that 'that force would then entrench itself and await the arrival of the reinforcements required for the subsequent operations.' This would, of course, be a strike at the 'industrial heart of the Kingdom'. The correspondent did not know that von Schlieffen had selected that stretch of coast between Great Yarmouth and Aldeburgh, little more than 100 nautical miles to the southeast and about the same distance, as the crow flies, from the outskirts of London.

The majority of the public and many of the defence planners saw *The Riddle*'s warning of German invasion as a signal either to pay greater attention to the physical defence of Britain's shores or to provide a Navy strong enough to ensure that the enemy came nowhere near. We have already seen how the Bolt from the Blue school, particularly the Army, saw the invasion threat. *The Riddle of the Sands* was very effective pro-Roberts propaganda and provided a good argument for the better defence of Britain's coastline by providing more men by compulsory military service and by giving funds to the Army, rather than to the Navy.[2]

The Blue Water school saw the Navy's role as defensive, an iron filter through which no one would dare penetrate with a force of any size. There was, though, another message concealed in *The Riddle* that the two warring factions did not spot. The invading force could be dealt with in three places; on the beaches, as the Army would have it; on the way across, as theNavy and the Blue Water school would argue; *or* at the place of embarkation. 'This,' the *Western Gazette*'s expert held, 'was Nelson's method when entrusted with the defence of England against the threatened invasion by Napoleon, and its wisdom is unquestionable.'

In *The Riddle*, Davies had stressed that this should be the role of the volunteers, the force that Warington-Smyth, Erskine and others had argued for so persuasively.

Davies was convinced that in shallow waters the small boat would play 'a mighty role' in a naval war, particularly if 'two well matched heavy battle fleets met early on and destroyed one another mutually.' 'It's then that the true struggle will set in; it's then that anything that will float will be pressed into the service, and anybody who can steer a boat, knows his waters, and doesn't care the toss of a coin for his life will have magnificent opportunities.'

Remember Davies' channel theory, where 'a small torpedo-boat could on a dark night cut clean through from the Jade to the Elbe and play the deuce with shipping there.' The *Westminster Gazette* saw sense in this:

> *If this volunteer force is established and made efficient, its operations need not be defensive. As Mr Childers points out, it could be utilised in offensive operations on the German coast, could make the preparation and dispatch of an invading flotilla almost impossible, and might effect much against the mercantile marine using the few German ports on the North Sea. This is in strict accordance with our traditional naval policy – to seek the enemy on his own waters and there deal decisive blows.*

The well-reasoned article ended with a prayer: 'It may be hoped that the proposals of the author may be realised and practical effect given to his suggestions.'

Some of Erskine's ideas were taken up, but one in particular, which he felt strongly about, was not. This had to do with charts. All through *The Riddle*, Davies, with his taste for amateur hydrography, heaped scorn on the accuracy and usefulness of the Admiralty charts of the sand-strewn coasts of Holland and Germany. In contrast to these insults, he praised 'German charts of excellent quality'.

The criticism came straight from experience, from hours of puzzling over *Vixen*'s position, using inadequate information or searching, with tired eyes, for something that might exist on the sheet of grey and white paper and was subsequently found to have moved or not to have been there for years. His brother Henry would have been able to bear witness to these moments of frustration. His son wrote, 'Dad helped to take numerous soundings to apply to the charts that Erskine kept.'[3] The taste for amateur hydrography not surprisingly was as strong in the crew of *Vixen* as it was with those aboard *Dulcibella*.

Erskine's complaint against the Hydrographic Office must have festered, for Molly Childers, in a letter to Frank Sidgwick, remembered how strongly her husband had felt.'He found the British Admiralty charts often seriously out of date and defective, whereas, when he procured them, the German charts not only of their own but also of British waters, were up to date and perfect. (And for Baltic waters it was the same.)'[4]

To Erskine such carelessness was dangerous and for this reason he publicised and brought to the notice of those concerned through *The Riddle* the gross inadequacy of British Admiralty charts and the apparent lack of appreciation of German developments. He bracketed both as perilous from the point of view of national defence and hampering to British mercantile shipping.[5]

Jackie Fisher turned his own spotlight on the chart-makers in the paper 'Naval Necessities' which he handed to Lord Selborne when accepting appointment as First Sea Lord on 20 October 1904. In Appendix I he concluded that the Hydrographic Department was inefficient and that business principles should be introduced. In his usual robust way he declared,'To have an efficient surveying service you must have a high sense of duty in the surveyors, or the work will be scamped; a naval training is superior to every other training in producing a high sense of duty. You must have a higher sense of duty than is necessary for ordnance surveyors or civilian ones; they cannot wreck ships and drown people, and marine surveyors can; their work lives after they are dead, and their capacity for producing wrecks lasts till the place is re-surveyed. (Example, HMS *Sultan*.).'[6] HMS *Sultan* grounded on an unknown rock in the South Comino Channel, Malta, on 6 March 1889, and sank, but was later salvaged.

Erskine was like Fisher in the latter's driving days. If he held a strong view, he did not just preach from some paper pulpit, but did all he could to right matters, even if it meant doing the work himself. So it was with his views on the inadequacies of the Admiralty charts of the Dutch and North German coasts. Erskine and his brother took their soundings and recorded the results on Erskine's own charts. He sketched 'views' and the shapes of lighthouses and other marks that could be seen and usefully identified from the sea. A fine example of this work may be found in the new *Unique Edition of The Riddle of the Sands* by R. M. Bowker.[7]

The chart is almost certainly the fruit of Erskine's and Henry's labours with lead line and pencil on *Vixen*, the First World War detail being added later. The original shows clearly that parts of the 'key' and the inset of Emden, with notes on oil and petroleum storage, are afterthoughts, as are the crosses labelled 'Anti-aircraft South of Borkum'.

It is now possible to put together the history of this remarkable chart, drawn so carefully on tracing linen.

The chart started as a fair copy produced from a rough, perhaps in the quiet of Carlyle Mansions, after *Vixen* had been laid up in Terschelling. It is tempting to believe that at this point Childers sent one to the Hydrographic Office, or to the Admiralty, but no record can be found of any correspondence of that date. If he did receive a brush-off from either, there would be firm background to the disappointment expressed in the Preface of *The Riddle* at the reaction of the authorities to the story told them by Carruthers. Whatever the truth of the matter, the charts and the log were a valuable resource when it came to writing the book.

The special chart, with the detailed view of Borkum from Borkum Reef in the east, with all the marks and lighthouses so well sketched, with *Vixen*'s log and his German charts, remained tucked away until the first days of the First World War. With this paper hoard were postcards and photographs taken from *Vixen*'s deck during the epic cruise, which had been useful in working up the views on the chart, as well as providing a valuable intelligence source.[8]

At the very outset of the First World War, Erskine was summoned from Dublin because of his special knowledge of the enemy's North Sea coast and posted to the seaplane carrier, the converted ferry HMS *Engadine* that flew Short 136s. He noted from the very start that the Admiralty could do no better than issue their own charts, already so suspect in his eyes. He hurried to his flat, by then 13 Embankment Gardens, and collected his own folios. The collection proved a valuable resource and later he took his own creation to West and Partners of 91-98 York Street, Westminster, for tidying up and reproduction.

HMS *Engadine*

Wests were owned then, as now, by the Hanrott family, Huguenots who had come to England from Alsace in the late seventeenth century. They started the drawing instrument and supply business in 1888. Harcourt Hanrott became a friend of Erskine's through maps or motorcycling, no one knows which, for the two were keen on both.

Whatever the reason, the production became much valued in the early part of the First World War by both the Royal Naval Air Service and later HM Coastal Motor Boats. Erskine served in both and was mentioned in despatches and subsequently awarded the DSC for his valuable work as an observer in the Middle East. His efforts on paper became widely known as 'Childers' Charts' and showed that amateur hydrography could pay off. He presented the originals afterward to Harcourt Hanrott.[9]

In following Erskine's crusade to improve the accuracy and reliability of Admiralty coastal charts other important events have been left behind. Perhaps this is an understatement, for in the first days of 1904 Erskine approached the run-up to the watershed of his life, for he married Mary (Molly), the daughter of Dr and Mrs Hamilton Osgood.

Erskine had had to be persuaded to go to America, to join the Honourable Artillery Company's call on the Boston branch contingent. He set off soon after *Sunbeam*'s return from the Baltic. Soldiering and ceremonials did not take up all and every day of the visit. Time allowed Erskine to enjoy another of his passions and tour the New England countryside on a hired motorcycle. Andrew Boyle, in his biography, tells how fate intervened. 'One day, as he roared up Beacon Hill, the machine spluttered and died under him. He wheeled it to a side of the street; and, examining the engine with the experienced eye of a man accustomed to fending for himself, he straightened up and walked without a second thought to the front door of the nearest large house.[10] There he met the doctor and, minutes after, his daughter, the girl he was to marry. Mary Alden Osgood had an elegant American face, sharp in profile with good bones, the sort of looks that improve with age. Molly, as he called her, had an attractive, yet determined mouth. This was no illusion. Her strong magnetic features advertised her character.

A birthday letter from Erskine written to Molly, after five years of marriage, sums up thousands of words contained on notes, on scraps and bundles of paper that this remarkable couple exchanged over the rest of their lives together.

> *My darling wife,*
> *I am so full of tenderness and reverence for you that words seem to fail me. I never come to the end of you, I am always to be just beginning to find out all you are in inexhaustible strengths and sweetness. That is the wonder of it, that the years are creative and with all the increasing joy they bring, bear in their womb infinite promise of more. Every one around turns to you and gets*

> *something from you in hope and self-reliance and joy. I have thrilled to see [you] bringing your darling influence into so many new lives this last year. I think you have more vital force in you than ten thousand. I feel so safe, my little mother/wife; safe in something more stable and immutable than anything in this world. The year seems to have gone like a flash, and I would grudge the speed only that I feel more and more that, whatever be the meaning of death it cannot affect our love and unity. Somehow I cannot tell now, there must be a harmonious end; it must all signify something unblemishably good.*
>
> *Happy birthday! My darling angel wife,*
>
> *Your husband.*[11]

Erskine was five years into the happiest period of his life when he wrote this letter and a year beyond the watershed.

Erskine and Molly made many new friends when they returned to 13 Embankment Gardens after their honeymoon. Among them was Sir George Clarke, a past secretary of the Royal Commission on Navy and Army Administration, and at that time on the War Office Reconstitution Committee, which led to the formation of what became known as the Army Council. He was soon to be secretary to the Committee of Imperial Defence and was later raised to the peerage as Lord Sydenham of Combe. He was also to write the Introduction, in 1915, to Howard D'Egville's booklet, *The Invasion of England.*[12] Erskine was particularly pleased when Sir George went away from a dinner party that he and Molly attended, carrying a copy of *The Riddle of the Sands*, given to him by H. Seymour Trower, the president of the Navy League.[13]

Erskine had been anxious from the start to show Molly the places described in *The Riddle*, and happily his father-in-law, Dr Osgood, gave them the perfect means as a wedding present, the twenty-eight-ton ketch *Asgard*, designed and built by the legendary Colin Archer, at Larvik, in Norway, and launched in the spring of 1905. They were not able to push off toward the Baltic, 'to wander far away – on from island unto island, to the gateways of the day,' for young Erskine was on the way, so they had to wait until 1906 for Molly to see those places. Sadly, they had to miss out the islands and siels, because of *Asgard*'s draft. Erskine had been denied the pleasure in *Sunbeam* too, for her requirement was only two inches less than *Asgard*'s six feet six inches. Erskine had stipulated that four feet was the maximum draft for yachts exploring the waters behind the islands.

There were no such physical constraints to thought and his mind at the start of 1906 was very much concerned with the coast of northern Germany. The cause may have been the publicity preceding the strengthening of the German fleet under the German Navy Law of that year, the Kaiser's plan for widening and deepening the capabilities of the Kiel Canal, or the need to send thoughts and ideas to a new government of his own persuasion, heralded by the Liberal landslide of January 1906.

The ideas so forcefully presented by *The Riddle* began to change in emphasis in the years following. It was not that Erskine lost interest in the possibility of invasion, but he saw that preparations and changes were being made by government to make this stark possibility more difficult for the Germans to achieve. He began to pay greater attention to the possibilities of attacking the German Frisian coast in time of war. It was as though Davies' channel theory was overtaking the invasion scheme discovered by Carruthers. A man who may have encouraged this change was Commander Edward Heaton-Ellis, a member of the outward crew aboard *Sunbeam* on the voyage to the Baltic in 1903. He had shared duties for two weeks with another naval officer, the Carruthers 'pretender', Captain Edward Charlton (see pp. 226–7). It is not possible to believe that the subject of *The Riddle* and, in particular, the method of invasion, Davies' channel theory and the use of marauding midgets, was not discussed in some detail as *Sunbeam* cruised among the Danish islands. Heaton-Ellis had a lively mind and the right bent, for he was to become assistant director of the Intelligence Division of the Admiralty War Staff from 1914 to 1915, moving on to command the battle cruiser *Inflexible*, whose celebrated gunnery did so much to assist the reputation of Admiral Hood's squadron at the Battle of Jutland.

Whatever the spur, early in 1906 Erskine wrote to Sir George Clarke, now a member of the Committee of Imperial Defence. He enclosed a paper entitled 'Remarks on the German North Sea Coast In Its Relation to War Between Great Britain and Germany – With a Note on the Dutch Coast'. He admitted at the start that 'The author of this memorandum, save in one passage, does not discuss grand strategy. He presumes though that Great Britain is acting as an ally of France and that the allied fleets have gained and are able to maintain command of the sea.' He realises in his usual deferential way that he is not an expert. He wrote, 'some of the propositions put forward might, under the stimulus of searching professional criticism, be expressed in different and perhaps more convincing terms.'

The first part of the document described the geography. He divided the German North Sea coast into three areas, the Frisian islands, the three great estuaries – the Jade, Weser and Elbe – and lastly, the North Frisian islands, or the coast of Schleswig-Holstein.

Under the first section, he mentioned economic activities on the islands and communications – in particular the Frisian loop railway. He emphasised, 'The islands are the eyes of the mainland. Should Germany lose the command of the sea and should the islands be occupied by the enemy, the mainland would be blind (or at least very short-sighted) as to what was passing in the offing.' Erskine gave solid advice on navigation around and behind the islands and the character of the bottom. He was emphatic: 'To the writer's knowledge, the vast majority of the banks are hard, firm sand affording good ground for heavy vehicles.' In fact, he could only remember one mud bank, just to the east of Norderney. He took some trouble over marks, saying that 'the channels are so tortuous and narrow that if one perch has disappeared, you may strike on an angle of the bank.' He said the currents were strong but never violent and 'the rules governing them are easily discernible. Behind each island is a "water-shed" or point where the sand reaches its greatest height. The streams flow to and from this point on the flood and ebb to the nearest sea outlet.' He discussed depth, mentioning the barge-ketches fitted with lee boards that drew from six to seven feet when loaded and that 'the writer's boat drew 4', without the centre-plate, and for three hours round high water he found he could use great latitude.'

When discussing the great estuaries of the Jade, Weser and Elbe, he gave a little detail but gave less on the North Frisian islands, for good reason: 'The writer has no personal knowledge of this region, but *mutatis mutandis*, he believes that it closely resembles the two others.'

He then presented the committee with Part II, headed 'Suggestions', and commenced by insisting that proper knowledge of the coast was vital. 'It cannot be too strongly laid down that nothing but personal experience can make a good pilot. But a *good chart is an indispensable source of assistance.* The British Admiralty charts (save for the open sea and main channels of the great rivers) are not good. They are on too small a scale, their engraving is defective, and they are not kept properly up to date. The writer has experienced this to his cost. The German charts; on the other hand, are very good; on a large scale, exquisitely engraved, and kept up to date as far as possible.' He suggested, therefore, a practical way forward:

> *It is submitted that all officers called upon to operate in these waters should possess, if possible, facsimiles of these charts. Further, that at whatever risk of alarming or annoying the German government, an attempt should be made to gain practical personal knowledge of the coast by sending young men (officers or otherwise) to explore it, and as soon as possible; men who shall be available thereafter to turn their knowledge to account either as guides, scouts, spies or in an executive capacity.*
>
> *The knowledge at a critical moment of one little by-way or bank, of the depth in inches at a certain point at a certain tide and in a certain wind, and of such-like details, may be of incalculable value.*

Erskine went on to discuss boats. 'What is wanted is a small, short boat, of the very least draught compatible with stability and a certain modicum of sea-going qualities, which, under skilled guidance, can navigate with the utmost possible freedom in shoal regions behind the islands and among the banks of the great estuaries.' He said that these would be constantly wanted in an invasion for patrol work, scout work, for offence or defence. He suggested that for offence these should be fitted with spar-torpedo apparatus. He gave further details, suggesting a maximum length of twenty to twenty-five feet and a draft of three to four feet, as these could then cross the watersheds.

Erskine then considered the number of offensive alternatives. The first of these was the 'blockade of the German coast with offensive and defensive operations appertaining thereto'. His enthusiasm for this idea is evident.

> *Given boats such as are described above, and given good charts, knowledge, skill and daring, the North Sea coast and, more particularly, that part of it which stretches from the Ems to the Elbe, affords unrivalled scope for enterprise of the most important kind. While the blockading fleet watches the offing, boats operate within the islands up to the great estuaries and within the sands of the great estuaries. There abound natural ambuscades, lairs, and fastnesses. A fast boat could travel from the Ems to the Jade in two tides, from the Jade to the Elbe in two tides, or even one. Scout boats could keep the fleet au fait with movements on the mainland. Boats would cut the cables running from the mainland to the islands, and thus to some extent make the mainland blind and deaf.*

He looked at the idea of 'blockading the Kiel Ship Canal'. He had obviously given the matter some thought, drawing, no doubt, on his knowledge gained aboard both *Vixen* and *Sunbeam*. 'In the opinion of the writer, one of the simplest and cheapest ways and one offering a very fair chance of success would be to send one of the boats described, or several in succession, fitted with spar-torpedoes at night against Brunspüttel [he always spelt it wrong] lock gates. The boat or boats would avoid the main channel altogether, cut across, or rather behind, the Medem Sands on a rising tide, and only enter the main channel a mile short of the lock. That mile would be the crux; but under favourable conditions, (e.g. storm or mist) and with men who valued their lives lightly, enterprises just as desperate have had success.' He concluded that 'if vessels were in the lock when the explosion occurred, the obstruction caused would be of long duration.'

Erskine's third alternative was the one nearest his heart – the seizure of islands and the invasion of the mainland. He saw that the seizure of an island or islands might be an end in itself or an adjunct to the invasion of the mainland. It was here that he gave his one quick thought on strategy. He foresaw that the seizure of territory would distract and embarrass Germany in her main strategic aim of crushing France by land. This would create a flank diversion. He realised that 'the military thinkers of Germany, cool, prepared and well informed, would not be frightened by a mere demonstration.' The offensive planners should not be under any illusions. The Germans' principal aim would be the possession of Paris and the loss of a few islands, their colonies and part of their trade would hardly dissuade them from pressing on toward this goal.

Erskine thought that, given the command of the sea, the seizure of an island or islands presented comparatively little difficulty, but if invasion of the mainland were contemplated at the same time, the two operations should be co-related. He felt that 'the attention of the enemy should not be drawn in advance to the point actually selected for the true objective.' This meant that if an island was to be seized it should not be opposite the mainland landing point, unless the whole operation was as one.

Erskine then concentrated on the 'seizure of an island or islands' and, in particular, 'the point for landing'. He gave the opinion that with the possible exception of Borkum and Wangeroog, none of the islands were fortified. The problem was, of course, the place to land. He at once argued against the North Sea coasts of the islands, as the landing force would be at the mercy of the weather and might well meet heavy surf. He argued that safer points existed inside the islands, but emphasised that this would require good pilotage. He also remarked that 'the sand hills of the islands afford excellent artillery positions,' though 'floating batteries may be thrown out nearer the mainland.' He then spelt out his recommendations. Borkum, Wangeroog and Neuwark were particularly important, for they commanded the Ems, Jade and the Elbe rivers. He thought that in the case of the Ems there was another alternative – the Memmert Sand. It was 'practically an island, with a fine sheltered roadstead adjoining', and should not be neglected. He also highlighted the Scharhörn Sand, northwest of Neuwark. Again it was 'practically an island, distant less than a mile, at its nearest point, from the navigable channel of the Elbe estuary'. Lessons of *The Riddle* were coming to the fore.

He then briefly turned his attention to the North Frisian islands, recommending an examination of Sylt, the Bosch Sand, the four-fathom roadstead behind, and two miles to the southeast of the Mittel Plate.

Having dealt with the islands in this way, he turned his attention to 'the invasion of the mainland', making general remarks first. The mainland shore presented conditions for a landing 'because it is sheltered from swell throughout its entire length. Not only can the landing be made without embarrassments caused by an open sea, but communication with the supporting fleet can be freely and confidently maintained.'

A separate class of boat, though, should be used for the purpose, distinct from those recommended previously for scout/patrol/offence/defence work. 'The landing boat must clearly be of very light draught, the lighter the better.' This interesting observation shows that he had moved away from the ideas of barges and tugs, responding to new possibilities and anticipating Admiral Fisher's Bolinder-powered 'K' lighters, which were built for just such a purpose but actually employed in the Dardanelles campaign a decade after this paper was written.

Erskine then contemplated the timing of the landing, putting forward various options and coming to the conclusion that:

> *... given good local knowledge and pilotage, and given the prospect or reasonable suspicion of resistance at the right point, the landing should be at comparatively low water, with (say) a mile of land to cross; so that the troops could deploy steadily out of rifle range, and advance to the attack by orderly military methods.*
>
> *The tide, while low, should be rising, so that once a footing was obtained on the shore, supports could be brought up the more rapidly, and the boats, being in no danger of stranding and drying off, could go to and fro for fresh loads or be free to anchor temporarily.*

He was anxious that 'dead low water should be avoided for landing, because it is just then that the muddy fringes of the channels, if such exist at the spot chosen, are laid bare to their greatest extent.' The experience of *Vixen*'s endless groundings and strandings was burnt deep into his memory. All through this memorandum there was the cry for proper information. 'It is urgently necessary that minute local information should be available.'

Erskine then gave particular advice on mainland opportunities and turned his attention to the channels leading to the ports and siels. Norddeich was just able to 'carry the ferry boat at low water, but it is unfavourable as a landing point, very narrow in its last stages, and very public.' The tidal channels 'leading to the village harbours, though they (together with the harbours themselves) would be invaluable when a firm footing had once been gained on the mainland, seem scarcely suitable to a landing. They are very narrow and tortuous, so that very few boats could travel abreast, and some of them, for a considerable distance outside the harbours, are dyked up with piles and brushwood, which, if just covered by the tide, would, without perfect pilotage and perfect orderliness, be a nasty obstruction and, naturally, it would be hard to effect a surprise at these points.' The sandy foreshore was much to be preferred and his principal recommendation was 'to choose one of the most desolate and least frequented spots on this desolate coast, and trust boldly to the sandy foreshore'. He did, however, feel that attention might be 'directed to the point where the "post-road" crosses from the mainland to Norderney. There can be no mistake as to the practicability of this approach at low water.' He pointed out that it had 'one of the shortest transits from the offing but passed through marsh land, submerged at high water, just before reaching the main dyke and that might cause difficulty.'

At the end of Erskine's 'Remarks', he added a note on the Dutch Frisian islands. He thought that the Committee of Imperial Defence should take into account the possibility that Germany might infringe Dutch neutrality and, therefore, the shoal region between the Dutch Frisian islands and the mainland deserved to be studied as carefully as the German seaboard. He made no particular recommendation beyond advising that intelligence should be gathered. His principal worry had a familiar ring, for again he was concerned about the absolute unreliability of the British Admiralty charts, singling out the stone breakwater that connected the island of Ameland to the mainland shore. Their lordships had marked this as stretching uninterruptedly across the sands, but Erskine had seen the gap in it and the natives confirmed that the deep channel through the obstruction had existed for many years.[14]

The Committee of Imperial Defence, then established at No. 2 Whitehall Gardens, replied with commendable speed. Assistant Secretary W. Nicholson wrote on 27 February:

I am directed by Sir George Clarke to thank you for permitting him to see your interesting notes on the North Sea German and Dutch coasts. It is evident that the Hydrographic Department of the Admiralty cannot maintain correct charts of such changeable waters on the sea frontier of a foreign power, and used only for local trade, without giving offence.

It is, therefore, of great importance that any fresh information gained by yachtsmen and others should be placed at the disposal of the government department concerned.

An invasion in the direction you mention appears to present very great difficulties, the distance at which the covering fleet must lay, the exposed position, the distance over which the invading force would have to be 'boat transported', and the distance when landed of any very important objective renders that portion of the coast as it is of comparatively doubtful advantage should an invasion be contemplated.[15]

The reply did not mention, of course, that Jackie Fisher had supervised the genesis of a plan for seizing the island of Borkum and for raiding Sylt, at the War College, Portsmouth, only a month before Erskine submitted his ideas to the Committee of Imperial Defence. Fisher's scheme originated as part of a series of war games played at the college and later given the status of war plans to refute Lord Charles Beresford's charge that the Admiralty had made no preparations for this sort of war.

The scheme was worked out in great detail and included the names of the ships to be employed and the size of force required to take and hold Borkum. Once this objective had been achieved, it was planned to control the Ems as far as possible, capturing the mouth of the Elbe-Jade canal at Emden, 'so as to prevent any torpedo craft being sent along it'. Fisher admitted that the operation would be most hazardous because of mines, but in justification he went on to say that 'if we hope to interfere with the advance of the German Army into Holland, it is probably the only way in which it can be done.'[16]

Erskine had seen the importance of Emden, for Davies had mentioned the utility of the canal that linked Wilhelmshaven to that growing port. In his 'Remarks' he had also had the same objective in mind, 'to create a flanked diversion, to check the German westward advance,' though he was less sanguine about the effect that it would have on the Germans' prime objective to push westward to Paris.

If Sir George Clarke had held the view that was attributed to him by his assistant secretary at the Committee of Imperial Defence, he was to change his tune later, for he supported Fisher's idea that the Navy should throw the Army ashore at some unexpected part of the enemy's coast, whence it could take the enemy army in flank or rear.[17]

This idea was to gain support in due course from important quarters. Winston Churchill, who had succeeded Lord Selborne as First Lord of the Admiralty in 1911, was foremost among them. In the chapter 'The Search for a Naval Offensive' in *The World Crisis 1911–1918*,[18] he explained how this came about and what happened to the plan.

> *In my earliest meetings with Lord Fisher in 1907, he had explained to me that the Admiralty plans at that date in the event of hostilities with Germany were for the seizure as early as possible in the war of the island of Borkum as an advance base for all our flotillas and inshore squadrons blockading the German river mouths. I was always deeply interested in this view. I found it strongly held by Admiral Lewis Bayly. In 1913, this officer, who stood in the very first rank of the younger Admirals of the Navy, had been employed on examining the methods by which the capture and maintenance of this island could be effected in the event of a war, and how the problem had been influenced in the meanwhile by new conditions. The new elements were formidable; to wit aviation, the submarine and the long-range gun. But they favoured or hindered both sides in various degrees at the different stages of the operation. As an alternative, or possibly as an accompaniment, the island of Sylt was also studied. Very careful models in relief were made of the German river mouths and of all the islands. Admiral Bayly's reports and plans were available in the staff archives. There was no possibility of using them at the beginning of the war. At least three or four brigades of the finest regular infantry we possessed were*

> *required for the storm of an island, though a smaller force would have sufficed to garrison it after it was taken. There was no possibility of sparing these troops from the decisive battle front in France. Moreover, as has been seen, the Navy had plenty to do on the outbreak of war in securing the command of the sea and in ferrying the Army across.*

Churchill, Fisher and, of course, Erskine were very much of the 'do something brigade'. Fisher's building programme had had Borkum and the later Baltic scheme in mind when he laid down the light draft cruisers *Courageous*, *Glorious* and *Furious*, the shoal-water monitors and the powered landing craft already mentioned.[19]

When the dark days of war did begin on 4 August 1914, Winston Churchill's secretary and Erskine's friend, Eddie Marsh, suggested that the unique knowledge of the author of *The Riddle of the Sands* might be pressed into service.[20] Erskine was pursued and persuaded to join the Royal Naval Volunteer Reserve, the body that his friend Herbert Warington-Smyth had done so much to create. Erskine posted to the Hydrographic Office a redraft of his 'geographical' notes on the 'Nature of Sands, Channels and Foreshore of German/Dutch Friesland'. His first official job for the Navy before joining HMS *Engadine* was to revise the 'Remarks' of 1906 for Captain (later Admiral) Sir Herbert Richmond, then assistant director of operations. The new paper was entitled 'The Seizure of Borkum and Juist' and again put forward the need to secure 'an important base' at the mouth of the Ems estuary for three good reasons. The first of these was to achieve 'a close blockade of the German North Sea coast', the second was 'to help in the softening up (or, as he put it, "digging out") operations by air, sea and land against German naval and military strongholds and roadsteads, e.g. Wangeroog, Schillig Roads (in the Jade River, north of Wilhelmshaven), Heligoland and the Elbe'. Finally his plan suggested an 'invasion on a grand scale, whether by Emden and the Ems Valley to the Essen-Dusseldorf Cologne region, in concert with an allied advance from France, or elsewhere.'[21]

Erskine saw this last objective as 'the greatest ulterior aim of the operations' but allowed that if the pursuit of any of these schemes 'provoked the German fleet into a decisive battle in the open, the highly important end would have been achieved.

Indeed, it was Admiralty thinking that the seizure of Borkum would precipitate a momentous battle between the two fleets.'[22] There were those within and without that organisation who welcomed such an outcome because it would shorten the war, and others who feared the finality of such a conflict.

Erskine worried about how far the seizure of Borkum would commit the Navy. Would they be able to achieve the first two of their objects without having to go on to the last? He thought they would, but again the only way, on land, of shortening the war was by a decisive invasion up the Ems Valley, using Emden as a base.

The ideas put forward so tentatively in 1906 had certainly developed in the eight years, and in the process Erskine had dropped the hazardous concept of blocking the Kiel Canal with his twenty-five-foot boats armed with spar torpedoes – 'mosquitoes with stings', as he had called those offensive small craft so many years before. Instead, he turned his attention to Zeebrugge and Ostend, with the plea that they be made 'useless to the enemy as ports, either by destruction of works or obstruction of channels or both'. Erskine had anticipated the plans of Commodore (later Admiral Sir Reginald) Tyrwhitt and Commodore (later Admiral Sir Roger) Keyes. He dined with the two on the former's flagship, HMS *Arethusa*, at Harwich early in 1915[23] and may have urged part of his battle-plan on them. He had realised that it would be difficult to capture Borkum or command the Ems while these ports were in enemy hands.[24]

Whatever anyone else thought about the invasion of Borkum, Captain Richmond was not convinced by Childers' arguments or those of anyone else. To him, the attack upon 'Danzic', the code name for Borkum, was 'quite mad. The reasons for capturing it are NIL, the possibilities about the same.... It remains with the Army, who I hope will refuse to throw away 12,000 troops in this manner for the self-glorification of an ignorant and impulsive man [Admiral Sir Lewis Bayly had prepared the scheme] ... To risk troops in waters full of submarines, depending on such precarious defences as we now possess against them is pure foolery,' or so he wrote in his diary for 4 January 1915.[25]

Whatever the rights and wrongs of the matter, Lieutenant-Commander Schwieger, the commander of U-Boat 20, left *Borkum* on 30 April1915 – just over four months after this entry – and sank the liner *Lusitania*.[26]

RMS *Lusitania*

Churchill's determination 'to do something' was encapsulated in his question 'is there no alternative to sending our men to chew barbed wire in Flanders?' The First Sea Lord was reflecting on the stalemate on the Western Front where Allied forces had suffered terrible loses. He added, in a bitter note, that 'no doubt several hundred thousand men will be spent to satisfy the military mind on this point'.

Childers was sent to Gallipoli and the eastern Mediterranean, on the seaplane carrier HMS *Ben-my-Chree,* the Engadine's successor, where he served as the ship's intelligence officer. 'It was just typical of our authorities at home,' wrote Captain L. B. Weldon, later Surveyor-General of Egypt, 'here they had a man who, I should have thought, would have been invaluable to them on account of his knowledge of the North Sea, and they promptly sent him out as an intelligence officer to a ship working on the coasts of Sinai, Syria and Asia Minor.' [27]

While aboard his previous ship, HMS *Engadine,* Childers had been visited by Churchill the First Sea Lord accompanied by Admiral Sir John Jellicoe.

However, Erskine did return to a task for which he was best suited, for in December 1916 he joined HM Coastal Motor Boats and judging from a memorandum written for the benefit of Lieutenant Bremner, he had succeeded, at last, in persuading the Hydrographic Department to produce two charts for coastal motor boats – the first taking in Heligoland, the Elbe river up to the entrance to the Kiel Canal and west as far as Langeoog island (X222) and the second from the Jade River to Norderpiep (the entrance of the Eider river), taking in, on a large scale, the region around Wangeroog and Schillig Roads, including Wilhelmshaven (X223). Only thirty copies of each chart were prepared, but he mentions that other large-scale charts were available, including those produced of the Thames Estuary by the Royal Cruising Club. He must have been delighted to be able to announce that 'a set of the German North Sea coast charts are in the possession of Captain Lynes, signed for by me at the Intelligence Department, Admiralty'[28] (Herbert Lynes, later a rear admiral, organised and commanded the blocking of Ostend, soon after Keyes' action at Zeebrugge). Erskine had to wait nearly three years into the war *and* produce his own charts before really reliable information of this sort was obtainable from the Hydrographic Office. It is perhaps surprising that it took such a time, for the volcanic Jackie Fisher, when advocating the close blockade of Germany, wrote in his war plans that 'the unreliability of our present charts of the German North sea coasts – which are constantly changing in contour – would call for the use of at least two surveying ships with the blockade.'[29]

Sir Frederick Sykes, one of the founders of the Royal Flying Corps, recalled how, in the closing weeks of 1916, Erskine took part in the daring attempt to raid the German fleet at anchor by means of coastal motor boats.[30] This dash was not amongst the Frisian islands but it was in a 'small torpedo boat', as suggested in *The Riddle*. Coastal motor boats in those days were forty-foot Thorneycroft stepped hydroplanes, capable of thirty-five knots, sliding a torpedo over the stern, and then swerving hurriedly out of the way to allow it to take the course of the boat to the target, which meant going faster initially than the torpedo.[31] Captain (later Admiral Sir Barry) Domvile, described Erskine then as a 'quiet little man with the courage of a lion'.[32]

Good charts and reliable intelligence were essential, as Erskine pleaded time and again. The assistant secretary of the Committee of Imperial Defence had argued in 1906 that it would be difficult, 'without giving offence', for the Admiralty to gather such information and, therefore, it was 'of great importance' that yachtsmen and others should play their part. Jackie Fisher had put forward the same argument about the German, Dutch and Belgian coasts: 'We find ourselves unable to proceed for want of information. We want to know more about possible landing places, sources of supply, the nature of the country, the kind of vessels required for the navigation of these shoal waters, how the channels are marked, if boats or lighters can be obtained locally, and where they may be found.' The Naval Intelligence Division could not have had a better invitation and the First Sea Lord was in no doubt how it might be organised.

> *This information can all be obtained in peace time by encouraging officers, when on leave, to keep their eyes open and to send in reports on their return home, and also by organising a system of secret service agents, whose business it would be to obtain it. It will be necessary to train both officers and agents to a certain extent, so that they should know what to look for and what to report. For this work we do not want plans of defence works and details of that nature, that would bring them into contact with local authorities on the charge of espionage, but we want accurate details of the physical features of the ground, and of the resources of the country that may be useful to us. Where defence works exist, it will be for the present, quite sufficient to indicate that the place is defended, and the details can be obtained later on, if necessary.*[33]

Erskine had certainly done his bit, for when he went to the Baltic in *Asgard* in 1913, the *Daily Mail*'s Berlin correspondent, Frederick William Wile, reported to Lord Northcliffe that Childers was 'watched' by German naval officers.[34]

Erskine though was not the only one to keep his eyes open or to place information at the disposal of the government department concerned. To begin with this was a little difficult, for the Naval Intelligence Division (NID) believed that such delicate material could only be gathered by naval officers.[35] The NID relied on captains of warships to see that their intelligence officers filled in specially produced questionnaires which were then correlated and analysed by the Admiralty in London. Indeed, when Rear-Admiral Sir Charles Ottley, who took over as secretary of the Committee of Imperial Defence in 1907, and his assistant, Captain Maurice Hankey, RM, looked at British intelligence organisations, they discovered to their astonishment that there was not a single British agent on the whole mainland of Europe at that time.[36]

Gathering intelligence was therefore difficult, to say the least. If more detailed information was required, special efforts were made to find out more, again using naval officers. And so it was that the cadet deck training ship, the first-class armoured cruiser, HMS *Cornwall*, under the command of Captain (later Admiral Sir Reginald) Hall, entered the port of Kiel in 1909, as part of a tour of German ports. He was anxious to obtain photographs of the harbour installations and, in particular, to discover the number of naval building slips. To assist him he had Captain Bernard (Barney) F. Trench, RMLI, and Lieutenant Vivian R. Brandon, RN. German security was tight and the task looked daunting until Hall managed to persuade the Duke of Westminster to lend them his high-speed launch *Ursula*, powered by two twenty-four cylinder Wolseley petrol motors. With Hall at the helm and Brandon and Trench disguised as engineers, they raced up the harbour, achieving something like forty knots, until *Ursula* 'broke down' off the slips so that they could be photographed through the conning turret.[37] Trench and Brandon then spent a little time ashore and discovered a good deal more. For this they both received expressions of their lordships' appreciation for their useful report on coast defences at Kiel.[38]

The Admiralty was not nearly as pleased with their exploits the next year, for in May of 1910 they were both arrested and charged with spying on the island of Borkum. Brandon and Trench had been invited by their immediate superior, Captain Cyrus Regnart, RMLI, to make a 'walking tour' of the German North Sea defences, particularly those on the Frisian islands.

It may be that Erskine's exhortation in his 'Remarks' of February 1906 'that at whatever risk of alarming or annoying the German government, an attempt should be made to gain practical personal knowledge of the German coast by sending young men (officers or otherwise) to explore it' was bearing fruit. The pair had read *The Riddle of the Sands*. Brandon admitted at his trial that he had done so three times, perhaps at the suggestion of Captain Hall, for the latter had made strong representations to the Admiralty, not only about their lack of knowledge of German naval installations, but because their charts of the North German coast were so out of date. Indeed, he held that the only accurate information on the Frisian islands was to be found in *The Riddle*.

Richard Deacon points out that:

> *In the 1903 edition of Erskine Childers' book, 'The Riddle of the Sands' (and in many other subsequent editions), there is the following note on page ix, 'the fragments of charts shown at pages 69 and 219 (of the first edition) are reproductions, on a slightly reduced scale and omitting some confusing and irrelevant details, of British and German Admiralty charts. Space precludes the insertion of those bulky engravings in full; but the reader who wishes for fuller information is referred to charts number 406 and 407 of the British series, and to number 64 of the German series.' It is, of course, astonishing that the Royal Navy was so unaware of the charting of this area by both the British and German navies that it took Childers' book to make them realise it. All Childers had done was to 'marry' the two sets of charts; this the N.I.D had failed to do.*[39]

The NID did not, however, omit to tell Brandon and Trench that if they were caught their activities would be disowned by the Navy.

In three weeks they visited the North Frisians, including Sylt and Amrum, they went to Cuxhaven, on to Heligoland, back to Wangeroog and worked their way west down the Frisian chain until they reached Borkum. In the course of this 'walking tour' they took photographs, noted bearings of guns and filled notebooks with sensitive information. Of Wangeroog, for example, the Leipzig court was told that Lieutenant Brandon had written:

> *Landing piers × high, × long, × broad. Milk and eggs come from mainland. Only five buildings on the west side. Seen no building which can contain mines. The beacon furthest out is occupied and has telegraphs.*[40]

The reporter had not been allowed to give the actual measurements.

On Borkum, the two found that security was strict and had to wait until nightfall to make their examination of a new battery. Captain Trench went first and managed to circumnavigate the barbed wire and to measure a number of the guns. Lieutenant Brandon then followed his route in to obtain further information. Before doing so he gave Trench all that he had in his pockets, except, and this proved disastrous, his camera. In the dark he stumbled on a sentry and was arrested. The films were developed and he was charged. Trench managed to reach their hotel room and hide the other papers. However, he too was soon arrested and it was not long before German security officers discovered who they were.

A celebrated trial took place and Brandon and Trench were sentenced to four years' confinement in a fortress – Brandon to Konigstein and Trench to Glatz.[41]

Erskine followed the trial with great interest and perhaps a twinge of discomfort, in light of his 'Remarks'. Both he and his book were the focus of attention and the *Daily News* of 29 October 1910 published an article by him headed 'The Common Sense View – Very Little Known That Was Not Known'. He started off:

> *Since my book, 'The Riddle of the Sands', has been referred to in the trial of Lt Brandon and Captain Trench at Leipzig, and since I have a fairly intimate knowledge of the coast which the two officers were exploring, I venture to think that my impressions of the episode may be of some little public interest.*

He went on to urge 'coolness and sobriety' on the British and German people, for the trial of a German Lieutenant Helm was about to take place in England for acts, apparently, somewhat similar. He pointed out that much of the information gathered by Brandon and Trench was available and easily accessible. He argued that it was not possible to prevent any individual from supplementing the published information by observations of his own on the characteristics of the country he is studying. 'Travellers of all sorts – motorists, cyclists, yachtsmen, mountaineers, scientists, economists, journalists, novelists – do in fact do this sort of thing every day and in doing so promote international amity.' He added that 'it may seem an ugly paradox that similar studies may be directed to war-like ends, but war itself is an ugly paradox.'

He thought that except for the information gained by entering the gun position at Borkum, all could be obtained from published maps and charts. He pooh-poohed the charge that Captain Trench had measured depths of water while bathing at Sylt and Amrum.

> *Well, that is within the right of all bathers, whether at Eastbourne, Sylt or anywhere else; but for my part, I should be content to rely for such measurements on the extraordinarily accurate and detailed large-scale charts of the German North Sea coast, published by the German Admiralty and obtainable at stationers in London, which give depth, whose accuracy I have myself tested, correct down to the tenth of a metre, beside all possible information about the rise and fall of the tide, the nature of the bottom and foreshore, the course of the navigable channels, buoys, 'booms', lights and beacons – all matters, in fact which are just as important to the peaceful sailor as to the general or admiral who plans a landing.*

He went on: 'I used these charts myself in the course of a long and delightful cruise through the fascinating Frisian region, without a thought, at the *actual time*, that they had any bearing on war.'

One of Erskine's friends was not so particular. He was a man of very much the same stamp, indeed they had been firm friends since they first met in 1909. Gordon Strachey Shephard has come into the story before. He was one of three sons of the Madras judge, Sir Horatio Shephard. Gordon, like Erskine, was to die early. He spun into the ground on 19 January 1918 at Auchel, in the Pas de Calais. At the time of his death he commanded the First Brigade, Royal Flying Corps, as a brigadier-general. He was only thirty-two.

Gordon Shephard was a very accomplished small-boat sailor and, like Erskine, a member of the Royal Cruising Club, in whose *journal* he logged some of the more adventurous of his cruises aboard the eleven-ton yawl *Sorata* and Erskine's own *Asgard*. Perhaps it was his keenness to transfer to the Royal Flying Corps that persuaded him of the value of being particularly watchful, keeping his camera ready and with his chart pencil noting what he saw as he sailed along the coast of Germany. He was just the type Jackie Fisher had in mind when he urged that officers be encouraged to 'keep their eyes open and to send in reports on their return home'. It may be that Erskine had shown Gordon the letter he had received from the assistant secretary of the Committee of Imperial Defence, in 1906, which had said much the same as Fisher.

Whatever the reason, Gordon set out on his 'yachting with a purpose' with some energy. His letter of 16 July 1912 to Winston Churchill at the Admiralty describes both the problems and the opportunities of intelligence gathering and shows that he did not always enjoy a 'soldier's wind'.

> *I have the honour to bring the following facts to your notice. I am a yachtsman of much experience, and have during the past few years made extended trips in a twelve-ton sailing yacht along the German coast and in the Baltic. As I am an officer in the Regular Army, a friend of mine who is an officer in the Naval Intelligence Department at the Admiralty suggested to me that any information I could procure regarding coast defences and channels in foreign waters would be of great service to naval intelligence. Since then, I have in the last two years made three extended trips along the North Sea coast and in the Baltic. The report on Borkum, which I now enclose, is the result of my last trip made in September, 1911 to that island; there are also several photos and sketches which I do not forward, but which are now in the possession of the Naval Intelligence Department at the Admiralty. The Admiralty and the War Office, and the officials who read them have recognised how valuable the information was. I made a request recently at the War Office for recognition for*

these reports. My suggestion was that some part of my expenses should be paid to me. I also proposed to make another trip this summer. The answer of the War Office was that reports on coast defences do not particularly interest them, and that they could not pecuniarily recognise the last trips, or give me leave to make another trip. The opportunity for the trip I suggested this summer, which could have been made under very advantageous circumstances, is now past as it is only possible to visit these islands during the summer tourist season, and I have taken up flying, which will keep me in England this summer.

I wish to say, however, that I shall be very glad to make another trip next year. The attitude of the officials that I have questioned on the subject left with me the impression that, though they do not care to undertake the responsibility of granting me the necessary leave, they are yet not altogether adverse to my proposals and I think that a hint from a high quarter would smooth the way. I have gained considerable experience in this branch of investigation, and am confident that I could obtain information without undue risk.

During my last trip, I had the misfortune to be arrested at Emden, but I had carried out investigations in a sufficiently prudent manner to prevent the German authorities having any grounds for taking legal proceedings, and after four days' detention I was released.

The account of this experience is enclosed and a copy was sent to the Admiralty in October, 1911. I do not undertake these journeys for the purpose of making money out of them, but rather with the hope to provide useful information and better myself in my profession. I have not, however, sufficient means to be able to defray all the expense of the trips myself, and my last two trips put me to a considerable amount of expense, but the only financial assistance I ask for is an amount sufficient to cover the cost of the voyage.

My knowledge of the channels on the German North Sea coast is great, and I think that I could be of service in war time in piloting destroyers in waters which necessarily are but little known to naval officers.

The Naval Intelligence Department at the Admiralty have full reports of my trips.[42]

He was quite right and they gave him a good reference, saying that he had visited Borkum and Sylt twice, Wangeroog once and the unfortified Frisian islands several times. He had also reported on the Kiel Canal and the Elbe and Kiel defences as well as providing information on the navigability of the Baltic Belts and Sound and the defences of certain Russian and Swedish ports. They also told the First Lord of the Admiralty that his information on Borkum and the other Frisian islands had been embodied in a notification to the War Intelligence Department's coast report and added that Gordon Shephard was the only person who could be said to have thoroughly reconnoitred Borkum (on Britain's behalf) since the fortification of the island was commenced. They continued, 'He is a good yachtsman and is familiar with German charts and sailing directions (he speaks German), and the knowledge he has acquired of the so-called secret channels round and about the Frisian group is probably unique among English yachtsmen.' Finally, they 'thought that £75 should cover the expenses of a month's trip, should it be thought advisable for him to make one next year'.

Gordon had further correspondence with Eddie Marsh, Churchill's secretary, but not a sou did he obtain from the government.[43]

Brandon and Trench were treated in an even more lickpenny way, for when they were pardoned by the Kaiser on the occasion of George V's visit in May 1913, they came home to an argument over expenses. Captain Regnart had promised them that the overheads of their walking tour would be recompensed up to £20. Their defence cost them £380 each and they had had to pay four shillings a day keep while imprisoned. The Admiralty were adamant that they would get nothing and it was not until Reginald Hall became director of the Intelligence Division of the Admiralty War Staff in 1914 that they were adequately repaid.[44]

The Admiralty, in spite of exhortations, did not make it easy for patriotic young men to follow the example of Davies and Carruthers. The author(s) of an anonymous cutting, undated and headlined 'Our View – *The Riddle of the Sands*', which can be found among the Childers papers at Trinity College, Dublin, need not have worried:

One of the prime needs of the hour appears to be a society for the suppression of

> *the publication of 'The Riddle of the Sands'. Not that there is anything improper in that brightly written little book – far from it, but we cannot view without alarm the increasingly rapid transference of the population of these islands to German prisons, for which the work in question appears to be responsible.*

The article goes on to describe the story and the interest that it might hold for those interested in national defence, 'especially among yachtsmen and members of the naval and military forces. The result might easily have been foreseen. Young men of patriotic instincts in whom the love of adventure was strong have chartered small boats and have cruised stealthily among the islands in question, to the great scandal of the authorities of the Fatherland, in whose blood the microbe of the spy mania flourishes exceedingly.'

'We do not suppose,' the article continued, 'that the same enterprising yachtsmen have been allowed to discover anything of great moment, even if there be anything of great moment to be discovered, but in Germany they take little heed of that. The offence lies in trying to find out something and it is punished with the severity to which we in this country are strangers, the net results being that we lose the services of a number of young men whom we can ill spare.'

In light vein, the article concludes,

> *Moreover, with every fresh arrest the sale of the book increases, and looking forward into the future, we can foresee a time when the key of a German prison will turn upon the last able-bodied Englishman, and when our country, defended only by women, infants and invalids, will be at the mercy of any unneighbourly neighbour who may choose to attack it. That is why a society for the suppression of the publication of 'The Riddle of the Sands' has become a national necessity and we can only hope that steps will shortly be taken to found such an organisation and carry on an active propaganda.*

Erskine would not have minded, even had they been successful, for he had long passed the watershed of his life. That mark on history was made in a letter he wrote to Basil Williams as far back as 19 October 1908. In this, Erskine remembered,

> *We had a very quiet but very happy holiday in Ireland including a jolly motor tour with my cousin [Robert] Barton through a good slice of central and western Ireland mainly to inspect co-operative societies in which he is much interested and in which Sir H. [Horace] Plunkett [and] a good many other well known people look for the economic salvation of Ireland.* I have come back finally and immutably a convert to Home Rule, *as is my cousin, though we both grew up steeped in the most irreconcilable sort of Unionism.*

The First World War had brought the adventurer temporarily to the fore again, a side of his character that was never to disappear completely. His mind, though, even in those strenuous years, was more and more on Ireland and its problems. He became disillusioned and had lost any hope of progress or sensible solution. His natural optimism ebbed from him, taking with it a good deal of his natural joy. As the war came to a close, Erskine Childers, the zealot, swiftly took the place of Lieutenant-Commander Erskine Childers, DSC, RNVR, the gifted adventurer. Gordon Shephard, had he survived, might have slowed the change and just possibly halted it. Erskine had written to Lady Shephard on his friend's death, 'He is one of my heroes and always will be so. Molly and I loved him. We saw great things and lovable things in him from the first and the friendship has grown closer all the time.'[45]

Basil Williams, in his *Sketch*, recognised this attachment. He saw Gordon Shephard as Erskine's most notable and dearest friend. It was not that William Le Fanu, Alfred Dennis, Ivor Lloyd-Jones and many of the old guard felt that 'they were drifting out of his life', it was more that 'he had a wonderful capacity for sympathy with men of a younger generation who showed his own spirit of adventure and of openness to new ideas.' Basil Williams cited now Captain Trench and Lieutenant Brandon had made 'a pilgrimage to the unwitting author of their mishap, and thereafter became his friends.'[46]

Molly, though, was the key and that is why Gordon Shephard might just have turned the tide, for she thought just as much of him as did Erskine.

Chapter 9

EPILOGUE

My journey had come to an end, though I had not found the answers to all the questions that had raced through my mind when I started my search for the background to *The Riddle of the Sands*. My early devotion to the story had kindled a fascination with the author. The three years of research, reading his words and the

On the Sands

words of others about him, meeting his son Bobby and daughter-in-law Christobel, happening upon those with claims and connections, had all fuelled my driving wish to know more. This need was reinforced by following the wake of *Vixen* under sail, examining for myself the siels and villages that he had visited, wandering around the streets of Esens and along the banks of the Benser Tief, to pause on the parapet of the bridge where Carruthers had rested. Through all this, Erskine seemed as close, just down wind of me and within hailing distance, as *Vixen* had been of *Medusa* on that day off the Scharhörn.

I had covered a slice of forty-eight years of Erskine's life – facets of ninety-two per cent of his span, and all through this he managed to retain my interest with the same freshness with which it had begun, yet I put down my pen knowing that there was more to discover. *The Riddle of the Sands* had a thick red line of truth running right through the plot. Erskine had pieced the evidence together in a masterly way; he later turned the tables and created his own invasion plan against Germany.

There is, though, one question to which I long for an answer. Why did he not awake the people of both his countries to the problems that confronted each of them over Ireland, with a story of the same power as *The Riddle of the Sands?*

It may be that his zeal paralysed him so that he could only see the question in stark, urgent terms, conditions that could not be gilded with description or twisted in any way to entertain.

Another thought came with this. Two books had nudged the course of the nation and the world at the time. *The Riddle of the Sands* had influenced Britain's plans for defence and the book had helped to awake leaders and people alike to the Kaiser's ambitions. Thirteen years before its publication, Alfred Thayer Mahan's *The Influence of Sea Power Upon History* had sparked off those desires and in so doing persuaded Wilhelm to follow a course that was to set the world on fire. Books could certainly influence events.

I thought it strange, too, that almost thirty years to the day after I had first picked up *The Riddle of the Sands*, a yet unpublished book was defeating the ambitions of new invaders – the Argentines in the Falkland Islands.

Ewen Southby-Tailyour, an officer in the Marines, was posted to those islands and from 1978 to 1979 and, in the peace before that war, charted the coastal waters for the use of yachtsmen. It seemed just as unlikely a venture as the amateur hydrography of Erskine and Henry Childers, and yet the results of that year, 'a comprehensive collection of notes, soundings, observations, sketches, photographs and watercolour paintings', proved invaluable to those who planned the liberation of the Falklands.

Port San Carlos was sketched as carefully as Erskine had charted the Ems and the approaches to Emden on his 'Childers Charts'. The difference was that Erskine's book was published *before* the invasion could take place, while Ewen's had to wait until *after*.[1]

Coming Ashore

Appendix

RIDE ACROSS IRELAND – AN ACCOUNT OF A BICYCLE TOUR BY ERSKINE CHILDERS

In 1889 Erskine Childers explored the west of Ireland by bicycle (see p. 47). The account that he wrote of his tour, showing the development of his style and descriptive powers, is published here in full for the first time.

It took me two days and four hours. The four hours came first, and good reason had I to commend my foresight in allowing that little overflow from the congested forty-eight hours that followed. Therefore behold me at three o'clock on a windy afternoon shooting down a certain carriage-drive between Roundwood and Rathrum, Co. Wicklow, with dear old Boreas (or rather his more westerly cousin) plunging along behind me, as if it was a positive pleasure to him to find I was going his way. I mention Boreas (and respectfully as you will observe) because in common with most cyclists I am rather sensitive about winds, they can make themselves so very unpleasant on occasion, that, once in the saddle, one grows to regard them as remorseless arbiters of destiny for they hold mortals who cross them in their laudable errand of filling a vacuum. Reflection at that moment would have reminded me that the aforementioned carriage-drive ran south-east, while my line of route for the next two days lay north-west, in other words that the vacuum that wind was hastening to fill lay somewhere in the direction of Cornwall, while the vacuum I desired to fill was situated in Mayo. But the road was hard, the air was fresh, the hills were a dream of purple and gold, and withal my heart was light and my limbs were strong, such being the circumstances, I am sure the sympathetic reader will wonder that clouds in the future were unthought of, and that the first three miles went by uncounted, for a vivid appreciation of the ecstasy of rapid motion, combined with vigorous physical exercise, give me but three things, a hard road, a following wind, and a well-oiled bicycle. Then may a man drink deep of a sparkling, giddying Lethe, then may he leave the grosser things of earth, and mingle his being with the etherial elements. While effecting the latter process, let me give causes and circumstances. I was on my way out to rejoin a fishing party on the West Coast, which I had left a week before. Having lately become the possessor of a 'safety' [bicycle] I had conceived the idea of a ride to Mayo. 'Ho there! An Atlas!' To count the counties to be traversed seemed a good preliminary step; then a crude attempt to measure the miles by walking a finger and pencil across the map – result, mental confusion: Why bother about petty details? Westward Ho! So here I am with an invitation in my pocket to sleep that night with a friend, on the other side of the mountains, and so start fresh for my inland ride.

Four rapid miles, and here is little Laragh, at the meeting of the valleys and peeping up each in turn, Clara, Glendalough, Glen Maceanass; as I round the corner for Glendalough a nasty gust of wind distinctly affects the ardour of my wheels, and as foreshadowing trouble ahead, appreciably disturbs the morale barometer. But it is but a mile and I get a glimpse of the loveliest spot in Wicklow; there is the Round Tower, grey old weather-beaten monument, but still strong and stout and as tenacious of its secret as ever, though generations of its critics have sunk with the dust, with its mystery yet unsolved. And there about it are the scattered ruins whose decay it has watched through centuries, instinct with memories grave and gay, of quaint pranks among reverend fathers and simple chieftains, of devoted sweetness and pious heroism in the hour of danger and trouble. Yonder, by the silver sands of Avonmore, is good St Kevin's dwelling house, beyond again, Our Lady's Church, in the gloom of surrounding elms, with that wonderful ivy-wreathed doorway that Scott dreamed lovingly over. Nearer, the massive corner stones and still graceful chancel arch of the tiniest edifice that ever grew august under the name of Cathedral: a speck in the valley to the west, little St Saviour with its queer mystical symbolism of carving and moulding and its tiny spiral staircase, worn down by pious feet. Then take a wider view and frame tower and ruins and the thousand memorial stones and haunts of legend in their natural rampart of gorse-covered pine-clad mountains. Follow it westward and pause at the armour grey gloom of the waters of the loch, whence grim Lug Duff rises frowning, all jagged rock and heather-tufted precipice, till kissed at his tawny summit by one warm sunbeam. You can guess at the spot, overhanging the white strand, where amid lusty young oaks stand the time-worn stones of the Reefert church, the good saint's earliest work (so the legend says) when he discarded the anchorite's robe and with a few devoted followers began a life of good works. And that tiny grey speck on the farther shore of the lake when the cliff recedes a little, less seen than imagined to be sure, that is the rough little structure, half chapel half cell, where the young monk – royal of blood and fair of face – first sought solitude from the world in the bosom of the hills. Nearer, in the face of the rock sheer up from the lake is the mall rock-hewn recess that legend calls his sleeping place, what time he fled from the eyes of most unholy blue and were it a few hours later I fancy would perchance grant a glimpse of a wan white-robed Kathleen still nightly roving the spot where she met her death at those loved hands.

But Glendalough is fading with distance as I ride up the little diverging valley of Glendasan, enroute for Wicklow Gap, the pass by which I was to cross the mountains. I am loth to forget St Kevin and his monks and that fair retreat of theirs, for now begins the hard and dreary labour of mounting to the head of a pass by a slow ascent, first through poor scanty cultivation – past many a derelict house, then through bleak bog and moorland. Two miles up, a deserted lead mine shows where in 'man versus mountain', mountain has won, and sleeps secure, its treasure yet untrove. There is something inexpressibly chilling in the prospect of such a derelict mine as this. The great gaunt driving wheels, clear-cut against the sky, the heaps of rusty rails and discarded iron work, the wheel-less trucks and rotting barrows, blasted boulders in tumbled confusion, skeleton cottages, roofless, doorless, ghostly and, running through all, the once fair mountain stream, discoloured with unsightly deposit. It is Desolation's Winter Palace. The road is delightfully smooth – one of those excellent military roads that traverse the Wicklow hills, but the wind is strong in my face, and the upward gradient considerable. Already I have given up the struggle and am leading my variant wheels on the way that they should go. Uh-rah! Clak-k-k-; an old cock grouse wings it off to report on the invading monster. Now I am high enough to see on my left Lough Nahanigan under a low cliff, not half a mile long but looking cold and cruel as a sword. Once upon a time it burst its banks and brought sorrow to many a cottage-home in the little valley, for the rest it harbours a forlorn spirit of obscure antecedents, whose only corporeal function is to wail bitterly. It is in mystic sympathy with a similar organism attached to Lough Oolah (another little tarn about a mile to my right) and in a snow-storm these musical phantasms sustain a very regular antiphony of mournful yells, whether to comfort or harass one another or merely to pass the time, I am not in a position to state. After two more miles of slow ascent, I top the gap, and pause for breath and a last look at East Wicklow, with the sea in the distance. Then again the saddle, feel after the brake with the right hand, leave the pedals to their own sweet will and begin the welcome descent, though the wind is almost a hurricane up here and proves itself no unworthy foe even of gravitation itself. This descent is all too short, for I am still a long way from the level plain: soon I am reluctantly feeling for the pedals again, and am toiling along through a country the desolation of whose aspect is only emphasised by an occasional scanty oat or potato patch near some smokey hovel. Low hills are on either side of the road, pinewoods in the northern distance and above a grey, stormy sky. My thoughts go back to St Kevin and his lonely watchings by the 'gloomy shores'. I can picture him leaving his cell at the call of duty, ministering to the simple country folk, feeding the very wild animals with food from his own hands, e'er the morning dew was dry, and at last at the call of the heaven-sent angel, descending to the valley to found a city where learning and piety should flourish hand in hand. And I follow the story of the ill-fated town of his founding through the first bright decades of prosperity till the shadow of blood and rapine fell on it, at the hands of the dreaded Northmen. Another steep ascent is before me, after crossing the King's River; but I know now that this is the last big hill before Co. Mayo is reached, and mount it lightly. Meet a man (the first since Laragh), he remarked that it is a sore job I'm after. At the top I meet a second (this must be a congested district). He says 'Ye will not jaunt down that?' I confess that that is my intention, and he moves on rapidly to avoid (I suppose) being called at the inquest. It is Hollywood Hill, steep but not too steep, thanks to the safety pattern it is negotiated in a couple of minutes, and I am quaffing a cheering cup in a diminutive tavern of Hollywood village, grateful to think that the mountains are behind me. Handmora: four miles now (I have come about eighteen) through a very different country, green fields, comfortable hay ricks, comfortable cattle bound for the milk pail. Dunlavin is passed – Dunlavin, with its bright little streets and incongruously grim town hall: it is growing dusk so I reach my destination, to receive a warm welcome, to pass a pleasant evening and to doubtfully think of the morrow. After dinner 'Maps of the Counties' is produced and my route discussed. We are just within the border of Wicklow – let us certify our position on the key map of Ireland. Impatient of details, I pitch on Athlone in West Meath. 'There I sleep tomorrow night', now for the route and Kildare King's County, the least shaving of Queen's County, and part of West Meath, are to be traversed; we trace it out, Monasterevin, Portarlington, Tullamore, Clara, Moate, Athlone, something near seventy miles. 'Hope you may get there,' says my friend.

Morning, and an anxious opening of shutters. 'Olola!' Boreas' first cousin rampant among the trees and Jupiter Pluvius distilling his divinity into everything in a most superfluous manner. I affect indifference and remember that rain keeps one cool (which it unquestionably does), strap on my valise; 'farewell!' and am away. At first I am doomed to perplexing little by-roads muddy of surface and of serpentine tendencies. The head wind is baffling. I am getting irritated, then careless: here is a hill to run down, now to show the wind god that I am independent of him, forgetful of slippery ruts, I am conscious of doing too many things at once, extracting my map, readjusting my pipe, and so on: what is this? The front wheel seems tired of the back wheel's company and starts off somewhere by itself. I am powerless to effect a reconciliation or even a compromise; posing as an arbitrator, I am simply shelved ... I am not altogether unused to this method of dismounting and accordingly after a decent interval for self-examination proceed philosophically to ascertain my liabilities and compute my assets. My machine was quite unable to move and seemed in great pain; a twisted treadle crank invited my inspection and was pronounced not calculated to disable: a short tour down the road, pipe, map and bell, which latter obstinately refused to attach itself again to such an untrustworthy machine. I assist my fallen steed to its wheel, though the motion wrung from it piteous moans and console it with oil, harden my heart and am off again.

At the little village of Narraghmore I turn into a bigger road and take a direct course for Monasterevin. The rain-mist is clearing away and shows me a country of the prosperously uninteresting type, though not monotonous, presenting alternatives of pasture and wood-land, like the hunting-country it is. I get my first 'refresher' at The Seven Stars, the tiniest of hamlets owning the tiniest of publics. Four miles on we cross the Barrow, four more, the bridge of the Gt S. and Western. Here through some splendidly wooded parkland into Monasterevin. Then I demand milk. Now on these occasions the same thing always happens: 'Have you milk?' No. I don't leave the shop, but appear stunned by the intelligence. 'Wait till I see if we have a drop' – and a jugful appears. I light my pipe and scan the map. Portarlington is the next place. 'Which road to Portarlington?' Ye'll go straight on under the railway and then ye'll cross the canal and wheel to the left till ye cross the canal again and then ye'll go straight and cross – bless the man! Am I to spend the day in crossing and recrossing this ubiquitous canal! But so it is: how the road had ever the heart to leave the canal after their entanglement at Portarlington, I could not imagine, but it tore itself away ultimately and started off across a bare shelterless stretch of country – the bleakest I had crossed since Wicklow Gap. For a mile or two I had a mighty hassle with the wind which wreaked particular force on me as the only protuberance in sight. Rain had ceased, but the sky was depressingly grey. I thought of Athlone with despair. A bend in the road, and lo! the canal. The road seemed delighted to cross it and promptly broadened and hardened and created unto itself two goodly hedges. Here was shelter, and I blessed that canal. Portarlington is left behind now (the last stage had been but two miles) and Tullamore is the next hope on the horizon. It seems about seventeen miles on the map. I have passed Geashill, a very English looking village with a goose green and a duck pond, and am getting along fast, when I suddenly realise that the wind is almost at my back. My first impulse is to vow a shrine to Aeolus, my second to ask, was that the road to Tullamore? 'Yes, but a long way round', which indeed seemed likely, when it appeared that I was going due south. I had better go to Killeigh my informant said, and I knew then that I had lost a couple of miles. The hotel at Tullamore looked too tempting to be passed; it was one o'clock and I feasted royally on chops, read the morning papers and counted the miles to Clara. Seven, it appears, and they are the prettiest seven I have ridden today. It may be that the chops throw a rosier glamour over things, but this undulating well-wooded country no longer mist-wreathed, but cheerful and wakeful, is most enlivening to the eye and strength-giving to the knee joints. The little silver river, as it ripples beneath the road to hide itself in the bosom of the broad old Shannon, is positively smiling under a momentary sun-kiss: it skirts the park of Coleraine House and soon I am bowling along through the shelter of oak and elm for a mile or so. Finally I bore through a miniature defile, gorse-clad and cottage-crowned and drop into the beautiful little town of Clara. It seems to be market day, and I spread panic among the dumb creation, exchange greetings with their garrulous masters, give my blessing to Clara and leave it behind me. The road to Moate is charming, chiefly past big parks and wealthy-looking farms. It is only six miles from Clara and in 40 minutes I can see its chimneys below me over the tops of the trees: conscious of compensatory steeps beyond, I made the best of it, and shot into a long, straight street at about fifteen miles an hour. The next moment I felt quite apologetic: the hamlet had such a funereally melancholy aspect that I felt as if I had trodden on a condemned convict's toe, and therewith slunk stealthily through the street as though I had no business there. It may be that spiritual Moate was depressed by a drizzle which had just begun, and material Moate showed a sympathetic change of complexion, or it may even be that the aforesaid drizzle had washed out the rose colour in my own spectacles. My last stage is before me now: it is only four o'clock and there are ten miles between me and Athlone. As the evening approached, the wind falls and the sky brightens and very pleasant miles they were. It is a consummation of physical bliss known only to cyclists and pedestrians – that of dropping quietly into a sunlit haven, after fighting weather and roads through the vicissitudes of a toilsome day. I felt it to the full this evening, riding easily down over slight inclines, into the valley of the Shannon. There is an added charm when the haven is a strange one, then can imagination work her own sweet will and deftly ply her magical brush over the virgin canvas with no fear lest familiarity with sweeping pitiless washes and insipid monotones should mar the daintiest touch and the fairy haze that she loves.

At 5.30 I may be seen in the yard of the Prince of Wales bending over an ancient servitor, by all the ties of hospitality and obedience, to attend to the material wants of my mud-spattered Singer. Then climax of bliss – a hot bath, followed by the milder dissipation of tea and eggs and bacon. Then my pipe precedes me down the gay little street and stops at the bridge. I stop too, and gaze up the Shannon, pink-flushed by the evening sun. My pipe breathes a puff of unutterable content and leads me past the black old fortress scowling down on the bridge and far along the riverside, till all the shadows are merged into one.

Looking at the map next morning was a more serious operation than I usually found it. The straightest route to Killary Bay seemed to lie nearly due west through Co. Galway, past Tuam and between lakes Corrib and Mask and so to the sea. But I recollected that reasons compelled me to pass Westport, whither I had sent my Gladstone and gun case, concerning which I desired an understanding with the station master. But the necessity gave a considerable curve to my route, pointing to a course by Roscommon and Castlereagh, almost due North, then due West to Ballyhannis, Castlebar and Westport, then due south to Leenane, Killary Bay. 'Sufficient for the day' etc. is a sacred saying to me and I had not thought of all this before. As matters stood, there was a little over a 100 miles to be traversed: this, I reflected, was an epoch in my lately inaugurated cycling career, and I felt quite important, as, after testing the loyalty of the ancient servitor, I mounted my machine in the presence of the waiter, the boots, the under boots, and a diminutive pseudo boots of no definite standing. I note with satisfaction that the sky, though grey, is bright and – the powers of nature be praised – that what there is left of the wind has shifted and will prosper me that day. The morning air and the swift motion over smooth roads are invigorating and intoxicating to a degree. The seventeen miles to Roscommon pass like a dream: I am aware that the country has widely changed in aspect, that contours are less pronounced, that trees are few and stone walls are many, that everything has a hardier greyer aspect and once – about ten miles away – wheels are forgotten in a pleasant five minutes with a parish priest, at whose house, at a lonely spot in the road, I enquire about a doubtful turning, but for the most part I give myself up to that rapt enjoyment of self-created motion which is our most perfect appreciation of the reality of living. I reach Roscommon without having had a glimpse of Loch Ree though I have skirted at no great distance for quite twelve miles. I am in no mood for delays, and after questioning about roads start up the street and out of the town enroute for Castlereagh via Ballymoe. The country is, if anything, barer and opener and generally poorer in appearance. By the way, a word about the habits of the dumb creation if surprised by a cycle, at the moment when they are reflecting that all the road belongs to them. A cow waits and looks till collision is imminent, then swings round its anterior parts, using its hind legs as a pivot, and sidles moodily away. Hens, wherever situated when the horrid thing comes revolving down the road, wait till the very last moment and then run straight across the track of the machine, escaping sudden death by a miracle. They even prefer this course to remaining quietly in a ditch and scoffing at the infernal machine with the insolence of security. Pigs make for the ditch, if not there already, and run before one up the road, till they get uncomfortably hot, when they stare very hard. A dog treats the whole thing as a personal insult of an aggravated character, and barks at the back wheel (which I suppose he thinks is being led into this audacious folly by the front wheel, and is for that reason all the more deserving of his contempt) until he sees a pig, when he worries that instead. The duck alone has judgement, she waddles respectfully though perhaps a little fussily, from the dangerous zone, and philosophises at her leisure over the unaccountability of events. At Ballymoe I am in Co. Galway; soon after I cross the Suck and the Roscommon boundary once more and Castlereagh receives one, somewhat weary and glad of biscuits and a drink in a charming sitting room of the little hotel. It was a great relief to feel that I could now ride due west and set my face for Westport. All was eminently satisfactory so far; sympathise with me when on entering the street I met – 'the blank monotony of rain'. I will spare the reader a detailed narrative of the next fifty miles or so. I see it all. Myself through a dim grey mist of saturated despondency. I was obscurely aware that the mud grew thicker and my clothes damper; that small sopping towns of uniform structure and uniform melancholy appeared and were passed about every ten miles; that at Ballyhaunis there was cyder, and at Claremorris milk-and-soda; that the road to Balla was a desolation of jagged stones and clammy ooze such as Milton never dreamed of; that passers-by still sent up through the mist the mocking greeting 'Fine day!' (it takes much to persuade an Irishman that it is not a fine day) and only when it was a hopeless, 'soft day', that at Castlebar I looked at the time and vowed no power on earth should bestir me from Westport that night. That once between Castlebar and Westport I dismounted and sat for ten minutes on a bank without being very vividly conscious of my position in the scheme of things in that I passed much by and many stacks of turf, that I climbed a very long hill, and saw others dimly (Croaghpatrick must have been visible on my left) and I flew down a long, steep descent into the town and stopped exhausted at the Railway Hotel. Then I bethought me of the station master and rode slowly up to the station and back, took some refreshment – 'and then a strange thing happened'. It may be that a chat with a man of heavy face and watchchain (who gazed solemnly at the barmaid between his periods), in the course of which he expressed much lofty pity at my misdirected energies, caused a reaction within my somewhat blurred understanding: probably too the strength gained by refreshment, the promise of finer weather, and the certainty of a warm welcome, had their share in the change; but however that may be, at a quarter to eight o'clock I detected myself in the act of elevating my soaking personality into the saddle again, having apparently steeled my heart for the eighteen miles of mountain road that separated me from Killary Bay. Westport is quite hill-locked and sea-locked. I climbed a hill to leave it on which it seemed a marvel that the houses could resist the force of gravity. Some day I shall return and find them a heap of tumbled ruins at the bottom. It rapidly grew very dark and a sighing wind began to rustle the heather and gather force. Three miles out a sou'-wester was blowing torrents of rain in my face, and the night was black as Erebus. I have rarely felt so completely lonely as on that (to me) memorable evening. Once at seven years of age, on my first night at a strange school, I woke up from sleep-walking to find myself alone in the darkness of the great bare schoolroom. I felt something of the same sensation now, as I struggled half-blinded through the driving rain. Through pure carelessness I had omitted to light my lamp at starting and now every match on me was wet. Houses were few and far between; the fatigue of ninety miles was definitely asserting itself. The road was a quagmire and a treadle-nut became loosened about every fifteen minutes. Under this accumulation of discomfitures, I progressed at about six miles an hour, over wild moorland, and beneath the frown of chill, black mountains, a presence not seen but felt. In somnambulism I am aware that my movements are erratic but though wide awake, I surpassed myself this night. My machine was constantly trying to put an end to all the bother and lie down quietly at the side of the road. That it did so quietly, was only due to the fact that our pace was not excessive: for the rest, some ditches were deep, some shallow, some rocky, some boggy – and I tried most kinds. None were wholly comfortable. I shall never forget the sensation of heart-sick impotence that followed the sudden rough jolts, while one wondered what one was falling into. In spite of the general humidity, I was afflicted with an unquenchable thirst, which, at intervals, when the plash of falling water fell on my ears, drove me into cramped fantastic attitudes beneath some overhanging rock. The river Erriff I knew must be on my right. I had once fished up as far as this, but landmarks were indistinguishable. At length I crossed the Erriff bridge and felt home-like for one instant, then passed into the region of blank, black mist. There were nine miles more I knew. An hour had passed after that – I should be disposed emphatically to deny that there were only sixty minutes in that hour- when I found myself splashing down a long hill, then plunging beneath trees, suddenly the bottom is reached, trees cease, the road swerves and I graze a low rock wall, twenty feet below which I hear the splash of waves, and beyond black emptyness. The Bay! I shudder and ride on as rapidly as I can. There are but two miles now. A small inlet is to be skirted – at its apex a swollen mountain stream comes racing beneath the road – then a promontory has to be rounded: just there the wind makes a last furious onslaught, as if conscious it was to lose me soon, but I forget the wind, for I faintly see the glimmer of a light in the distance. Five minutes later I pass through the few little houses that make up Leenane village, then up a little hill and over a bridge, and at 11.15 I am pelting with gravel the solitary lighted window in Leenane Hotel. Ejaculations – long pause – footsteps, somebody's hearty welcome – dishevelled waiter – tea – more tea – beef – more beef – sleep, more, more, more sleep!

Notes

1 A VOYAGE TO FRANCE

1. John Rider, *English–Latin, Latin–English Dictionary*, Oxford, 1589.

3 ERSKINE CHILDERS – CORINTHIAN SAILOR

1. Erskine Childers, *The Riddle of the Sands*, London: Sidgwick & Jackson, 1972.
2. Burke Wilkinson, *The Zeal of the Convert*, Gerrards Cross: Colin Smythe, 1978.
3. Erskine Childers, *A Thirst for the Sea* (ed. Hugh and Robin Popham), London: Stanford Maritime Press, 1979.
4. Tom Cox, *Damned Englishman*, Hicksville, NY: Exposition Press/Hicksville Press, 1975.
5. Basil Williams, *Erskine Childers, 1870-1922: A Sketch*, London: privately printed, 1925.
6. Basil Williams, *Dictionary of National Biography*, 1922–30, Oxford: Oxford University Press, 1931.
7. Letter to Basil and Dorothy Williams from Molly Childers, Dublin, 1 September 1922.
8. *Irish Times*, 25 November 1922.
9. Haileybury School essays, unpublished, *c.*1885.
10. Childers Papers, Trinity College, Dublin.
11. Andrew Boyle, *The Riddle of Erskine Childers*, London: Hutchinson, 1977.
12. Williams, *Childers*.
13. *Royal Cruising Club Journal*, 1896.
14. Alasdair Garrett and Trevor Wilkinson, *The History of the Royal Cruising Club, 1880–1980*, London: R.C.C. Press, 1980.
15. Letter to Walter Runciman from R.E.C., House of Commons, 19 March 1896.
16. Alan Palmer, *The Kaiser – Warlord of the Second Reich*, New York: Charles Scribner's Sons, 1978.
17. The Salisbury Papers, quoted in Palmer, *The Kaiser.*
18. Leipzig, 1920–1.
19. Raymond Sontag, 'The Cowes Interview and Kruger Telegram', *Political Science Quarterly*, 1925, vol. 40.
20. Brooke Heckstall-Smith ('Bookstall'), *All Hands on the Main Sheet*, London: Grant Richards Ltd, 1921.
21. E. F. Benson, *Edward VII – An Appreciation*, London: Longman's, Green, 1933.
22. Christopher Hibbert, *Edward VII*, Harmondsworth: Penguin, 1982.

23. Count Phillipp zu Eulenburg, *Aus 50 Jahren*, Berlin: Gerbrüder Paetel, 1923.
24. Baron Hermann von Eckhardstein (then Chancellor at the German Embassy, London), Leipzig, 1919–20.
25. T. G. Cuthell, *A Sailing Guide to the Solent and Poole Harbour*, London: L. Upcott Gill, *c.*1890.
26. Linton Hope, 'Small Boat Racing', *British Sports and Sportsmen – Yachting and Rowing* (ed. 'The Sportsman'), London: British Sports and Sportsmen, 1916.
27. W. R. McKay, 'Mild Drudgery', *The Table* (Journal of the Clerks to Parliament), London: 1972–3, vol. 41.
28. A. G. Bagot, *Shooting and Yachting in the Mediterranean*, London: W. H. Allen, 1888.
29. Frank Cowper, *Sailing Tours: The Yachtsman's Guide to the Cruising Waters of the English Coast*, part 2, London: L. Upcott Gill, 1893.
30. Thomas Packenham, *The Boer War*, London: Weidenfeld & Nicolson, 1979; Futura, 1982.
31. Edward T. Cook, *Rights and Wrongs of the Transvaal War*, London: Edward Arnold, 1901.
32. Boyle, *Childers*.
33. Paul Kennedy, *The Rise of Anglo-German Antagonism, 1860-1914*, London: George Allen & Unwin, 1980.
34. Childers Correspondence, Trinity College, Cambridge, 1143.
35. Letter to the author from Professor Walter Childers (Henry's son), 16 February 1983.
36. Letter to the author from Professor Walter Childers, 16 February 1983.
37. Cowper, *Sailing Tours*.
38. S.V.S.C. Messum, *East Coast Rivers*, London: J. P. Potter, 1903.

4 THE EPIC VOYAGE OF 1897

1. Letter to Walter Runciman from R.E.C., London, 23 March 1898.
2. Maurice Griffiths, 'What Was It Like? Cruising on the East Coast 50 Years Ago', *Yachting Monthly*, August 1983.
3. Letter to the author from Group Captain Frank Griffiths, 1 January 1980.
4. John White, *The Lifeboat*, Cowes: Kinsam and Co., 1883.
5. Letter to the author from Maurice Griffiths, 12 February 1980.
6. Letter to the author from Eric Hiscock, 16 February 1980.
7. Letter to the author from Ted Watson, 1 January 1980.
8. Letter to the author from Frank Carr, 1 March 1980.
9. Letter to the author from Dick Stower, 18 January 1980.
10. Letter to the author from Grahame Farr (hon. archivist of the Lifeboat Enthusiasts Society), 3 July 1980.

11. Letter to the author from Grahame Farr, 3 July 1980.
12. Letter to the author from Howard Biggs (hon. sec., Broadstairs Branch, RNLI), 27 July 1980.
13. Adrian Nelson, C. E. Dixon Kemp and G. Christopher Davies, *Practical Boat Building and Sailing*, London: L. Upcott Gill, 1900.
14. Letter to the author from Frank Carr, 1 April 1980.
15. Major R. Ridding, 'Victualling – *HMS Warrior* (1860)', unpublished, 1982.
16. Ridding, 'Victualling'.
17 Letter to Walter Runciman from R.E.C., undated, but probably written from *Vixen* on 26 October 1897, because it is addressed from 'Sonderburg, N. Germany'.
18. Letter to Dulcibella Childers from R.E.C., 8 October 1897; Childers Papers, Trinity College, Dublin.
19. Letter to Dulcibella Childers from R.E.C., 28 October 1899, written from Hotel de Lion d'Or, Souillac, Dordogne; Childers Papers, Trinity College, Dublin.
20. E. F. Knight, *The Falcon on the Baltic – A Coasting Voyage from Hammersmith to Copenhagen in a Three-Ton Yacht*, London: W. H. Allen, 1889.
21. Harry Vandervell, 'Through Holland by Sleep-boot', *Yachting World*, December 1897.
22. G. Christopher Davies, *Cruising in the Netherlands*, London: Jarrold & Sons, *c.*1890.
23. G. Christopher Davies, *Practical Boat Sailing for Amateurs*, London: L. Upcott Gill, *c.*1890.
24. Raymond Flower and Michael Wynn-Jones, *Lloyd's of London*, Newton Abbot: David & Charles, 1974.
25. 'Memoranda to Accompany a Sketch Model of Operations at HMS *Lutine* during the Years 1894 to 1898', Lloyds of London.
26. He was so described from Lloyd's archives in a letter to the author from Peter Green (the then chairman of Lloyd's), 16 April 1981.
27. H. da Haan and R. Ijbema, Engelsman Plaat, Paescens-Moddergat: Fishery Museum.
28. Hans Jürgen Hanson, *The Ships of the German Fleets, 1848–1945*, London: Hamlyn, 1974.
29. Conway's, *All the World's Fighting Ships, 1869–1905*, London: Conway Maritime Press, 1979.
30. Chart No. 64, Die Ostfriesischen Inseln, 1:100000, 1897.
31. Chart No. 99. Emsmundung, 1:50000,1973.
32. *Waddenzee*,Netherlands Nature Conservancy, 1976.
33. *The Standard*, 26 March 1908.
34. *The Times*, 23 August 1910.
35. Mark Brackenburg, *Frisian Pilot*, London: Stanford Maritime Press, 1979.
36. Hamburger Yacht Club Chart, 'Die Heligolander Bucht', 1897; republished in *Yachting World*.

37. *The Times*, 23 August 1910.
38. Letter to Dulcibella Childers from R.E.C., 8 October 1897; Childers Papers, Trinity College, Dublin.
39. *The Times*, 8 May 1913.
40. Paul Kennedy, *The Realities Behind Diplomacy*, London: Fontana, 1981.
41. Holger H. Herwig, *Luxury Fleet – The Imperial German Navy, 1888–1918*, London: George Allen & Unwin, 1980.
42. George Nye Steiger, *China and the Occident*, New Haven, Conn.: Yale University Press, 1927.
43. Marina Warner, *The Dragon Empress*, London: Weidenfeld & Nicolson, 1972.
44. Jonathan Steinberg, *Tirpitz and the Birth of the German Battle Fleet – Yesterday's Deterrent*, London: Macdonald, 1965.
45. 'Germany: Coast Defences and Coast Defence Ordnance', *[The Naval Baedeker]*, London: Naval Intelligence Division Report No. 579, September 1902.
46. Admiralty Chart No. 2593, Ameland to Jade River, engraved by Davies, Bryer & Co.
47. Captain Tip Sneider, coxswain of the Lauwerswoog Lifeboat *Gerbroeders Luden*.
48. *The Times*, 23 August 1910.

5 THE MAKING OF AN AUTHOR

1. 'The Londoner's Cruising Ground', *The Times*, 28 July 1908.
2. *The Times*, 28 July 1908.
3. Letter to his sisters from R.E.C., 18 October 1896; Childers Papers, Trinity College, Dublin.
4. 'Cruising in the West Indies', *The Times*, 12 May 1908.
5. Letter to the author from Professor Walter Childers, 16 February 1983.
6. Letter to his sisters from R.E.C., Grenada, 24 November 1898.
7. Basil Williams, *Erskine Childers, 1870–1922: A Sketch*, London: privately printed, 1925.
8. Herbert Warington-Smyth, *Sea Wake and Jungle Trail*, London: John Murray, 1925.
9. Herbert Warington-Smyth, *Yachting Monthly*, February 1932.
10. Certified copy of Attestation; Childers Papers, Trinity College, Dublin.
11. Williams, *Childers*.
12. Letter to Basil Williams from R.E.C., 5 January 1901; Childers Papers, Cambridge University Press.
13. Paul Kennedy, *The Rise of the Anglo-German Antagonism, 1860-1914*, London: George Allen & Unwin, 1980.
14. Kennedy, *Anglo-German Antagonism*.

15. Letter to Flora Priestley from R.E.C., 8 January 1901; Childers Papers, Trinity College, Dublin.
16. Letter to Basil Williams from R.E.C., 19 January 1901; Childers Papers, Trinity College Library, Cambridge.
17. Jim Young in conversation with the author; 24 May 1982.
18. *Evening News*, 11 August 1939.
19. R. Stower, 'The Riddle of the *Dulcibella*: Some Thoughts on an Old Boat'; unpublished paper.
20. Letter to the author from Ted Watson, 1 January 1980.
21. Letter to Molly Childers from C. H. Gibson, 14 June 1948; Childers Papers, Trinity College, Dublin.
22. A. A. Raines in conversation with the author, 6 March 1982.
23. Letter to Molly Childers from C. H. Gibson, 14 June 1948.
24. Letter to the author from Group Captain F. C. Griffiths, 19 January 1980.
25. *The Spray* (magazine of the Slocum Society), June 1957.
26. Erskine Childers, *A Unique Edition of The Riddle of the Sands*, with Historical Postscript by R. M. Bowker, Old Bosham: Bowker & Benram, 1976.
27. Letter to Basil Williams from R.E.C., 23 January 1901; Childers Papers, Trinity College, Cambridge.
28. Letter to Basil Williams from R.E.C., 13 February 1902; Childers Papers, Trinity College, Cambridge.
29. Letter to Basil Williams from R.E.C., 28 February 1902; Childers Papers, Trinity College, Cambridge.
30. *Dictionary of National Biography* (compact edition), Oxford: Oxford University Press, 1975.
31. Letter to Basil Williams from R.E.C., 24. March 1902; Childers Papers, Trinity College, Cambridge.
32. Letter to Basil Williams from R.E.C., 24 April 1902; Childers Papers, Trinity College, Cambridge.
33. Thomas Packenham, *The Boer War*, London: Weidenfeld & Nicolson, 1979; Futura, 1982.
34. Letter to Basil Williams from R.E.C., 12 June 1902; Childers Papers, Trinity College, Cambridge.
35. Letter to Basil Williams from R.E.C., 12 June 1902.
36. Letter to Basil Williams from R.E.C., 29 August 1902; Childers Papers, Trinity College, Cambridge.
37. Letter to Basil Williams from R.E.C., 29 August 1902.
38. Letter to Basil Williams from R.E.C., 25 February 1903; Childers Papers, Trinity College, Cambridge.

39. Letter to Basil Williams from R.E.C., 25 February 1903.
40. Letter to Basil Williams from R.E.C., 14 January 1903; Childers Papers, Trinity College, Cambridge.
41. Letter to Basil Williams from R.E.C., 1 May 1903; Childers Papers, Trinity College, Cambridge.
42. Karte des Deutschen Reiches – 141. Esens, 1895.
43. Letter to Martin J. Turner from John Murray (Publishers), 22 April 1931; John Murray Archives.
44. Andrew Boyle, *The Riddle of Erskine Childers*, London: Hutchinson, 1977.
45. Michael Mclnerney, *The Riddle of Erskine Childers*, Dublin: E. T. O'Brien, 1971.
46. I. F. Clarke, *Voices Prophesying War, 1763–1984*, London: Oxford University Press, 1966.
47. P. L. Stevenson, *How the Jubilee Fleet Escaped Destruction and The Battle of Ushant*, Hertford: Stephen Austin & Sons, 1898.
48. Erskine Childers, *The Riddle of the Sands*, New York: Dover Publications, 1976.
49. Brigadier-General Gordon Shephard, *Memoirs of Brigadier-General Gordon Shephard, DSO, MC* (ed. Shane Leslie), London: privately printed, 1924.
50. Public Record Office, Kew.
51. Herbert E. Julyan, *Sixty Years of Yachts*, London: Hutchinson, *c.*1950.
52. Letter to the author from Professor Walter Childers, 16 February 1983.
53. Letter to the *Spectator*, 12 August 1955.
54. Letter to Frank Sidgwick from Molly Childers, undated; Childers Papers, Trinity College, Dublin.

6 BOLT FROM THE BLUE

1. Selborne Papers, Trinity College, Cambridge.
2. Committee of Imperial Defence, 'Draft Report on the Possibility of Serious Invasion', 11 November 1903; Public Record Office, Kew.
3. H. R. Moon, 'The Invasion of the United Kingdom – Public Controversy and Official Planning, 1888–1918', 2 vols, PhD thesis, London, 1968.
4. 'Débarquement d'un Corps Expéditionnaire en Angleterre', June 1897 (Moon, 'The Invasion of the United Kingdom').
5. Lieutenant-Colonel W. R. Robertson, 'The Military Resources of France and Probable Method of Their Employment in a War Between France and England', 27 December 1901; issued by Committee of Imperial Defence, 2 November 1903. Public Record Office, Kew.
6. Arthur J. Marder, *The Anatomy of British Sea Power – A History of British Naval Policy in the Pre-Dreadnought Era, 1880–1905*, London: Putnam, 1940.

7. Marder, *British Naval Policy*.
8. Marder, *British Naval Policy*.
9. W. E. Cairns, 'The Problem of Invasion', *National Review*, November 1900.
10. Moon, 'The Invasion of the United Kingdom'.
11. John Leyland, 'The Invasion of England', in T. A. Brassey (ed.}, *Brassey's Naval Annual*, Portsmouth: J. Griffen, 1902.
12. Later editor of *Army and Navy Gazette* (1904–9) and of *The Navy* (1910–12).
13. Marder, *British Naval Policy*.
14. Arnold Forster, 'Notes on a Visit to Kiel and Wilhelmshaven, August, 1902, and General Remarks on the German Navy and Naval Establishments, 15th September–November, 1902' (Moon, 'The Invasion of the United Kingdom').
15. W. T. Stead, 'The German Menace – Why Germany Requires a Fleet', *Review of Reviews*, March 1897.
16. 'Naval and Military Notes', *Royal United Services Journal*, February 1896.
17. Marder, *British Naval Policy*.
18. Marder, *British Naval Policy*.
19. Moon, 'The Invasion of the United Kingdom'.
20. Marder, *British Naval Policy*.
21. Marder, *British Naval Policy*.
22. Richard Hough, *First Sea Lord*, London: George Alien & Unwin, 1969.
23. Committee of Imperial Defence, 'Draft Report on the Possibility of Serious Invasion'.
24. *The Times*, 6 March 1903.
25. Inverkeithing High School, *The Story of Rosyth*, Fife Educational Resources Centre, undated; notes supplied by the Port Admiral, Rosyth, 1983.
26. Arthur J. Marder, *The Road to War, 1904–1914*, London: Oxford University Press, 1961.
27. J. Lennox Kerr and Wilfred Granville, *The RNVR – A Record of Achievement*, London: Harrap, 1957.

7 OPERATION AGAINST ENGLAND

1. Paul Kennedy (ed.), *The War Plans of the Great Powers, 1880–1914*, London, George Allen & Unwin, 1979.
2. Jonathan Steinberg, 'The Copenhagen Complex', *Journal of Contemporary History*; 1966, vol. 1, part 3.
3. Kennedy, *War Plans of the Great Powers*.
4. Letter to the author from Professor Ivo Lambi (University of Saskatchewan}, 2 June 1981.

5. 'Naval High Command Files on Operational Plans Against England', Admiralty Library, London.
6. Jonathan Steinberg, 'A German Plan for the Invasion of Holland and Belgium – 1897', *Historical Journal*, 1963, vol. 6, no. 1.
7. Jonathan Steinberg, *Tirpitz and the Birth of the German Battle Fleet – Yesterday's Deterrent*, London: Macdonald, 1965.
8. Steinberg, *Tirpitz*.
9. Steinberg, *Tirpitz*.
10. Gordon Craig, *Germany, 1866–1945*, Oxford: Oxford University Press 1981; Steinberg, *Tirpitz*.
11. Kennedy, *War Plans of the Great Powers*.
12. Memorandum to Admiral von Knorr from Graf Alfred von Schlieffen, 14 December 1897; Admiralty Library, London.
13. Letter to the author from Professor Ivo Lambi, 2 June 1981.
14. H. R. Moon, 'The Invasion of the United Kingdom – Public Controversy and Official Planning, 1888–1918', 2 vols, PhD thesis, 1968.
15. Steinberg, 'The Copenhagen Complex'.
16. Steinberg, 'A German Plan'.
17. Steinberg, 'The Copenhagen Complex'.
18. Letter to the author from Professor Ivo Lambi, 2 June 1981.
19. Moon, 'The Invasion of the United Kingdom'.
20. Moon, 'The Invasion of the United Kingdom'.
21. Letter to the author from the Pressedienst, Deutsche Bundesbahn, 15 February 1984.
22. Imperial German Navy Staff Memorandum, 31 May 1900; Freiburg: A.3369 Bundesarchiv Militärarchiv, Bestand RMS/v. 880.
23. Letter to the author from Professor Ivo Lambi, 2 June 1981.

8 THE CHILDERS PLAN

1. Letter to Frank Sidgwick from Molly Childers, 9 November 1938; Childers Papers, Trinity College, Dublin,
2. Richard Shannon, *The Crisis of Imperialism, 1865–1915*, St Albans: Granada, 1976.
3. Letter to the author from Professor Walter Childers, 16 February 1983.
4. Letter to Frank Sidgwick from Molly Childers, 9 November 1938.
5. Letter to Frank Sidgwick from Molly Childers, 9 November 1938.
6. Lieutenant-Commander P. K. Kemp (ed.) *The Papers of Admiral Sir John Fisher*, vol. 1, London: Navy Record Society, 1960.

7. Erskine Childers, *A Unique Edition of The Riddle of the Sands*, with Historical Postscript by R. M. Bowker, Old Bosham: Bowker & Bertram, 1976.
8. G. E. Livock, *To the Ends of the Air*, London: HMSO, 1973.
9. Charles Hanrott and R. M. Bowker in conversation with the author, March 1984.
10. Andrew Boyle, *The Riddle of Erskine Childers*, London: Hutchinson, 1977.
11. Letter to Molly Childers from R.E.C., 14 December 1909; Childers Papers, Trinity College, Cambridge.
12. Howard D'Eguille, *The Invasion of England*, London: Hodder & Stoughton, 1915.
13. Boyle, *Childers*.
14. Erskine Childers, 'Remarks on the German North Sea Coast In Its Relation to War between Great Britain and Germany – With a Note on the Dutch Coast', February 1906; Public Record Office, London.
15. Letter to R.E.C. from W. E. M. Nicholson (assistant secretary to the Committee of Imperial Defence), 27 February 1906; Childers Papers, Imperial War Museum.
16. Lieutenant-Commander P. K. Kemp (ed.), *The Papers of Admiral Sir John Fisher*, vol. 2, London: Navy Record Society, 1964.
17. T.124 Commander Russell Grenfell, RN, *Sea Power*, London: Jonathan Cape, 1940.
18. Winston Churchill, *The World Crisis 1911–18*, London: Thornton Butterworth, revised: edition 1931.
19. Arthur J. Marder, *From the Dreadnought to Scapa Flow*, vol. 2, London: Oxford University Press, 1965.
20. Boyle, *Childers*.
21. Marder, *From the Dreadnought to Scapa Flow*.
22. Marder, *From the Dreadnought to Scapa Flow*.
23. Boyle, *Childers*.
24. Erskine Childers, 'Seizure of Borkum and Juist', Chatham, 1914; Childers Papers.
25. Arthur J. Marder, *Portrait of an Admiral: The Life and Papers of Sir Herbert Richmond*, London: Oxford University Press, 1952.
26. Sir Julyan Corbett and Sir Henry Newbolt, *History of the Great War, Naval Operations*, 5 vols, London: Longman, 1920–31.
27. Captain L. B. Weldon, *Hard Lying, Eastern Mediterranean, 1914–1919*; London, Herbert Jenkins, 1925.
28. Lieutenant Erskine Childers, RNVR, HM Coastal Motor Boats, Memorandum for Lieutenant Bremner; Childers Papers, Imperial War Museum.
29. Kemp, *The Papers of Admiral Sir John Fisher*, vol. 2.
30. Sir Frederick Sykes, *From Many Angles*, London: Castle, 1942.
31. Harald Fock, *Fast Fighting Boats, 1870–1945*, Lymington: Nautical Publishing, 1973.

32. Temple Patterson, *Tyrwhitt of the Harwich Force*, London: Military Book Society, 1973.
33. Kemp, *The Papers of Admiral Sir John Fisher*, vol. 2.
34. Letter to the author from Dr Paul Kennedy, 25 January 1981, referring to report by *Daily Mail* correspondent on 5 July 1913 (Northcliffe Papers, British Library). The *Times*, 3 January 1981.
35. Richard Deacon (George D. K. McCormick), *The Silent War, A History of Western Naval Intelligence*, Newton Abbot: David & Charles, 1978.
36. Nigel West, MI6, *British Intelligence Service Operations, 1909–1945*, London: Weidenfeld & Nicolson, 1983.
37. Admiral Sir William James, *The Eyes of the Navy, A Biography of Admiral Sir Reginald Hall*, London: Methuen, 1955; Montague Grahame White, *At the Wheel Afloat and Ashore*, London: G. T. Foulis, *c.*1935.
38. Letter to Major Donald F. Bittner, PhD, VSMCR, from A. J. Francis, Admiralty Library.
39. Deacon, *The Silent War.*
40. N. C. Bywater and H. C. Ferraby, *Strange Intelligence: Memoirs of Naval Secret Service*, London: Constable, 1931.
41. James, *The Eyes of the Navy.*
42. Brigadier-General Gordon Shephard, *Memoirs of Brigadier-General Gordon Shephard, DSOMC* (ed. Shane Leslie), London: privately printed, 1924.
43. Shephard, *Memoirs.*
44. Deacon, *The Silent War.*
45. Shephard, *Memoirs.*
46. Basil Williams, *Erskine Childers, 1870-1922: A Sketch*, London, privately printed, 1925.

9 EPILOGUE

1. Ewen Southby-Tailyour, 'Ask Me One on Beaches', *Royal Cruising Club Journal*, London: R.C.C. Press, 1982; *Falkland Islands Shores*, London: Macmillan London, 1985.

Select Bibliography

Bagot, A. G., *Shooting and Yachting in the Mediterranean*, London: W. H. Allen, 1888

Bayly, Admiral Sir Louis, *Pull Together! The Memoirs of Admiral Sir Lewis*

Bayly, KCB, KCMG, CVO, Forewords by Franklin D. Roosevelt and Admiral Sir Roger Backhouse, London: Harrap, 1939

Benson, E. F., *Edward VII – An Appreciation*, London: Longman's, Green, 1933

Boyle, Andrew, *The Riddle of Erskine Childers*, London: Hutchinson, 1977

Brackenbury, Mark, *Frisian Pilot*, London: Stanford Maritime Press, 1979

Brassey, T. A. (ed.), *Brassey's Naval Annual*, Portsmouth: J. Griffen, 1902

Brassey, Sir Thomas, *The British Navy – Its Strength, Resources, and Administration*, vol. 2, part 2, London: Longman's, Green, 1882

Bywater, H. C. and Ferraby, H. C., *Strange Intelligence: Memoirs of Naval Secret Service*, London: Constable, 1931

Childers, Erskine, *The Riddle of the Sands*, Introduction by Ralph Hammond Innes, London: Collins, 1955

Childers, Erskine, *The Riddle of the Sands*, Foreword by Lord Longford, London: Sidgwick & Jackson, 1972

Childers, Erskine, *The Riddle of the Sands*, Introduction by Norman Donaldson, New York: Dover Publications, 1976

Childers, Erskine, *The Riddle of the Sands*, New York: David McKay, 1977

Childers, Erskine, *Unique Edition of the Riddle of the Sands*, with Historical Postscript by R. M. Bowker, Old Bosham: Bowker & Bertram, 1976

Chitty, Jean, *The River is Within Us – A Maritime History of Lymington*, Lymington: Belhaven, 1983

Churchill, Winston, *The World Crisis 1911–18*, revised edition, London: Thornton Butterworth, 1931

Clarke, I.F., *Voices Prophesying War, 1763–1984*, London: Oxford University Press, 1966

Clews, Graham T., *Churchill's Dilemma*, Imprint of ABC – CLIO, LLC, Santa Barbara, 2010

Colomb, Captain J. C. R., *The Defence of Great Britain: Sketches of Its Naval, Military, and Political Aspects*, London: Edward Stanford, 1880

Compact Dictionary of National Biography, 1901–1960, entry on Erskine Childers by Basil Williams, Oxford: Oxford University Press, 1961

Conway's, *All the World's Fighting Ships, 1869–1905*, London: Conway Maritime Press, 1979

Cook, Edward T., *Rights and Wrongs of the Transvaal War*, London: Edward Arnold, 1901
Cooke, Francis, *The Corinthian Yachtsman's Handbook*, London: Edward Arnold, 1913
Corbett, Sir Julyan, and Newbolt, Sir Henry, *History of the Great War, Naval Operations*, 5 vols, London: Longman, 1920–31
Cowper, Frank, *Sailing Tours: The Yachtsman's Guide to the Cruising Waters of the English Coast*, part 2, London: L. Upcott Gill, 1893
Cox, Tom, *Damned Englishman*, Hicksville, NY: Exposition Press/Hicksville Press, 1975
Craig, Gordon A., *Germany, 1866–1945*, Oxford: Oxford University Press, 1981
Cuthell, T. G., *A Sailing Guide to the Solent and Poole Harbour*, London: L. Upcott Gill, *c.*1890
Davies, G. Christopher, *Cruising in the Netherlands*, London: Jarrold & Sons, *c.* 1890
Deacon, Richard (George D. K. McCormick), *The Silent War, A History of Western Naval Intelligence*, Newton Abbot: David & Charles, 1978
D'Egville, Howard, *The Invasion of England*, London: Hodder & Stoughton, 1915
Drummond, Maldwin, *Salt-Water Palaces*, London: Debrett, 1979
Fisher, Admiral of the Fleet Lord, *Records*, London: Hodder & Stoughton, 1919
Flower, Raymond, and Wynn-Jones, Michael, *Lloyd's of London*, Newton Abbot: David & Charles, 1974
Fock, Harald, *Fast Fighting Boats, 1870–1945*, Lymington: Nautical Publishing, 1973
Garrett, Alasdair, and Wilkinson, Trevor, *The History of the Royal Cruising Club, 1880–1980*, London: R.C.C. Press, 1980
Hanson, Hans Jurgen, *The Ships of the German Fleets, 1848–1945*, London: Hamlyn, 1974
Hassall, Christopher, *Edward Marsh, Patron of the Arts – A Biography*, London: Longman's, Green, 1959
Herwig, Holger H., *'Luxury' Fleet – The lmperial German Navy, 1888–1918*, London: George Allen & Unwin, 1980
Hibbert, Christopher, *Edward VII*, Harmondsworth: Penguin, 1982
Hislam, Percival A., *The Admiralty of the Atlantic – An Enquiry into the Development of German Sea Power, Past, Present and Prospective*, London: Longman's, Green, 1908
Hough, Richard, *First Sea Lord*, London: George Allen & Unwin, 1969
Hunt's Universal Yacht List, London: James Imray & Son, and Norie & Wilson, 1898–1903
Hydrographic Department, Admiralty, *North Sea Pilot*, vol. 2, Northern and Eastern Coast of Scotland, From Cape Wrath to Berwick, 11th edn, London, 1959
Hydrographic Department, Admiralty, *North Sea Pilot*, vol. 3, East Coast of England, From Berwick to the North Foreland Including The Rivers Thames and Medway, 9th edn, London, 1922
Hydrographic Department, Admiralty, *North Sea Pilot*, vol. 4, The Eastern Shores of the North Sea, From Nieuport to the Skaw, 9th edn, London, 1934

James, Admiral Sir William, *The Eyes of the Navy, A Biography of Admiral Sir Reginald Hall*, London: Methuen, 1955

Julyan, Herbert E., *Sixty Years of Yachts*, London: Hutchinson, *c.*1950

Kemp, Lieutenant-Commander P. K. (ed.), *The Papers of Admiral Sir John Fisher*, vols 1 and 2, London: Navy Record Society, 1960 and 1964

Kennedy, Paul, *The Realities Behind Diplomacy*, London: Fontana, 1981

Kennedy, Paul, *The Rise and Fall of British Naval Mastery*, Basingstoke: Macmillan Press, 1983

Kennedy, Paul, *The Rise of Anglo-German Antagonism, 1860–1914*, London: George Allen & Unwin, 1980

Kennedy, Paul (ed.), *The War Plans of the Great Powers, 1880–1914*, London: George Allen & Unwin, 1979

Kerr, J. Lennox, and Granville, Wilfred, *The RNVR – A Record of Achievement*, London: Harrap, 1957

Kerr, Mark, *Prince Louis of Battenberg, Admiral of the Fleet*, London: Longman's, Green, 1934

Knight, E. F., *The Falcon on the Baltic – A Coasting Voyage from Hammersmith to Copenhagen in a Three-Ton Yacht*, London: W. H. Allen, 1889

Livock, G. E., *To the Ends of the Air*, London: HMSO, 1973

Ludwig, Emil, *Kaiser Wilhelm II*, London: G. P. Putnam's Sons, 1926

McInerney, Michael, *The Riddle of Erskine Childers*, Dublin: E. T. O'Brien, 1971

Mahan, Captain Alfred Thayer, *The Influence of Sea Power Upon History (1660–1783)*, London: Sampson, Low, Marston, 1889

Marder, Arthur J., *The Anatomy of British Sea Power – A History of British Naval Policy in the Pre-Dreadnought Era, 1880–1905*, London: Putnam & Co., 1940

Marder, Arthur J., *From the Dreadnought to Scapa Flow*, vol. 2, London: Oxford University Press, 1965

Marder, Arthur J., *Portrait of an Admiral: The Life and Papers of Sir Herbert Richmond*, London: Oxford University Press, 1952

Marder, Arthur J., *The Road to War, 1904–1914*, London: Oxford University Press, 1961

Messum, S. V. S. C., *East Coast Rivers*, London: J. P. Potter, 1903

Military Correspondent of *The Times*, *Imperial Strategy*, London: John Murray, 1906.

Neison, Adrian, Kemp, C. E. Dixon, and Davies, G. Christopher, *Practical Boat Building and Sailing*, London: L. Upcott Gill, 1900

Packenham, Thomas, *The Boet War*, London: Weidenfeld & Nicolson, 1979; Futura, 1982

Palmer, Alan, *The Kaiser – Warlord of the Second Reich*, New York: Charles Scribner's Sons, 1978

Patterson, Temple, *Tyrwhitt of the Harwich Force*, London: Military Book Society, 1973

Popham, Hugh and Robin, *A Thirst for the Sea*, London: Stanford Maritime Press, 1979

Rider, John, *English–Latin, Latin–English Dictionary*, Oxford, 1589
Shannon, Richard, *The Crisis of Imperialism, 1865–1915*, St Albans: Granada, 1976
Shephard, Brigadier-General Gordon, *Memoirs of Brigadier-General Gordon Shephard, DSO, MC*, ed. Shane Leslie, London: privately printed, 1924
Southby-Tailyour, Ewen, 'Ask Me One on Beaches', *Royal Cruising Club Journal*, London: R.C.C. Press, 1982
Southby-Tailyour, Ewen, *Falkland Islands Shores*, London: Macmillan London Ltd, 1985
Spender, J. A., *A Short History of Our Times*, London: Cassell, 1934
Steinberg, Jonathan, *Tirpitz and the Birth of the German Battle Fleet Yesterday's Deterrent*, London: Macdonald, 1965
Stevenson, P. L., *How the Jubilee Fleet Escaped Destruction and the Battle of Ushant, or Two Episodes in the Career of a Naval Officer*, Hertford: Stephen Austin & Sons, 1898
Stone, Norman, *Europe Transformed, 1878–1919*, London: Fontana, 1983
Sykes, Sir Frederick, *From Many Angles*, London: Castle, 1942
T.124 Commander Russell Grenfell, RN, *Sea Power*, London: Jonathan Cape, 1940
Taylor, A. J. P., *The Struggle for Mastery in Europe, 1848–1918*, Oxford:. Oxford University Press, 1954
Thornbury, Walter, *Old and New London*, London: Cassell, Petter, Galpin, 1881
Tuchman, Barbara W., *The Proud Tower – A Portrait of the World Before the War, 1890–1914*, Basingstoke: Macmillan Press, 1980
Van der Molen, S. J., *The Lutine Treasure*, London: Adlard Coles, 1970
von Tirpitz, Grand Admiral A., *My Memoirs*, 2 vols, London: Hurst & Blacken, 1919
Ward, Philip, *Invasion Road*, London: Cassell, 1980
Warington-Smyth, Herbert, *Sea Wake and jungle Trail*, London: John Murray, 1925
Warner, Marina, *The Dragon Empress*, London: Weidenfeld & Nicolson, 1972
Weldon, Captain L. B., *Hard Lying, Eastern Mediterranean, 1914–1919*, London: Herbert Jenkins, 1925
West, Nigel, *MI6, British Intelligence Service Operations, 1909–1945*, London: Weidenfeld & Nicolson, 1983
White, Montague Grahame, *At the Wheel Afloat and Ashore*, Foulis, *c.*1935
Wilkinson, Burke, *The Zeal of the Convert*, Gerrards Cross: Colin Smythe, 1978
Williams, Basil, and Childers, Erskine (eds), *The HAC in South Africa*, London: Smith Elder, 1903
Wyatt, Harold Frazer, and Horton-Smith, L. Graham, *The Passing of the Great Fleet*, London: Sampson, Low, Marston, 1909
zu Eulenburg; Count Phillipp, *Aus 50 Jahren*, Berlin: Gerbruder Paetel, 1923

Index